Dream
of the
Walled
City

Dream of the Walled City

Lisa Huang

Fleischman

POCKET BOOKS

New York   London   Toronto   Sydney   Singapore

POCKET BOOKS, a division of Simon & Schuster, Inc.
1230 Avenue of the Americas, New York, NY 10020

ISBN: 0-671-04228-9

First Pocket Books hardcover printing September 2000

10 9 8 7 6 5 4 3 2 1

POCKET and colophon are registered trademarks of Simon & Schuster, Inc.

Book design by Ruth Lee

Printed in the U.S.A.

For my mother and father.

Acknowledgments

I am grateful for the encouragement, assistance, and sheer dazzling ability of my agents, Jandy Nelson and Danny Baror, and of my editor, Greer Kessel Hendricks. I would also like to thank the following people, who entered heroically into the spirit of this enterprise, devoted time to an interest not their own, and always gave good advice: Elizabeth Bernhardt; Milagros Estrada; Eric Friedberg; The Honorable John Gleeson; Roberta Golden and Faith Coleman; Evelyn Konrad; Edward Lazarus; Yula Lin; Maris Liss; Tim Macht and Laurie Abraham; Geoffrey Mearns; Deborah Morowitz; Peter Norling; Ethan Nosowsky; Sean O'Shea; Peter J. Powers; Victoria Ruiz; Leslie Shad; Alexandra, Mike, and David Sloan; Fran Siegel; Kathy Simonetti; Stephen Stickler and Jeff Toobin.

Pronunciation Guide

With only one or two exceptions, the Chinese names herein are rendered in pinyin, the modern romanization method. Pinyin uses particular letters of the Roman alphabet to approximate Chinese sounds, specifically, sounds in Mandarin, rather than Cantonese, which often formed the basis for the old-style Western names. For example, *Mao Tse-Tung* is now spelled *Mao Zedong.* The following names in pinyin are followed by a rendering of their pronunciation.

Pinyin	*Pronunciation*
Xiang	Shi-ang
Qing	Ching
Cai	Tsai

Certain words, however, such as *Canton* (as opposed to *Guandong*) and *Chiang Kai Shek* (as opposed to *Jiang Jie Shi*), are so common and evocative in the old-style spelling that it seems a shame to change them now.

EARTH

I

$\mathcal{T}$his person speaking is Jade Virtue, and Old Liang, the late chief magistrate of the city, was my father. He was important in life, and may still be so, out there among the dead. In the empire of China, in the red-earth province of Hunan, in the ancient walled city of Changsha, his mansion stood as one of the finest of the great houses. The manor flaunted its shiny green-tiled roofs, its carefully tended wisteria vines, like a proud woman in fine clothes. The outer walls were painted a fresh bright red every new year. Sunlight reflected from a hundred glass windows, while the windows in the other houses of the city were made of oiled paper. The great red-painted front gates were studded with brass, polished every day to shine like the gold rings on the fingers of my mother and of my father's concubines. A hundred servants scurried through the dozen courtyards, cooking live shrimp in boiling rice whiskey, pouring fine wine, steaming the crinkles out of silk garments, planting flowers, all for the pleasure of Old Liang and his women and children.

I was born in the year 4588, or 1890 by Western counting. The first ten years of my childhood were passed entirely within the walls of that house. I knew the great rooms, whose floors were wiped every day with soft cloths by the maids on their hands and knees, and the crowded servants' courtyards, where they would boil tea and spit into the gutters. Rich and poor, fat and thin, old and young—all lived under our roof, walking to and fro as men do on the face of the earth. But I knew, too, those parts of the house that were like the depths of the sea, or the caves in the mountains. I knew the four blue tiles in the corner of the bathhouse floor whose cracks, traced by my small finger, formed a perfect spider's web. I played with the dusty old birdcages lined up in a row on a windowsill in the grain storage room. I watched the slow tide of tarnish spread from one corner of the copper mirror that hung forgotten in an unused room, watched as over the years it seeped across the surface of the metal and slowly blinded it. And I knew the alley between the kitchen courtyard and the banquet hall, which was always damp and muddy, even on the hottest day. When it rained, a pool of water would form, resting lightly on the dark red mud, the footprints of the servants protruding from under the edges of the reflected silver sky and early moon and black tree branches, an entire planet drawn upside down into the heel mark of a serving girl.

We had frequent guests, visiting officials and imperial soldiers with messages, all of whom were lavishly entertained by my father with banquets and gifts; but unlike those of us who lived there, they entered our walls and left again when their business was finished, and being temporary, they seemed somehow not quite real. Of our entire household, only my father ever went outside the walls regularly, to preside over the criminal court or to attend council meetings at the governor's palace. My mother and the concubines rarely ventured out. Guei Xiang, the First Concubine, passed for a scholar among women, and would sometimes read us stories when she became bored. Xiao Zhuang, the Second Concubine, must have been very young herself, for she liked best to play dolls with us, and even cut up her own silk scarves to make doll clothes. I don't know how they occupied themselves otherwise, since only my mother, the Big Wife, ran the household. She held all the money, and ordered all the food, and when the concubines gave the servants any but the most insignificant kind of orders, the servants would always ask my mother first if they might obey. Guei Xiang and Xiao Zhuang were always very excited on the few occasions when they left the house to go outside, either to accompany my mother on a formal visit or, following a few steps behind my father and mother on feast days, when they went to venerate my father's ancestors. Sometimes my father would take Guei Xiang to a poetry-writing party, and then she made a great production out of leaving, clutching her inkstone and brushes importantly. As far as I was concerned, they simply mysteriously disappeared and then reappeared. I could not understand why they were so eager to go outside, since going outside the walls was like dropping out of the world.

But the very beginning of this new Western century, the Western year 1900, was marked by many strange portents. The Boxers, the heaven-sent rebels, with their black headbands and clenched fists, killed many in the great cities of the north, and were killed in their turn by the foreign armies that marched into Beijing and Shanghai. Stars fell; distant waters flooded their banks and spread out over the defenseless fields. In Changsha, frogs

clambered out of the Xiang River by the thousands, to be eaten by peasants and degree candidates, who are always hungry. Strange flocks of black
birds roosted in the trees. And that summer, my father fell mysteriously ill
and lay in his bedchamber, sweating through many layers of silken bedding.

In our family at that point in time there were only three children remaining. My elder brother Li Shi, aged thirteen. Myself, personal name
Jade Virtue, aged ten years. And my younger sister Graceful Virtue, aged
seven. All of us, as far as we knew, the children of our mother. Before and
behind and between us had come eleven other children that my father had
sired, but the spirits of infants were more fickle in those days, and fled this
earth easily, and all of them now lay under the rough red earth along the
eastern wall of the city cemetery. For fear that our spirits might be just as
unreliable, we children were kept strictly away from our sick father, and after a while his illness ceased to fascinate us and became merely a part of
our life in the house. Li Shi continued to take lessons every morning with
his tutors, preparing for the day when he would sit for the imperial examinations, and Graceful Virtue and I simply played together, or with the servants' children. But my mother and the concubines took turns nursing my
father, one of them always present in his bedroom. Guei Xiang was there
most often, because she answered all his letters for him as she always did,
kneeling on the floor by his bed to take dictation, brushing the characters
very quickly onto the rice paper spread out in front of her. Indeed, my father often joked that there were several officials in the capital who thought
Guei Xiang's excellent calligraphy was his own. Sometimes if my father
awoke and found my mother or Xiao Zhuang there, he would send them
to fetch Guei Xiang, because she was the only one who could read to him.
Then Xiao Zhuang would weep quietly outside his door, whispering to my
mother that the Old Master did not care for her. My mother listened to
her, nodding, but the serene expression she always wore on her face did
not change.

That year, autumn came early and harshly to Hunan. It grew unusually cold, and then it seemed to me as if my father became worse. There
were no more letters sent out, or reading aloud; my mother began sitting
up all night at his bedside. Curtains were draped over the lattices of the
doors and windows, and we could no longer see inside to where he lay. A
long column of doctors, including the governor's own physician, came to
my father's bedroom. The door would open slightly to admit them and

shut behind them again immediately. They always left with serious faces, plucking at their long sagacious gray beards with their pale fingers, the skirts of their dark silk gowns rustling amongst the brown leaves lying on the stones of the courtyard.

Ever since my feet were bound the year before, the pain sometimes woke me in the middle of the night. Usually, I simply lay quietly so as not to disturb Graceful Virtue, who had a tendency to get sick when she hadn't slept. I would gnaw my fingers, or rub my temples, or count my breaths until light showed at the window. But one night, as the knife edge of winter began to show, with windless chill and frost on the roof tiles, I could not keep still, and finally got up and wincingly pulled my shoes on over my foot bindings. Cold air sometimes relieved the excruciating throb in my ankles, so I wrapped myself in my quilted coat and opened the door of the room and looked out into the central courtyard.

Across the open space, under the unmoving bare branches of the ginkgo trees, I could see the dull glow of the lamps from my father's bedroom. I could see my mother's shadow inside, moving against the white curtains. I thought about the shadow puppets in a play that a traveling puppeteer had put on for the entire household last summer, waving his little paper figures behind a white screen lit from behind by lanterns, while my father and his women laughed and clapped along with the servants. But there was something about my mother's shadow just then that disturbed me—there was an awkward, frantic quality that was alien to her usually graceful, restrained manner. If I hadn't clearly recognized my mother's profile, I would have thought that some strange woman was in my father's room. Then I saw her shadow drop a bowl, and I heard it crack into pieces on the stone floor, and watched as she put her hands to her head in despair, and heard her low groan float across to me on the night air. The sound of the crash drew me across the icy courtyard toward the light behind the curtains. I found the door ajar and slipped inside, shutting it behind me.

All the lamps were burning, and I blinked a moment in the sudden glare. My father's bed was at the far end of the room, and the curtains were mostly drawn—I could see only his bare forearm lying on the mattress. My mother had her back to me, crouching on the floor and picking up the pieces of the bowl. There was no one else in the room. Without thinking, I walked up to my father's bed and took his hand as I normally did, for my father was affectionate with us. But his arm flopped back unresistingly, his fingers did not close on mine, and his skin was oddly cool. I drew back in surprise, and when I turned I saw my mother staring at me, her mouth open. Her upper lip was covered with perspiration, even in the chilly air of the room. It was the fearful look on her face—her eyes staring in panic in a way I had never seen before—that frightened me, and I opened my mouth to cry out, but before I could make a sound she had rushed forward and put her hand over the lower half of my face.

"Hush," she whispered, and held my head very tightly in her hands for a moment. Then she leaned back and looked at me. The panicked look had gone from her face, and she had instantly put her usual calm expression back on. But I saw that the rabbit fur of her collar was quivering in the still air and her hands were burning hot, and then for the first time in my life I saw my mother's serene face as a mask, now not quite firmly fixed at the edges, and I was even more frightened by the sharp new thought that I did not know her at all, and perhaps had been tricked all along.

"Be a good girl, and don't make a sound, or you'll disturb Baba." She took her hand away from my mouth.

"Baba isn't here," I said immediately, for reasons that remain unclear to me to this day.

My mother straightened and looked down on me, her eyes moving about in the stillness of her face as her gaze flickered over me. She seemed to reach a decision, for then her eyes came to rest in mine. "No, that's right. Baba has gone now, gone forever. But we can't tell anyone yet."

"Why?" I asked, too astonished to think about what it meant for my father to be gone forever.

My mother crouched down again and took my shoulders in her hands. "Listen, Jade Virtue. You are old enough now to understand things. Your father has gone to his ancestors. But for certain reasons, we cannot let anyone know he has departed. We must keep this between ourselves for a few days. Do not tell your brother and sister. Do not tell Second Aunt and Third Aunt—especially do not tell them. Do not tell any of the servants. You must promise Mama and help her in this matter."

No one had ever asked me to keep anything secret before, and I was so troubled my chest felt tight, as if my mother had introduced something sinister into the life of the house.

"Do you promise?" she demanded, in the same hoarse whisper.

"Yes," I said tremblingly, afraid of the new shadows in the world.

She said nothing further, but stood up and went over to the bed and, half clambering onto it, turned my father's body over onto its side under the quilts, so that his back was toward the door. Then she moved the charcoal brazier to the far end of the room from the bed and opened two glass windows, letting in the freezing night air.

"It's cold, Mama," I said, going to her. "This month has never been so cold before." She rubbed my hands between hers. Her hands were damp with perspiration, the moisture turning cool on my fingers when she let them go.

"The gods are helping us," she murmured. "It's late. Go back to bed."

In the courtyard, the night was more frigid than ever, and the frost crunched beneath my steps. I paused for a moment to let the anesthetizing cold of the tiles seep through the cloth of my shoes into my feet, which burned and ached so much that I felt the pain all the way to my teeth. Waiting for my nerve endings to deaden, I looked up at the gallery that ran the length of the second story right above me, and realized that someone had to be standing there in the darkness, because I could see a puff of breath curling out into the cold air. I peered more closely, and an elderly man, wearing a long white beard and a somber silk robe like the other doctors who attended my father, emerged from the darkness of the gallery and looked down at me. I bit my lip. I had just been sworn to secrecy by my mother, yet now I was lingering foolishly in the courtyard and one of my father's doctors had seen me, and might call down to ask questions about my father's condition. The old doctor put his hands on the railing of the gallery, and I saw for a moment in the glint of moon and stars and the faint lamplight behind me that he was wearing a thick gold ring with a large green stone carved to look like a bird. I glanced quickly over my shoulder, but I could not see my mother's silhouette in the window. When I looked back up at the gallery, the old gentleman was gone. I ran back to bed quickly to avoid meeting him, and lay there all night, unable to sleep for the chill that had settled into my bones.

"He hasn't asked for either of you," my mother told the two concubines at the door of my father's room the next day. "In fact, the noisiness of the household and your quarrelsomeness disturbs him and makes him sicker. So everyone should stay away just now." She shut the door firmly, and the two younger women looked at each other, Guei Xiang with anger in her face. But my mother was the Big Wife, and they had no choice but to obey. During the day, servants brought food on trays to the door and my mother took them inside. That night, I left my bed again and went to my father's room, where I found her eating a little from each of the dishes. I sat with her awhile, but she was afraid I would become sick, with the windows open as they were, and she sent me back to bed.

On the second day, my mother leaned out the door and told the cooks that my father wished to eat salt fish and thousand-year-old eggs. They protested—such stinking fare was too strong for the stomach of an invalid. But she shook her head, and said, "I don't dare disobey the Old Master, especially when he is ill and cannot have his wishes crossed in anything." The dishes came, and the fish and pickled eggs could be smelled through the windows into the courtyard.

Very early the next morning, the morning of the third day, there was a tremendous bustle at the front gates of the house, and the sounds of many excited voices in the front courtyards. A manservant ran into the central courtyard, where I was trying to amuse a small puppy, and crouched by the door to my father's room, whispering, "Madame! Madame!" My mother emerged, her face utterly expressionless, but I was afraid of her fingers, which were twisting in each other like eels, brought up in baskets from the bottom of the sea.

"The Emperor's messengers," the manservant gasped, his whole body quaking with excitement.

"Bring them," my mother said. The man ran off. My mother looked at me and beckoned with a secretive gesture, her fingers uncoiling and coiling back again. I left the puppy and ran to her, and she drew me inside.

"Jade Virtue, I need your help now. Imperial messengers have come with a gift from the Emperor for your father. I have been expecting them every day. But they must leave here thinking that your father was alive when they delivered the gift, or they will take it back. Do you understand?"

I didn't, but I nodded anyway.

"We must have this gift, because we will need it in the years to come. So you must get underneath your father's bed and when I bring the messenger to the doorway, you must groan as if you are in pain, in as deep a voice as you can. Can you do this?"

I climbed under the bed, and my mother pulled the quilt down over the edge to hide me. But I could just see past the corner of the bedding, to the door beyond. I cleared my throat.

I heard the clang of spurs outside as the messengers arrived in the central courtyard. I heard a rising din of voices; word had spread so quickly that the entire household had gathered to look at them. I saw my mother prostrating herself just outside the door, touching her forehead to the floor. Then a strange creature like a giant hard-shelled beetle emerged from the glare in the doorway and stepped into the room, its antennae waving. I started in my hiding place, before I saw that it was a man in armor, his joints encased in leather, bamboo and steel mail, small pennants whipping above his head at the end of long, thin sticks fastened to his back.

The messenger carried a small box wrapped in silk, which he presented on one knee, holding the box in front of him. My mother stood to one side, looking at the direction of the bed.

"Chief Magistrate," the man said. "His Imperial Majesty has deigned to grant you an inscription, written with the Vermilion Brush itself, together with a trifling gift, in token of your most recent services to the realm."

I sat in terrified silence under the bed.

"Don't approach; the doctor says he is contagious," my mother said softly, moving toward the bed. "As you can see, he is very ill." At that moment, I managed to groan, faintly but audibly. The messenger looked up at my mother, who simply knelt at the edge of the bed and began whispering into my father's cold ear. I groaned again.

"I'm sorry he cannot greet you properly," my mother said, turning back to the messenger, "but he has been ill for so long. He can barely speak, even to me. Only the thought that the Emperor was sending him a personal message kept him alive."

The messenger came to his feet with a clang of armor, his hand on the hilt of his long sword. He gave the box to my mother, who pressed her hands together and bowed before taking it.

"Chief Magistrate Liang expresses his humblest gratitude to His August Majesty," she murmured. "He remains, as always, the loyal and devoted slave of the Emperor, and the Empress Dowager."

The messenger nodded with approval, and turned to leave. My mother set the box on the table and with hardly a backward glance at it followed him outside, closing the door behind her. I ran to the window and looked out carefully through a slit in the cloth drapery, watching as the imperial messengers strode away out of the courtyard, the entire household of a hundred persons or more bowing to the ground as they passed. Then I ran to the box and slid open the carved wooden cover. Inside was a strip of calligraphy on rice paper, which I lifted impatiently. Underneath were four gold ingots, each with the imperial seal set into the middle. I had seen gold before, in the form of jewelry, and I recognized it in this incarnation as well, and for the first time it occurred to me that the substance might be valuable.

My father was said to have died that very afternoon. My mother emerged from his room at sundown, her hair pulled out of its golden hairpins and falling about her face, crying out for Guei Xiang and Xiao Zhuang. They came running, and collapsed onto each other's shoulders when they saw he was dead. Frightened by the hysteria, and perhaps finally realizing that my father was never to return, I wept too and had to be taken away to my room. At the news of his death, the servants set up a great cry that went on all night, wailing and sobbing and tearing their clothes in every corner of every courtyard—it felt as if the entire house were being shaken to its foundations by these gathering storms of interruption. Lying in my bed in the dark listening to them, I wondered that my father should have been so beloved that the lowest stable hand should spill tears for him. But I was a child then, and I did not understand that with every death, many different things are mourned at once. For with every death, we are at the end of time.

2

Xiao Zhuang was sitting in a spindly lacquered chair in my mother's bedroom, weeping into her thin fingers. My mother sat across a small table from her, her hands perfectly still in her lap. Guei Xiang was pacing angrily on the small square of Xinjiang carpet that lay in the middle of the stone floor. I was standing outside with my brother Li Shi, peering through the crevices of the latticed windows, and every time Guei Xiang in her pacing turned toward us, we ducked back behind the shadowy drape of the curtain, which was looped up to one side.

"How can you do this to us, your sisters?" Guei Xiang finally cried, her hands balled into fists. "Have you waited all these years for the Old Master's death just to throw us out of the house? Have you nursed some grudge I have been unaware of, Eldest Sister? You know, I can't help it if you can't read and write."

At this, Xiao Zhuang looked up in shock and gave a little cry of protest. My mother shook her head, very slightly, as if she wished to conserve energy. "You know that's not true," she said, wearily.

"I don't know it!" shouted Guei Xiang, arching her neck. Her elaborately coifed hair slid out of its hairpins, and one gold pin fell to the stone floor with a sound like a key turning in a lock. "Why won't you keep us with you?"

My mother glanced away a moment and then looked back. "I can't," she said. "I mean . . . Guei Xiang, I have lost all interest in this world since my husband died. I intend to sell the house and all its contents and live very simply and devote myself to the education of my son. It's best for you to go elsewhere. Old Liang did not give you your freedom in his will, and he never made you his proper wives. I could have sold you like slaves. But we have lived together like sisters all these years; we have buried children together"—at this my mother and Guei Xiang both glanced guiltily at Xiao

Zhuang, who looked stricken and began to sob harder—"and I could not see such a fate befall you."

Guei Xiang crossed her arms on her chest.

"Now," my mother continued, "Old Li has told me that he wishes to take Xiao Zhuang into his house as his fifth concubine, to live in his house in Canton."

"That's so far away," moaned Xiao Zhuang.

"That's no surprise," Guei Xiang snorted, interrupting. "Old Li has had his eye on her for a long time. Every time he came to dinner he would spend the entire evening leering at her from behind his wine cup." She resumed pacing, her hands on her hips, her elegant dark brows drawn together in a frown.

"Xiao Zhuang doesn't have to go," my mother said firmly. "If she wishes, she can return to her own home, and I will give her one hundred gold pieces. If you wish to go home, Guei Xiang, I'll give you the same. Or you can marry the farmer Chung. He isn't educated, but he is very wealthy and he is willing to make you a proper wife. You'll have all kinds of rights with him that you didn't have with the Old Master. Your children will inherit his property."

Guei Xiang stopped again and looked at Xiao Zhuang. "Well, what do you plan to do, Younger Sister?"

Xiao Zhuang looked up plaintively, her wide almond eyes filled with tears. "I will go to Old Li," she whispered. "I don't want Eldest Sister to waste one hundred gold pieces on me."

The other two women looked at her. I can see their faces to this day, my mother's face melting into gratitude and Guei Xiang's tightening mouth shaping itself into a combination of tenderness and frustration. The three of them remained in silence for a moment, and then my mother and Guei Xiang looked at each other over Xiao Zhuang's bowed head with an air of perfect understanding, and an utter lack of affection. Looking back at them now, with these eyes of mine that have seen much more since then, they must have looked like a married couple who no longer loved each other, but who each knew all too well what the other was about. I would never have mistaken them for friends, but they looked as if they were conspirators.

"Well," said Guei Xiang, breaking the silence and turning back to pace on the carpet as before, "I'll take the money. I won't marry Chung the farmer, I won't be the means by which he climbs in society. I'll return to my parents' house in Shandong instead and think about what I wish to do now, with the rest of my life."

"What do you mean, what you wish to do?" murmured Xiao Zhuang in genuine bewilderment. "What can you do, except marry again?"

"We'll see," Guei Xiang said.

I glanced at Li Shi, standing beside me, and was surprised to see how angry and unhappy he looked. When the two concubines left my mother's room and were crossing the courtyard, he ran after Xiao Zhuang and called to her. Guei Xiang only glanced back as she walked away, but Xiao Zhuang stopped at the sound of his voice. "You won't have to leave," I heard him say. "I won't allow it, now that I am the master." She turned to him, her long silken sleeves fluttering, and put her arms around him, wiping the tears from his face with her sleeve. He was as tall as she was and already broad and strong; when he put his arms around her waist, it was as if a grown man were embracing her. I turned my head to look back inside my mother's room. She was sitting in her chair as before, unmoving, her face as still as usual. Then she looked up at the window, moving her eyes only, before I had a chance to hide, and her eyes narrowed, like fists clenched with anger. Shocked, I recoiled, thinking she was angry at me, and panic-stricken, because among the women only Guei Xiang dared display a temper, which she had even to my father, who always seemed to enjoy placating her. But then I realized that my mother did not even see me, that her eyes were fixed on the courtyard behind me, where her son clung to the youngest concubine for comfort, much as his father must have done.

The concubines left on the same day as all the servants, except for Cook and one housemaid, who would be going with us to our new house. It was midwinter and very cold, but the sun was shining, making the icy air glisten. In a few weeks, it would be the lunar New Year, but there were no preparations. Fresh red paint on the gates, casks of wine carried through the kitchen courtyards on the backs of sweating workmen, Xiao Zhuang cutting delicate little gilt paper decorations with her crane-shaped embroidery scissors—all these things that we might expect to see were missing, and all the courtyards were empty. Instead, two sedan chairs sat in the front courtyard, and boxes and bundles were being loaded onto bullock carts outside the front gate. The servants were lined up weeping in the courtyard as my mother gave each of them their wages and an extra gold coin. From where we three children sat on the steps at the far end of the courtyard, we could not hear what any of them said, but many of the women were weeping as they took their money. One young man was angry, and snatched his money out of my mother's hand, and stormed out through the gate.

Then Guei Xiang and Xiao Zhuang emerged from the central hall, where they had been paying their last respects to my father's ancestors, burning incense and prostrating themselves before the long totemic wooden plaques that bore the ancestral names. The crowd of servants parted to let them through to the sedan chairs. Guei Xiang paused a moment to speak to my mother, and although they had both always been rather cool with each other, now my mother touched Guei Xiang's cheek tenderly, briefly, and Guei Xiang covered my mother's hand with her own, resting her face in my mother's palm. The First Concubine looked back at us sitting on the step, and smiled, very slightly, the way she used to when she was going out to a party, as if to reassure us that she would be right back. I saw she was holding her inkstone and brushes, and for some reason the sight made me worry for her, for what I understood even then to be the frailness of her weapons. Then she climbed into her sedan chair.

Xiao Zhuang was still weeping, and her face was red and swollen, making her look even younger. She clung to my mother's shoulder sobbing. Then, as she was about to climb into her own chair, she suddenly turned and flew across the courtyard like a bird, and threw herself on us, embracing us and kissing us all, and burying her face passionately in Graceful Virtue's hair. Li Shi clung to her especially, and she to him, and he wiped away his own tears angrily, ashamed of acting like a woman before the rest of us.

"Don't forget me," Xiao Zhuang wept. "Don't ever forget me. When I am dead, my ghost will guard you, all of you."

"We won't forget you, we won't," we all murmured together, caressing her silk-clad arms and nestling against her, smelling for the last time the sweet citrus perfume she wore on the back of her neck. Then she was gone, stumbling toward her sedan chair. The sedan carriers, with a groan, heaved both chairs into the air, and they stepped out through the gates into the street, one after the other. The last that I saw of them, framed in the open gate, was Xiao Zhuang's hand reaching out of her chair high above the bearers' heads, to brush Guei Xiang's outstretched fingers before they were pulled apart, in opposite directions, and then the two women fell outside the frame. I never knew what became of them afterward. At the moment of parting, you can hardly believe that your paths have diverged forever. It is only in retrospect, when you look down the length of the years that have passed, that you realize that your last glimpse of someone's face, had you but known it at the time, was indeed final.

That night, only six of us remained in the vast, echoing mansion. All of our things were packed, my father's books and papers in boxes, the few beds and tables and chairs that were coming with us bound with quilts and ropes to protect them while being moved. The cook and one housemaid who would be going with us to our new house were in the kitchen, cooking our last dinner and carefully wrapping straw around the pots of eggs and pickled vegetables we would take.

After we had eaten, my mother drew me into her own bedroom. She said almost nothing, but pushed me down onto the side of the bed and squatted to take off my foot bindings. I stared in amazement at her. It had been my mother who had insisted on binding my feet. My father had found Western notions attractive and had flirted cautiously with the new anti-foot-binding movement. But my mother had insisted that no man would marry me if my feet were allowed to go unbound and berated my father for condemning me to a sad destiny. She had been so implacable on this point that I had assumed that I would have a life of incessant pain, of frail and atrophied calves, of feet so divorced from the rest of my physical person that they might simply fall off my ankles in cold weather like dead wood. Of course, like all the girls my age, I could hardly wait for my first visit from the foot binder.

"Well, it's been less than a year, so your feet have changed very little," my mother muttered as she busily unwound the white cloths. "A few weeks of walking, and they will resume their shape. It is just as well; I don't think I could have made your feet into golden lotuses anyway." My mother's own feet were golden lotuses, a mere three inches long. She had hoped that with luck I might have the inferior silver lotuses, four inches long. Gritting my teeth through the binding process, I had wondered if I were capable even of silver lotuses. Perhaps there was a descending scale of lotuses, made of baser and baser metals, and I would end up with copper or brass lotuses to stand up on. Tonight I had found out my destiny. I would have iron feet.

My mother stayed awhile longer, massaging the blood back into my insteps. "We no longer have your father, so our lives will be different from now on. There will be no servants to walk you. I will not have us end badly."

My mother provided no further commentary—it was not her way to be obvious. But as I sat on the edge of my bed looking down onto the top of my mother's carefully coifed black hair, I came to my first true understanding about life in this world. That nothing remains the same. That change comes to the powerful as well as the weak, to those who are fortified as well as those who are unready. And feeling the painful gush of circulation reentering my twisted feet, I learned too, that the pain of release can be as great as the pain of confinement.

We left our home the next morning. My sister and I and the servants cried. Even my brother bit his lower lip and dragged his feet, turning again and again to look at the grand house and courtyards where we had lived. But my mother shut the gate firmly behind her. She walked in front of us up the street to where the hired moving carts stood waiting. I watched her straight, black-clad back. She had lived in that house as a bride and a wife and a mother, for almost twenty years. The gardens had been her pride— she had grown the flowers, tended the carp in the pond, designed the crooked little footbridge that led to the pavilion. I had heard her speak to my father once, when they had both been drinking rice wine in the garden one summer evening, about how together they might watch the plum trees grow old. Yet she walked away without a shiver. She did not turn around once, not even when we got on the cart and the wooden wheels rumbled beneath us.

The outside world spun around us, a chaos of noise and dirt and dun colors, incomprehensible to our eyes and ears. When we climbed from the cart outside our new house, which huddled in a crowd of other small houses, a group of children playing in the street stopped to stare at us. We stared back—we had never seen children play in the street before. The garden wall was painted a faded red, the small gate that served as an outer door was a plain black. My mother fumbled for some keys—the first time I had ever seen her with keys, for she usually knocked for a servant to admit her—and unlocked the gate. When I stepped inside, I had a sudden sense of the world having gotten very small and close, as if I had been marooned on a tiny island. In the old house, we never stopped finding new places to play among the dozen courtyards, the galleries, the walled gardens, the many closets and halls. Here was only a single courtyard, with single-story rooms arranged around three of its sides. A long strip of paint had peeled from one of the pillars, and bent over backward as if to get a better look at us. The fact that I could see the entire house from the entry gate made me very unhappy, and I started to cry.

"What is wrong with you?" my mother hissed. To the hired moving men, to the remaining two servants, she shook her head. "The poor thing misses her baba," she murmured, and they nodded sympathetically. Actually, I couldn't tell whether I missed him or not. He was always kindly, but only Li Shi had ever spent much time with him. But I missed the walled mansion where I had spent my first decade of life. In all the decades that have intervened between then and now, I have never yet felt the same about any other place. The feeling of being at home is, I suppose, the first thing that leaves us, and it does not return. From the very first night in that new house as a child of ten, until this very day, when my life is so close to its finish, I have always slept badly, as badly as a restless guest in a poor country inn.

That night we unpacked our things. My mother took care that the first thing she did was to set up a tiny altar to my father's ancestors, a pitiful replacement for our great ancestral hall at home, with its forest of stone and wood name tablets. The last thing Guei Xiang had done in our house was to copy all the names on the tablets on slips of paper for us to take with us, and now my mother pinned the slips of paper to the wall behind the altar. She gave me and Graceful Virtue the task of unpacking her own clothes and jewelry, thinking this would amuse us and keep us quiet. Graceful Virtue tried on my mother's dresses and shoes, and I picked through the little rosewood jewel boxes that my mother had personally carried into the house. At the bottom of one, entwined in the coils of a long, twisting jade necklace, I found a heavy gold ring with a stone carved to look like a bird.

"When did you get this ring, Mama?" I asked.

She glanced over absently. "That was your father's father's ring. The Empress gave it to him—see, the bird is the phoenix, the Empress's symbol, just like the Emperor's is the dragon."

"Oh. It looks a little like that doctor's ring."

"What doctor?" my mother called back, her voice muffled as she bent over some leather clothing boxes.

"The one I saw in the upper gallery the night"—I glanced around to make sure we were alone—"the night Baba really died."

My mother straightened up quickly and looked at me for a long time, her eyes speculative and nervous. "Come here," she said, dropping her voice so that Graceful Virtue and Cook, who were in the next room, would not hear. "There were no doctors in the house that night," my mother whispered. "Was it your grandfather that you saw?"

"I don't know what Grandfather looked like," I replied reasonably, but my mother seemed hardly to hear me.

"You saw him wearing this ring?" she demanded.

"I'm not sure if it was this very ring . . ." I began to say. But my mother sat down suddenly on the floor, as if her legs had given way.

"Old Sir, forgive me," she murmured, her eyes gazing past me into the empty spaces beyond. "But it had to be done."

I never quite understood what my mother meant by her words—whether she was asking for forgiveness for disguising my father's death with the rank smell of old fish and eggs, for tricking the Emperor out of his gift, for selling the house and its contents, for dismantling the ancestral hall. As for the old gentleman on the gallery—well, I don't know what I saw that night, but I know what my mother saw as she was sitting on the floor of the new house, muttering prayers to the dead. The ring itself is long gone, sold to pay for my brother to go to university in Nanjing. But I feel its weight in my hand still. The phoenix is the beast that dies and comes back to life again, over and over. It stands to reason. In the entire realm of existence, there is not one thing that is permanent. Why would death be the exception?

There was some disapproval of my mother's swift actions among my father's old friends, at the way she dispersed Old Liang's household and sold his house with the furniture still standing in it. She bore the criticism quietly. But then my mother let it be known that she intended, for the sake of Old Liang's memory, to live humbly, away from worldly concerns, waiting only to join him and serve him in the next world. Her wifely sacrifice and humility then won their praise, and her otherworldliness, their admiration. But at home, her humble exterior barely disguised her relentlessness. She wrung our livelihood from the few lands left to us. When the farm laborers shrank back in superstitious awe from the black flocks of birds who descended to feast on the tender shoots of the rice plants, my mother shamelessly ran out into the field herself, trailing the thin cotton of her widow's weeds, and chased the birds away, flapping a great red cloth at them and throwing stones until they took flight. At night, she pulled up a tile from the floor under her bed, and counted again and again the money she had saved, and buried it once more, stamping down the earth with her embroidered shoe.

Someone else bought our old house and lived there, and now it no longer stands. But once I dreamed that the mansion where we had all lived became a lair for thieves, and a nesting place for rooks. When in my dream I dared to enter the broken gates one more time I saw that grass grew between the paving stones, and every single one of the one hundred glass windows was broken. A swaggering aristocrat had become a blind, deaf beggar. Broken wood and shreds of porcelain covered the ground. It was as if a mighty god had taken up an entire world and turned it upside down and shaken it, and emptied everything out, tumbling, into the great universe.

3

Changsha was, and I suppose still is, the capital city of Hunan, a province in south central China shaped on the map like a man's head facing west. It was then a walled city, girdled on all sides by its massive stone bulwarks, on top of which people would stroll, and entered through four great gates, one in each cardinal direction. The site of the city had been occupied in one way or another for three thousand years—indeed, the city archives extended back almost that far, moving backward through time on first paper, then silk, then bamboo strips and thence to the very oldest records, etched on the shells of tortoises. Long lists of governors, granary contents, verdicts of conviction and acquittal, irrigation projects, the census in times of both famine and plenty, lay buried in the cool stone vaults under the imperial buildings, gathering in numbers, aggregating, accruing, multiplying, until the city sat on a foundation of bureaucratic records.

The city was a large provincial town, rather a backwater in those days, stewing in the steamy heat of central China, somewhat run-down and shabby, as was to be expected of a city that had reached its peak of importance eleven hundred years earlier. But there were some signs of more recent activity. The city's buildings became newer and newer as it spread east until it came to the railroad station at the far eastern edge of town. There the lines ran north and south, curving around the city outside the ancient imperial walls, through factories and mills and abattoirs. Beyond these signs of industry and changing times lay the green rice fields for which the province was famous, the rice plants raising their heads out of the flood of muddy water and the bloodred, iron-rich soil. In Hunan, the redness of the soil stained everything—the sides of buildings, the undersides of carriages, the legs of beasts, and the souls of men. Throughout the years of my childhood, when I was planting vegetables in the garden or carrying water from the well or buying chickens at the market, I came home with my skirts streaked in rusty bands and my cloth shoes dyed a dark oxblood shade. Permanent red half-moons formed beneath my fingernails, which I would dislodge with the corners of the pages in my books. The red soil and the heat are my strongest memories of that time and place.

In the year 1908 by Western counting, I was eighteen years old. And this entire year was eaten up by drought. Day after day, the heavens were like lead, the air as dry as the gray dust that swirled from the fields onto the roads, seeping into the seamed faces of the farmers and into the cracks of the houses, clogging the spokes of the wagon wheels. Behind the drought, like a faithful wife, came the famine. The farmers fed their children with musty rice left over from the year before and then with the seed grain; they turned their cattle loose to graze wherever grass could be found. Fearful of thieving neighbors, they tied their oxen up inside their houses at night, with the entire family sleeping all around it, guarding the beast's flesh with their own.

The governor rationed the food in the province strictly, handing out tickets of yellow paper, stamped with the imperial red stamp of dragon and phoenix. He announced that to increase efficiency in the distribution of food, large shipments of rice would be brought from Szechwan and Canton, a task he naturally entrusted to his brother-in-law, who would serve the state at only a modest profit.

We all stood in long serpent lines at the food stalls, each person clutching the required number of yellow tickets, which we thought were more precious than gold. But too many tickets were printed, and too many sold on the black market, and too many shopkeepers dealt them about like playing cards, and so their value became debased. My mother told us, "Do you see? All paper money is the same—good only for wiping your behind. If money doesn't make a noise when you drop it on the table, it's worthless."

Those of us who had metal coins—and my mother was forced to dig them up from under the tile on the floor beneath her bed, unearthing them like an artifact of history—spent precious coppers bribing the Triad gangsters who smuggled food from the coast. But the poor began to eat the grass from the sides of the road, and I saw them staggering along the highways with their mouths and tongues stained green. Their women went from door to door of the great houses, offering to wash clothes, to clean latrines, to sleep with the lordly men who lived there. But no man in the great houses, accustomed to the perfumed white flesh of the concubines, wanted a woman from the fields, the sunburn still around her neck like a hempen rope. The farmers, burdened with their wives and children, were afraid. Among men who were hungry and fearful there always appeared the Elder Brothers of the Eight Trigrams.

The Eight Trigram Brotherhood was a secret brotherhood, with a long trail of bloody deeds with sword and knife, of burned granaries and rich men hanged from their own ornamental fruit trees. The society had been suppressed and reborn several times. Its origins were hidden from the common person, but it was known that the founder had been the son of a demon. It formed and reformed over the decades, emerging from starvation and trouble, a bird of prey whose egg hatches only in evil days, brought forth from despair and bad dreams, when the soil was like iron. They were fearsome because they were violent, and even more fearsome because no one knew what they wanted, other than disruption.

Rumors of the Eight Trigram brothers now filled the ears and mouths of the province. Day after day, they spun from tongue to ear through the villages and towns, carried on the backs of market carts and in the hands of itinerant peddlers, exchanged like coins. A minor tax collector had been beaten by a gang of men in masks late one night, after he followed a young woman in mourning dress out of a tavern, and the incident was blamed on the secret brothers. A wandering mystic, dressed only in a rough robe of sacking and carrying his begging bowl, announced in the marketplace that he had dreamed of a ghost dressed in red garments and with one foot bare, with a face painted black like the disinterested judge in the opera, stealing the Emperor's jade flute. He refused to confess his involvement with the Trigrams, even under interrogation. A sorcerer threatened to call up a great wall of flame and was put to death by slicing for his treason. There were many such wild prophets in Hunan in those days, and we believed all of them to be in league with each other. When I think about it, it seems we took a sort of comfort in blaming a single organization of men, knowable and identifiable, even if unseen.

My brother Li Shi had gone to the university at Nanjing four years before, after years of lessons at home with me and Graceful Virtue. We were all clever at school, but of course Li Shi, being a boy, was the only one to go to university. How angry I had been when he left! I thought that all my learning had come to nothing, that he would always be the one to explore the great world, while I remained trapped at home in a muddy provincial city. But I missed him anyway, and I was glad when, in the midst of those hard days, he came back home to take up a minor office at the governor's palace in Changsha. Li Shi had not taken the imperial examinations, which had been abolished in a fit of modernity three years before. He arrived home with an office already in hand, a new pair of round spectacles on his face, and a cynical view of advancement that horrified our mother.

"The examinations are no more," he told us, standing in a distinguished manner by the dining table. "And it's about time. The fastest to rise are the ones who show an ability for practical application, and for that, it's best that I start in some smaller arena. Of course, those that buy their offices rise quickly as well."

"You are talking about corruption," my mother thundered angrily, cutting Li Shi's laughter off at the throat. "I did not raise my son to be a corrupt man. Will you take bribes, as well, to buy a higher office, once you have squeezed the meat juice out of this one?"

"Sit down, Mother," Graceful Virtue murmured. "It isn't good for you to be standing like this." I pulled out a chair and pushed it underneath my mother.

"Of course not," Li Shi replied, surprised and indignant. "I'm not a bribe taker. I'm not dishonest. But I've seen how the world works."

My mother was silent for a moment.

Li Shi knelt by our mother's chair and wiped his hand over his forehead. "Listen, Mother. There was no point in going to the capital. I would have gotten a much lower position than the one I have now. And here I can show myself off to the best advantage."

"But you would be in the imperial bureaucracy! In Beijing!" My mother waved her hands in exasperation. "Not here in the provinces. Your father began in the Ministry of Punishments in the capital. What has happened to this world, that learning counts for nothing?"

Li Shi patted her knee, and rose to his feet. "Learning counts. You just have to learn different things now. Besides"—he glanced out the window into the courtyard—"it's better not to be in Beijing these days."

"What do you mean?" I asked. I kept my voice low, to match my brother's. My eyes followed his gaze out the window, realizing that Li Shi was for some reason keeping watch in that direction.

Li Shi leaned on the sill and put his face against the shutter. "Being in the Emperor's service now—I would be a man buried up to his neck in the ground. Unable to move, and any passerby could kick my head off." He shifted the position of the wooden shutter. "Don't worry. This is all part of the plan. I'll go to Beijing one day. But I'll go in a big way, as part of great national undertaking. The wise wolf first circles the prey."

My mother's voice was dry as paper when she answered. "I am sorry, my son, that upon entering the imperial service, where you might best benefit your nation, you then begin thinking of yourself as a wolf."

With Li Shi living at home again and working at the governor's palace, it fell to me to bring my brother his lunch almost every day. On a day in late August, a few months after his return, when the town lay under a blanket of heat and dampness, I brought him salt pork and mustard greens. My hair stuck to my neck, my clothes stuck to my back, and my eyes were slitted against the glare as I moved mechanically through the streets, taking care to hide the tin box of food under my sleeve, away from the bulging eyes of the hungry on the street.

The governor's palace sat on top of a small rise overlooking the city. I arrived at the outer gate, guarded by six soldiers in blue, and passed quietly through the open door into the first courtyard, then through to the second inner courtyard. A steady stream of people passed in and out, officials in their gowns and caps and petitioners with small scrolls clutched in their fists. A crowd jostled with weary anger at the gate, crying for food. The eyes of the soldiers moved over the crowd.

At the second courtyard, and at the tired nod of yet another soldier, I ascended the outside steps. My brother's office door opened onto a second-floor gallery that overlooked the courtyard below, where he usually ate his lunch. Li Shi, looking up from his wooden desk in his small office, followed my beckoning hand and emerged onto the gallery. He still carried his reed fan. I sat next to him on the stone bench while he opened the tin box and began to eat.

"I can't even think about walking back now," I complained. "It's too hot."

"Stay for a while, then. Sit here on the porch. There is a breeze every now and then." He handed me his fan while he wielded his chopsticks, and I took turns fanning us both.

"Don't drop any grease on your gown. It's really hard to wash."

"Hmm," Li Shi said, his mouth full. His round wire glasses slid down his nose. I put my head back against the stone balustrade and closed my eyes, dozing. Through the fog of my sleepiness, I heard my brother remark, "How strange. Those peddlers down there—the open baskets on their backs are empty. I can see into them from up here."

Without opening my eyes, I replied, "What do you expect? There is no food to sell."

"Then why are they here at all?"

A shout sprang up from the courtyard below, followed almost immediately by more shouts, which ricocheted off the walls, echoing madly. Li Shi jumped up, chopsticks still in hand, and looked over. I craned over his shoulder.

Fifteen or twenty peddlers ran into the courtyard. They had sun-reddened skin, and white strings tied around their foreheads. As the officials on the upper gallery stared, the men pulled knives from under their peddlers' baskets and ran for the stairs. Sounds of fighting came from the external gates. The officials on the upper gallery started to shout in fear.

A blue wave of guards from the outer courtyard came running, and the peddlers turned to fight them with their long knives. The courtyard boiled over with the struggle, the combatants bursting into each other's hostile arms. Looking down from where I stood on the balcony above, I thought the courtyard looked like a nest of furious scorpions, stinging each other to death. Several of the peddlers broke away, hacked furiously at the soldier at the bottom of the steps and flung his body aside.

But before the peddlers on the steps got to the top, a burst of fire and sulfur exploded in their midst. One man fell over the stair railing and struck heavily on the flagstones. Li Shi and I and everyone else looked toward the source of the shot, to the balcony opposite us across the courtyard. The governor's twelve-year-old son, drawn to the noise from his lessons, had apparently called for his fowling piece. I stared at him in disbelief; the boy seemed quite calm and only mildly interested.

Li Shi dropped his tin lunch box and ran for the stairs. I grabbed at him. "Don't go down there! You have no weapon!" I cried. He threw off my restraining hand and ran to the top of the stairs, in time to launch a kick at the peddler just reaching the top. The attack was unexpected, and the peddler lost his balance, falling back onto the long knives of his comrades, but not before he slashed Li Shi's kicking foot through the thin leather sole of his shoe.

Li Shi stumbled back, cursing in pain and anger; I saw the blood spring from his instep, and I leaped forward and threw my arms around him. The next peddler, pulling his knife out from under the body of the first man, jumped up the last two steps and raised his blade. Li Shi flung himself forward and grasped the man's upraised arms in both hands; his glasses clattered to the marble as they struggled. I grabbed the man's hair and pulled his head back. The peddler spun his head around, twisting out of Li Shi's hands and snarling in fury at me, but even as I ducked back, a large blackening hole suddenly opened up in his chest, widening like a great mouth about to cry out, and he was dead before he sank to the floor. The governor's son, circling a little further on the balcony across the way, had once again demonstrated his excellent marksmanship. The boy now stood unblinkingly with his arms crossed, while his personal guard crouched beside him, frantically reloading the gun.

The remaining peddlers, about a dozen or so, were defeated and pinned to the ground by the soldiers. Of those, nine were dragged to their feet alive and tightly bound. The others lay on the flagstones, one with his feet still twitching. I clung to Li Shi's arm. He patted my hands.

"Your hair is a mess," he panted.

"Your foot," I murmured, stooping down.

"Never mind," he said. "Leave it. I have to go see the governor. I'll get someone to see you home." He rubbed his scratched glasses with the end of his handkerchief and hobbled off. But in the end, I staggered home unaccompanied, since everyone else was now necessary at the palace. Before leaving, I remembered to retrieve the lunch box and chopsticks.

The nine who had been caught alive were beheaded two days later. "All of them from the Elder Brothers—the sect of the Eight Trigrams," Li Shi told the family over bowls of noodles after the public execution. "They could once claim ten thousand men in central China. In my father's time, they tried to assassinate the Emperor inside the Forbidden City itself." He paused to daub chili paste on his chopsticks and then swirled them in his soup. "The signal was the donning of the white headbands."

"Did they really think they could reach the governor, with so many soldiers guarding him?" Graceful Virtue asked.

"Maybe. One or two men can succeed in reaching even a well-guarded man, as long as they don't care about coming out alive. Remember Minister Yu, so many centuries ago. He was killed in his bed, under a dozen feather quilts, in a locked, windowless room at the center of a hundred-room palace, guarded by a thousand men whose own lives depended on

Minister Yu's safety. The Emperor executed all one thousand guards, so perhaps it was a suicide conspiracy of a thousand men. Anyway, there is no such thing as a safe place."

"But what did they think would be accomplished?" I asked.

"They thought the people would rise to support them once they had seized the palace and murdered the governor." Li Shi snorted with contempt. "The people rise. Ha. The people never rise. The people attended their executions instead, that's what they did, and ate oranges and peanuts and blew their noses while their saviors' heads were being chopped off. Oh, by the way. The governor told me he's very pleased. I was the only non-soldier to be wounded."

"You should have seen him, Mama," I interrupted, looking at Li Shi with pride. "He was very brave, fighting off the Elder Brothers without any weapon."

"I am thinking of trying for the military assignment," Li Shi said.

My mother shook her head. "No one advances with the military assignment. It's only for mediocre bureaucrats."

"Not true anymore," Li Shi replied. He wiped his mouth and pushed his noodle bowl toward the center for more. "In any case, I'm not talking about a bureaucratic position. I want a commission as an officer in the military. Which costs money."

"Why do you want to be in the army?" my mother asked, with a slight grimace, as she filled his bowl again.

"Haven't you noticed how everyone is a soldier these days?" Li Shi asked. "This is where the power will lie, more and more. The world is turning into an armed camp."

"Where will we get the money to buy a commission?" my mother demanded.

Li Shi's face fell a little. "I don't know. It will cost five thousand taels, I have estimated." He bent over his soup. "Of course, we could always sell the girls."

We all glared at him, until we saw he was laughing silently into his bowl. "Really, Li Shi," my mother drawled, trying to sound disapproving. Graceful Virtue threw an orange at him, which he deftly caught.

I had insisted on going to the execution and had refused to avert my eyes at the blows of the executioner's heavy sword. The condemned men knelt hunched over on the ground on their knees and elbows, mumbling to themselves, reciting over and over again their mystical eight-character incantation, which I could just barely hear over the slow deep throb of the drums. "Eternal mother in our original home in this world of true emptiness," the men chanted.

The executioner moved aside each man's pigtail with a gesture almost tender, as if brushing aside the hair on the forehead of a small boy. With every head chopped off, the chant lessened in volume, until only one man's voice remained. The lines of imperial soldiers, like beetles in their jointed metal armor, did not move or look. A stiff breeze whipped at their flags. The last man continued chanting without hesitation, until he too met the sword in mid-incantation, and was in this fashion finally sent away from his original home, here, in this world of true emptiness.

4

*M*y best friend was Xiang Jin Yu, a daughter of the wealthy and prominent Xiang family. The family practiced respectability and scholarliness, without really being scholars. There had been no energetic man to increase the family fortune in many generations, but neither had there been any wastrels or opium smokers to fritter it away. The Xiangs did not plant more profitable crops or build a mill on the riverbank to improve revenues. But they did not sell good bottom land in order to buy earrings and silk for dancing girls. Year after year, they collected their rents and hoarded their gold. But they had been supporters of the anti-foot-binding campaign and had helped endow a school in Changsha that was actually completely for girls. I had introduced myself to Jin Yu in a bookstore, urged by my mother, who was eager that I should make the right sort of friends.

"Your father was Magistrate Liang?" Jin Yu had asked me, in her authoritative way.

"Yes," I answered, flustered. "I am his elder daughter, Jade Virtue."

"I am Xiang Jin Yu. My father had a case before Magistrate Liang, a long time ago. The magistrate was a very just man."

"Your father won his case?"

"He lost," she said coolly.

Jin Yu herself was a remarkably beautiful girl, with an elegantly modeled face that was as quick and hot and pale as the edge of a flame, changeable as a storm, strongly marked with thick dark brows arched like a gull's wings. Many men wanted to marry her, but Jin Yu's approach to the question of marriage was simple. She refused. Her parents brought into their house a number of fine young men, all of excellent family and good prospects. Each suitor was treated to stunning displays of rude and coarse behavior, with Jin Yu alternately picking her nose, singing lewd songs overheard from the fisherman at the river docks, and vigorously criticizing the young man's clothes and opinions. Yet the Xiang family was rich, their ancestors were powerful spirits, and their daughter possessed of a lovely face, so the young men kept trying, goaded on, perhaps, by her reputation for high spirits.

Right after the sudden rushing onslaught of the rainy season, Jin Yu invited me to the Xiang house on the day she was to meet yet another youth in this long line, this one the second son of a Shanghai magistrate. Her family's mansion was in the old town like the other truly ancient houses, rather than on the outskirts, where the new great houses sat sleek and shiny. Indeed, the Xiang house was barely visible behind its faded pale rose walls; only the austerely decorated eaves showed, and the dark mossy tiles of the roofs. I arrived at the western gate, which was in fact nothing more than a large wooden door painted a discreet black and devoid of ornament, in the midst of a storm. In fact, I had strongly considered not coming, since it had become clear that the storm was now approaching the outer edges of the city, boiling into the valley from the distant coast. But I didn't think I could get a servant to go out in the rain to give my apologies, so I came myself. I was escorted through the garden by a maid with an umbrella, through the vestibule by a second maid with a towel to dry the rain from my hair and a third with slippers to replace my wet shoes, and then through three successive doors separated by long hallways by a majordomo with a long goatee. A manservant flung open each door as we approached, and murmured, "Miss Liang has arrived," in a manner like a benediction.

The Xiangs left us alone in the guest hall with the suitor, on the condition that I, who was considered responsible, remain to chaperone. Normally, both parents would have sat in the room as well; I took it to be a sign of their desperation that they would leave us all alone. Or perhaps they had simply reached the end of their desire to be shamed before strangers.

We all sat in a circle around a small table, where a teapot and some cups were set out. I shifted on my hard chair and watched Jin Yu humiliate the boy by asking detailed questions about the loss of virginity and when it was best undertaken, generally speaking. But this boy was more determined than the others. He refused to be stirred, and when Jin Yu finally told him to leave, he stubbornly held his ground.

"I won't leave your presence until you consent to the arrangement," he told Jin Yu firmly.

"Then I will commit suicide," Jin Yu replied. The young man did not move, but sat with a smile intended to express mastery of the situation. Idle threat, his smile said. I knew Jin Yu much better, and I began to get nervous.

"Please be reasonable," I pleaded with the young man. "She is crazy."

The young man only crossed his arms and sat back.

"I will burn myself to death," Jin Yu warned. Still the young man did not move.

Jin Yu reached into a little box on the table and produced a wax match. She lit the match. The young man's face paled, although his smile remained fixed. He looked at me.

I started from my seat, snapping, "Jin Yu! Stop!"

My alarm frightened the boy more, and he looked about wildly for assistance. Jin Yu struck the match and dropped the little flame into her lap, where the cloth of her dress immediately began to burn.

I turned on him. "Get out!" I shouted. The young man leaped from his chair and bolted from the room. Jin Yu calmly pulled off her burning dress and stamped out the flames on the floor. I wiped the sweat from my forehead.

"One day," I told Jin Yu, "you will go too far."

"I've burned my hand a little," Jin Yu said to the maids who appeared, openmouthed, at the door. "Go get me some ointment. And here. Take this dress to be fixed."

"What did you do, Miss?" one of the girls asked.

"I was burning my dress. Nothing for you to worry about."

When the maids had left, Jin Yu patted my arm. "Don't look that way," she said. "It had to be done. You didn't want me to marry him, did you?"

I sat down with a great sigh, my hands on my knees like a farmer. "If he hadn't run out, would you have stood there and burned to death?"

Jin Yu looked surprised. "Of course. I don't make empty threats."

"But then you would have defeated yourself."

"Well, I wasn't expressing defeat. I was committing an act of aggression. It's only that it could have cost me my life, and I was willing to risk that. It's not the act, it's the intention behind the act that is important."

"That is a dangerous point of view," I replied. "Anyway, I certainly wish you would choose a less alarming path. What do you think you are going to do now?"

Before Jin Yu could reply, her parents appeared at the door. They appeared frightened of their daughter, but then they always seemed that way, as timorous as mice in her presence.

"What happened?" her mother asked. "The maids said you were standing here in your shift, and you burned your dress."

Old Xiang looked around. "Where is the guest, Jin Yu?" he asked, in an attempt to be stern.

"He suddenly remembered he had an appointment elsewhere and ran out." Jin Yu smiled.

The Xiangs looked at each other. Madame Xiang buried her face in her hands and began to sob. Her husband patted her shoulder. Jin Yu strode past them with determination and went to her study. I murmured a few words of consolation to the Xiangs, and followed Jin Yu. I closed the door to the little study behind me.

"I hope you are ashamed of yourself. Your parents are terribly distressed."

Jin Yu shrugged, but I was glad to see that her face was slightly troubled. "It had to be done. I had to break their feudal habits of thought, and sometimes only pain can do that. But I wish it were not so."

"What will you do, now that you have frightened away the last unmarried man in China?"

Jin Yu's face brightened. "I will continue my studies. There is no place for girls to study here in Changsha after they have finished the middle school. But I have arranged to study privately with Teacher Yang."

"The lecturer at First Normal?"

"Yes, him. A brilliant man. I will do political theory with him."

I felt a surge of envy that overcame all my previous reservations. "You are very lucky, Jin Yu. How I wish I could do this."

Jin Yu came to sit near me and took my hands.

"Come with me to the study group. We'll do it together."

I shook my head. "I can't. I'm getting married."

Jin Yu simply stared at me for several seconds. "What is it you are saying you will do?" she asked, her voice disbelieving.

I looked at the floor. "I'm marrying Pan Wang Mang," I said. I wasn't ashamed of my engagement, but Jin Yu had a strange way of making me feel as if every minor action of mine were somehow a setback for society.

Jin Yu let go of my hands and jumped up to pace the floor furiously. "I can't believe you will do this mad thing instead of studying with me. It's finally come to pass. You are falling back into the morass of the old ways."

"Jin Yu, try to understand. I can't afford to do this with you, although every part of me wants to. I must marry Pan."

Jin Yu shrugged, although she was still angry. At the bottom of Jin Yu's impatience with me was a shady tinge of self-absorption that made me shiver, even in the humid warmth of the day.

"If you loved him, I would only embrace you and be happy," she said, her voice still edgy with disdain. "But I know you cannot love this man."

"I don't understand why we have to marry for love anyway," I protested. "His father was an old friend of my father's. He is educated and of my social station. He is accounted good-looking. I have no reason to think we will not be compatible."

"What feudal thinking!" raged Jin Yu, starting to pace again. Then she stopped, crossed her arms, and looked down at me. "What is the real reason you are marrying him? Are you pregnant?"

"Of course not!" I replied with asperity. "But if you must know, and I know you will hound me until I tell you, I am marrying him to help Li Shi."

Jin Yu raised her eyebrows.

"Li Shi needs five thousand taels to buy a commission in the army. The Pans are very rich. I am sure once I am Wang Mang's wife, I can easily raise the rest. He is their only son and heir, after all."

Jin Yu sprawled into a chair. "Well, you surprise me all the time, Jade Virtue. I never realized you were such a cynic about love."

"Romantic love," I said, with all the assurance of the very young, "is fundamentally unreliable. This way, I have money and position. My mother need not fear for her old age, and I can make sure Li Shi is placed in a good position. Anyway, I'm sure Wang Mang and I will be as happy as any other married couple."

"Now, why does your cynicism sound like a sort of idealism? I hope you know what you are doing."

"I do. I am completely capable of handling the situation. Don't worry."

"Well, and what do the beneficiaries of your heroic self-sacrifice feel about all this?" Jin Yu asked.

I did feel as if I was making a heroic self-sacrifice, but it was irritating to hear Jin Yu speak of it so sarcastically.

"I haven't told them my real reasons, of course. I never intend to say anything to them about that."

"Yes, yes, best to suffer in silence," Jin Yu murmured. "No sacrifice is so noble as the one made in secret."

I ignored her. "I just reminded them that old Pan and my father had spoken of betrothing us when we were children. Li Shi and my mother think it's a suitable match."

Jin Yu gave a great sigh. "A suitable match. How mundane that sounds."

Young as I was, thinking only of great things and ignorant of the degree to which our lives are determined by small matters, I said, "Well, of course. Only politics is exciting, Jin Yu. This marriage business is quite mundane and easily disposed of. I don't expect it to make much difference in our life's work. What about you? You don't even want to marry."

Jin Yu looked over at me in surprise. "Of course I do. But not now, not when I have so much work and study in front of me. And when I do marry, I will marry a true revolutionary. Someone whose soul resonates with mine. Together, we'll change the world."

Her eyes glittered in such a strange way that I laughed to cover up my confusion. "Well, this romantic notion doesn't sound at all like you," I said.

Outside, the rain splashed the shiny broad leaves of the trees in the garden, the tamarind and the ginkgo and the plum, and dripped down in rapid pulses to the moss-green ground. Jin Yu opened a window and let the rain fall into the room. "It's good; we will have an excellent view of the storm. It will roll in right over our heads. I love storms. You will of course stay until it has passed. I don't think it will last overnight."

Jin Yu read aloud some poetry in French, with so much dramatic expression that I could guess at the meaning of the alien language. We drank green tea, and ate mangoes which Jin Yu sliced herself, slitting the green-and-red skin and pulling it smoothly away with the golden flesh still intact, releasing the jungle fragrance into the air, punctuating her remarks with the silver knife in her elegant hands. The heavy crash of the rain was continuous but somehow pleasurable, like the drums of an army, like the quickened beat of my heart.

5

The Pans lived in a giant ivory-colored house of fourteen linked court-yards, bound by carved wooden galleries along the second floors and stud-ded with elaborate window shutters. It was not far from where we used to live when my father died, in that same district of fine mansions and wealth. The house had originally been built two centuries earlier, by a founding ancestor who had made a separate courtyard for each of his wives and concubines and hung a birdcage in each one with singing birds, to symbolize the harmony of his household. Curiously, however, each passing generation of the family became smaller and smaller, instead of more and more populous—the women of that house were cursed with a tendency to bear only one or two children, if they had any at all. It was dif-ficult to blame the women for this infertility, since they came from many different families and cities. Instead, the problem was said to lie with the house, which was not properly aligned along a heavenly axis.

At this time in their history, the Pan family had reduced itself to only Old Pan, Mrs. Pan, their son Wang Mang and the last of Old Pan's concu-bines, Peaceful Beauty. As a result, most of the outer courtyards had been closed, their treasures of paintings and books and fine furniture shut up in-side, waiting for a new generation to open them and appreciate them. There had also been an older daughter who had gone away several years ago, and whom no one ever saw. Sometimes Mrs. Pan would speak about the letters she received from her daughter, who she said was now presti-giously married in Kunming. But Wang Mang and his father and the con-cubine had never been heard to mention her name, once she had left home.

The Pan house was near ours when my father lived, and he and my mother had included them on their rounds of visits at New Year's. My fa-ther was friendly with Old Pan, although he didn't approve of having so

many concubines in the modern era—when I was small I think there were
at least seven, in addition to Mrs. Pan—but he and Old Pan were part of
the same circle of men of affairs. They had all attended councillors' meetings at the provincial governor's palace. They had worn the robes of office
and had put their seals to memorials to the Dragon Throne. They were
part of several thousand years of imperial history, and their tragedy was
that they arrived just as it was ending.

The Pans insisted on holding an engagement party, with all my father's
old friends to be invited. My mother had not visited the Pan mansion since
my father had died, eight years before, and I was startled to see how excited she was about returning. Of course, my mother never expressed any
excitement by word or gesture, but her eyes shone, and she fussed a little
about what we would all wear. She dug up her hoard of gold coins to have
a fine silk dress made for me. I was pained at seeing her this way. My
mother had walked away so resolutely from her old life of privilege. I had
never considered that she perhaps missed her old house and her old life
and that her avoidance of our former district came as much from a fear of
memories as from practical necessity. She had never once spoken of it with
longing. She had never said anything about what I, now that I was older,
recognized must have been my father's mismanagement of money, a foolishness that left her after his death unable to continue in the position in
which she had lived. She had to pay off his debts secretly and pretend a desire to live humbly thereafter, all to preserve his reputation. Her happiness
now felt like an implied criticism of my father. I was angry at her for this
betrayal and at myself for my own sudden recognition of his flaws. Seeing
my mother's longing, I pitied her for her loss, but I wished I had not seen
the vulnerability in her character that made that longing exist.

The silk dress was made, in pink, and my hair dressed in two braids.
With Li Shi in our father's gray silk gown with a squirrel collar—for winter
was hovering nearby, and the fallen leaves clustered timidly on the lanes—
and Graceful Virtue in green and my mother in her best dark blue dress,
we walked to the Pan house. All the lights were on in the front courtyard,
and a maid greeted us at the gate with a burning torch. Inside, all the men
of my father's generation and their wives and grown children were already
drinking wine in the main hall and admiring the garden.

They set up a cry when I walked in, everyone shouting, "The bride!
The new bride is here!" and crowding around us to offer their congratulations. The go-between was there as well, and she accepted congratulations

on the fine match she had made, although, in fact, she had only conducted
the formalities. I myself had made the match.

"Perhaps their condolences would be more in order," Li Shi hissed in
my ear. I glanced at him and felt as if I could rub the pursed expression off
his face with the heel of my hand. I refused to look at him for the next two
hours, and I could tell he was surprised at the fury of my reaction. He tried
to get my attention or speak to me several times, and I always found a reason to turn away.

The great hall was beautiful, with many fine paintings collected by the
wealthy Pans hanging between its red-lacquered pillars. We were all
brought to admire a specimen of Ming painting by the great, the immortal
Chien Lung, hanging in the middle of the western wall, called "The Sages
Visit the Peach Orchard." The scroll as a work of art had been devalued
somewhat because the Xianlong Emperor had inscribed a dedication to
one Pan Ming Zhuong on it in his neat, undistinguished calligraphy. But as
an example of the family's connections to greatness, it could not have been
better. As she gestured at the painting, Mrs. Pan's fingers glittered with
jewels, and I saw she wore jade bracelets on both arms.

We ate supper in the adjacent hall, where hired caterers and the Pan
servants set forth an enormous banquet of rock crabs, pink-scaled perch
from the Xiang River, dark wine from Li Shui, koaliang wine from Shan-
tung, and yellow wine from Fen Chou-fu. For the first time, I was able to
observe my new in-laws. Old Pan was still hearty, although thinner now
than I remembered him, his flesh drawing in like an autumn evening. Mrs.
Pan was tiny and birdlike, vivacious and pleasantly plump, her skin still
very smooth and white. Peaceful Beauty was apparently not at the dinner.
And seated next to me was my future husband, Pan Wang Mang, elegantly
slender in gray silk.

It was curious that I only noticed him as a sort of afterthought. He was
smoothly handsome, with a well-mannered air and a low voice. He did not
make any hurried or ungraceful movements. But I was only eager to see
signs of their wealth and standing, eager to see passing into my hands the
means to buy Li Shi's commission and to reintroduce my mother into her
old world. My impressions of my future husband that night were slight,
but on the whole good. His looks pleased me, and he seemed a little distant and remote, which meant he would not bother me much or stand in
my way. When he spoke to me, he was courteous, and he helped me to
food from the dishes. Whenever he put a morsel of food on my plate, I

gave him a grateful look, and the entire company would smile fatuously at us. It was flattering to realize that they all thought we were a rather good-looking couple. He would do, I thought. I did notice, though, that his nails were bitten to the quick. A bridegroom's nerves, I thought.

But one question occurred to me. Why were the Pans marrying him to me? They were rich; their son was not deformed. I was fairly pretty, but far from a beauty. Although I came from a good family, I had no money, and yet knowing this, they had entered into the contract. It seemed they could do better than me. I whispered this to my mother in the hallway after supper.

"The Pans are old aristocracy," my mother said softly. "They are not like these new rich ones, who raffle off their sons to the highest-bidding heiresses and care only for their fortunes. Your father was a great man, and you are his eldest daughter. Your family is very worthy, Jade Virtue." She looked happily around at the elegant surroundings.

After dinner everyone wandered around the central courtyard, admiring the carp in the pond and the last of the flowers and leaves. The rooms around the courtyard had all been thrown open, their treasures exposed for the delectation of the guests. The lanterns blazing in each room, doors wide open to the night, made every room like a brilliant scene from the opera. I stood in the darkness of the center and watched the silhouetted figures of the guests crossing back and forth against the lights. The servants scurried about from side to side, crossing under the stars, serving wine. Red lanterns bobbed on the trees. The night air was a little cold.

"Very successful, Younger Sister." Li Shi's voice was at my elbow. He drew me away to one side, in spite of my reluctance, smiling our excuses to the other guests. When we were alone in one of the corners of the courtyard, he said, "Are you speaking to me yet? Or can I thank the heavens that you have stopped nagging me forever?"

This was too much, and I spat angrily at him, "It makes me furious that you talk to me this way, and look down your nose at this fine house, when this whole marriage is being done by me for your sake. So go away and leave me alone."

"For my sake? What are you talking about?"

"We will have the money for the price of your commission because I am sacrificing myself for you. When I am married, I will be able to borrow on my expectations as Wang Mang's wife. All for you, you ungrateful lout." I shoved his hand away and turned my back. He grabbed my shoulder and spun me around. His face held so many different feelings that it had simply gone blank.

"What exactly is it you are telling me? That you have agreed to marry this man for the money?"

"Yes, I have. Not just for you. For Mother now she's getting older, and for Graceful Virtue. Look around. This family, this house—their good fortune is vast."

Li Shi took off his eyeglasses and rubbed them on his sleeve. "Jade Virtue, I know you mean well. And I know the kind of person you are. I'm afraid you are burning to sacrifice yourself for some larger cause. But don't do this for my sake. If you make a mistake with this man, I do not wish it on my head."

"Listen, Li Shi. It's the solution to everything. He's an appropriate husband"—Li Shi nodded in agreement—"and I will make an excellent wife for him. And it solves all our problems. Money won't be tight again."

We sat down together on the stone steps leading to the walkway that ran around the edge of the courtyard.

"Are you certain about this?"

"Of course," I assured him cheerfully. "Don't worry. I'm not romantic. I don't believe in romance. I think marriage is a practical undertaking. I'll be good to Wang Mang and his family. You'll see."

Li Shi sighed and sat back. "Well, perhaps you are right," he said. "It certainly comes at a convenient time. I'll have the commission in a month or two, then."

"Sooner."

My brother started to laugh. "Of course, you aren't right when you say you aren't romantic. You just aren't romantic about marriage. All this self-sacrifice is just another kind of romance."

I shrugged.

"Let's stay away from the party awhile," he said, "and look around the rest of the house."

"No, that's too impolite."

"Why? It will be your house soon. We'll go quietly."

We followed the stone walkway out the side of the courtyard, between the buildings, and down a long, high-walled alley. We stumbled into a second courtyard, but this one was utterly dark, and only the distant sounds of the party disturbed its stillness. We walked around the perimeter, feeling our way, but all the doors were locked.

"Can you see anything?" I asked Li Shi, who was peering through a latticed doorway with his cupped hands.

"It's empty. Must be a storeroom. Although the ceiling beams are
fancy for a storeroom."

I strained my gaze over his shoulder. "Even their storerooms are nice,"
I said.

We left the courtyard by another way, on the opposite side of the way we
had entered, and wandered through some overgrown grass to the next
courtyard, which was just as shuttered as the first. The quiet of the night and
the coolness of the air must have mesmerized us, because we kept wandering, Li Shi holding my hand and leading me in and out of the buildings. We
chatted softly but contentedly, talking about what Li Shi would do when he
was commissioned. All the doors were locked and the rooms were darkened.

"We might be getting lost. I can't even tell where the servants' quarters
are," Li Shi murmured. "It's cloudy—I can't tell which way is north. This
house is a maze." We were now too far away to hear the sounds of the
party. But the crickets creaked pleasantly at the edges of the buildings, and
from time to time the moon gleamed unexpectedly on a tree or patch of
stonework.

"Li Shi, why do you think they are letting me marry Wang Mang?"

"Who?"

"The Pans. They could have gotten someone much richer and prettier.
Mother says it's because Father was a great man and they respect that."

"Probably. Changsha now is filled with vulgar new strivers. The Pans
would never want to open their little closed society to any of them. So
they chose the daughter of a man whose bloodline they knew all about.
They are richer, but our family has always been more distinguished, so it
helps their prestige too. They are trading money for honor."

"Mother said almost the same thing, but it sounds bad coming from
you."

"You aren't the only one who is unromantic."

As we were talking, we found ourselves in a long paved alley walled on
both sides with tile-topped whitewashed walls. Our cloth shoes made soft
shuffling noises. We turned the corner at the end and came into a small,
poorly kept courtyard with a single lighted window. Stalks of grass grew
through the pavement, which were made merely of rough fired bricks instead of tile. As we stood confused in the center of the yard, a woman
came to the door and looked out.

"I'm sorry," Li Shi called out. "We are guests at the engagement party, and we became lost. Could you direct us back to the main hall?"

We walked to the door where the woman stood. She was perched on the rough wooden threshold, and the lamp behind her cast a backhanded glow on her tired face. Her hair was twisted into a knot on the top of her head, but she wore only a simple jacket and trousers. The room behind her was bare except for the lamp and a low wooden bed with a straw mattress.

"I am Peaceful Beauty," she said. "I'll take you back toward the party."

She led us through the courtyards and along the walls.

"Madam, why aren't you at the engagement party? It's very festive," Li Shi asked.

"I stay away from all those things now. I became a Buddhist. I was just reading my scripture when I heard your footsteps."

She passed through a shaft of moonlight, and I saw the cotton wadding escaping through the seams of her jacket. She unlocked several doors and led us through the rooms, which were either empty or filled with objects covered in white sheets against the dust, which lay thick on the floor.

"It looks as if these rooms are rarely visited," Li Shi said.

"When I first came to this house, all these rooms were open and people lived in them. Now, the family is so small . . ." She was silent a moment. "I have no children myself."

Then we began to hear the sounds of the partygoers, and saw the glow of the lanterns spilling over the tops of the walls.

"Through this gate, cross the small court, and on the other side of the building there."

We bowed again and again, holding our hands folded before our chests.

"Please. No need to thank me." She turned to Li Shi. "Are you a classmate of Wang Mang's?"

Li Shi smiled and bowed again. "No, madam. My sister here is Wang Mang's fiancée."

Peaceful Beauty stepped into the light and looked at me. "You are the bride, then?" she asked. I nodded and bowed. She looked at me a long while before reaching out and taking my hand in hers. She gave it a light squeeze. Then she turned and was gone.

Peaceful Beauty died not long after, before my wedding. The Pans held a modest funeral for her, which was vastly overshadowed a month later by the national ceremonies held for the death of Dowager Empress Cixi and the ascension of the infant emperor Puyi to the Dragon Throne. When I came to the Pan manor to live, I recollected Peaceful Beauty's tired face in the slanting light from the red lanterns, and the touch of her hand. I went looking for her room, in the hope of finding her scripture book, or her hairpins, or some sign of her. But although I went to search often, I never found that little ruined courtyard again.

6

On a large stretch of land that used to lie between the Hunan First Normal School and the place where my mother now lived, a complex of imperial granaries shouldered each other. Those squat, windowless buildings were now filled with grain and rice again, as the year of the famine had passed, and the unrest in the province died away. But aside from the happy fact that grain was present in quantity, the plot of land on which the granaries stood was otherwise desolate and harbored only the charcoal-blurred outlines of old structures that had burned down decades before, a few half-standing walls, and foundations partially filled with debris. It was a place of half measures and broken wood; robberies and anonymous beatings took place often in the shelter of its hidden places.

At night, most people avoided this barren plot. But that evening I had stayed late in the curio market, examining the objects for sale, and now I was in a hurry to get home. I hesitated only momentarily before crossing the site. I stumbled a little among the boards and ash heaps, but only quickened my step. There was still light in the air, but it was uncertain and failing swiftly. The shadows shifted, tricky and elastic.

I climbed over a small rise and faltered suddenly. A small group of young men—six or seven, at a glance—were walking toward me, walking in a loose-limbed, predatory fashion that made me think of the packs of stray dogs that wandered the refuse heaps of the poor, sometimes snatching babies from the shacks. But I continued, attempting to look calm, picking my way carefully and keeping my eyes down. A prickle of sweat emerged on the back of my neck. I glanced around covertly from under my eyelashes, but saw no one else within hailing distance.

The young men were shouting to each other, laughing loudly, but when they saw me, they dropped their voices. This sudden discretion made me more anxious. Sometimes a single word would jump out from their murmurings with sinister clarity. "Liang," I heard one of them say. I glanced to the left and right, but there was no clear path on which to walk away at an angle. I thought that if I tried to cut away and run off, they would be after me, baying at my heels, and would bring me down like a stag in the mountain ravines. Instead, I walked straight, and the men passed me on either side, very closely, hunting dogs forcing a deer into a narrow track.

Then a voice spoke softly. "Why, Miss Liang," it said. "What a lovely surprise." I started and gasped. Pan Wang Mang stood before me, his face mostly in shadow, his teeth gleaming in a smile. The others stopped and stood around in a lounging fashion. I now recognized them all as sons of old families in the province, all expensively dressed in fine silk gowns, and I had a moment of relief. But then I saw that their faces were dissolute and unshaved, their eyes red-rimmed, and the silk gowns stained with rice whiskey. One of them was eating a raw radish, sinking his teeth into it ferociously.

"Mr. Pan," I said. "Good evening."

Pan Wang Mang executed a graceful bow. "Miss Liang, good evening to you." He glanced around him, at the empty yard. I could just see his dim profile, still handsome, although blurred with drink. His eyes were weary and prematurely pouchy with dissipation. But he smiled at me, tilted his head to one side, and affected an expression of serious concern. "Miss Liang," he said reprovingly. "Do you really think you should be out here by yourself? It's almost nighttime. I understand that dangerous men haunt these broken buildings." His breath was sour with wine.

"I am on my way home now, Mr. Pan," I said firmly, refusing to meet his eye. "In fact, I am late. My mother will be worried. If I may . . ." I began to move sideways, away from him.

"Don't go yet, Miss Liang," Pan Wang Mang said. His hand shot out from his embroidered sleeve and seized my forearm, holding it lightly. Alarmed, I began to pull away, but his grip tightened so quickly and painfully that I stopped and stood submissively, my feet together and my knees shaking. I stared at his hand on my arm, at the soft fingers and badly bitten nails.

"My friends," Pan announced to his companions. "I don't know if you have all met Miss Liang. If not, you will get to know this lovely blushing flower very well. May I present my fiancée to you, gentlemen. I—whose calligraphy falls so far below the accepted standards for a gentleman—may count myself a lucky man."

Pan's voice was elegant and calm, and he spoke in a courtly tongue, with as much formality as if he had been drinking tea with the Dowager Empress. Ugly ragged sniggers came out of the twilight, and someone imitated the howl of a dog.

Pan loosed my arm. "Be careful, Miss Liang," he said silkily, moving away into the night. "The world is full of alleyways. Bad for an educated young woman like yourself. Please be very careful." He called over his shoulder as he moved away. "As a personal favor to me."

Pan and his friends disappeared into the gloom of the empty lot, the gleaming backs of their silk gowns suddenly quenched by the darkness. I could only watch them with a dagger gaze. I rubbed my pained arm. I knew I would say nothing to my mother or brother, nothing to Jin Yu. Marrying Wang Mang had been my idea, and so marry him I must. My pride has taken on more trouble than I can handle, I thought. Above me, I heard a whirring noise. In the dimming night sky I felt a rush of air on my face, saw a hooked beak, a tangle of soft wings, and heard a dying caw. I watched as a falcon brought down a small brown bird, leaving a smear of blood and feathers on the darkened plain.

On the day I became a wife, I rode to my husband's home in the curtained sedan chair sent by the Pan family, sitting stiffly in my red embroidered gown. I kept my mouth shut and eyes averted all day, jumping up only to serve my mother-in-law. "Have you ever seen a more modest, demure, or better-behaved bride?" the guests murmured. "He's wealthy, and she's nice looking. Everything you need for a real romance," they said, nodding to each other. My mother and sister wore masklike smiles and whispered to each other in corners. Li Shi glanced at me several times, his face carefully neutral. Jin Yu said nothing to me on that day, but only drank her cup of wine and smiled her half smile.

That night, a crowd of raucous younger guests gathered outside the windows of our bridal chamber on the second story of the large, red-gated house of the Pans. Pan Wang Mang and I appeared at the window briefly, my jaw bruised and aching under the carefully reapplied white powder, where my husband had already favored me with his attentions. The well-wishers stayed long into the night, playing drums and banging iron pots together, and singing loud, drunken songs. Inside, lying on my back on my silken bed, Wang Mang's sweat dropping onto my chin, I shut my eyes and put my hands over my ears, the noises of the merrymakers below the window drowned out by the roaring inside my own head.

In the middle of the night, Pan Wang Mang rose from his bridal bed and went out with his friends, leaving me, his new bride, alone under the covers. I clutched the edges of the quilt with desperate fingers. I should have felt only relief at his absence, but instead my heart was twisted into a knot of battling emotions. I felt a failure, I was alone in a vast strange old house, I was ashamed that others would know he left me on our wedding night, when a man is most enamored of his wife—all these things and more were my midnight sustenance, and I wished him back in bed with me just as hard as I had wished him gone forever.

The following morning, I arose before dawn. Wang Mang had not returned. I crept through the long cold corridors of the alien house where I now lived, past the stately rooms with their rows of red-painted pillars. Courtyards, galleries, tiny hidden gardens, endless doorways—I thought I might walk to Canton and never leave the house.

Down in the kitchen, I found several fresh bird's nests sitting in a pile in a basin. Squatting on the floor by the dim light of a guttering candle, I painstakingly picked out every tiny pin feather and bit of down from the bird's nests and at the end of two and a half hours of such blinding work, cooked a soup with the nests. When my parents-in-law arose, I served them the soup, as I had been instructed to do.

I watched them eat with a kind of dread fascination. They were an imperial pair, who sat squarely and heavily like ancestor portraits, stocked to their back teeth with appetite and discontent. They took up every ounce of air in the house. At one point, my father-in-law, Old Pan, stopped and fished about in his mouth with his forefinger, producing a bit of feather. The old couple glared at me, and I crept forward and took the feather off Old Pan's digit. I murmured abject apologies and touched the corner of my eyes with my sleeve. Old Pan and his wife only turned their backs and went on eating.

Sitting quietly in a corner listening to their slurps, trying to hide my tears—my vision spotty from cleaning the nests in the bad light from the candle—I thought about how many more mornings like this would have to take place before these two demanding progenitors died. They looked to me as if they were destined to be long-lived.

My personal unhappiness only increased my desire to help Li Shi buy his commission, and in my youthfulness I seized on my sufferings as a noble price to pay for the advancement of my brother. I waited for a month to pass after my wedding before I tried to borrow the money for Li Shi's commission. I would have preferred to wait longer, but Li Shi and I were afraid that someone else would buy the commission, and my brother harried me every day. So I left the house early one day with a market basket and met Li Shi at a noodle shop near the bridge, and we hurried to the street of moneylenders.

There were banks in Changsha then, and even the common people—those who could be made to trust the bank more than they trusted their own straw sleep mats or a brick in the wall—would deposit their money there. But I was a married woman, and I would not be able to borrow money without Wang Mang's permission. To make things more complicated, the banks would demand something of value as collateral, such as jewels or silver or gold. Of course, if I had such things, I would have no need to borrow money. But the moneylenders down on Pawnbrokers Street were known to lend money on the strength of expectations. A young heir might borrow gambling money because his elderly father was sick. As Wang Mang's wife, I stood to inherit their fortune through my husband, and I could use that to stake the loan.

Pawnbrokers Street was in many ways the strangest street in Changsha. It was an ordinary dirt lane with a runnel of wastewater down its center and one-story wooden buildings lining both sides. The pawnbrokers were on one side of the street and the moneylenders on the other. There was one in particular we came to see, a man who sat in bed all day on a raised platform at the back of his shop, his quilt drawn over him. I don't know how Li Shi came to get his name, but we went to him first.

The shop was dark and musty, three rooms long and one room wide; a sack of grain spilled out near the entrance. Rice grains hung between the warped wooden planks of the floor. We stood in the vestibule and strained our eyes. The day was dim with midwinter, and the only source of light was a single window in front of us, at the far end of the third room. Below the window was the bed of the moneylender Sui, and Sui's own head was silhouetted against the oiled paper pane. We moved toward him in an embarrassed shuffle. He looked up languidly from his bed, where he reclined propped up on one elbow.

"Well, and here you are, Mrs. Pan," was the first thing out of his mouth.

"How do you know my name?"

"I know your husband very well."

Li Shi and I looked at each other.

"We are here because we wish to borrow five thousand taels," Li Shi said.

Sui sat up cross-legged and took out some tins. He proceeded to roll a cigarette from a variety of odds and ends of tobacco, and licked the edge of the paper. His thumb and forefinger were stained a deep yellow from the smoke.

"Sit," he said. "I see the young lady makes a face. Don't worry, there are no lice."

We perched at the edge of the platform bed.

Sui blew out the white breath of his first puff. "What can this poor moneylender do about that? I am always on the verge of bankruptcy because I am so softhearted and kind to the guests who borrow from me."

"I need five thousand taels to purchase a commission," Li Shi said. "I know other young officers have come to you. I am the one taking out the loan and will be responsible to pay you. I will of course have an officer's salary, and I can be relied upon to pay you in full."

"Including nineteen percent interest?" Li Shi opened his mouth in anger, but Sui interrupted. "You won't get a better interest rate on this street. You can go and ask."

Li Shi hesitated a moment. "I can pay," he said.

"But why should I lend you anything? Young officers—well, they are all young bucks, and must always spend their money on women and drink and horses. They always say they will pay, but they are often bankrupt also, and when they go bankrupt, I go bankrupt."

"But sir," I said, distressed, "if you go bankrupt all the time, why do you continue in this business? Why not find another trade?"

Sui threw me a suspicious glare, and looked over at my brother.

"She knows nothing about this," said Li Shi, pinching my arm very hard. "This is my sister, Mrs. Pan. She is willing to stake the loan."

"Ah, a good sister. Well, Mrs. Pan, what do you stake the loan with? Do you have jewelry?" Sui was laughing through the smoke that wreathed his head, his open mouth a dark hole in the whiteness of the smoke and the light from the window behind him.

"I have my expectations," I murmured. "I have married the heir to the Pan fortune. The Pans are elderly . . ."

"And in good health," said Sui dryly.

"But old," I insisted. "My husband will inherit everything, and I am sure I will be able to make good a mere five thousand taels."

"What do you suppose he will inherit?"

I was confused. "Why, the fortune."

"Which is precisely what?"

"The house," I stammered, shifting uncomfortably at the edge of the bed. "The orchards and rice fields. The paintings and antiques that fill the house. I am sure there is gold and silver in Old Pan's strongbox . . ."

I could not continue. Sui had thrown back his head and was laughing in complete silence. He did not make any sound, but he shook with glee, and tears of mirth ran down his cheeks. Li Shi and I stared at him. Sui lay on his back on the bed and pounded his fists on the quilt. When he had laughed this way—without so much as a grunt—for a long time, he sat back up again and pounded the bed.

"Hey," he shouted down. There was a scrabbling noise under the bed which made me jump up in fear of rats. Then a pair of small brown hands emerged, and a large head, and a dwarf scrambled out from under the bed. I smothered a scream with my hand. "Did you hear?" Sui asked the dwarf, who nodded and laid her hand on Li Shi's knee. Li Shi stood up and gave the dwarf a great push which sent her flying into the corner.

"Li Shi . . ." I gasped, and stooped to help her, although when she grabbed my hand to stand up I felt revulsion. Li Shi bent over the bed and snatched up Sui by the greasy collar of his gown and wrenched him into a kneeling position. The veins on my brother's hands bulged.

"I won't be made a fool, Sui," my brother snarled. "What do you mean by this, hiding a spy under your bed? This was confidential business, and I was told you were a man who could keep secrets."

Sui's face flattened like a dog's does when it lays back its ears. "No confidential business will find its way out of this room, unless you bring it out yourself," he murmured.

"Will you lend me the money?" Li Shi shook him until his teeth clattered together.

"No. You have nothing to stake the loan."

"What do you mean, you thief? What about my sister's inheritance?"

A glint of amusement sparked again in Sui's flat black irises. "She has nothing. The Pans have nothing. There is no gold, no silver. They have been selling things out of their house for years, piece by piece. The harvests from their fields have been mortgaged in advance for the next one hundred years. Your sister's grandchildren—assuming she has any—will not eat their fruit. We unworthy ones in this street all know it. It is only you quality folks who have been deceived."

"How can this be?" I cried.

Sui slid his eyes over to me, peeking over my brother's gripping hands. "Expensive habits, young madame. Gambling. Concubines. Hush money. And the most expensive habit of all is to put on a good show for the neighbors."

Li Shi threw him down roughly. "You lie, you dog."

Sui felt his neck tenderly. "Why would I lie about such a thing? Wouldn't I want my nineteen percent?"

"What hush money?" I asked.

Sui shook his head. "Best not to ask about the daughter. Anyway, professional ethics keep my mouth closed. I happen to hold that loan."

I looked at Li Shi in the dim light from the window, and my own shock and panic receded somewhat at the sight of defeat dawning in his face. It was then that I realized that the dwarf still held my hand. When I glanced down, she jittered at me, but I could not understand her words.

Li Shi crossed his arms. "I suppose it would do no good to go to another money lender," he said to Sui in a matter-of-fact tone that was at odds with his recent violence.

Sui nodded in equally businesslike fashion, as if he viewed such incidents as part of his work. "Every moneylender on this street holds accounts receivable from the Pans."

Li Shi turned and walked out of the room. I heard the door slam behind him, and through the latticed side window I saw him standing on the street. I looked again at Sui.

"No wonder they chose you," the man remarked. "The father of an heiress would have demanded a full accounting. But your lot gets by on the glory of your ancestors and never thinks to ask questions about the cash."

He picked his teeth with his gnarled thumbnail.

"Was there anything else, young madame?" he asked carelessly.

I just shook my head. I disengaged my hand from that of the dwarf, who released me gently, looking up into my face and making soft noises. Then I stumbled out into the street.

Li Shi was waiting for me in a side street. I ran up to him. "Li Shi, we'll get the money somewhere."

"Of course we will." His voice was very calm.

"We should visit every moneylender in this street."

"No. Sui is telling the truth." I watched him walk away. I spent the rest of the day visiting the other moneylenders, and they all told me the same thing. I had no expectations of wealth, and I was in peril even then.

I walked home and sat down in exhaustion in one of the reception rooms. I had admired from the first the spare richness of the decor in the reception rooms. But now I looked around more carefully. I got up and walked through the ancestral hall and the other rooms. On almost every wall, I saw for the first time a lighter square or rectangle where a painting had once hung or where a chest had once stood. I thought about all the locked doors in the other courtyards, the rooms closed off from my view.

"I haven't done anything wrong, Mother, to get this commission," Li Shi snapped. "I can see you are very suspicious, but there is no reason. I helped a friend from university pass the mathematics civil service exam. His father was so grateful for the career I saved for his son that he used his friendship with the governor and obtained the commission for me."

"How does he have this power over the governor?" my mother asked, her voice very dry. "Is he blackmailing him?"

"They were at school together."

"Hah. No doubt blackmailing him." My mother rubbed her forehead. "I was unhappy with the fact that we have reached a time in history when army commands might be purchased, but that at least is a straightforward transaction, without hidden costs. This . . . influence brokering makes my mind very uneasy. I yearn for the days of the examinations. The best scholar was given the best position at court, as it was in your father's day."

Li Shi merely shrugged and looked out the window. "It hasn't really worked like that for a long time, Mother," he said. His voice was barely audible.

When my mother and Graceful Virtue had left the room, I touched his sleeve.

"What was the name of the friend you helped pass mathematics?" I asked.

Li Shi did not turn his head. "Why, it was Gao Bao."

"Gao Bao?" I said, astonished. "But he's an idiot. He could never pass mathematics, Li Shi. Did you have to tutor him day and night?"

Li Shi neither replied nor looked at me. Out the window, I saw the newborn buds of the trees trembling in the chilly breezes. I tried to follow his gaze, but saw nothing in particular. Then another thought came to me.

"Did you actually tutor him?" I asked, trying not to sound too doubtful. I hoped he would say yes.

"I took the university graduation exam for him." His lips were pressed together whitely. "I went up to Nanjing, as you know. While I was up there, I went to the exam hall and presented Gao Bao's identity papers. There must have been several hundred of us taking the exam. I am glad to say we passed with honors. Gao Bao is now in the national budget office, no doubt hampering its work. His father paid me. His father, I understand, made his money in opium smuggling, so it is a messy business all around."

"Li Shi, what have you done?" I was horrified.

Li Shi's voice was cold. "What had to be done. You women don't understand. We had undertaken the purchase of the commission. How could I back out? I had to get the rest of the money somehow, so I got it through corruption. And now there is no point in crying about it."

I was weeping softly. We were hissing at each other so my mother would not hear. "I feel as if it were my fault," I sobbed, muffling my voice in my sleeve. "I married for your sake, but I made a terrible mistake, and I couldn't get the money that way. If you have been corrupt, it is because my failure has forced you."

Li Shi stood by the window with his arms crossed. I could not read the expression on his face, but I sensed that he was indeed angry, at both himself and at me. I wiped my eyes on the sleeve of my sweater and put my hands on his arm. We were silent awhile before he spoke again.

"Well, that is the thing about corruption. It spreads to everyone. Never mind. The world is stuffed full with these kinds of things. Better to be the scissors than the cloth."

When I look back on that conversation now, I realize that it was the end of my brother's boyhood, the end of his intransigence, and the beginning of that endless flexibility that was to mark him as a man.

7

The following autumn passed into the winter, and charcoal braziers were lit in every room in the house. I myself carried one into the old Pans' bedroom, staggering under its weight. Afterward, I could not brush away the dark charcoal smears on my dress and went into my own bedroom to change. Wang Mang was already there, standing in the middle of the room and looking around him.

I passed by him and went to the wooden chest where I kept my fresh clothes. I said nothing to him, for frankly I was afraid of his tongue; his words were quietly vicious, like circling hawks, and as quick as well-placed arrows. I kept my back to him as I changed clothes.

"What's this?" I heard his unwelcome voice. I turned.

"That's a new book Jin Yu gave me," I explained, with slightly exaggerated patience. Would he detect the tone in my voice? Had I made it subtle enough?

"Oh? What's it about?" he asked innocently.

"What does it say on the cover?" I replied, as innocently.

"Why, I believe it says *The Changing Industrial Economy*. Published originally in Japan, I see."

"That, then, is the subject of the book." I allowed myself a small smile.

"Very interesting. And I suppose it tells us that the world is changing, and soon all the old ways will be obsolete. Does it not?"

"Ye-es," I replied, cautiously. I could not tell which way this conversation was going.

"All your books tell us that, don't they?" Wang Mang flipped open the book in his hand and regarded the printed page with solemnity. He frowned and tugged at the corners of his mustache in concentration. "Why is that, my dear wife? Do you wish all the old ways to disappear?"

I only stood and watched him. I did not wish to give away any more of my heart's secrets, no more than those he had already squeezed from me simply because I lived with him. I felt that the protection of my mind, if not my body, lay in what I kept from him.

Wang Mang sauntered over to the charcoal brazier, held the book out over the burning embers—just long enough to see the alarm jump into my face—and dropped the book onto the white heat. I darted forward with a little cry and attempted to wrest the book from the flames, but the thin, crusty paper had caught fire immediately, and I pulled my burned fingers away. I set my face like wood and turned my head so I would not have to see him.

Wang Mang's own anger immediately surged in response to my refusal to look at him. "What?" he shouted, coming very close to me and taking my dress deliberately between a contemptuous thumb and forefinger. "What? Are you angry? What are you daring to be angry about? Is it not enough for any man to be married to a woman who wishes for the day when his whole house will crash down on his head?" He yanked at my dress. The housewife's pocket in front ripped, and a small cascade of coins scattered onto the floor.

Wang Mang, on seeing the coins, immediately pushed me out of the way, then bent to gather up the coins. He placed them in his own pouch, under his gown, and started for the door.

"Wait!" I cried. "You can't take that money! It's for the house. What will I do if you take that money?" I rushed at him and clung to his arm. "Please, husband. Leave me the money—at least leave me some. Everything is tight now. I can hardly pay our accounts. Think of what your mother and father will say!"

He shook me off, taking my wrist and peeling me away from him. "I have a better use for the money. I will spend it on wine and dice and women with gold teeth, who will laugh at my jokes." He leaned close and patted my cheek gently. "The ancient poets say, one cup, and a thousand griefs will vanish."

After he left, I sat down on the floor and tugged despairingly at my hair. I braided it and rebraided it until my fingers ached. I wondered why a man who possessed so much wit tried so hard to corrupt and erase that wit. I recognized in Wang Mang some dark element, a hard contempt, a subterranean stream that was poisoning him. But I did not know the source of that bitter river.

Five small bruises appeared on my forearm later, a souvenir of Wang Mang's hard grasp. I drew my sleeve down to hide them from my mother, but I went to tell Jin Yu. I found her in her small study, writing a letter which she casually covered up when I was brought in. I saw this, and in the midst of my concerns about Wang Mang, I felt a pang of hurt and jealousy. Ever since I had married, there were secrets between Jin Yu and myself.

"This is a surprise." Jin Yu smiled, looking up. Then her smile faded. "What's wrong with you?"

I was suddenly reluctant. I had been eager to tell Jin Yu about my dealings with Wang Mang, but now the peaceful fastness of the study made my story seem like a sordid thing. But I came forward and stood at Jin Yu's desk.

"You look as if you have something to tell me," Jin Yu said.

In reply, I merely pulled up my sleeve.

"A mark of affection from my husband," I said, showing the prints on my skin.

Jin Yu's face immediately darkened with fury, in that rapid way of hers. The speed with which her anger always surpassed mine, overtaking me and passing me like a hunting dog, never failed to take me by surprise.

"He is always hitting you or insulting you—why do you stand it?" Jin Yu snapped. "You must tell your mother about this. You must tell Li Shi. If you won't, I'll tell them."

"Telling them would only grieve their hearts, and produce no other result. As it is, my mother still thinks they are rich and that therefore my life is in easy circumstances."

"Does Li Shi know the truth about their money?"

"Yes, he does." I leaned against the edge of the desk with a sigh. "I just can't understand them."

"Don't bother to understand them," Jin Yu spat. "That is typical of you, always trying to understand. The Pan family is very old and arrogant. They claim they trace their ancestry back to the dukes of Chin. So do we, for that matter." Jin Yu snorted in disdain. "As if that made a difference. This ancestor worship. What a disease. Descent from the dukes of Chin should be a criminal offense."

I rubbed my eyes with the heels of my hands. Sometimes, Jin Yu's concepts of right and wrong irritated me. She had as much regard for bloodline, it seemed, as the Pans did, only she would punish what the Pans would glorify. "Don't be silly, Jin Yu. How can you punish people for their ancestors?" She looked away with a shrug, as if I failed to comprehend her.

My flare of annoyance passed, and I sat down on a chair across the desk from Jin Yu. I suddenly felt weak in the stomach, as if I were hungry. "Frankly, I'm afraid of him. He's already earned himself a wicked reputation—he gambles and drinks; he plays cruel jokes. I heard he had an insane fit at the Painted House just a few days ago and broke all the furniture and beat the businesswomen."

"Don't you know why?" Jin Yu asked. "I heard this from one of the cooks, who heard it from her cousin who is cook at the Painted House. I meant to tell you when I saw you next. Wang Mang was infatuated with one of the whores there. So the Pan family purchased the girl and sold her to a mule driver going to the north, in exchange for the ivory toothpick the driver happened to be cleaning his teeth with at the moment. When Wang Mang went back to the Painted House, they brought him a different woman. The favorite was gone forever. So he went mad. Almost as if he were grief-stricken." Jin Yu drew her eyebrows together thoughtfully, as if she had surprised herself. "How strange I never thought of it before. He *is* grief-stricken."

"What would he be grieved about?" I asked. "Not some prostitute, surely?" And was immediately ashamed at what I had said.

Jin Yu looked at her hands. "Who knows? But the world has changed. Pan Wang Mang, whatever else he may be, is not stupid. He knows he is fit for nothing except to be an old lord's son." She paused thoughtfully and chewed a thumbnail. "My father said that he heard the Pans actually want to sell land. It's a bad sign."

The two of us sat in silence for a while.

"The only thing I can do is commit suicide," I finally said.

"Don't," Jin Yu said, sitting up in displeasure. "Poison him instead."

But I shook my head. "I can't be a murderer. But I can kill myself, and punish them by the shame of my death."

She came around to my side of the desk and put her arm around my shoulders in her old affectionate way. "We'll think of something. There is always a second path through the mountains."

"I thought you would want me to do something dramatic," I sighed, leaning against her.

"I'm trying to teach you to be effective. Your death won't punish them nearly as much as it will punish you. If you really want to punish them, then stay among the living."

My mother was invited to the wedding of Miss Zhao, who was to marry the second son of a great house, a family that owned many rice fields and orchards and whose warehouses were always full to bursting. She brought only my sister, since Li Shi hated weddings and refused to attend. I myself also attended the wedding with my mother-in-law, Mrs. Pan, and without Wang Mang, who was missing from home that day. Each of us carried a fine present wrapped in red silk. The guests gathered at the groom's house, overflowing the main courtyard onto the galleries of the buildings and out onto the streets, to await the arrival of the bride's sedan chair. An old friend of Mrs. Pan snatched at my dress, smiled a sugary smile, and asked the same coy question she always asked whenever she saw me. "When are we going to drink the wine for your first baby, my dear girl?" She made a rounding motion with her hands in front of her belly. I leaned against a wall in misery.

The bride's sedan chair appeared at the rise in the street, elaborate with swags of red silk and gold brocade, the girl herself concealed behind heavy curtains. Jade bridle bells hung on the chair tinkled merrily in the clear air. "Eight sedan chair carriers," murmured the guests, impressed. A band of musicians appeared behind the chair, carrying their lutes and timbrels. The guests clapped their hands and shouted greetings. A few of the men indulged in spicy jokes for the groom's benefit.

When the carriers set the chair down, the groom stepped forward to catcalls from his school friends. He parted the curtains and leaned inside. He staggered backward with a terrified yowl, and fell fainting into the arms of the guests behind him. As the horrified wedding party watched, the body of Miss Zhao slid slowly into view, flopping out diffidently to hang upside down, half in and half out of the curtained recess. Her stained face was white with rice powder; the front of her red embroidered gown was soaking wet. The long glint of metal in her hand fell to the ground with a click. Miss Zhao had cut her own throat in the bridal sedan chair. All around me, there was a thick hush, which broke apart into the terrified screams of the guests, running as fast as they could, away from the wedding, away from the evil luck that Miss Zhao had brought down on them. My last glimpse as I was rushed away by my mother and mother-in-law was of Miss Zhao's bloodless hand, dangling above the straight razor she had used to erase her name from the tablets in the family temple, and I wondered, even as I fled, how Miss Zhao had held her hand so steady all the way through.

The next day, I told Jin Yu all that I had seen at the wedding. I buried my face in my hands.

"No one knew she opposed the wedding," I moaned.

"Did anyone bother to ask?"

I shook my head. "No, of course no one asked. Her family is paralyzed with shame. Neither family wants the responsibility of burying the body, so it's still lying unwashed in the police hall. They're already arranging another marriage for the groom."

"I suppose they'll keep this new bride away from sharp things."

I looked up at this. "How can you be so cold about poor Miss Zhao?"

"Poor Miss Zhao should have saved that razor for her father-in-law's neck."

I sat up and rubbed my face. "I won't commit suicide now," I told Jin Yu. "Miss Zhao's white face haunts me. I had a terrible dream last night."

"What was your dream?" Jin Yu asked more gently.

"In the dream, I slept on a wooden pallet in a bare room in an isolated country inn. Behind a curtain, Miss Zhao's body lay, waiting to be buried. As I lay there with my eyes closed, I realized that the corpse had moved, had stood up, and was bending over me, watching for any movement of mine. Her breath was poisonous, but I had to lie still. When the corpse turned away for just a moment, I leaped up and ran to the door and out into the night. But Miss Zhao's corpse chased me, gnashing her teeth with rage. I ran through the black forest, the branches reached out to snatch me and trip me—all I could hear was the thumping of my heart and the pounding of Miss Zhao's black-bound feet behind me. When I awoke, I was covered with sweat."

Even as I told the story, my lip broke out with perspiration. Jin Yu frowned with concern and wiped it away with her silk sleeve.

"Don't be frightened," Jin Yu said. "It was only a nightmare. I'm glad you've decided not to kill yourself. Stay and fight."

"I won't kill anyone, Jin Yu."

"I know," Jin Yu said. "But go down with your teeth in their heels, like a snake."

8

*M*y only advantage lay in the fact that Wang Mang liked to drink and gamble in the dance halls with his friends throughout the night, and would only come home in the early mornings, his gown grubby and his breath humid with wine. In his absences I would sit quietly in a ground-floor room, reading or sewing, enjoying the garden from the window. One early evening, my shutter clattered open, and Xiang Jin Yu put her pale face into the room. The effect was the same as if she had flung a flaming brand into the house. I ran to the window.

"Jin Yu, you go too far. Why are you at the window, like a burglar?" I was laughing like a child through my words of reproach, and I clutched my friend's arm.

Jin Yu leaned against the sill insouciantly, like a stableboy. She was wearing a plain black gown, and her pale face stood out sharply against the darkness of the garden. "I came to break you out of prison," she said casually. "Come to my house. I have some friends there, all the young teachers from First Normal. Here, just push that footstool over here and step up on it. I'll help you."

I looked around guiltily. "I don't like stealing out of the house."

"I agree. If it were me, I would walk out the front, and slam the door on my way. But since it's you, let's just make do with the window."

"How arrogant you always are," I snapped, as I hiked up my dress. "It's your least attractive quality." I tumbled out the window, collapsing in a heap onto the geraniums. I laughed, and was sternly shushed by Jin Yu. We ran through the dark streets to Jin Yu's house.

The young teachers who taught at First Normal were already present and drinking tea. They welcomed me warmly. "Welcome, welcome," they said. "Speak freely. We are all New China here." I plucked a few leaves from my hair and smiled. No one seemed surprised at my bedraggled appearance.

The men wore Western trousers and wing-tipped leather shoes under their gowns. One of the young women even carried a watch, on a chain pinned to her dress. I recognized them all from protest demonstrations in the town and from reform-minded political societies. The young woman with the watch was known to have very pronounced views on the rights of women and had taught herself English in order to read about British suffragettes. Men and women alike, they all talked a great deal, and it all sounded like treason.

"My eldest brother is in Beijing," said one of them, inhaling the fragrance of his jasmine tea and rolling the warm teacup around in his hands. It was a soft night, and the shutters were open. "He did very well in the examinations, back when they gave examinations, and now he is an official in the Ministry of Revenue. He said he submitted a very long memorial about how, every year, the imperial administration is able to collect fewer and fewer taxes owed to it. My brother says that is a sign of the decay of government. He got it back with a note about his calligraphy style. No one cared about the contents of the report."

The others nodded in confirmation. "Exactly," said the young lady who wore the watch. "Remember what Kang Yuwei said. Relying on the reactionaries to save China is like climbing a tree in search of fish."

"And they drove Kang Yuwei into exile in Japan. Meanwhile, we remain here, under the thumb of the foreign powers."

"In Shanghai," said Jin Yu, who had recently visited that city with her father, "there is a sign in the park. 'No dogs, no Chinese.' I wept when I saw it."

I enjoyed their free talk and easy manners, so different from the sullen mood at the Pan dinner table. I enjoyed their air of authority. I sat and listened with pleasure to the crisp purpose of their voices and the hint of danger in the criticisms they made.

Then I glanced out the open window into the dark garden. I jumped up wildly and upset my teacup, which cracked sharply on the floor.

"What is it?" Jin Yu asked, alarmed.

"Wang Mang is outside," I whispered, trying to keep the panic from my voice.

"How does that adder know you are here?"

"I don't know."

Within seconds, Wang Mang had pushed his way into the room, shoving aside the servants roughly. He grabbed my arm and started to drag me out.

"How dare you burst into my house like this?" Jin Yu exclaimed, trying to block the way.

Wang Mang sneered. "Can even you come between husband and wife?" he asked insultingly.

"Don't," I begged. "It will only be worse for me if you interfere."

Jin Yu fell back, her face burning with fury and frustration.

As we left, the young lady who wore the watch hurled her cup out the window in sudden anger, and we heard it shatter on the tiles around the goldfish pond.

Wang Mang hauled me home by my hair, twisting the black length around his hand and forcing me to stumble behind him, bent double and clutching at his gown for support. Louts in the road pointed and jeered, and shouted obscene suggestions. My face burned with shame.

Once inside our bedroom, I bore Wang Mang's blows silently. He shouted insults loudly enough for the entire house to hear, pushed me around the room, and pulled my hair out of its hairpins. "Don't think I won't always know where you are!" he shouted. "I always know! Where else would you go, except to that damned woman?"

I felt I could not bear my own silence any longer. "Why do you do this?" I screamed, choking on my anger. "You don't ever wish to see me yourself—why do you care if I go to Jin Yu's house? I have never dishonored you."

Surprisingly, Wang Mang turned me loose and replied coolly. "I know you haven't. Do you think I would care if you did? Sleep with the boys who read books, Jade Virtue, if that is what you want."

I raised my head and brushed aside a veil of loosened hair. My hands were shaking and my scalp ached, but my eyes were wide with astonishment. "Then why do you behave like this?"

Wang Mang turned away and threw himself down into a chair, which creaked at the sudden weight. He picked up one of my books from the table and began with great deliberation to tear pages out of it, one at a time. He shredded each page into very small pieces. His eyes were in shadow, cast by the wooden window shutter, but the yellow light of the oil lamp struck his lower face harshly. I noticed for the first time that he had a slight tic in his upper lip, as if a moth were fluttering under his skin.

"Why should anyone want to be away from me?" he finally asked, with a small, tight smile.

At first, Wang Mang always came home from the gambling halls and taverns in the early hours of every morning, drunk and reeling. But in another year he started to be absent for a night and a day and night at once, and would arrive home groggy and uncertain in the middle of the afternoon. I said nothing, but I noticed that he was becoming thinner. After one such occasion, when he had been gone three days, he stayed home in the evening, to recruit his strength on homemade wine and a large meal.

After eating dinner, he sat lounging in a chair, looking out the window at the fading light, and flicking seeds to the songbirds in their cages on the sill. A cool and pleasant breeze drifted in from the small garden and nudged at the shutters. I sat nearby and wrote a letter to the tradesman who had that very morning presented a large bill to me for wine. I was cross with Wang Mang's free spending and answered him coldly. But Wang Mang did not appear to notice.

"I see your brother has recently distinguished himself," Wang Mang remarked. "Li Shi will be promoted for this. Everyone was talking about it in the taverns yesterday."

I rattled the abacus loudly before answering. "I don't know. I don't listen to people in taverns."

"Well, his strategy captured Pang the millstone maker. It couldn't have been easy, since Pang and his followers had tunneled into the very sides of the mountain."

"Li Shi has always been very brave."

Wang Mang sighed. "Ambitious too, or so I hear. I see he has cut off his queue and started to slick his hair, like the other young cocks in the army. He doesn't seem to need eyeglasses anymore, for that matter, now that he no longer sits behind a desk."

I turned my head slightly. In the corner of my eye, I could see my husband, but he was merely looking out the window, a careless expression on his face. I sensed potential trouble for my brother, hearing the envious whispers of tavern dwellers and rumormongers echoing in Wang Mang's offhand comment.

"Not really," I said, equally offhand, shuffling paper and scratching my pen busily. "Li Shi is very dedicated to his duty. He has no personal ambition. If he did, I would know, since I am his sister, and I would tell you, since you are his brother-in-law."

"Well, the governor is going to promote him. Is he too shy and retiring for that?"

"It would be Li Shi's duty to accept whatever position the governor wanted him to take. You know that."

"Hmm. Pang the millstone maker will be put to death by slicing in a few days."

"They seem to be using that method more now."

"Yes. It's very ostentatious, but it sets a good example to the other Elder Brothers. If Pang is an Elder Brother. There are so many clandestine brotherhoods now, all promising the universe. I hardly know which one to join to enter heaven." Wang Mang smiled at his joke.

"Don't let Li Shi hear you say that," I said briskly. "Or it would be his duty to arrest you."

Wang Mang eyed me narrowly, but only shrugged. He took out a silk pouch and a pipe, and began to stuff the pipe with soft filling from the pouch. I frowned, a little bewildered—I knew Wang Mang chewed betel, but I had never seen him smoke.

I watched him suck greedily at the pipe, smelled the strange sweetness of the smoke, and felt my own head grow light. I saw Wang Mang's eyes grow foggy and distant, even as his fingers twitched along the length of the pipe. Opium, I thought. He has become one of the opium eaters. I remembered the waxy, weary countenances of the opium smokers I had seen, the rich old ladies and the wastrel sons in the halls of the big houses, the skinny wrinkled anonymous men who leaned out of the upper windows of brothels. I knew that the opium smokers drifted away from the living. I watched my husband carefully. I walked in and out of the room several times to test his reaction, but he did not appear to notice—his dulled eyes remained far away. From then on, I often prepared his pipe for him.

WOOD

9

The midwife confirmed my first pregnancy before the New Year, and the astrologer predicted a son. As a result, the Pans held an unusually large New Year's celebration that year. Dozens of hired cooks from the town arrived with their own clay stoves, which they set in a row in the courtyard and stuffed with glowing coals. From their iron pots, they turned out fat dumplings swimming in soup. From their great flat pans, they produced whole fish, striped with silver and freshly caught in the Xiang River that very morning, steamed with garlic and sesame oil and spread thick with scales of ginger. Great pieces of snowy pork were sliced with their heavy cleavers and flung into skillets of hot oil; the oil roared and snapped back, spackling the hands of the cooks and raising little puffs on their skin.

The guests arrived with boxes of cakes; Wang Mang's friends arrived with flasks of wine. The Pans hugged their happy secret to themselves. Outside the walls of the Pan family house, some small children squatted like pond frogs in the midwinter dark, rubbing their hands and feet together against the February chill, hoping that the leftovers would be handed out to them from the gates.

Ten round tables, with ten guests each, were set up in the main hall of the Pan house, which had been decorated with red paper. I sat at the center table, in a new black silk dress, a gift from my mother-in-law. Madame Pan spent all evening picking up food in her chopsticks and placing the pieces almost shyly on the edge of my plate. "Is that piece good?" she would ask. "If you don't like it, I'll pick out a better piece for you, and I'll eat the bad one." At the end of the supper, before the sweets, Madame Pan picked up the entire plate where a whole fish had rested an hour before and poured the juices into a bowl of rice. "Eat this," she said, handing the bowl to me. "It's good for you." She leaned close to whisper, "Then you'll have as many eggs as the fish." She laughed at her own joke and patted my shoulder.

My mother sat at the next table with Graceful Virtue—Li Shi was eating New Year's dinner at the governor's palace. She wore the carefully attentive expression of a meditating Buddha. But she was worried. At some point in the evening, she whispered to me, "It's bad luck to celebrate so early, even inside one's own heart. It will attract bad luck."

"I'm just grateful everyone is so pleased," I replied, my heart buoyant at the eager attention being paid to me.

"Pathetically grateful," my mother murmured in a low, dry voice. "Try not to look so pathetically grateful."

Wang Mang greeted the guests with a smile and a nod, but did not shout or sing. He drank a great deal, prompting a worried look from his mother; I myself averted my face crossly from him, even though he often looked over to me, as if seeking reassurance. But now I was the stronger one, since I carried the grandson inside my stomach, and I meant to indulge my feelings just a little. When the dinner was over and the guests had left, he made to follow me down the hall to our bedroom.

Glancing back, I saw Madame Pan take his arm. "Son, your wife is very tired," I heard her say. "You should let her sleep quietly." But Wang Mang only shook off her hands and followed me.

I undressed and lay down in my cotton shift. I did not look at him, but only turned over on my side with my back toward him and said, "Turn out the lamp when you're ready to come to bed." Then I lay there, waiting for his weight on the mattress, for his breath on my neck and his hand under the bedclothes. But the bed was undisturbed, and I remained alone, the light still gleaming brightly. Opening my eyes, I saw Wang Mang's shadow on the wall before me, its gray shape flickering in the lamp flame. He was sitting very still.

I craned my head over my shoulder and saw that Wang Mang was sitting on a chair by the bed. He had taken off his shoes, but he was still fully clothed. His face, freshly shaven for the New Year, was ruddy and irritated from the newly-sharpened razor, and his eyes were dark with fatigue. He seemed, however, wide awake.

"Well, what is it? Are you sick?" I asked brusquely.

He waited a long time before answering. I turned over onto my back and looked at him more closely.

"I had a dream last night," he said simply.

"Is that all?" I began to turn my back to him again. "You started drinking before noon yesterday. I'm sure it was a bad dream."

But Wang Mang answered, "When I awoke, I felt my heart had been broken, like a glass window, and a cold wind blew inside."

I turned to him again and regarded him in amazement. He merely continued to sit, looking at some place on the farthest wall.

"What was the dream?" I asked, sitting up in bed. Wang Mang rubbed his eyes tiredly. When he did not answer, I said, in a softer tone, "Tell me your dream."

Wang Mang replied, "I was lying in a field, and I had been sleeping the entire day. I could feel the sun on my closed eyelids and dry lips. Then I felt a weight on my chest, and I opened my eyes to see what it was. There was a little girl sitting on my chest, just a few years old by the size of her. She was so pretty, and I reached out to touch her."

He hesitated.

"What happened then?" I asked. I felt a cool draft from under the door, a rush of air, and I held the edges of the silk quilt tightly.

"Then I saw her eyes. They were white and empty. Not like a blind man's eyes, with a milky film, but white and vacant like the plains of a desert. When I saw her empty eyes, I knew she was not a little girl. I knew she was a ghost."

"No," I whispered.

"She opened her arms wide, as if to embrace me. I was frightened. I sat up and pushed her away. Then she raised her arms to the sky and flew away, into the setting sun. I jumped to my feet and called for her to come back. Again and again I cried out. But she did not return."

Wang Mang put his head in his hands. "I wish I had not pushed her away."

"What can this mean?" I cried. "What kind of dream is this? Wang Mang! Answer me!"

But Wang Mang did not answer. He remained where he was, with his face resting against his palms.

When my daughter was born, she was named Lai Di, which means "bring a younger brother." My second daughter was named Zhao Di, which means much the same thing. Neither child survived her first month, and neither of their small spirits sent a brother to take her place.

·   ·   ·

As the years passed and Wang Mang smoked more opium, his desires for wine, dice, and women decreased, and he became content to live his pleasures only in his mind. Behind his eyes lay the entire universe of good and bad things. He would lie on a reed mat in a room on the second story of a gambling hall in the town with the other smokers, served a pipe by a tired woman with betel-blackened teeth. Eventually, I would send a servant to fetch him home, to eat and sleep and begin the immortal cycle over again. I met with Jin Yu and her group as often as I pleased. The moments when he was clear in his mind, sarcastic and callous and sharp, grew fewer and fewer, and one day disappeared altogether. Wang Mang the man sank out of sight as if he had drowned, and only his empty body still bobbed lightly on the surface of his river of smoke.

But the opium itself remained, extending its power, witchlike, beyond the confines of Wang Mang's rapidly wasting body to the rest of the house, sucking in what was left of the riches of the Pan household with an unending appetite. Gold, jewels, land, servants—all these things were eaten up in Wang Mang's pipe.

On a winter's day, my mother passed by an orchard owned by the Pans and saw the unfamiliar figure of a stocky man in early middle age, walking around, looking at the trees and patting their trunks, crunching the light frost under his shoes. The great gray winter sky stood like a wall behind him, and the barren branches of the trees fingered it gingerly.

"You there," she called to him, coming to the edge of the property. "You are trespassing in the Pan orchard."

The man looked up at her in surprise. Then a wide smile creased his broad brown face.

"My orchard," he shouted back, in unmistakable satisfaction. "I bought it yesterday."

My mother's face reddened. "I'm sorry," she murmured. "I was unaware." She looked at the ground in shame.

"Never mind, madam. A very recent change of ownership. But I've had my eye on this piece for a long time. I knew I only had to wait and it would come into my hands. The property needs a lot of time and effort, but I have both."

My mother listened, holding her face carefully still.

"A thousand taels only. Ah, the Pan properties. Fruit drops from the rotten tree. I stand underneath with my waiting basket." He chuckled richly.

"I see," my mother said. "Yes. Well, I must go. Good fortune with the new land, sir."

"Thank you, thank you," the man called out, already on his way to inspect the rest of his trees. "If you are passing by in the summer, you may rest in the shade. I don't mind. Just tell them you have permission from Cho the landlord."

Looking back at him as she hurried away, my mother remembered the man's broad black coat moving clearly among the trees, sharp against the iron skies, bulking large with ownership.

She ran directly to our house, where she found painters at work repainting the outer walls a new ocher red. She entered and found me sitting in the middle of the central hallway on a small wooden stool, reading a book. There was no coal in the brazier, and I was wearing several layers of clothes and had wrapped a bed quilt around my waist. The air had a damp chill and rested unpleasantly on the skin.

"Mother." I smiled, getting up.

But my mother was angry. "Where is your fire?" she demanded, pointing at the hollow brazier.

I sighed. "We save the coal for formal dinners now."

"Indeed? Saving money, are we?"

"Mother, why are you angry? What's happened?"

"But there are painters outside, painting the walls red."

"For New Year's. We do it every year. You know that."

She sat down on the stool I had just vacated, sat with her gowned knees apart, her small hands balled into fists on her thighs. She glared into the middle distance.

I felt a little afraid. "Mother," I said. "Mother? Take off your coat. Come sit on a more comfortable chair. Mother, please. I don't know why you are acting this way. I'll get something for you to drink."

"No. Sit and listen."

I sank obediently to the floor by my mother's feet.

"I blame myself," she began. "I was blind; I accepted appearances as if they were reality, me of all people. But now the Pans have sold their orchard." And she told me about her meeting with Cho the landlord.

"It's just an orchard. Cho the landlord is a very low person. He used to be a barber until he made money."

"Have you no sense? The Pans are not barbers or salt dealers or blacksmiths. They do not make money from anything except their land. And now that land is going. Cho may be, as you say, a low person—and it is they who have taught you to speak this way—but now he has the orchard and you do not. It is not the first piece of land they have sold, is it? Tell me the truth. If you lie, heaven will punish you."

I hung my head. "It's true."

"Selling cheaply in order to sell quickly."

I nodded.

"To pay for what?"

I was too ashamed to answer.

"You cannot let things go on as they are," my mother said. I felt her eyes boring into my own, a gaze like a diamond drill driving her own resolve home to her daughter. "Close down the unused wings of the house. Surely the four of you can live comfortably in one set of rooms. If you do this now, you may still be Wang Mang's widow with some small amount of money. His time is not long."

I shook her head. "The Pans won't live that way—how will they face their friends?"

"Their friends?" my mother asked. "Their friends?" She gestured around her, at the large empty room in which we sat. "Where are these friends? Do you see them?"

I looked away and shrugged.

"You can act either richer than you are or poorer than you are," my mother snapped. "I suggest the second course of action. And I suggest it soon. The meat is already very close to the bone. I would rather see you wear cotton in two rooms under a roof, my daughter, than wear dirty silk in the street."

"The Pans won't do it," I pleaded.

My mother leaned very close to my face. "Then you must make them," she said.

10

*T*here had been no bird's nest soup for many mornings now; I began to bring tea to the elder Pans in the morning, before switching to plain hot water. White tea, as we called it. But I brought the boiled water in the same covered bowls that the soup and the tea had been served in, so that the water looked like something better. I paid each of the servants some coins from a precious hoard I was learning to keep and dismissed them one by one over the days, until I was left with only a single maid for all work. Wang Mang in his fog did not notice, and the Pans pretended to see nothing.

Finally, I hired two men to move some beds and chairs into a few chambers in the front of the house. The kitchen, the ancestral hall, a bedroom for each of the Pans and one for myself and my husband, when he was there—that would be our world now. That afternoon, I walked through all the dozens of abandoned rooms, closing the window shutters as I went, dropping the latches into their slots with a metallic click of finality.

When I got to the central hall, I found Mrs. Pan waiting for me, standing in the slanting blaze of sunlight that poured through the windows. Her tiny shadow was black as anger on the stone floor.

"You have not asked my permission," Mrs. Pan shouted, her face whitened with temper. "You have sent away my servants and closed off my house. In broad daylight! Everyone has seen this thing! You are a thief and a vandal."

I said nothing, not trusting my own tongue. I shut a window and moved to the next one.

Mrs. Pan shouted, "I am speaking to you! Have you lost your mind?"

I walked the entire circuit of the room, shutting one window after another without hesitation. As I moved around the hall, the glaring white wash of sunlight began to dim, thinning like a drying river, fading into Mrs. Pan's shadow until the entire room was a blank-faced twilight gray.

Mrs. Pan was incensed. "You fool! You slut! You unspeakable slut! You have shamed me before all my friends!" She stood quivering in fury in the center of the hall and stamped her feet on the floor.

I locked the last window and walked toward the door. As I passed Mrs. Pan, I came to a stop. Without turning my body, turning only my head, I spoke in a voice that was almost a whisper.

"You will have to eat your shame, because there is nothing else. As to the reason why, you will have to ask your son."

I left the room. Behind me, I heard Mrs. Pan hurrying to the room that now held her bedstead, and heard the door slam. I ignored the old lady and simply spent the afternoon stacking dishes and quilts in the rooms where the family now would live. At the end of the day, my work completed, I sent the serving girl to the market for some salt beef, which I reasoned would come more cheaply than fresh meat. I walked through the abandoned rooms and ended up back in the central hall.

Once there, I was suddenly tired, and squatted on the floor like an old market woman, looking at the darkness. Through the slats in the shutters, I could just make out a few stars in the night sky.

There was already dust on the furniture in the closed rooms. I rubbed my face with my sore, cracked fingers. After only one day, I thought, the house was already dead. It will not breathe again. Soon I will have sold all the ornaments and furniture. Bit by bit, like a burrowing worm, I will dismantle the body of this house until it is only a skeleton, its white parts sticking out of the ground. I wonder if grave robbers ever feel as I do now.

That night, I could hear my mother-in-law pacing in the next room, and smelled the lantern burning in the old lady's window. I eventually brought myself to go to Mrs. Pan's room and put the old woman back to bed, murmuring soothing words.

"Will there be enough money for my burial?" groaned the old lady, as she climbed obediently beneath the covers.

"Of course," I said. "Don't worry. A long life yet to come."

I pulled the covers up over the birdlike body. Mrs. Pan, surprised at these small attentions, patted my hand and sighed before turning over under the quilt and closing her eyes.

"Don't leave," she murmured.

"I won't," I said, and sat on a chair nearby, trying to make myself comfortable for the remainder of the night. The moon filled the room, paling and softening Mrs. Pan's old face. Poor thing, I thought with genuine pity. I can't even get her a fine coffin ahead of time, for her to look at while she's dying. I hope for her sake she runs out of life before we run out of money.

I began to sell more items from the house. But I had many unpleasant surprises in store. Some of the more unused rooms were already completely empty, the fine furniture and books and porcelain and paintings that had ornamented them gone far away to other people's houses. The Pans had indeed sold precious things cheaply, with no idea of their true value, for the sake of swiftness and secrecy. They had eaten out the center of their own wealth. And Mrs. Pan's jewels turned out to be paste. The jeweler shook his head at me, holding out a coral necklace, embarrassed for my sake. I fled from the shop, my cheeks burning with shame. Selling my mother-in-law's jewels was bad enough, I thought, wiping away a tear when I was around the corner. But to try to sell fake ones was for some strange reason even worse. My shame was bottomless in those days.

But to feed Wang Mang's parents while Wang Mang fed his opium pipe, I realized I had to do more. I finally went to Jin Yu, whom I had been avoiding since the downturn in my husband's family's fortunes. Jin Yu, returning from what was no doubt a stimulating tutorial with the famous Teacher Yang, found me outside the Xiang gate, leaning against the wall wordlessly. Only cloth shoes separated my feet from the light dusting of snow on the ground, and my face had begun to show lines of wear, for worry always brings age with it, no matter how young and beautiful you are.

Jin Yu approached and took my hands in her own.

"I'm sorry you have to see me like this, my sister," I said.

Jin Yu drew her eyebrows together disapprovingly. "Don't abase yourself," she said. "There is no need to be this way. It is a needle to my heart. Am I not your friend?"

She led me inside. The tracks of my cloth shoes in the light frost, leading into her gate, were soon erased by the falling snow.

"Why don't you just leave them? Leave that whole house to sink into its swamp of decadence." Jin Yu was sitting across the dining table from me, watching me hungrily eat cold rice and pickles. "Don't lick the bowl, Jade Virtue. There's more food in the kitchen."

"I can't. You don't understand. I would be ashamed to abandon them now. I can't marry Wang Mang when I think he's rich"—I faltered a moment, thinking about the paste jewels in the bottom of my drawer—"and then desert him when I find out he's poor."

Jin Yu shrugged before turning to the cook. "Bring Mrs. Pan some salt eggs. I know we have some," she ordered. She turned back. "Do you want a loan? I'll get my father to lend you money. He'll do it because your father's memory is respected."

"No, no! A loan would be the worst thing. This opium sucks our blood—I don't want it to suck anyone else's. More money would just be put into Wang Mang's pipe and smoked away. Do you have any tea eggs too?"

Jin Yu gestured silently for more dishes. She watched me eat, and her white face was thoughtful.

"I can think of only one thing," she said finally. "You will have to go to work."

I looked up from my rice bowl, my mouth full and my chopsticks still at my lips.

"Yes, I said work," snorted Jin Yu. "You can teach at the girls' middle school. Teacher Yang knows the principal. I've told Teacher Yang all about you."

"You have? What did you say?"

"Have you ever met him? Spoken to him?"

"No, I've seen him, but I've never spoken to him. What did you say about me?"

Jin Yu leaned forward and opened her mouth. I had been balancing a piece of salt egg on my chopsticks, and I impatiently put it in Jin Yu's mouth.

"I told him," Jin Yu said, swallowing the sliver of cooked yolk, "that you were a brilliant young woman with a fine mind, but that you were not going to be a revolutionary."

I looked at Jin Yu a moment. I looked away into the distance, past the dining room door, down the long hallway that led to the kitchen. I could only just see the figures of the cook and the kitchen maids moving about like shadow puppets, with sudden, jerky movements, mysterious because I could not see the whole of what they were doing. One of them was bending over, one of them was moving her arms about, but I could see only fragments of motion from where I sat, and the true meaning of their movements remained hidden.

I picked up some more food. "No, I am not," I agreed. "I am not like you."

Jin Yu spoke again. "But Teacher Yang suggested that you teach. The girls' school will hire you."

"I've never taught school."

"You are an educated person. Why can't you start? Schoolteachers are very honorable."

I was still hesitant. "My in-laws would be so ashamed, a married woman going out to work like that. I have to think about it."

Jin Yu only remarked dryly, "Just tell them you are going to be paid."

II

*I*n spite of Jin Yu's words, however, I hesitated about starting to work. Indeed, there were too many other things to worry about. Wang Mang was often sick, and I was kept busy nursing him. He spent most of the burning summer of the year 1911 in bed, feverish and tossing, the covers thrown off in the summer heat. I sat beside him with a pan of cool water in my lap, and from time to time I sponged his face with a rag. Heat radiated in waves from the wooden ceiling, so close to the sun. I was often drowsy with heat and boredom, and my head nodded. I was twenty-one, and I had been married three years.

That year was also the 267th year of the Qing dynasty. In Wuhan, in Hunan, in Nanjing, strikers thronged the cities—railroad workers and ironmongers and charcoal burners. They formed militias without guns or uniforms, but they poured sand into the new combustion engines and broke the legs of the horses that carried the Qing soldiers. When the imperial government sold off portions of the railroad to Japan and France and England to enrich itself, the strikers dug up the iron rails, and locomotives jumped their tracks, coming to crash in the dense soil. The bodies of the strikers who were caught dangled from the telegraph poles, sagging heavily on their ropes like grapes near harvest.

All around me, China heaved with rebellion and fury, but I was secreted in a room under the eaves of the old mansion, watching a man poison his blood with opium and counting the holes drilled by wasps in the ceiling beams. I could not bear to dwell on my own thoughts, could not bear to think that my life—which I once believed might affect all of society—had been reduced to this room, and this sick man. The pain came not from the fact that I was not doing what I dreamed of with my life, but from the realization that I would never do it, ever. A slow, choking desperation was building in me that I could barely keep down inside. I had very

little resilience to resist the most evil thoughts about myself, and I was easily upset. I will have to become a wooden woman, I thought, who feels
nothing, or I won't be able to go on living.

Wang Mang remained sick through the autumn. The air cooled
slightly, but his skin remained hot to the touch. And even in the little room
where I tended him, I could sense the tension in the city. My brother rarely
visited us anymore, me or my mother, and was constantly occupied with
the affairs of the army. Jin Yu left to go to Nanjing. Their unexplained absences made me feel as if they were keeping secrets from me. When I
glanced out the window, over the top of the walled garden, over the
rooftops and chimneys of Changsha, I saw only the daily to and fro of life.
But there was a strange humming, which I felt rather than heard, that told
me of some vast anger at our own weakness and corruption, at our impoverished state, at our continuing humiliation before the great Western
powers, an anger that only increased with every attempt to appease or suppress it.

Then in October, there came bits and pieces of news, about bombings,
and about mutinies in the army, none of which I understood. I heard only
the gossip of the markets that the servant girl, Yong Li, brought back to
me, and that was disjointed and contradictory. I sent Yong Li with a message to Li Shi, but she returned saying that he had been too busy to see her.
Every day, I sat by Wang Mang's bed and saw the thunderclouds gather,
framed in the window a few feet away.

From the sickroom I heard in the distance a sound like the roar of a
river in spring. The sound was quickly growing louder and closer, and in
the midst of that expanding roar, I heard the noise of pounding footsteps.
I jumped from my seat, upsetting the pan of water, and rushed to the window. From the second story, where I was, I could see a vast crowd of bobbing, black-haired heads, a swarm of men thrusting and rearing through
the streets like the multiple parts of a great snaking monster, flicking its
tentacles down each alley as it passed. The roar of voices surged with what
sounded very much like anger.

I looked wildly around the room, my heart lurching madly in my
chest. The mob had finally come to attack the rich men's houses. What
could I save from this devastation? In my opinion, the only really valuable
thing left in the house was the cask of brine-salted shrimp in the cellar—
that would be a terrible loss, after all I had gone through to purchase it under the counter, below cost, from the grocer's embezzling assistant. They

were welcome to what little was left of the furniture. The mob would find
the Pan house an empty shell, and in their fury they would burn us all out.
I would have to try to get Wang Mang and the old Pans out of the house,
to some hiding place, and abandon this mockery of a great manor to the
invaders.

I looked out the window again, but this time, to my surprise, I saw
that the crowds were already beginning to pass through the streets of the
area without pausing. Then half the city seemed to be running past, shouting and waving fists in the air, trouser legs and banners snapping in the
rush. The big banners, held aloft on bamboo poles, dipped perilously back
and forth as the banner men ran, and the poles scraped along the top of
the walls that guarded the Pans from the street. A red banner caught momentarily on the broken glass that was cemented along the top of the wall,
before it was ripped away. I dodged from window to window to follow
their progress.

"Where are you all going?" I screamed above the roar. Now I could
hear gunfire in the distance, and little puffs of white smoke rose above the
rooftops.

"To the governor's palace!" someone shouted back without breaking
stride.

"What is it? Why are people going to the palace?"

"Seize the palace!" came the answer, sounding like a command. I
threw a look at Wang Mang. He seemed to be sleeping. The blood rushed
through my veins like wine, overflowing. I pulled on my shoes and ran out
the front door, heedless of its banging behind me, and joined the crowd,
and heard my own voice above the others, rising in exultation.

The skies were darkening rapidly above the elegant yellow-tiled roofs
of the governor's palace. By the time I arrived—carried along by the
crowd, almost without my feet touching the ground—great gray thunder-
heads had gathered overhead, but as yet no rain fell and the atmosphere
was humid and as thick as mud. The red-painted gates shuddered from the
force of a hundred pounding fists, echoing the bursts of thunder in the
skies; stones whistled through the air and landed on the parapets above.
Lightning whitened the faces of the crowd.

Now my excitement was tempered by anxiety, for I began to fear that
we would be shot. My eyes scanned the tops of the walls, but saw no one,
no helmeted heads, no banners, no lances or guns. "Where are all the soldiers?" I shouted to a man next to me.

"The army has rebelled against the Qing!" he shouted back. "You can hear them shooting in the garrison!" He pointed toward the army post, and I followed his finger to the smoke on the other side of the hill. Where was Li Shi? I looked around and saw among the crowd many faces I knew—almost all the young teachers from the First Normal School and their students, the editor of the literary review, the telegraph operator, the young physician who had been to Harvard to study and so was nicknamed "Ha-Fu." They clutched eagerly at the great wooden battering ram that had been brought, laying their soft white hands alongside the soil-blackened fingers of the farmers and rickshaw drivers that they were eagerly directing.

One farmer tried to nudge the young physician away. "Move aside, sir," the countryman said. "Don't strain yourself. You aren't used to this. This kind of work is for strong oxen like us."

The physician shook his head firmly. "Indeed not," he said. "We are all equal men here." He bent and braced his slender shoulder against the end of the beam. "On the count of three, yes?"

The farmers grinned with pleasure and pounded the young physician on the back so hard his spectacles slid down his nose.

The gates split open with a loud crack, and the bronze hinges splintered away. The crowd streamed into the inner courtyard, led by the Normal School teachers, who made straight for the governor's suite. Determined to be among the first inside, I elbowed some others aside and ran along with them. The teachers impatiently pushed aside the few lower-level mandarins and clerks still in the building, huddling fearfully in the corners, and these were quickly engulfed by the rough crowd that followed. In the scuffle, some of these clerks died under a farmer's quick knife or scythe, their lives pulled away merely in passing, like a silk scarf catching on the horns of a bull. I saw the crowd roll over them like an ocean wave, and then the unlucky ones were lying on the ground. I opened my mouth to shout in horror, but my cry was drowned out by the thunderstorm, which broke before we reached the other side of the courtyard.

The crowd spread out through the palace. They looked in cabinets, searched through closets, overturned furniture, sampled the food left on the stoves in the kitchens, pulled out drawers and left the contents strewn all over the floors, stuffed the steel pens and brass rulers and little cloisonné boxes into their pockets. A steady buzz and murmur hung in the air.

The governor's office was empty, its piles of paperwork still scattered on the desk, a cup of jasmine tea still warm under its ceramic lid. The young teachers shouted joyously, squeezing behind the governor's desk and sitting on his chairs. They opened a box of Virginia cigarettes and passed them among themselves. The farmers huddled at the doors, leaving grimy handprints on the white-painted walls. The rain blew in through the windows in great powerful gusts, and those that remained in the courtyard pushed to shelter under the eaves and bowed their shoulders against the downpour, watching the heavenly waters purge the paving tiles of blood-stains and debris.

I thrust myself into the room, just in time to hear the noise of a struggle in the back. The crowd rippled like a snake's belly, and a terrified clerk was produced, thrown to the floor in front of the crowd. One of the farmers, a big, broad-shouldered man, leaned in from the open window.

"Where is the governor?" the farmer demanded, and the crowd of peasants on the galleries outside pushed further into the room. The man began to cry. "Stop blubbering. Be a man. Where is the governor?"

"He left," wept the clerk, his voice almost drowned out by the roar of the rain. "He left with seventeen baggage wagons before dawn, on his way to the imperial garrison at Guelin."

"Where is the garrison commander?" the crowd howled from the windows and doors. The young teachers at the governor's desk sat up in surprise and looked around them. The man wept more. The big farmer strode to the terrified clerk and snatched a handful of his hair, bending his head back.

"Stop, don't hurt him!" shouted the young teachers, alarmed.

"Tell us!" the crowd roared, as loud as the storm.

"The Qing commander is the prisoner of Captain Liang Li Shi and his company. Captain Liang is holding him in the garrison jail. Please, that's all I know."

I put my hands to my face in surprise.

"We must eliminate the commander!" One of the men, a broad, husky young man of twenty or so, with a wide, flat-boned face, now spoke for the first time. His face was known to me, from the school and the protest demonstrations, but I couldn't remember if I had ever known his name. He had remarkable brown eyes and a mole near his mouth, and he was certainly not an ordinary peasant. The others shouted their agreement.

"No, no, what do you mean? There is no need for violence, since the man is already in prison!" cried "Ha-Fu" the physician. But the crowd of men outside the room, thrusting their heads through the doors and windows, bellowed until his voice was drowned out.

The young man with the mole shook his head decisively. "If we leave him, there might still be loyal troops who will gather around him!" he cried. "We must cut off the head so the body dies!"

The terrified clerk edged toward the door, forgotten among the shouts of the argument. I shifted position to let him past. With the bodies in the courtyard in mind, I leaned forward and whispered to him, "Leave quickly." The clerk did not pause. He dropped instantly to his hands and knees and crawled rapidly out the door, through the forest of legs and feet.

Almost before I saw his heels disappear, the forest began to move, and soon the entire crowd of peasants, led by the young man with the mole, began streaming out of the governor's palace, looking from this distance like a great army of red ants. I followed them, as fast as my legs could carry me, along the crest of the slope toward the garrison several hundred meters away down the hill, on a naked stretch of land that had been shaven bare of trees.

The first men to arrive at the garrison launched themselves like a wave at the gates, which, as it happened, were not locked. The soldiers were armed, but put up very little resistance, letting the mob push past them. I looked anxiously for Li Shi, but I did not see him, though there was a light on in the window of the officers' quarters.

When the rebels reemerged from the buildings, they dragged with them the Qing commander, a middle-aged man with a slight paunch and a square jaw. He wore the old armor of leather and metal, but someone had broken the pennants on his back, and now the sticks jutted up like broken fibulas. There was a moment in all the jostling and struggle when I came face-to-face with him, and I felt a sudden terrible stab of pity for this ordinary-looking man. None of this is his fault, I thought. My pity turned almost instantly into sheer terror of the wild crowd around me. They pulled him out of the garrison and started down the street into the center of town, the entire city baying like wolves from the sides. I ran after, trying to grab at the commander's arm to slow his progress, shouting desperately to let him go, and praying that Li Shi would come out with his soldiers and rescue the man. But my voice was not heard above the thunderclaps and hatred, or if heard, was not listened to, and the man was snatched from my grasping hand and hanged in the square. I stood in the crush of the mob and watched as he struggled for a while at the end of the rope, and thought that I would now always be afraid of angry crowds, which so easily took on a demonic and uncontrollable life of their own. At nightfall his corpse was still there, but his boots were gone, by that time miles away on the running feet of a thief.

I found my brother that night, now in command of the army in Hunan. He had not yet moved into the dead commander's office, but sat in his own smaller one, smoking cigarettes. Cigarettes had become a recent habit with him. I dropped into a chair across the desk from him, and the soldier who had escorted me inside shut the door behind him as he left.

"Where were you when they dragged out that poor man to be killed?" I snapped, in a voice that just missed being a shout.

"Here. In this very office." He looked at me unflinchingly.

"Did you try to stop them?"

"No. I let them do it."

"Then in fact you killed him," I said.

"That seems a fair way of putting it."

We were silent awhile.

"Thirteen days ago, in the Russian concession in Hanjou," my brother said, "some of Sun Yat Sen's revolutionaries were making a bomb. They weren't soldiers, but intellectuals, so they blew themselves up by accident. The authorities arrived and found in the wreckage lists of names of all the officers in the army who were planning to rebel against the Qing. So we had to act immediately. The Wuchang Eighth Engineer Battalion rose the next day, and the rest of us followed."

"Was your name on the lists in Hanjou, Li Shi?" I gasped.

"Don't be silly. I would never let my name appear on any list. Until today, the rebels—I'm sorry, the revolutionaries, I should call them, since they've succeeded—weren't certain I was with them. I'm sure they were relieved to find that I was."

"Were you certain where you stood before today, my brother?"

Li Shi shrugged. "I was prepared to go in any direction necessary. Look, I know you are wasting sentiment on the old commander, but his fate was preordained. The mob demanded nothing less, and it is best for all the troops that there be no confusion about the chain of command."

"What will happen now?" I was suddenly too tired to sort out my feelings about what my brother was saying. I was almost too tired to feel.

"The new commanders are in place all over China. We are making certain demands on the Qing. That the provisional assembly elect Yuan Shikai as premier and allow Sun to return and be our president."

"Where is Sun?"

"In Kansu City."

"What's Kansu City?"

"It's in the middle of America somewhere. It's the capital of an American province called Kansu. This is a new world, Jade Virtue. We are sweeping aside the old one." My brother's usual sardonic expression lightened, and for just a moment, he looked eager and ardent, the way he used to when he was a boy.

12

*T*he crowd that gathered every day at the governor's palace to watch the deliberations of the provincial assembly roared its approval. The speaker was a man in the earliest years of old age, with long iron-gray hair, a long gray beard like a sage, and a gray silk gown. He stood clutching a black umbrella and looked like an unbending old oak, knotted with strength and sinew. His deep voice carried considerable displeasure. This was eminent Kantian philosopher, Teacher Yang.

"It has been several weeks since Sun became president, and Yuan is now premier," the old man boomed. "But now we want nothing less than to abolish the dynasty that feeds off the people, a foreign dynasty of Manchus. It is a court filled with all manner of eunuchs, opium smokers, and aborigine whorehouse owners. The boy emperor Puyi must abdicate. We will have a republic with Sun Yat Sen as its president!"

The crowd roared again. I applauded enthusiastically. Several army officers—Li Shi's men—nodded their heads in approval, but otherwise remained silent.

It was late January 1912. I had come to the assembly every day in the hope of learning what was to happen to my country, my appetite for politics made boundless by my now unrelenting desire to escape the bounds of my life. I sensed the advent of great changes, but I didn't know when they would arrive or what form they would take, or even if they would be good or bad; I knew only that I wanted to be carried away with them. Li Shi had not bothered to attend the assembly, since apparently he already knew the future, but he always sent some officers to report back to him on the proceedings. We all sat in the winter chill that pervaded the hall and watched the speakers' breath curl out into the air. I thought of Jin Yu, now in Beijing, organizing demonstrations for the abdication of the Emperor. She was at the center of things, I thought, and I am here in a shabby, unheated hall in the provinces. Then I thought of the Emperor, who was still only a little boy, and I felt sorry for him. Where would he go?

Yong Li brought me the news from the marketplace in early February. She ran into the rear courtyard, where I was washing dishes in a basin. She was panting very hard, in spite of her youth and slenderness, for she had raced all the way home. She leaned forward, her hands on her trousered knees, and strained for breath.

I stood up, wiping my hands. "Is it true?" I asked, excitedly.

She nodded. "The Emperor has stepped down," she gasped. "Yesterday."

I turned and walked through the courtyard and into the long hallway behind it. Grass was growing through the cracks in the pavement. The Pans were waiting for me at the top of the steps leading into the ancestral hall. Old Pan clutched at his wife's arm. Their faces were haggard with anxiety.

"Has it happened?" he croaked. "Can it really have happened?"

"The Emperor has abdicated the Dragon Throne," I said, with a sort of horrible satisfaction, knowing it would shock them.

"How can the Son of Heaven abandon his people?" Madame Pan sobbed. The Pans clung to each other, rocking back and forth and weeping. They fell to their knees and bowed again and again, crying out for the Emperor, whom they had never seen. I stood and stared at them, open-mouthed, moved by their despair. I had hoped to see this day come, to see new ways triumph over the old, but when I saw the effect of the departure of the boy emperor on the Pans, I was overcome by a terrible, unforeseen grief. Whatever else the child Puyi might have been, he was the Son of Heaven, and the last one China would ever see. It was as if history itself were coming to an end. Without thinking, I fell to my knees and elbows and bowed my forehead to the tiles again and again, bowing to the Pans and to the ancestors in the hall behind them, trying with this display of ancient piety to soothe their fears, and my own sudden, enormous sense of loss.

Bewildered, I went to the assembly and sat again in the audience. The room was full, in spite of the winter rains, but the crowd was quiet today, as if they had not fully recovered from the shock of getting exactly what they had demanded. Teacher Yang was there, although he did not speak. I also saw the broad-faced young man with the mole in the crowd, the one from the governor's palace. An army officer stood up and spoke.

"Yesterday, President Sun resigned his office and recognized General Yuan Shikai as the new president. Captain Liang Li Shi asks that everyone remain calm and hopeful. General Yuan has pledged to the officers of the army to hold general elections as soon as can be managed . . ."

Teacher Yang stood up and picked up his umbrella. He walked across the round open space in the center of the assembly, past the speaking officer, who looked at him in consternation but did not pause in his words. The double doors creaked open and then swung closed behind the old man.

I told myself to stay in my seat and listen to the other speakers. I told myself I would only be embarrassed chasing after him. But the irrational thought came to me that if I did not catch up to him, I would be left behind in this life of mine and never be able to get out. Then my heart will burst in my chest, I thought, because it has been pressed down for so long. I clambered out of my seat and past the people sitting in my row. By the time I had extricated myself from the crowded room and run out into the courtyard, I could see only the back of his gown disappearing through the gateway, the black umbrella unfurled and bobbing jauntily over his head. I ran after him, sliding on the icy wet tiles. I was soaked to the skin immediately, and I stopped to pull off my shoes, which were my only pair and could under no circumstances be sacrificed to the elements. I finally caught up with him on the stone-paved road leading down into the town.

"Teacher Yang, wait for me," I panted, stumbling up to him. He stopped and looked back at me. My hair streamed into my eyes, my clothes ran rivulets of rainwater, and I held my soaked shoes in my hands. The hem of my dress was bedraggled with Hunan's red mud, and my feet were very dirty. Teacher Yang did not seem to notice my condition or think it strange. He gracefully extended his arm and held his umbrella over my head. The rain slid down his own hair and beard.

"Did you call me, Mrs. Pan?" he asked courteously.

"You know me?" I gasped, breathing hard.

"Xiang Jin Yu is one of my pupils. She studies political economy with my private study group."

"Jin Yu told me you are a great man, sir," I said. Teacher Yang smiled and shrugged modestly.

"That surprises me. Jin Yu never thinks I am radical enough. She is in Beijing now, as you know."

I nodded. Then I blurted out, "I was told you could help me get work."

I blushed furiously. "Please, sir. I meant to ask you months ago, but my husband . . ."

"Did not approve? But now? He approves now?"

"He doesn't care now." I looked away shamefacedly. Long drips of rainwater flowed to the ends of my hair.

"Have you considered this carefully?" Teacher Yang asked, his face very serious. "Do you know what an association with me entails? I have not been a friend of the state. And since our civilian president has been only too eager to hand the nation over to that ambitious general, I am still not a friend of the state."

I nodded. "China cannot remain as she is," I said. Then somberly, I added, "I cannot remain as I am." I hoped my tears would be invisible in the rain.

Teacher Yang laughed. "I think we had better get out of the rain. Come to my house. My daughter can make you comfortable. When the rain lets up a little, I will send a maidservant home with you."

All the way back to his house, Teacher Yang insisted on holding the umbrella over my head.

"Please, sir, you are the elder," I protested.

"But you are wetter, Mrs. Pan."

Teacher Yang lived in a large, comfortable house on the outskirts of the city, suitable to the contemplative life of a scholar. He opened the gate with his own key and led me through the garden onto the veranda outside the glass-paned front door, which was open.

"You there inside! Come help us!" he called.

A maidservant appeared at the door, then ran off to get towels. When she reappeared, she was followed by a young woman who, judging from her superior dress and manners, was clearly not a maidservant.

"My daughter, Yang Kai Hui. Kai Hui, this is Mrs. Pan." Teacher Yang stopped rubbing his hair with the towels long enough to make a casual gesture of introduction.

"Things went as expected at the palace," Teacher Yang announced to his daughter as he shed his wet shoes. He turned to me. "Kai Hui is a little angry at me because I wouldn't let her go to the assembly. But I thought in such an uncertain moment it was best she stay away. I know I am an over-protective father."

Kai Hui bowed her head politely. She had a round, pretty face that wore no expression and revealed absolutely nothing; she seemed to be shading her eyes with her eyelashes to prevent me from looking inside her. Her hair was cut short like a boy's.

"Please come in," she said. "We'll make you some tea. I can lend you a dress to wear until yours dries." She said nothing about the events of the assembly and asked no questions about what had happened that day.

"Mrs. Pan is the very best friend of Xiang Jin Yu," Teacher Yang said, bending over at the waist so his beard fell straight down, the better to rub it dry.

I had turned sideways to wring out my skirt over the flowerpots as Teacher Yang said these latest words, and I glanced up at his voice. Directly in front of me was the glass-paned front door, propped open against the wall, and reflected in that glass was Kai Hui's face. At the mention of Jin Yu's name, it underwent a startling change. Not a nerve or a muscle twitched, but the shuttered expression, so carefully neutral, shifted suddenly, subtly, into a white mask of fury. I was transfixed by the image in the glass. I twisted around to look at Yang's daughter, but Yang Kai Hui's face was blank again, blank as the shuttered front of an empty house. I stared at the girl, but Kai Hui looked steadily back without rancor. I could find no trace of trouble in the smooth white planes of that perfectly closed face.

Less than half an hour later, I was sitting quietly with Teacher Yang in the main parlor, both of us now in dry clothes, rolling a cup of tea in my hands and perspiring a little from damp. I wore one of Kai Hui's best dresses, at her insistence. My own dress had been taken to be hung over a fire to dry. Then Kai Hui, with a polite smile, withdrew from the room.

Teacher Yang sat across from me, folding his hands around his cup. "I'm rather afraid that with the big emperor gone, the company commanders—and perhaps your brother—will be happy to be little emperors with small armies." Teacher Yang sighed. "Who knows? It might be better. But they might also be even harder to dislodge in the future."

"How can you be so confident of what the commanders will do? Of what my brother will do?"

"I asked them, of course." Teacher Yang smiled. "Surprised? I thought so. Your brother and I have had several friendly contacts recently. Captain Liang is a very practical man."

He chuckled in a manner so frank and free of delusion that I immediately decided that I liked him very much. Then he leaned forward and tapped my knee with his finger. "However, let's discuss the more immediate questions about you. I'm being rude to neglect you. In addition to the state of the nation, I'm afraid you have other troubles as well?"

I nodded.

"You are beginning to feel as if you must . . . earn a living." He waved a hand modestly. "I hear things."

I was angry at the needy position I was in, and angry that Teacher Yang knew all about it, and galled by that wave of the hand meant to soothe me, and angry at Jin Yu for telling him, so when I spoke my voice was harsh. "It seems to me, Teacher Yang, that judging from the membership of your study group, only those with money can be revolutionaries."

Teacher Yang only nodded, in the same grave fashion. "Does that surprise you, Mrs. Pan? One day, we will all be full-time revolutionaries, because revolution will be the full-time business of society. But for now, the study of revolution is only for those with education and leisure. Those who are in possession of these good things are known as . . ."—and here, Teacher Yang shrugged slightly, and rolled his eyes upward—"the vanguard. Do I sound dreadfully pedantic? Now you are laughing instead of furious; I'm glad. When I first read that, I thought it very silly and very elitist. But it's true. People who have to earn their rice are too busy to make revolution. But one day, when China is ready, all hands will join in."

I looked down and smoothed Kai Hui's dress. I sipped the tea. Teacher Yang stood up and came to sit next to me.

"Don't be upset," he said. "I will help you. Jin Yu tells me you should teach at the girls' middle school, and I think I agree. I will speak to the principal for you—Principal Chen and I were at university together. He is more moderate than I—more like you—but he is a good and sincere man. Work for your living, Mrs. Pan. Work will educate you."

Relenting, I smiled at him in gratitude and bowed my head. "How will work educate me?" I asked.

"We will have to see the outcome when it comes."

"But what will I teach?"

"What do you like?"

I wrinkled my face, a little embarrassed. "I'm afraid I'm good at mathematics and accounts. It's not very refined, really, I'm ashamed, but . . ."

Teacher Yang held up his hand sternly. "Please. Life seems to me to revolve around one's accounts. More so than around poetry or art, I'm afraid. Don't look down on the mundane. I'll speak to Old Chen tomorrow—you should start this coming autumn semester."

"I've never had a job before."

"At first it seems artificial. To have the whole day divided up into periods by the clock. But after a while, you will become used to it. Unless I read you very wrongly, you will find the discipline soothing."

Teacher Yang stood up as he was speaking and walked back across the room to where he had left his teacup. As he sipped, he glanced out the window. I watched as a frown slipped onto his face.

"What is it, Teacher Yang?" I came to stand beside him, looking out into the front garden.

It was no longer raining. In the garden, by the gate, stood Kai Hui. Over her head, we could see that the gate was partly open. Kai Hui appeared to be speaking to someone who stood just outside the walls, hiding that person from view with her hunched and furtive posture.

Teacher Yang pressed his lips together. "Speaking of poets," he murmured. He strode to the window and threw it open; the sound turned Kai Hui's head. When she turned, the person outside the gate stood revealed. I recognized him as the broad-faced young man with the remarkable eyes and the mole near his mouth. The one who had been so sure that the death of the Qing commander was necessary.

"Why, I recognize him," I murmured.

"Yes, perhaps. He was in the anti-Qing militia. He is my daughter's ardent admirer, and a student of mine. His family had arranged a marriage for him back in Shaoshan, where he's from, but he repudiated it. Now he is Kai Hui's suitor. I suppose they will marry someday." Teacher Yang watched as Kai Hui pushed her lover out of the threshold of the gate and shut the door. She came up the garden path slowly, her face averted from us in the window.

"Will you approve their marriage?" I asked, my curiosity overcoming my manners.

"Doesn't matter. I don't believe in arranged marriages, everyone has to be free to choose their own spouse." Kai Hui reentered the house, and Teacher Yang shut the window. He picked up his cup of tea again, and grimaced when he tasted its coldness.

"I don't suppose I disapprove, really," he said. "The boy is brilliant. Very, very brilliant. Just a little strange."

"What's his name?" I asked.

"Mao. Mao Zedong."

13

*I*n the years that followed, my daily life became a routine in which I went from one extreme to another between sunrise and sunset. In the early morning I left the Pan mansion. Wang Mang lay in bed smoking; Old Pan and Madame Pan sat in the central hall by the weak heat of the only brazier. I walked swiftly to the girls' middle school to teach. In the evening, I walked slowly home again, to find Wang Mang and his parents in the same places where I had left them. So I reversed the great journey of life every morning, awakening in a cemetery and spending the day in a nursery. I have never been happier in quite that same way than when I was in school, not before or since. Of course at the time I did my best to look miserable, and gave sad sighs, and wiped my eyes on my sleeve whenever someone was visiting.

"Poor thing," the neighbors whispered. "What a good wife. Eating opium is like eating silver. She needs the money. You can tell that working outside the house is an intolerable burden on her modesty. At least she doesn't have to take in other people's washing."

Part of me disliked the charade, but my mother shrugged philosophically.

"A little acting keeps the neighbors in their place," she told me. "And costs you very little."

Even Madame Pan and Old Pan said nothing to me about my new position, but only held out their hands for the small heavy coins I brought home at the end of each month.

The school itself was small and, to my eyes then, as lovely as a jewel box, although in truth it was a very plain, square brick building without fine carving. It sat on the outskirts of town, a number of simple rooms arranged around a single courtyard where a large magnolia tree had been planted. The air seemed fresh and serene inside the courtyard, the shouts and struggles and violence of the city seemingly distant and meaningless. The bone-cracking tension and misery of the Pan house was two miles away. The rich girls came in rickshaws; the daughters of the prosperous merchants and craftsmen rode into the courtyard on newly fashionable bicycles. Their good manners were a balm to my heart, which was tired and torn with neglect and loneliness.

At first, without caring anything at all for the actual education of my charges, I was grateful simply to be allowed to come to the school and stay there all day. But as I became a more experienced teacher, my work began to gather moral weight, and I began to feel its importance. I had very few girls who distinguished themselves in my eyes as great minds. But there were some who nevertheless found in our books fuel for their wit, and some who found whetstones to sharpen the fighting swords in their souls, and some who found the shivery exultation of a bird flying before the storm. And in seeing all this, I was content.

But China in the second decade of the century was wild and uncontrolled. All around us, all around the dead center of the Pan house, where the dead sat and talked, all around the living heart of my school, the land spun like a potter's wheel. Every day on the way to school, I passed bands of soldiers. As the years passed, their makeshift uniforms changed, the colors of their ragged pennants changed, their young unshaven faces changed, but the beat of their drums and the sharp metal of their weapons remained the same. They still marched, or smoked and flicked their cigarette butts into the pathway, or had prisoners on the ends of thick ropes they trailed behind them like mule halters. They ran through the streets with rifles—or with wooden clubs and hoes if no real guns could be gotten—and skirmished in the alleys with each other. They burst upon the students protesting in the squares and dispersed them harshly, descending with the grating caws of carrion birds.

The streets were frequently impassable, crammed with bodies, living and dead, with wagons and donkeys and the occasional sedan chair with a man inside who was either rich or armed. Pickpockets and thugs roamed the byways. Wherever you stood in the city, shouts of anger reached your ears, and indeed, when I think of it now, my main memory of that time is of enormous, unceasing noise, roaring like blood along the veins and arteries of the city and the province, throbbing, building, crashing, exhausting, draining. Noise from demonstrations, from gunfire, from clashing military units, from angry gangsters or nervous shopkeepers. An entire people in full howl, never silent long enough to hear the frightened beating of their own hearts, realizing too well that silence now would be a sign not of serenity but of desolation.

The Dragon Throne, which had ruled my country in one incarnation or another for several thousand years, had been uprooted like a giant oak and blown away—one night I dreamed I saw it spinning upward into a whirlwind, bearing its last and weakest incarnation inside, yellow silk imperial robes flapping with the sound of a giant bird's wings—and had left behind every sort of predator, crawling about hungrily in the rotting roots.

A military strongman named Yuan Shikai had emerged momentarily from these confusing times. There is no reason to discuss him very much, except that we acquiesced to his ascension because of his strength, because in interesting times we yearn only for calm, and because we were beginning to see that democracy might be the kind of thing that has to be imposed on a people, odd as that might seem. My brother supported Yuan, because my brother always knew that the need for strength outweighed all other needs. At first he hoped that Yuan would be that rare thing, an unselfish warlord, but he never expressed any disappointment or anger at the way things turned out. When Yuan Shikai dismissed the assemblies in 1913, Li Shi said merely that China needed a strong leader. When Yuan dismissed the governors who belonged to Sun Yat Sen's Guomindang Party and dissolved the party itself, driving Sun into exile in Japan, Li Shi only said that he himself would govern Hunan until a new governor could be sent out to us. When Yuan had himself declared emperor in December 1915—and ordered a forty-thousand piece porcelain dinner set—Li Shi only shrugged and murmured that this world was one of endless betrayal, and what did we all expect? Then Yuan died, and the other warlords fell to squabbling among themselves, and dividing up the nation into bits and pieces, to be ruled by their private armies. The sardonic expression of Li Shi's face grew darker still, and he smiled even less often than before.

But Li Shi was always practical. Taking measure of the way things were headed, he gathered his troops and built a compound in a new quarter of the city, pouring concrete for the walls instead of piling up stones, and topping the fence with barbed wire, now in common use because of the great war in Europe. He had initially announced that the compound was to be a sort of police station, to pacify the area until such time as le-

gitimate central authorities could come to Hunan. But one legitimate authority after another was kept busy in Beijing, fighting off the claims of all
the host of competing legitimate authorities, and no one ever came, so Li
Shi now had a stronghold inside the city walls all to himself.

Li Shi contented himself for the time by collecting taxes to pay for his
army and maintaining order in the southern half of Changsha, and left the
northern half to General Feng, a huge man, a former barber, head-shaver,
and minor sorcerer, who had risen from the ranks of noncommissioned
officers—or rather, had raised himself from the ranks when the strange
death by poisoned arrow of Feng's own army commander presented a
convenient opening at a sensitive time. Feng filled his belly with the rich
and oily meat of half a dog every day, and kept foreign women from Japan
and Russia in his harem.

As a result, a number of families moved into the southern half, because in those days Li Shi still wore his European-style army uniform
smartly and kept no permanent concubines, and there were rarely fights in
his half of the city. He hung thieves summarily from the lampposts and
paid reparations to the families of innocent men hung by mistake. A uniformed soldier swept the street frontage of Li Shi's compound every
morning, but outside Feng's fortified house, piles of chicken bones and
empty wine bottles sat for days. But Li Shi, like Feng, had to go to considerable trouble to find money to run his army. Li Shi controlled the rail lines
into and out of Changsha and imposed all sorts of made-up duties and
taxes, while Feng reinstituted opium growing in the fields outside his portion of the city wall. Between them, these two men—bitter enemies from
two different Chinas—controlled the city.

My mother and I rarely went to Li Shi's compound, since it seemed
like an army barracks rather than my brother's house, and we felt uncomfortable. But Graceful Virtue moved there, to help keep house for Li Shi. I
could not blame her, since in those days, there were few acceptable places
for a young woman to go for the society and attention of young men. The
fact that it was her brother's house gave the entire undertaking a curtain of
respectability. Before long, Graceful Virtue became engaged to a young
lieutenant, whose late father had been an army sergeant. The bridegroom
Mo Chi was tall and straight-backed and had a pleasant, open manner, and
there was nothing in his background that would have caused shame. But
some of the wives of my father's old friends shook their head.

"My dear Mrs. Liang," they said to my mother at the time of the engagement. "Educated people—daughters of magistrates, even dead magistrates—don't marry into the army. Not even officers." They sipped their tea in agitation.

"Do sneak thieves steal from your houses at night?" my mother demanded of all the old ladies, in strong tones. "Do your daughters have money snatched from them as they walk about the city? Must you go everywhere with a hired man as your escort, for fear of these bands of thugs that are now eating up the province?"

They all nodded, openmouthed.

"Well, none of that happens to me. Because of my son's soldiers. I married Jade Virtue to the well-educated son of a well-bred family, and now she has to go out to work to feed them." They all looked at me, and I looked away. "But if I marry Graceful Virtue to an army officer, perhaps she can know some peace. The world is a different place from the one I grew up in—it feels so long ago now. Then, our society was like a walled city, ordered and secure. Now, it is an open battlefield, covered with confusion. It strikes me that on a battlefield, an army officer is a useful man."

When they had all gone and I was helping my mother pick up teacups, I said to her gently, "You are right, you know. This young man is the best Graceful Virtue can do in these hard days, when we don't know what's up and what's down. You must not be distressed."

"Necessities don't distress me," my mother said, balancing half a dozen little ceramic cups on her hands and straightening slowly. "Compromises don't distress me. Not even change distresses me, since it is inevitable. Only foolishness distresses me. But I have to admit . . . " Her voice died away as she walked toward the kitchen with the cups.

"What?" I asked, following with more cups. I couldn't balance them along my wrists as my mother did; I just inserted my fingers into their mouths and carried them that way. "You must admit what?"

My mother stacked the cups on the stone walkway in the yard and squatted down at the water faucet, recently installed by Li Shi's men. She tucked her skirts around and rolled her sleeves up.

"Here, let me wash," I said. "It's too much strain on your knees."

"I was thinking that myself actually," my mother said, with the faint glimmer of one of her rare smiles.

I squatted down and turned on the water and began picking up the cups. "Admit what?" I asked again, as my mother rolled up my straying sleeve for me.

But she shook her head. "Nothing," she murmured. "Never mind. There's never any point in looking back."

Li Shi gave Graceful Virtue's wedding banquet at the compound, which was then still new, the bared ground around it still raw from the scars of construction. The wedding guests were an uneasy mix of soldiers in full uniform, soldiers in half uniform, and soberly dressed civilians. Once, these guests would have worn their best clothes to a wedding, but now those that had not sold or pawned their finery were unwilling to walk out in them, advertising their own ripeness for theft.

I was there alone. Li Shi had written a brusque note to the Pans, indicating his wish that they not attend. My mother and I were horrified at this breach in manners. The Pans sulked and were rude to me as a result, since they were rarely invited anywhere anymore. But sitting at Li Shi's side now, I was glad.

A great deal of food was dished up by the frantic cooks hired for the occasion and now busy in the mess kitchens. Drink was served—wine for the guests, and an extra ration of rice whiskey for the enlisted men in their barracks. Boxes of cigarettes were passed around for everyone sitting at the round tables that had been set up on the cement floors of the indoor drill square, which had been built in one corner of the compound. Red paper covered the iron doors, and dainty red tassels blew from the iron bars of the windows. Outside, red lanterns glowed all over the exercise yard. Graceful Virtue looked quite happy, and her groom very protective. I felt I hardly knew my sister, since I had married and moved out when she was still young. She was a cipher to me. But my heart was pleased for her.

Graceful Virtue and Mo Chi sat at the center table, and Li Shi sat at a table far to one side, next to me. But Li Shi seemed to be at the center instead. Every face kept turning toward him, and when he told jokes or toasted the newlyweds, the entire roomful listened and laughed. I had a distinct impression that the room was lopsided, its balance turned half inside out, simply to accommodate the weight of Liang Li Shi. I was fascinated with the variety of expressions that swiveled in our direction whenever he spoke. Admiration, obedience, a subtle envy, eagerness, caution—all these emotions, sometimes alone and sometimes mingled with one or two or three of the others, blurred the features of the guests. From behind my smile, I inspected them all closely, trying to make note of those who I thought might harbor ill will for Li Shi. And I saw that all these expressions, without exception, were shadowed by a kind of servility. No one cringed or bowed excessively to my brother, and he greeted everyone with the straightforward assurance of a military man, shaking hands in a good democratic manner. But I have seen a dog approach a larger dog in the street and simply stand in a way I can only describe as "lower," and this is how the guests behaved.

Partway through the wedding, a messenger arrived with a sealed letter for Li Shi, who read it quickly and stepped out of the room, making gracious excuses. Every eye followed him out, and the room seemed noticeably less merry while he was gone. When he came back a half hour later, the laughter and singing grew again, as if for his benefit, and there was a palpable sense of relief in the banquet hall. For the first time, I began to acquire some sense of who my brother was, and what he had become.

The wedding ended on a very happy note—Li Shi announced that he had requisitioned an empty house a few streets away for the newlyweds to live in, and gave Graceful Virtue a red envelope—"furniture-buying money," he said, smiling. Everyone laughed raucously and loudly. Mo Chi clasped Li Shi's hand and bowed again and again, and Graceful Virtue let Li Shi kiss her cheek in public—a new Western fad that our brother had recently picked up.

My mother went home with an escort of Li Shi's soldiers. I stayed to spend the night in Li Shi's rather bare and austere room, to help with the housekeeping the next day in the aftermath of the wedding. But when I passed Li Shi's study on my way to sleep, I saw through the half-open door that his makeshift bed, a field cot, had not yet been disturbed. A candle burned inside. I put my head in and saw my brother sitting at his plain wooden desk, writing letters. He had taken off his uniform jacket and hung it on the back of his chair.

"Why aren't you in bed?" I asked, laying my hand on his shoulder.

"I'm taking care of a few things first," he replied, patting my hand absently. "Don't read over my shoulder, please. This is not women's work."

"Sorry." I moved away and sat in a nearby chair, picking up the books on his table and rifling through them.

"How much money did you give Graceful Virtue for furniture-buying?" I asked, after a little while.

"Quite a bit. Why?"

"You never gave me furniture-buying money."

"When you were married, I had none to give. Besides, Mo Chi is one of my men, I have to do right by him. I gave a pretty sum to another young officer a month ago when he married, and his bride wasn't even related to me. That Pan you married is not my burden, thank heaven."

"You don't need Pan's loyalty either," I snorted.

"That too." Li Shi went on writing in silence. If I had hoped to insult him, I was disappointed. He had my mother's habit of naming things plainly.

"Can you tell me what's going on?" I asked finally. "What letters can you be writing at this time of night? Even your boots are still on."

Li Shi sealed the letters and rang for a soldier. A young man burst in almost immediately, from where he had been waiting in the hallway. Li Shi handed the messenger the letters and snapped, "Telegraph." The messenger disappeared, with a salute and a great clang of spurs and saber.

"It's nothing, I'm afraid. I got a telegram during the wedding banquet that told me that the premier won't appoint a provincial governor this year. There has been some dispute between the Shandong warlords. So I'm to hang on a little more and act in their stead. Whoever 'they' are."

"Surely you don't mind that," I remarked. "It's nice to be important."

Li Shi leaned back in his chair and lit a cheroot. His face was tired, the vigorousness that usually made its home there missing. The cheroot's smoke rose cautiously above his head.

"When I began my career," he said in a low voice, "I hoped to rise quickly in the government. I know you think of me as a vulgar opportunist, but I wanted to help my country too, and I really thought it was best for China if we new men assumed control quickly—to really change things swiftly and permanently. I think my father would have agreed. Now there is no government, however hard we try to pretend it exists. So I am alone out here. I am promised a new governor, and no new governor arrives. I built a police station for the protection of the people, and instead it is a warlord's fortress, and I am the warlord inside it."

"Li Shi, be honest with me and with yourself. Do you really want a new governor to arrive, and be the power in Changsha instead of you?"

My brother regarded the end of his cheroot. "I used to. I used to sincerely wish for such a man—so that I could serve him well and gain his approval and make a name for myself with the central authorities. One day, I thought, I'll go to Beijing and be part of a great national undertaking." He puffed lightly. "But now, I am beginning to wish for the new governor not quite so hard as before. Because I am beginning to enjoy my local eminence here. And I am sorry I am turning this way. It can't be a good thing. My father would be ashamed of such disloyalty in his son."

I stood up and went to his side. I put my hand on his shoulder again. I smoothed his hair, an old gesture from our youth—I had not done it in a long time.

"Li Shi, just resign," I pleaded. "You are not even thirty years old. Go home and live with Mother. Or get married. Become a teacher and teach the poetry you love to read so much. Put this all away from you."

Li Shi smiled wryly at me. "Ah, no. That's just what I cannot do. In this short space of time keeping order in my little area of the city, I have made enough enemies of the various ruffians and bandits who run through the other quadrants—not to mention that dog-eating Feng—that my life is not safe if I let go of my troops. Not to mention your life and Mother's and Graceful Virtue's. So here I am, Younger Sister. And here I must stay."

I knelt by his side, clutching his arm. "How can it be that the end result of all this"—I gestured around me, taking in the barbed wire, the walls, the sleeping soldiers in their barracks, the locked gun cabinets in the armaments room—"is to place you in a trap?"

He leaned forward and extinguished his cheroot very deliberately on the concrete floor beneath the heel of his boot.

"The lessons of power are hard," he said, his face close to mine. "Once learned, they are forgotten only at one's own peril. But there are advantages to my situation too. And I can't say I would alter it, even if I could."

He laughed dryly.

"Frightening, how one changes, isn't it?" he asked.

14

Jin Yu had taken to traveling a great deal, and staying for months at a time in Beijing, where she was corresponding for a number of women's suffrage societies. She had even been arrested at a suffrage demonstration in the capital. She had written me an angry letter from the jail where she was held for two days before the charges were dropped. "Can you imagine in this day and age?" she wrote. "The new law denies voting rights to, and I quote directly from the relevant legal statute, 'illiterates, opium smokers, bankrupts, those of unsound mind, and women.'" I was proud of her, and also disapproving of her for having gotten herself arrested. But perhaps the disapproval was, as it often is, a way of keeping envy at bay.

In 1917, in the middle of my fifth year of teaching, Jin Yu finally came back to Hunan to teach school and to study French at the secondary school that had been opened by Yale University of America. She promptly set about trying to turn me into a revolutionary, and took me with her to a meeting of Teacher Yang's newly formed Marxist-Leninist study group. The meeting took place on a Saturday night, when there was no school the next day, because all the young teachers who attended had taken advantage of the Saturday half-day to travel to Teacher Yang's house from their country schoolmasterships all over the province, and would use Sunday morning to go back again. The rural teachers left their muddy, straw-soled cloth shoes outside the door to dry in the stiff winter winds and carried in blankets in varying degrees of threadbareness, which they would later use to sleep on Teacher Yang's floor.

I stood shyly to one side and watched them as they came in the door and greeted each other like long-lost friends, employing a sort of private language filled with slang and obscure references to incidents I didn't know about. They gave me friendly nods, but rushed to embrace Jin Yu as a comrade, hugging her and clapping her on the shoulder and teasing her. In return, she bestowed her half smile, as if they would have to do more to impress her, to make her curved mouth turn all the way up at the corners. I can never be her, I thought, my favor would never be so eagerly sought after. Watching them, these comrades in arms, I felt a deep yearning to be one of them, to have what they had, to be greeted as they greeted each other, a friend for no other reason than because I agreed with them. But even as I thought about my desire to belong with them, I felt uneasy as well, as if one part of my brain were at war with another. Agreement was a slippery basis for friendship. There was another thing, too, that made me uneasy. They were all full of unfailing confidence in their cause, driven by their belief in historical inevitability. Unfailing confidence makes me nervous, since it always seems a little inhuman.

"I'm giving them a good meal," Teacher Yang whispered to me as bowls of meaty-smelling dumplings and tangy soy and vinegar were passed around the room, and two dozen chopsticks clicked like crickets. "These country teachers get nothing for their labors. They live as poor as peasants."

"One questions," said a husky voice near me, "why intellectuals shouldn't be as poor as peasants."

Teacher Yang and I turned toward the voice, I with curiosity, and he with a thinly veiled impatience.

"If you wish to attract clever men to the teaching of others, they must receive something for their pains," said Teacher Yang.

"Market mechanisms," replied Mao Zedong. "Patriotic men aren't swayed by them." He gave us a broad and friendly smile, then edged around me to join a small group of the others.

"He must know better," I murmured to Teacher Yang. "It is a very rare patriot indeed who will give up eating."

"He likes to provoke," Teacher Yang whispered back edgily. "I've never known anyone better at the dialectic. But naive, as you might expect, coming from a family with money as he does. He seems to think you can perfect human nature. Some of the others in this room think the same way."

"Come on over, Teacher," called Jin Yu. "We are ready to start. And I want to introduce Jade Virtue to our brothers and sisters in arms."

We sat in a circle, some of us perched on chairs, some of us crosslegged on the floor. Jin Yu sat down on the floor with an air of purpose and pulled me down next to her. Teacher Yang sat in his great leather armchair.

There were several new people, and we were made to give brief histories of ourselves.

"I am Cai Hesen," said a slender, somber young man with a high nose-bridge and an unexpectedly harsh grate in the bottom of his voice. He hesitated an instant. "I am Cai Chang's brother." His eyes swept the room in anxious defense. The rest of us looked away in embarrassment.

"Cai Chang's brother is welcome here," boomed Mao in his great voice. "Your sister is a true revolutionary." Cai Hesen smiled suddenly and warmly at him, and I had my first glimpse of Mao's unusual ability to affect the morale of others, even of strangers.

"I teach middle school in Changde," Cai Hesen continued, more at ease. He added meaningfully, seeming to release his words in Jin Yu's direction, "I teach at the girls' middle school. I'm one of only two male teachers there." A little burst of applause greeted this disclosure, and Jin Yu awarded him with an approving look. Cai Hesen blushed furiously when he met her eyes, and I remember wishing as I sat there that I affected men that way.

Teacher Yang nodded kindly toward Cai Hesen. Then it was my turn. Jin Yu patted my knee encouragingly.

"This person is named Liang," I murmured. "My personal name is Jade Virtue. My husband is Pan Wang Mang." I faltered a little under everyone's gaze. "I teach at the Zhounan Middle School here in Changsha."

A moment of silence. "Tell them what you teach," whispered Jin Yu.

"I teach mathematics and accounting," I said.

A little more silence.

"Mrs. Pan supports her husband and his family entirely with her earnings," said Jin Yu. I stared at her, a flush of anger and shame rising up my throat.

The others clapped their hands and smiled at me, Mao most of all. Jin Yu brought her pale face close to mine—her voice glided toward me under the applause. "They don't consider it a shame," she murmured in my ear. "They think you are very capable."

"How many girls at Zhounan, Mrs. Pan?" Mao asked, his voice burly above the reedy fluting of the others.

"About one hundred and fifty," I said.

"And how many of those are scholarship students?" Mao was sitting on the edge of a wooden chair on the other side of the circle from me. He leaned forward as he spoke, resting his forearms on his knees and clasping his large hands in front of him.

"I . . . I don't know what you mean. What do you mean by scholarship student?" I stammered.

"You know. Poor girls on scholarship. How many of the one hundred and fifty are poor girls on scholarship?"

I was devastated. All my pride in the value of my work was gone, whirled away by the force of his question.

"None. There's no money for scholarships. No one at the school is really poor."

"I suppose it hasn't occurred to anyone yet to teach poor girls. And the girls you do teach. What good is their learning to them?"

"Why, they are better people because of it," I replied, in a soft, annoyed tone.

"I'm sure they are. Don't be angry, Little Sister Liang. I agree. But the question remains. What do they do with what they now know? Where do they go with it?" Mao sat back. The expression on his face was thoughtful. There was nothing in its broad planes that suggested the slightest ill will— indeed, he acted as if he were merely objectively considering an interesting fact, placed before him for dissection. "Because really, they have nowhere to go."

Most of the rest of the meeting took place in front of me, with very little of my participation. My mind seethed with anger at myself, anger at my delighted acceptance of the serenity of the school grounds and the sweet faces of the students. But all along, I thought in a fury, all along, that serenity and sweetness hid the rankest injustice. My stomach felt hollow.

"Nudism may be the answer," I heard Mao say from his side of the room. "I've been giving it much thought. So much of our modern social inequality is based on how we dress. How we admire the silk gowns and jewels of the wealthy! Better we should all be equal, dressed only in our own skins. Then we would all look alike."

"I'm not sure," Cai Hesen said slowly, "that would work." His thin, thoughtful face turned up toward Mao. "The bodies of the rich and the poor don't look alike, you know. The rich are plump and their skin is smooth and white. The poor have calluses, sunburns, and scars; their skin droops off them like old bags. You would still be able to tell."

"Why don't you just dress everyone alike, Zedong?" asked one young woman wryly, smoothing her own rather fashionable clothing. "Identical trousers and tunics for everyone. That would put us in the right frame of mind for perfect equality."

Jin Yu and I walked home afterward. She was not very pleased with me.

"You sat there with nothing to say," she snapped. "Your brilliant mind was silent as a grave."

"You talked enough for both of us."

"Everything I said was exactly to the purpose. Tell me what is wrong. Did Mao make you uncomfortable in some way? I noticed you fell silent after his remarks to you. Don't be affected like that. Mao's mind leaps around. He always has to contradict. He often changes his mind. More than anything in the world, he hates to be bored. The way you and I fear hunger or pain, he fears boredom."

I stood still in the road, heedless of the whipping night wind, and looked at her. She stopped and turned to look back at me, standing a short way ahead in the shadows of the evening. "But Jin Yu, he's absolutely right."

She shrugged, her pale stern face expressionless. "That's the irritating thing about him. His criticisms usually are right. It's just his ideas for improving matters that are often strange."

"But it's worse than that. Why didn't I see it myself? Why am I so blind?" I stared at the road beneath my cloth-shod feet. "Why am I such a fraud?" I muttered.

Jin Yu came to my side. "You aren't a fraud," she said, as gently as I had ever heard her. "You were just so happy to be a part of the school—happy for the first time in years—that you didn't examine its limitations. Now you know better."

15

There was in those earlier years of my teaching a girl called Family Rich, who had been a very good student at the elementary school. She was a daughter of the farmer Chung. Old Chung was wealthy, having risen to the point where he owned two hundred acres of rice land, and a team of oxen he hired out to others for labor, and a great granite millstone brought from the quarries along the Yangtze, on which Chung's men and Chung's beasts took turns slowly grinding grain into flour, for three coppers a half bushel, payable in advance. Chung was nicknamed "the Millstone" by his neighbors, for he shared its qualities.

Every teacher at the elementary school praised Family Rich's quickness and ability. As she was the only one of the three daughters of that family to be sent to school at all, I worried that Chung would take her home after she finished the lower school, before she could come to us. But someone told Chung that it was the fashion among the most wealthy and cultivated families to acquire educated girls as wives, and so Chung determined to send his youngest daughter to school for a few years more. In preparation, he changed her name from Family Rich to Elegance.

When she arrived, I liked her immediately. Elegance was a lively, attractive girl who came to school willingly and stayed late to read borrowed books. She was witty, with a natural facility for making up rhymes. I taught her with pleasure, anxious to encourage her voracious reading, and assigned the girls in my math class to take turns composing verses to start the class each day, partly to encourage Elegance, who liked poetry and wasn't very good at math. Her only flaw was a certain superficiality, as if her mind often worked a little too quickly and led her to glib conclusions. But I thought she might have reserves of depth she would reach as she became older.

I asked her if she would give any thought to being a teacher. To my surprise, she shook her head merrily and began to laugh. Her carefully combed hair flew, scattering about the shoulders of her neat black day-dress.

"No, I can't teach. Papa means for me to marry Old Yeh's eldest son."

I raised my eyebrows. Yeh was an ancient name, and it stood in an ancient house, and traced its bloodline to great lords of the Ming. Chung flew very high, I thought. But Yeh's fortunes were scanty these days, and money not ready to hand. So perhaps Chung knew his altitude after all.

"I'm sorry to hear that. You have the mind to be a reasonably good scholar."

"I hope so," the girl answered. "But I think I would rather be Yeh's wife. The school is lovely, but it is so quiet, so removed from life. I don't just want to teach girls. I want to meet the great men of our day. I want to talk to them, right to their faces, and hear their ideas from their own mouths, and dispute with them if I dare. If I marry Yeh—my goodness, his family knows them all."

I covered my disappointment, rubbing it away from the corners of my mouth with my fingers, along with a faint twinge of envy. "Well," I said, "as Young Yeh's wife, it's best that you yourself be learned. You'll have to entertain his friends at dinner. The wives of the friends are sure to be edu-cated women, since Young Yeh has been to university."

"That's what I think too," said Elegance with a knowing air. "So Papa lets me read and mind my appearance. I don't have to do chores on the farm like my sisters, because they don't go to school, and because labor will make me an ox. As they are, I guess." She looked troubled for a mo-ment, but her natural high spirits flowed back to her. "Well, I'm the youngest, so it's natural I'm the one who's spoiled."

I wasn't sure if I agreed with this attitude, but I nodded. There was nothing to be done about Elegance's oxlike sisters anyway. In a family risen from the land, it was common enough that one child should be sent to school and treated like a scholar, with books and new shoes, and the other children kept home to work.

"When I marry Yeh," Elegance added, "I shall read books and look at paintings all day."

I taught Elegance for two years. On the last day I saw her in school, she wore a new dress with a white linen collar, and all her friends admired it. She recited a poem that she had written for class, and which I remember to this day, even now, when so much else has been lost to me. She stood at the front of the little classroom, her voice bright with youth.

Even the beauty with almond eyes
Has been left by a lover.
Even the general with a hundred red flags
Has lost a few battles.
Even the emperor with a hundred palaces
Has stumbled in his garden.

We all applauded when she was done.

"What is the title?" I asked.

"'The Wise Man Views Profit and Loss As the Same,'" Elegance replied with a smile, putting her hands behind her back in a parody of scholarly posture.

"Well, they aren't the same!" a clever and rather practical girl named Patience exclaimed, and all the classmates laughed.

"What about Teacher's poem?" Elegance asked, smiling in my direction.

I stood up behind my desk and recited the one I had written.

I am a long way from the capital,
And the mountain paths are steep.
Ahead lies an old temple,
Where I will pillow my head on my hands.
Turning on my horse to look back,
I think I see a ghost in the trees.

The girls clapped their hands, and Elegance bowed to me, graciously.

The next day, Elegance did not come to school. At first, I was not alarmed, as I merely thought she was ill—she had been somewhat flushed looking the day before. In any case, some of the peasant families—even the rich ones—still kept their daughters home some days during the planting and harvest seasons, when every pair of hands was needed. But as the week finished, I began to worry. The following week, I watched for her from the school gates as the other girls arrived, but she did not come. More frightening still, her classmates had heard nothing of her. Even

Patience, who was quite friendly with her, and had even been invited to the Chung house to eat dinner, did not know what had happened. The other teachers told me not to worry, but from the corners of my eyes, I saw them shake their heads at each other.

Finally, at the end of the second week, Patience came to me before class. I sat reading essays at my desk, the early morning sunlight warming the old wooden forms where the girls sat, glinting where it touched upon a steel pen or on a hairpin wedged into a crack. When I looked up, Patience stood before me. Her round, merry face was strained.

"What is it, Patience?" I put down my papers. "Are you hurt? Are you sick?"

"Teacher Liang. I saw Elegance." Her eyes filled with tears even as I looked into them, and the tears ran down her cheeks.

I jumped up and rushed around the desk to put my arm on her shoulders. "What has happened, Patience? Is Elegance dead?"

"It would be better if she were dead," the girl wept. I was shocked, scarcely believing these harsh words, but I held my silence, waiting for Patience to tell me.

She gasped out the story with great effort, her face streaked with salt, her chest heaving. "She's at her father's farm. I went to see if she was sick and wanted me to come play dominoes with her. She was behind the wooden fence. She was hauling a bucket of water from a well to swill the pigs in the sty. She was wearing some dreadful trouser suit, not like our Elegance at all. I ran to the fence and called to her, but she only looked at me as if she didn't recognize me. She . . . she turned her back on me, and wouldn't answer my calls, and ran into the house. I felt like I was watching her ghost disappear. Oh, Teacher Liang. What happened to her?"

The rest of the day was insufferable. I sent Patience home, since she was ill with her distress, and I didn't want the other girls to question her or gossip until I could find out what had befallen Elegance. I made several efforts to lecture and gave up, explaining that I was feeling queasy, which was certainly true enough. I assigned some equations instead and could hardly bide my time until school let out for the day. I ground my teeth with frustration as I sat at my desk, jingling my watch chain every time I searched yet again for the hour.

In the midafternoon, the students flew home eagerly as swallows, their neat black dresses sailing behind them. I followed immediately, bolting down to the road that would take me to Chung's farm. I walked partway;

then in my impatience I hailed a passing man with a tin wagon attached to his bicycle, and paid him a few coins to carry me the rest of the way.

I got out a hundred yards down the road from the farm, so that I might approach quietly. The large whitewashed house edged into view at the place where the stone fence changed into one of split willow rails. I heard chickens, I heard pigs, I heard distant calls from the men in the open field behind, and from inside the house itself, but I saw no one. The muddy yard in front of the door was cluttered with fine metal tools, rakes, and new wood for building. Fat white chickens shuffled and hopped on the edge of a stone well, leaving white droppings on its wooden cover. A torn piece of red paper painted with the character for wealth fluttered above the door, which had also been painted bright red and boasted a fine brass lock. I stood quietly outside, just behind the split-willow fence, and waited.

I think I must have stood for almost half an hour when two women emerged from the house. I ducked back behind the stone portion of the fence. At first I could not tell what age these women were, but soon I realized that they must be Elegance's sisters. They were still young, but their bodies were heavy with muscle and calluses, and their skins burnt and oily with the sun. They moved about the yard in a businesslike fashion, before leaving for the field beyond. I waited a little longer.

Then Elegance appeared. Her long hair had been cut, bluntly, straight across at the level of her ears, and scraped back from her face. Her downy scalp, with the slight peel of sunburn, showed at her temples. She was wearing trousers and a tunic of heavy cloth, stitched stoutly for strength. She went to the well and pulled off the cover. A pebble must have fallen in then, because I heard a hollow clatter and a splash.

"Elegance," I whispered. Elegance looked up at the sound of my voice. She dropped the bucket and crept to the fence like a whipped dog. When she reached me, she gripped the rail with both hands and put her face as close as she could. She was crying.

"Elegance, what has happened?" I whispered. "Tell me, my poor girl. What is it? Why are you not in school?"

Elegance wiped her tears with her fingers, leaving grubby streaks on her face. She clung to the rail again.

"Old Yeh refused Baba's proposal. Old Yeh said he wouldn't have his son marry a peasant's daughter. Old Yeh said that teaching me to read and write was like training a monkey in order to gull fools into thinking it is human. But he knew better than to be fooled by a trained beast."

"No, oh no," I whispered. "That terrible old villain."

"Teacher Liang, I wish I were dead."

Her knuckles were white on the rail. I put my hands on both of hers, feeling the new roughness on her fingers. "Elegance," I said. I rubbed her hands and warmed them, and tried to think of what to do. "Elegance, listen to me."

"My name isn't Elegance," the girl sobbed. "Not anymore. Baba changed it." She put her head down pitifully on the backs of my hands, and I turned them over to hold her young face. As she wept into my palms, her tears seeped out between my fingers and stained the wooden rails of the fence.

A shout came from the yard. Elegance spun around. Chung had emerged from around the corner of the house and ran up to us at the fence. He struck his daughter, and she fell to the ground and huddled like an animal in the mud. She covered her face.

I pushed the gate open angrily and strode to where Elegance lay shivering and stood over her, as close to Chung himself as I could. "I have heard you were a hard man, Old Chung," I said, "but I never heard it said that you ever raised your hand to your children."

"You have no right to come in," Chung shouted, his face alarmed.

"I am here," I snapped. "Try to make me leave against my will, and you will regret it."

Chung hesitated and scowled, but did nothing except stand over his daughter, squaring his shoulders and clenching his fists.

"Why have you taken her from school?" I demanded.

"That is my business," Chung snarled.

"Make up your mind to tell me, because I will not leave until I have your answer." I folded my arms and stood squarely like an oak, my heart throbbing with fury in my chest, pounding so loudly I could hear the blood in my ears.

"Well, there is no use in sending her anymore." Chung shrugged, but a vein beat powerfully on his neck. "She failed to snare the Yeh, the miserable cow. She will marry a farmer like me, and a man like me has no use for a wife who will read instead of work hard and bear strong children and make him rich."

My heart sank, for the girl's father had absolute authority to decide her future, and it was not for me to question it, now that she was not in school anymore. I almost turned to leave. But then what Mao had told me came into my mind, about how I had to do more than simply fill my students with learning while they sat in my class. About how I had to try to give them someplace to go with that learning. With a great effort, I lowered my arms and my voice, and put away my pride, my desire to avoid other people's messy disputes, and my unthinking acceptance of the old ways.

"Please, sir," I pleaded. "You are a rich and important man. Everyone knows it. Surely you can afford to spare her from the farm. I know you have many workers who labor for you. What difference does one weak, silly girl make?"

"I have money because I don't waste it where there is no return."

"Then let her work," I entreated him. "There is no shame in doing both. I have done it myself. Let her do work here and also attend school. I know she is willing to do chores when she comes home."

Chung hesitated. "No."

I saw that Elegance's huddled shoulders began to shake.

"Then let her come to me for private tutoring in the evenings when she has finished her work here."

Now Chung grew angrier still. "So she can become as you are and look down on her family, on her father?"

"She doesn't look down on you!" I cried in protest. "I don't look down at you! Time and again, I have said to people I know, that if there was one man I honored, it was Old Chung, because he thought to send his daughter to school when so many others, from ignorance or ill temper, refused."

I thought I saw Chung hesitate again. But then he dashed his fist into his open palm. "No! No! Again no! Her learning has gotten me nothing. Her sisters are jealous and cry to me daily about her. Her mother favors her so openly, and sews her such fancy dresses, that I cannot stand it." He drew suddenly very close, and I smelled the onion in his breath. "I have spent hundreds of taels," he gritted, "for nothing!"

"It is not for nothing!" I cried, stung to my core. "Her prettiness must fade—and I see you are doing everything to ensure that. But she is clever. Her mind will waste away if you keep her here—it doesn't matter how many things you can buy her! You are burying her alive!"

"Get out!" yelled Chung, his face black with anger. He raised his fist and stepped forward, his body filled with threat, but then Elegance stirred herself and flung her arms around me.

"Baba, no!" she whimpered. "You cannot strike her. Liang Li Shi is her brother." Elegance twined her arms around my neck.

Chung fell back, his face working and twisting with frustration. But my brother's name was a shield.

Elegance clung to me tightly. "Please go," she whispered into my ear. "There is nothing here now."

I looked into her pained face, and touched her cheek.

"Get out!" Chung screamed. "Get out!" His face was screwed up into a reddened knot. And I saw with a shock that he was crying.

I held Elegance's face tenderly. "My poor girl, try to remember what you have learned. Practice in your mind."

She shook her head. "I shall try to forget everything. Memory will only make me sad."

I left then, glancing back at the girl standing white-faced and stricken in the yard. She stood very still, like a statue, her hands clasped and pressing on her chest, as if she would keep her heart inside it by force. Behind her stood Old Chung, who was rubbing his eyes with his fists like a child. Beyond them, several of Chung's workers were beginning to gather, open-mouthed, drawn by the shouts and sobs of their master.

"I've seen it before." Teacher Yang sighed deeply. "Sometimes these parents don't know the value of what you teach their daughters. They send them to school for silly and shameful reasons, because they think an educated daughter will be worth more. And so she is, but not in the way they think. She won't catch a rich son-in-law—for that, she only needs to be pretty." He sighed again. "They never can grasp the importance of having children who have even a single thought in their heads."

I lifted my head. My fingers were clenched together very tightly, and I thought I might not, just at this moment, be able to conquer my fear that nothing I did meant anything. "Sir, I have a question to put to you now," I said. Teacher Yang nodded again, waited, listening. "Sir, what is the value of what I have learned?"

Teacher Yang leaned back in his chair. When he spoke, he formed his words carefully. "There are too many people in this world who are poor and weak for me to sneer at the need to obtain money and power. And learning can, if you are also strong and lucky, bring you those things. But that is not all. Learning teaches you what to do with money and power, teaches you their proper place in this world, and teaches you too, when those things become unnecessary. It gives you a sense of . . . proportion. Disproportion is a kind of evil, in its own way."

He became momentarily abstracted in thought, his gaze shifting slowly from me to the photographs that sat on the top of his bookshelf. But then his eyes sharpened once more. "Think of yourself. You see that your early education has enabled you to earn the rice which feeds the Pan family. Please, don't squeak these rote protests. No covering up the family shame which everyone knows about anyway. But it isn't just the coins that your literacy has gained. You belong to no one except yourself. You can pay your creditors. You do not need to crawl to tyrannical relatives, nor to moneylenders, and submit to their degrading terms. Nor do you sigh for fine silk and jewels, because you know the precise worth of things like that, which is precisely nothing. You are not a slave to your basest desires."

He leaned forward across his desk. His eyes were dark with urgency. "It matters not if you have nowhere to go. The great world is not always in our control. But you are in your own control. If people speak nonsense to you, you know enough to disregard it. If people speak wisdom to you, you know enough to listen to their voices. You hold up your head. And what is inside your head cannot be taken away from you. Do you see?"

I nodded, and felt that sweetness, the beginnings of understanding.

Teacher Yang leaned back again, satisfied by what he saw in my face. He stroked his long beard a moment before he spoke again. "Learning might make you rich, or powerful, or admired. But now you know that most of all, above everything else, it makes you free. It makes you free in the one stronghold that can never be taken by force." He reached and touched my temple gently with his forefinger. "This is your fortress. It cannot be conquered."

It was not the last time I saw the girl. I was on the market road several years later, in the middle of a flat gray winter, my rubber soles melting through the rime of frost that crusted the rough, mud-mortared cobblestones. My head was down, and I was blinking the sugary snow from my lashes. But across the road, I saw her walking, her pregnant belly wrapped with an enormous quilted silk coat. In the slipping frost, she stepped on a corner of her coat and fumbled for balance.

I ran across the road. I grasped her hand warmly, reached out to touch her cheek, and opened my mouth to greet her. In that brief instant before I could speak, I saw the thickness of her coat, the fur lining peeping out over the collar's edge, and the powder and rouge on her face, dropping dustily into the outer corners of her eyes. She wore heavy gold rings on her slightly thickened fingers and a jade bracelet on her wrist. But she gave a little cry, her eyes widening, and she pushed me off with such force that I almost fell. She shambled away as quickly as her pregnant stomach would allow, staggering on the slippery stones beneath her feet, her hands planted tightly over her ears, as if she were afraid she might hear me calling to her.

Later I heard that she had taken to pretending that she could not read, and although I saw her from time to time, I never tried to greet her again. She had married another farmer, a man almost as old as Old Chung, and even richer. Another day I saw her with a new gold tooth, which would have cost a teacher at the middle school a half-year's salary to buy. I was glad she was surrounded by many fat children; I was glad she could open her purse and buy fine cakes in the pastry shops; I was glad she could throw down coins at the gambling tables. I hoped these things would be enough to comfort her. I remembered that she was no longer called Elegance, but I never found anyone who could tell me what her name had become.

16

At one end of the Northern Road, at least the way it looked in 1919, lay the Xiangs' great house, ancient, ordered, discreet and hushed behind its walls and gates, keeping its secrets like an old concubine. The house basked quietly beneath its glazed tiles and delicate lacelike painted shutters. The hummingbirds in the garden, the faint splashes of the carp in the pond, and the whispers of the servants all mingled like smoke fumes, curling softly at the edges of awareness.

At the other end of the road, miles distant, lay the iron-and-concrete rail station, a long, shed with a corrugated tin roof, setting its great raw concrete legs over several sets of railroad tracks, rising out of the piles of stone and sand and dust bred of its perennial construction. Inside the station, the engines shivered and squealed on their metal wheels, and puffed out huge clouds of damp gray smoke into the faces of the crowds pushing onto the platforms, turning the sweat on their foreheads into grime. The pounding and shuffling of feet, the shouts of the porters, filled every corner and bounced in aggressive echoes from every wall. The iron door of a locomotive would clang open, briefly throwing a glare of light and heat onto the bare-chested man bent over the coal bin.

On the morning Jin Yu left for Paris, we walked all the way to the station from the Xiang house. Her luggage was sent ahead in a hired cart, for a porter to load onto the train. The train would take her to Canton, where she would board a steamship that would eventually land her in France. I stood by the front door while Jin Yu bid her parents farewell in their hall, surrounded by a crowd of their servants and bondsmen.

"I will not take a maid with me to France," Jin Yu snapped, exasperated.

"Take at least one small one," Madame Xiang wailed, grabbing a short

girl in her early teens at random from the gathering of servants and pushing her forward. "She doesn't need to pack anything. Just take her."

The servants held their breaths, staring openmouthed at Jin Yu, hardly
daring to look at each other. But Jin Yu shook her head angrily.

"I am leaving precisely so that I can put behind me this feudal foolishness. I will thank you not to mention it again."

The servants let out their breaths. From where I stood, I saw the serving girl's mother wipe her upper lip with sudden relief.

Jin Yu left roughly, slamming the door behind her. We went out to the
road. It was still early in the morning, and the sun hung its head down near
the horizon. The shadow of the moon was still visible, very high up, behind the waving leaves of the silver birches that began to line the road as it
wound out of the older parts of the city, shrugging away the twisting alleys to lie down in the broad straightness of the fields and canals. The air
seemed warm, but there was an underlying chill, even though the leaves
had not yet begun to turn.

I walked beside Jin Yu, my hands in my pockets. We walked almost
two miles in companionable quiet, listening to the creaking calls of the
birds and crickets, and the distant shouts of men in the fields.

"I'm so excited," Jin Yu said finally. "I can't wait to get to France with
everyone else." She put her arm through mine. "How long I've wanted to
go there! I even envied those laborers that went there a few years ago to
dig graves for the soldiers in that war France and England had with Germany. I would see long lines of them waiting to take the cattle-car trains to
the ports, and I wanted to go with them."

"I think they would rather not have gone to that sausage factory, but
for the money," I answered dryly. "There is an entire Chinese cemetery in
France for those men. I trust your experience in France will be different
from theirs."

"Of course," Jin Yu said, nodding her head in a self-reproving manner.
"I did not wish to make light of their fate."

"Aren't you afraid of being homesick? I would be very excited too, but
I would also be sad to leave China and my mother."

"I won't be homesick. I will return, and in better circumstances. I'll
come back equipped to help our country. But now, I have to train myself,
like a soldier."

I sighed.

"Jade Virtue," Jin Yu said at once. "I'm sorry. You know I wish you were coming. It doesn't mean that I won't miss you. But I can't lose sight of what this means."

I looked at my friend's pale, changeable face, examined closely her heavy swallow's-wing brows.

"I want so much for you to succeed," I said. "There is nothing you want for yourself that I do not also want for you. But I'm sad that you are leaving me. And I wish I could go too."

"You said you couldn't leave the Pans," Jin Yu said, a little acidly.

"I can't," I replied simply. "Who would care for them? Who else will hold their spirits to their flesh? I worry for your parents too, Jin Yu. They are getting old. You are entirely right to take this chance to go to Paris, but I wonder that you do not worry more for those you leave behind."

Jin Yu's face looked stormy. "Nothing will happen to my parents. Nothing has ever happened to them, why should anything start happening now?"

I said nothing, but walked on.

"Your sentimental view always prevents you from seizing an opportunity," Jin Yu finally said, a distinct edge in her voice. "Your sense of obligation drags you down."

I stopped in the middle of the road. I turned and looked her in the eyes, holding her arm.

"Listen," I said. "Whatever else the effect may be, I'm certainly not dragged down. I am as free as any man in China. As free as any of the warlords. Even as free as you. Maybe I'm the only one who can see it, but I see it."

I walked on. Jin Yu stared at me. The surprise in her face was very gratifying.

We arrived at the train station with very little time to spare. We put our arms up in front of our faces and began pushing inside, toward the tracks, wriggling between broad backs and sharp shoulders. I jammed my elbow into a man in front of me.

"Porter!" I shouted over the din. "The Canton train!"

The porter shouted something incomprehensible and pointed toward a train puffing and straining on the third track. Jin Yu thrust her hand out from behind a woman carrying a box of chickens and waved her white ticket under the porter's nose. He grabbed her waving hand and brought the paper close to his spectacles. He shouted and gestured and wiped sweat from the end of his nose.

"What?" Jin Yu cried.

"He says the manservant loaded your luggage already!" I screamed in her ear. "Go to cabin eight!"

We struggled to the train. The crush of people pushed us this way and that way, as if they were paid to try to separate us with their elbows and boxes. I clung to Jin Yu's hand, and we dragged each other forward.

We finally crushed up against the side of one of the train cars. I took a little bag out of my pocket.

"A surprise," I said. "Salt plums. Your favorite." My voice was breaking.

"Don't cry. Don't be upset." Jin Yu, for all her superior resolution, was clutching my arm very tightly. "I'll come back to you one day. Just like always."

The whistle blew, and I watched Jin Yu climb up the steps to the sleeping car she would occupy. She pushed her way inside, past the tightly packed mob in the aisle, climbing over the bags and crates stacked up outside the compartments. For a few minutes I lost sight of her, but I followed her progress by the shouts of indignation from those crowded into the aisle, shouts that rippled along the car as she passed. Then a window fell open, and Jin Yu waved and smiled. In her other hand was the little bag of salt plums. Her voice could hardly be heard above the din, but she mimed taking a plum out and eating it. She rubbed her stomach in feigned pleasure, and I laughed.

When the train pulled out, many people ran alongside, shouting last words, putting a few last bits of food or a last letter into the clustering rows of outstretched hands reaching from all the windows. But I stood very still and hugged myself and watched Jin Yu's face fading into the gloom at the far end of the station before bursting out into the glare of the sun as the train left the building. It seemed as if it would always be this way, Jin Yu traveling and seeing the world, and me staying in the same provincial town in which I had been born. I stood until even the smokestack had sunk below the distant line of land, leaving only its smoke, and the train from Canton was pulling onto the track from the opposite direction. The Canton passengers tumbled off their train in a huge crowd, drowning the last of my view.

17

Something more than a year after Jin Yu left, I was stirred from sleep by a shower of pebbles on my bedroom window in the early morning. I glanced at Wang Mang, who was sleeping at home more now, but he had not shifted. I put back the quilts and went to the window. The entire courtyard below me was filled with fog. In the dawn mist, I could only just distinguish several shadowy figures beyond the gate. I swung open the casement.

"Who is it?" I hissed.

"Teacher Liang! Teacher Liang! It's us. Patience and Orchid." I recognized Patience's pleasant voice. "We have Fragrant Forest with us. We need your help."

Feeling alarmed, I pushed my feet into my slippers and stole downstairs. I let the girls into the courtyard.

"What are you young ladies doing here? What have you done wrong?" I demanded.

Fragrant Forest immediately started to cry.

Patience looked pleadingly at me. "Teacher Liang, please help us," she begged. "Fragrant Forest's parents have arranged a marriage for her." Patience's velvety little face was wide-eyed with disapproval.

"So?"

"They are going to make her marry young Master Luo."

"Oh. Him."

"Yes. She would rather die than marry him. We said we would help her escape."

I frowned at this. "Escape? Escape to where?"

"Her friends in Canton will take her," Orchid said, bending down to speak quietly in my ear. Orchid was very tall. "She's run away from home. We just have to hide her all morning, until we can sneak her onto the Canton-bound train at noon. But her family already knows she's gone, so we need your help to hide her. There's another boy," she added, as if it were an afterthought. And the two girls looked at Fragrant Forest.

"Why come to me?" I demanded. "I am your teacher. I am your authority."

Patience and Orchid looked at one another. "Teacher Liang," Patience said, "I knew you of all people would not fail us. You are a true revolutionary."

I felt a tiny drift of pride infiltrate my surprise and worry. I pushed it away with a show of irritation. I turned to Fragrant Forest, a slender girl with a twist of passion to her mouth. "Well, are your friends talking all your words for you?" I demanded. "Who is this other boy?"

Fragrant Forest looked at her feet, and replied, "He is the scholar Tung."

A cat knocked over some pans left to wash in the courtyard by the kitchen door. It leaped out of the gray mist like an apparition and scurried around the corner of the house. The girls jumped in fright, and I looked around with a gasp.

"Look, young ladies," I said sternly, annoyed at having been startled. "All this romantic business is silly. I'll go speak to your parents and try to persuade them to call off the match. Tung is not objectionable, and maybe I can help him find a teaching job. Then you can marry him."

Fragrant Forest shook her head, her twin braids flying. "No, no. It won't do any good. They've signed the contract already. Old Luo has offered a lavish wedding, and he doesn't mind a small dowry, he's so anxious to find a bride for his worthless son. I have three sisters, and my parents just want to marry us off inexpensively. If I can get to my friends in Canton, Tung will meet me there."

"Do you know how serious an elopement is?"

"I don't care. I read the translation of *A Doll's House* in *New Youth* magazine. I'll be just like Nora and leave everything behind."

"Please don't be a fool," I snapped. "Nora is just a character in a play. What happened after she left home, that's what I'd like to know."

"Well, at least, no matter what happens, that Luo pig-ghost won't want to marry me anymore," the girl wept, wiping the tears from her eyes. "If I can't get away from him, I'll set myself on fire. I will." Another arsonist like Jin Yu, I thought to myself. But I knew Fragrant Forest had a will of iron. These dreamy, romantic girls were always the most ferocious, insisting as they did that their lives match their fantasies.

Patience and Orchid added, "We've pledged to help her or die trying."

"Oh, don't be so melodramatic." I stood and thought furiously. Hiding her in my own home was impossible—Wang Mang would not care, but the Pans would give her away in an instant. Helping the girl to elope was almost too lunatic to bear thinking about, but here the girl was, standing in my courtyard. I looked down into Fragrant Forest's face. The girl's almond eyes were fevered with determination.

"Wait here," I said, and went back inside. In the still-dark house, I moved about in silence. I went back to the bedroom and dressed, pulling on a quilted jacket over my suit. I glanced frequently at my husband, but he went on sleeping the peculiar, deadly sleep that came over him just after the drug had crept down his veins. Watching him over my shoulder, I dug out some money from the bottom of an empty face-cream pot and put the coins in my pocket. I gathered some brushes, paper, and an inkstone from the study.

The last thing I did before leaving the house was to wake the maid and tell her I was going drawing on the river with some students. "Yong Li, at ten o'clock, bring us some food to the dock. I'm hiring Grandfather Fang's boat." Yong Li tried to rise and go with me, but I ordered her to remain at home. "Don't forget, ten o'clock food. Some sesame buns and fried noodles and a pot of tea, I guess."

With that, I left the house, taking the three girls with me. As we hurried down the back alleys to the riverside, with the morning coolness on my skin, I felt my blood springing like a river, gathering strength.

The Xiang River was still swathed in woolly folds of fog, but the air was warming and clearing. We had no trouble finding Grandfather Fang. An ancient fisherman who no longer had the strength to go fishing in the more distant reaches of Tung Ting Lake, he plied the river itself, ferrying passengers or taking families on pleasure rides. He slept on his boat, and the girls woke him by shouting and flinging stones. He emerged sleepily.

"What is it? Who dares to throw stones? What? Is that you, Teacher Liang? What do you want at this hour?"

"I want to hire your boat. I want to take my students drawing on the river. The early morning light is beautiful, don't you think?"

Grandfather Fang looked up into the sky thoughtfully, his mahogany skin, seamed and cracked by years on the river, wrinkling in serious thought.

"I suppose so," he said, a little uncertainly.

"Well, let us on the boat, then."

He pulled the boat closer to the dock and put out a plank. With tottering steps, and a few cries at the shakiness of the planks, we were on board. Sails creaking, the boat floated slowly out into the middle of the river.

I held out two silver coins to Fang. His old eyes widened greedily. "This is for your boat," I said, handing him one. "And this is for your silence," handing him the other. He only smiled, and took the coins. His smile turned to a look of astonishment when the girls started to pull up the floorboards of the deck, which were laid loosely and without nails on top of the framework.

"Here now, what are you doing? Don't look under there—it's not your business!"

"We aren't interested in your contraband," I snapped at him. "Look to your money for comfort."

A mottled sunlight spilled into the hold. Beneath the floorboards was a smallish space, with a few inches of water swishing lazily about the bottom. Fragrant Forest jumped down, and the others put the floorboards down over her. Then I rubbed dust over the place with my foot and flung down a coil of dirty rope. It looked as though no one had taken up the floorboards in a hundred years.

"Sit down, girls. I order you to draw. Draw the view of the town from the river." With that, we all seated ourselves and began to sketch the city of Changsha. After opening and shutting his mouth a few times, Grandfather Fang shrugged, placed the coins in his shirt, and settled down to smoke a peaceful pipe.

The sun glinted on the green water, and the river breezes were cool, ruffling the edges of the paper and blowing wisps of hair into the artists' eyes. The mist was now wholly gone, and the day clear and hot. Changsha then had a certain haphazard charm when seen from the river, as I suppose it might still have now. Blossoms of smoke from the cookfires on shore curled tentatively into the air. It was almost pleasurable to paint like this. The only one who suffered was Fragrant Forest, crouched in the warm stuffy hold with her feet damp. She sat down on a large bale wrapped in coarse sacking cloth; a moment later she called up that the bale was full of tobacco.

"Untaxed tobacco, no doubt," I pronounced, throwing a cold glance at Grandfather Fang. He began to search the sky for signs of a change in the weather.

"Teacher Liang," said Patience in a low voice, hardly looking up from her paper. "On the dock."

I glanced up very carelessly. Several small figures were on the dock, waving to us. Young Luo, Old Luo, and Fragrant Forest's father, Old Dai. I waved back gaily and pretended not to hear the shouts as they reached me over the water.

"Good morning to you too," I called back.

The three men on the dock promptly spotted a small rowboat and shouted at the man dozing in it to bring it over to where they stood. I watched them with burgeoning anxiety as they started to climb in.

"Can our boat outrun them?" asked Orchid.

"No," I replied. "Anyway, then they would know we've done something wrong. Sit still, and let them come. Fragrant Forest?"

"Yes?" The girl's voice sounded muffled, coming through the floorboards.

"Sit still and be quiet."

"Well, now, here are some visitors coming," said Grandfather Fang, coming around from the other side of the boat.

I hissed at him, "Not one word from you about the girl under the deck, or I'll have you beaten. And I won't spare your gray hairs when I do it."

Grandfather Fang went back around to the other side of the boat.

When the little rowboat pulled up close to the larger fishing boat, Old Dai shouted, "Teacher Liang! Where is my daughter?"

"Which one? You have four daughters, and they are all my students." My heart was pounding, but my voice sounded steady enough.

"Fragrant Forest, that one. One of my maidservants saw her running down the road toward your house, in company with those two unspeakable girls, Yu and Cheng, and your servant told me you suddenly went drawing on the river. Yu and Cheng are sitting right there with you—I know they stole my daughter away from my house."

"Teacher Liang!" roared Old Luo, who was a formidable character. "The girl is to marry my son here. I know you have her."

I stood up and cupped my hands around my mouth to make myself heard. "Why would I do a thing like that? I am the deputy head of a school. Why should I take part in such a silly escapade?"

"Your reasons are your own," Old Dai shouted back. "But you have hidden her."

"I have not."

"You are lying!" This was Young Luo, a youth with the appearance of a wasted crow. He now stood up in the boat, pulling his slipshod robe more tightly around his thin frame. I bent a fierce glare at him. "Tell me, boy. Do you speak to your betters in this way?" To his father, I snapped, "Teach your son some manners." I would rather die than let Fragrant Forest marry such a fellow, I thought furiously. And now I am just like these silly girls.

Now Old Luo stood up in the boat. "I apologize for my son, Teacher Liang. He is young and has no manners. But we want the girl."

"Well, I hope you find her, then. It has nothing to do with me. She is not even a very good student."

"We want to search the boat. You cannot stop us." Old Dai was red-faced with anger and embarrassment, and in his agitation was rocking the boat alarmingly. The boatman began to bail the rowboat with a tin cup, glancing about with apprehension.

"Hey," he said to the party. "If you sink my boat, you'll have to pay." They ignored him.

"Do you hear me, Teacher Liang? We want to search the boat. We are coming now." Under the floorboards, I could hear Fragrant Forest crying.

"Come search it then!" I strode to the railing and pounded my fist on it, and the old, sea-soaked wood cracked slightly. "Search this boat, like hoodlums! If you find her, take her. But you have harassed and slandered me, in front of my own students. If you don't find her"—I shook my fist menacingly—"I will go straight to the magistrates and lay charges against all of you."

A hurried discussion took place on the boat. They looked at me balefully as they argued. I stood and scowled at them as fiercely as I could, letting my resolve show in my face. I blinked my eyes, yet when I opened them again, the men were still there, conferring in the little boat. They shall back away, I thought desperately, because it is my will.

Finally, Old Luo shouted, "We are not coming, Teacher Liang. But I will not forget this."

"Neither will I, Master Luo," I replied. The old villain drew his brows together in anger. But he silenced his son, who was shouting that he would swim all the way to Fang's boat.

The maid from my house appeared on the dock, a little spot of pink against the weathered grays and browns and lichen green of the harbor. She carried a pail of food and an iron pot of tea. As the rowboat with the three men was turning back to shore, I called again to them.

"Master Luo!"

He turned in the boat.

"My maid Yong Li is on the harborside there with food for us. Would you be so good as to send your rowboat back to us with her?"

Close to the hour of noon, we stepped off Old Fang's boat. I looked at Fragrant Forest, and I realized I was sorry to see her go. I handed the pail of food to her.

"Don't worry about her," said Patience. "She'll eat sesame buns and fried noodles all the way to Canton."

I watched while the girls disappeared quickly into the side streets that would lead them to the train station. I could not risk being seen at the station, so I merely went home.

The house was still darkened and quiet when I came in. Yong Li was waiting for me.

"Elder Sister, do you want me to make you something more to eat?" she asked me. Her eyes widened slightly. "Why, what happened to the pail I brought out to you?"

I looked around, as if in confusion. "Um, I don't know," I said. "I must have left it on Grandfather Fang's boat. I'm sorry. It doesn't matter."

I started down the hall. "Are the master and the old ones awake yet?" I called back to her.

"The master's in bed still. The ancestors are sitting in the garden drinking tea. Oh, there's a letter for you with a foreign stamp. I put it on your bed."

"How do you know it's for me?" I asked, looking down the long, dim hall to where she stood in the faint light that seeped in from the shuttered windows.

"You're the only one who gets letters," she replied.

I hurried to my bedroom. Wang Mang was still asleep, as the girl had said. I saw the envelope on my side of the bed, but I did not pick it up immediately. I waited long enough to open a window, flooding half the room with sunlight. Wang Mang stirred a little. Then I took up the letter, feeling the thin crackling paper between my fingers. I examined the red seal, enjoyed the foreign postage stamp, before sitting down in the sunshine to read it. Jin Yu, I thought, did not write me often enough. But after what I had done that day, I felt her presence close to me, almost as if she were in the room and I could hear her breath.

In fact, she wrote to say she had married. "You may remember Cai Hesen. We have contracted a revolutionary union. He is an editor of the underground journal that Chinese students have here in Paris, in which I have published many articles on women's suffrage. The production of the journal is a model of cooperation and equality. We recently gave Deng Xiao Ping the honorary title 'doctor of mimeography' for his help in the printing. We told him that this was the farthest he would ever go, because he is too short to become a leader!"

I smiled at the rare flash of humor in the letter, at odds with Jin Yu's angry black handwriting. She always pressed the pen down so hard that the ink soaked through the page, and the nib of the pen made occasional small holes. Even when she was writing words of affection, her calligraphy style always boiled with indignation, her words like black ants on the march.

"I enclose a copy of our wedding photograph. Please don't write me to say my bridegroom is handsome. The only important things are a noble mind and a brave heart."

I looked at the studio photo of Jin Yu and her new husband. The bride and groom stood side by side, dressed in ordinary dark blue street clothes, posed a little stiffly. Well, I certainly wasn't going to be writing Jin Yu that her groom was handsome. I looked more closely. The two of them held a book in front of them, clasping it between their four hands like the four corners of the earth. Had they become Christians? I looked more closely still, and saw that it was a copy of Marx.

A bird chirped, and I looked out the window. On top of the wall below me, I saw Patience's round face and hands. She was clinging to the wall, her feet planted against its side. I stood up to lean out the window.

"The train left," she called up softly.

I smiled.

"Orchid and I have sworn that we are going to live for love too."

I leaned out further.

"Go home now, Patience," I whispered out to her. She grinned at me, then dropped to the ground. Beyond the wall, I saw her running down the street, turning one last time to wave merrily to me before she disappeared around the corner.

I sat down to read the last words of Jin Yu's letter.

"I hope you realize that you are a revolutionary too. Every blow, no matter how small, brings us closer to the new world."

.   .   .

I kept Jin Yu's photograph—the only one I ever had of her—for many years, through the days when the possession of it could have meant my death. Finally I had to leave it behind me, like everything else. But when I was much older, I saw her picture again. Someone else must have had a copy of the photograph, because her face was put on a postage stamp by the new people's republic, the first in a series entitled "Women Heroes of Labor." I saw it on a letter that had been smuggled out of China in the sole of a one-legged man's shoe.

"Why are you laughing?" Wang Mang spoke from the bed, his voice blurred with sleep. But on this day, I was invincible, and I looked back at him fearlessly from where I stood in the window.

"Husband," I said, leaning on the sill. "Sometimes I look up at the dizzying clouds, and I feel my soul on the currents of air far above. Do you ever feel that way?"

Wang Mang reached for his long slender opium pipe, propped against the wall beside him.

"Wife," he chuckled. "I feel like that much of the time."

18

Graceful Virtue and her husband Mo Chi had their first child within a year after they married, a daughter they called Suan-Suan. In spite of the fact that the child was only a girl, Mo Chi was a very doting father, who liked nothing better than to feed the child and play with her and put her to sleep in her bed at night. Privately, I did not think Suan-Suan was very pretty, but Mo Chi thought her the most beautiful child in the world. He was different with his daughter than with anyone else, unreserved, as if she and she alone could be trusted with his innermost thoughts.

"He is being held prisoner by our daughter," Graceful Virtue said in vexation one day, looking out the window to where Mo Chi was sitting in the garden comforting Suan-Suan, who was crying over not being allowed to join us at the table.

"You're lucky he takes care of her when she's upset, so you don't have to," I said, sitting back in my chair and sipping tea.

"Well, the way he encourages all her little problems. Every time she says she doesn't feel well, Mo Chi acts as if she has a terrible disease and we have to call all sorts of doctors. He will turn her into a complaining kind of person who always thinks there is something wrong with her health."

"It's nothing." I yawned, bored. Graceful Virtue always talked about the most mundane matters, about her husband and child, about her house, about her clothes or her furniture. About herself all the time, really. She was never offensive—in fact, many people found her far more charming than I, since she was more placating and always turned away from any argument or confrontation—but I occasionally felt impatient with her. I wondered if she was keeping a part of herself hidden, but in Graceful Virtue, I suspected, the hidden part didn't actually exist.

I was fond of Suan-Suan and bought her presents, which always made Graceful Virtue happy, since she liked Suan-Suan to have nice clothes and toys. But I didn't have much to do with my little niece until a young soldier knocked on my door in the middle of a summer night in 1920. I was actually awake, as usual unable to sleep, with the covers thrown off because of the heat, listening to the crickets outside. When I heard the staccato banging of a fist on the wooden gate, I sat up in alarm. Wang Mang merely groaned. I heard Yong Li answer the door, and then she came to fetch me, and followed me anxiously down the stairs. The soldier gave me a nervous bow when I appeared, and without any preamble said, "Please, Mrs. Pan. Your brother-in-law, Captain Sung, has sent me to fetch you. I'm afraid something terrible has happened."

"What is it?" I asked. "Is my sister ill?"

"I think," the young man said discreetly, "that it may be the little girl."

I rushed upstairs to change my clothes. I sat in the horse-drawn carriage as it hurried through the darkened streets, nervously fingering my handbag. I had thought that Mo Chi was away from Changsha, but apparently he had returned. When we arrived at Graceful Virtue's house, I did not wait for the soldier to step down from behind the carriage and help me out, but climbed out myself and ran to the gate.

"Open up, open the door!" I heard the soldier shout from behind me, and the gate swung ajar. Inside, all the lamps were lighted, and the hall was filled with people—maidservants; Mo Chi's soldiers, who lived in the barracks nearby, hastily half-dressed in pieces of their uniforms; and a physician's assistant, standing outside a closed door with his back against it. When he saw me approach, he admitted me into the room beyond.

The room was Suan-Suan's bedroom, and my three-year-old niece lay on her bed, her eyes closed and her fingers clutching the sheets. A half-dozen lamps burned all around. There was a doctor leaning over her, partially obscuring her from my vision. Graceful Virtue was crying softly by the bedside. Mo Chi was there as well, but he stood with his back to me and I could not see his face.

"What is it?" I exclaimed, stepping forward. "What has happened?"

Graceful Virtue turned and saw me then, and threw herself into my arms, crying incoherently. I stared over her shoulder at the doctor, who turned to look at me and shook his head. I could see from his face, and from the flush that was rapidly fading from Suan-Suan's face, retreating like a tide, that Suan-Suan was dead.

"I should have been called sooner," the doctor said gravely. "I should have been called yesterday."

"I didn't return home until this evening," Mo Chi said, his back still to me. His voice sounded bizarre, as if he were being strangled.

Graceful Virtue raised her face from my shoulder, streaked with tears. "Mo Chi, I didn't think it was anything, I didn't! Please, don't blame me, I didn't think it was anything except a hot flush, what children always get when they run around! I didn't even think about it! Please understand!" Her face was tightening, as if she were getting ready to scream, and I was afraid she would become hysterical.

"Graceful Virtue," I said sternly, turning her face to look at me. "When did you find out Suan-Suan was sick?"

"She had a fever yesterday at noon," Graceful Virtue groaned. "She was running around, and I thought she was just hot from running around."

I held her tightly.

"I didn't really think about it," wept my poor sister, racked with remorse. "I didn't understand it was serious."

The doctor simply shook his head again and left the room.

Mo Chi stood very still for what seemed to me to be an eternity, stood without speaking, his face turned away. I tried to soothe my sister, murmuring to her that it was not her fault and that she had done nothing wrong.

"Mo Chi," I said, in a very low voice. "Please. You can't blame her. Try to be understanding."

Mo Chi turned around. His angular, agreeable face was absolutely white with agony. But he drew his wife into his arms and stroked her hair. "Hush," he said. "I do understand. I don't blame you. You just didn't realize it was serious."

Watching them, I was grateful that my sister had married a man who was always so kind to her and protective of her feelings. But as I stood listening to his voice soothing her gently, I had the odd sensation that this scene was not new to them, that they repeated it in some form or another almost every day, with Graceful Virtue always unable to recognize things and Mo Chi always understanding. It is a crack between them that he tries to bridge, I thought, but cracks follow the universal law of cracks and only widen. I shook the thought out of my head and sat outside in the hall and wept for poor Suan-Suan.

Graceful Virtue and Mo Chi had another son and daughter, but those children were not born for many years after the death of Suan-Suan, almost as if the parents were afraid to have another. We buried Suan-Suan, at my mother's suggestion, in the same grave as my father.

"When I die," my mother said, "then our little girl can lie between her grandparents, and we can look after her for eternity."

Mo Chi took my mother's hand in gratitude and gripped it very hard. Her face became more tender, and she touched Mo Chi's face briefly with her fingers, in a gesture that, strangely, made me think of one of my father's concubines, on the day they left long ago. There's something about a gesture of farewell that always looks familiar.

Everyone in the family, including Mo Chi, tried to comfort Graceful Virtue, everyone assuring each other that she was not to blame. Except Li Shi, who was furious with our sister, but told only me of his anger.

"She never knows what to do. She never sees what's happening outside her own skin. The whole world exists only for her, to pet her and reassure her."

"Li Shi, she didn't do it deliberately," I said.

"I don't think she did," he said, twisting his mouth a little to one side in an expression that hovered very close to being sheer contempt. "But she may as well have, because the outcome is the same."

As best as I can remember, I went to Mao's wedding feast the year after Suan-Suan died, in 1921. Mao invited Graceful Virtue as well, but she was still mourning for Suan-Suan and could not bear anyone else's happiness. I remember, too, that from the street, standing outside the walls of Teacher Yang's house, the only sign of the celebration within was the sound of human voices rising above the crash of the storm. Only a faint reflection of the lights could be seen in the night sky, reflecting a hard glitter from the black rain that poured from the heavens. But once inside the gate, the blaze of lanterns from the windows was a fiery glare, a molten river sliding down the wet and winding garden path.

The house itself was so full of guests that many people had no place to stand inside, and gathered under the slanting roof of the veranda, crowding close to the walls of the house itself to avoid the long and continuous drippings of water that laced the eaves. From inside, plates of food and cups of wine were handed out to them; chopsticks, oranges, pecans and cigarettes were passed to the clutching hands reaching through the windows into the main room.

In the house, the guests jostled for food and space—China in miniature, I thought—and pushed past one another to greet friends. We all shouted above the roar of the rain, and shook hands above people's heads. We brandished our chopsticks in the air as we talked, and got grease stains on our best gowns, and wiped our mouths on the backs of our hands when we ran out of napkins. Steam heat rose from everyone's damp clothes and ran down our faces as perspiration. The noise was deafening.

At the center of the main room, Teacher Yang sat on a great carved chair, inlaid with abalone shells. On either side of him stood his daughter, Kai Hui, and her bridegroom, Mao Zedong. They were already living together. Kai Hui wore a flowered cotton dress, and Mao stood up in an unornamented dark blue gown. The three posed for wedding photographs, holding their solemn expressions for minutes at a time while the photographer burrowed under his black cloth. Then there was a blinding flash, and a gust of flash powder puffed out over the room like a sandstorm. The three portrait subjects rubbed their eyes, Mao laughing in delight.

The photographer straightened and frowned at Mao.

"Don't smile please, sir," he said, annoyed. "You have to look serious for a wedding photograph. Now, again."

Teacher Yang held up his hand. "Stop," he said. "Take pictures of the bride and groom. I'm finished."

"Let me see the camera," cried Mao. "I want to see this machine."

Kai Hui said nothing at all.

I looked around the room. Those who had gone to France had not yet come home, yet I kept imagining their presence. I saw a young man rubbing the beginnings of a beard on his chin with his hand as if he were an ancient sage, and for a moment I thought he was his elder brother. I saw young women who knew Jin Yu. They were splitting a pomegranate, but when I looked around the circle, Jin Yu's white hands were not among those held out for pieces of the fruit. Around me, the crowding bodies of the other guests moved and thrusted, without an inch of air to spare. But I saw only empty places, blank spots where a face or a gesture should have been. In all that vast, mobbed room, I felt as if I were by myself.

"We can hardly wait until we get there!" shouted Patience into my ear. I dragged my eyes back to look at her, pressed against me. She and the four girls now talking and giggling around us would leave for university at the end of the summer. They had all been very excited at having been invited to the wedding, a mark of their new status as university students.

"I notice that all five of you college girls are always in each other's company now," I observed as tartly as I could, to cover my feeling of being disconcerted. "You all manage to look both self-important and falsely nonchalant at the same time. In fact, you are doing it now. Quite an achievement."

"Oh, Teacher Liang, don't criticize us!" cried the young ladies. "We can't act like schoolgirls anymore! We graduate tomorrow. We have to be like intellectuals."

"Don't be like intellectuals, please. Be intellectuals in fact, but conduct yourselves humbly, and then you will make me proud," I said.

They smiled at me, their round young faces turned up toward me, devoid of doubt or fear or hunger. In my pocket, I could feel the outlines of the little tin pencil box Patience had given me on the last day of class. What a riot of feelings I am having tonight, I thought, quelling my emotions forcibly by swallowing hard. It's not even my wedding. I peeled an orange to focus my concentration and passed the segments to the girls, who ate eagerly from my fingers as if they were still small children.

At the other end of the room, I saw that Teacher Yang was now sitting, and being served a small covered lacquer bowl. Kai Hui sat down next to Mao on a small settee, but in a second, Mao jumped up again and was moving about the room, his broad shoulders shoving everyone aside, his big hands clasping the outstretched hands of the guests leaning in through the windows, or pounding the backs of the men who gathered around him. Kai Hui remained sitting. Her face bore its customary lack of expression, yet there was an intensity to her gaze I had not seen before, and she watched her new husband closely as he circulated the room. Her head turned in minute increments, like an insect's antenna, at the sound of his boisterous voice.

People behind me were talking.

"Well, the bridegroom certainly seems well-pleased."

"Where's his family?"

"Not here. You know he repudiated the arranged marriage. Actually, I heard that his parents indulged him about that, but they had to stay away out of respect for the other girl's family."

The crowd separated to let the photographer leave, carrying his camera above his head, the tripod legs waving dangerously. His assistant followed with the carved chair, held upside down with its legs in the air and bobbing up and down like an enormous beetle.

"Zedong is back before everyone else."

"He didn't go nearly as far." There was some light laughter.

"What in heaven's name did he do in Beijing?"

"Well, he was a laundryman in Shanghai for a while, I'm told."

"Not really?"

"My brother-in-law's brother told me." This was said with an air of finality, and the others all murmured, *"Aah."*

"In Beijing, he started a number of literary magazines, then had to abandon them for lack of funds."

"Lack of readers, you mean."

"Same thing. Now, here he is again."

"You've just described a failure. So how is it that he's appointed the new principal of the elementary school?" An excellent question, I thought, exactly what I myself wanted to know. I could not imagine what a laundryman and failed magazine editor had done to change his fortune so well.

"Yes," broke in a third voice, heretofore silent. "It's very mysterious."

"Good friends," replied the knowledgeable one. I saw the speaker nod in the direction across the room. Our eyes all followed there and rested on a group of clean-shaven, straight-backed young men, smoking cigarettes and speaking together. They wore Western trousers and pointy-toed, shiny leather wing-tip shoes under their austere silk gowns, and carelessly put their hands in their pockets. An economy of movement, expressing itself as physical elegance. They all seemed indescribably modern and new, as if they were chrome engines. Next to them, I thought, Mao would look like a great big grinning peasant.

"Guomindang Party officials," said the knowing voice again. "There is nothing mysterious about their friendship these days."

Mao emerged from the edges of our private view, stopping amid the billowing clouds of cigarette smoke to speak to the men we were examining so closely. I peered curiously at him, for he seemed a changed man. He was a little older, the boyishness that once softened his face now gone, his body broader and thicker. His wide grin was the same, and his crooked teeth, and his gratingly thick Hunanese accent. But he also had a new quality, a kind of readiness of purpose I had not seen in him before. His titanic energies no longer blew in every direction—something that had made him rather endearing in the past. I sensed nothing about him of force being dissipated now, but only of force being gathered. I had thought he would look coarse and fat next to the elegant Guomindang officials, but instead he looked like a fortress looming over a slender grove of birches, and he bristled with strength the way a fortress bristles with cannon. Mao now gave the impression of being a much larger man than he once had been—indeed, at first I thought that he had gained weight—and everyone kept looking at him.

When I looked away again, my eyes met those of Teacher Yang's, over the top of his lacquered bowl. The expression in them was a strange one.

I crossed the room with difficulty—it took me almost twenty minutes to get twenty feet. I leaned over Teacher Yang, who sat eating warm rice wine with a spoon.

"Teacher," I said softly.

"Hmm," he replied, wiping his mouth. Then he stood to greet me.

"I am so happy you could come today, Mrs. Pan," he said with grave courtesy. "Yours is one of the faces I most wanted to see."

I bowed my head to him. "Congratulations, sir, on giving away your daughter. Many, many grandsons in the future."

Teacher Yang snorted. "Have I not taught you better than that? Don't talk to me about many grandsons, it's feudal talk. You sound like those dowagers over there." He gestured with his head in the direction of several old ladies, whispering, wide-eyed, into each other's ears. "Their voices sound like mice in the eaves."

He sat down again. "Sit, sit," he said. I looked around and could see no chairs. I squatted on the floor at his feet.

"By the way," I said carelessly, "who are those men with your son-in-law?"

Teacher Yang glanced over briefly.

"Men of the Guomindang Party," he answered dryly, stirring his rice wine with his spoon. "You've heard of them. They are some of the new appointed officials here. Mao came down from Beijing in their luggage. As shiny as rifles, aren't they?"

"What a curious way to describe men."

"The Guomindang are the successors to our brother Sun Yat Sen's revolutionary alliance. Their party is still small, with only a few offices held, but it will become very powerful. They are all soldiers, that is why."

"Surely there are men besides soldiers who become powerful?" I asked.

"Mrs. Pan, the first two decades of this century thus far prove you quite incorrect. One day, perhaps, the ones who rule the nation will not need an army to maintain themselves. But I will not live to see it, and nei-ther will you."

"Sir," I said, putting my hand on his arm.

"Now, don't be upset," he said instantly, smiling at my troubled face and patting my hand. "I am losing my daughter today, so I am sharp-tongued."

"Take comfort, sir. She loves him very much. I can tell."

We looked uncomfortably at Kai Hui, sitting in monumental silence in the middle of a knot of women and girls, all of whom were gossiping and taking turns fixing plates of food for the bride, which they ended up eating themselves. Surrounded by this comfortable feminine bustle, Kai Hui sat and watched Mao—only watched Mao—strained to see Mao—through all the crowd of guests.

"She loves him indeed," Teacher Yang said grimly.

I took away his empty bowl of rice wine and replaced it with a filled one. "Brilliant but strange, you once said." I smiled.

"Well, he's still brilliant. He has learned statecraft." Teacher Yang stirred the new bowl as he said this, and breathed in its sugary fragrance.

"He's too blunt," I said.

"Wrong," Teacher Yang replied firmly, stopping a moment to sip some rice wine. "How delicious this tastes. It shows I'm in my dotage now, when a bowl of rice wine makes me feel so good and the histories of Ssu-Ma Chien have no effect on my mood whatsoever. Mao only seems blunt. He always knows how to seem—it's quite a strange gift. He is a Marxist, as we all know, but he has persuaded the other Reds to ally with the Guomin-dang, who hate Communists. They will join forces to wipe out warlords and foreigners and unify the country."

"But that's good! Those are the results you've always wanted too."

"Yes, but what then?" Teacher Yang snorted. "What then? Someday, we will find that a marriage of convenience will breed nothing but a good civil war."

He paused with the bowl at his lips to look at me. "How is your hus-band?" he asked.

My eyes sought the floor. "He's very ill," I murmured.

"I know. I've heard."

"I shouldn't even be here tonight. I should be at home, nursing him." Teacher Yang was silent. Still he looked at me, and I felt his gaze like a nee-dle. "But I couldn't be so rude as to not come to the wedding. The old Pans were angry for my leaving—the old lady said I didn't care if they all died—but I told them that it would be a shame on the house if I failed to go to my teacher's daughter's wedding. I told them that Wang Mang would be well until my return."

"You have exhausted yourself nursing him, my child," Teacher Yang said gently. I looked away, out among the crowd. "Everyone knows of it. Everyone has heard of your devotion. You sleep only an hour at a time, on a straw pallet at the foot of Pan Wang Mang's bed. You cannot eat a midday meal, because you run home from school to comfort him. You hold him up when he is on the chamber pot. You feed him like a child, chewing the food in your own mouth first to make it soft."

I stared dully ahead.

"Yet I know you have no love for him," he said. Across the room, Kai Hui looked at me and looked away. "Surely this goes beyond appearances?"

"I want him to die." I did not turn my head toward him, but continued to watch the crowd. "I want to lay down this vicious burden that I have carried for thirteen years. And it is because I want him to die that I work so hard to keep him alive. I cannot fail to do a single thing for him, because I will always wonder if the failure was deliberate. Any failure on my part would be like murder."

"The word 'failure' is much on your lips when you discuss yourself tonight."

"Am I too hard on myself?" I smiled a bit.

"Oh, no." Teacher Yang leaned back and began eating again. "Be as hard on yourself as you can be. All the best people do it."

As I was leaving, I embraced Kai Hui. She put her arms around me and hugged me with surprising strength, but I sensed that her very flesh shrank from me.

Mao clasped my hands, engulfing them in his own broad palms, and shook my arms up and down with great energy.

"Congratulations, and many fine children," I said.

"Thank you," he boomed at me. "I was very pleased to see you, Little Sister Liang, after so many months. I looked forward to your presence here tonight, when we are so happy. Here, let me walk you to the gate."

He walked out with me into the thunderous storm. I held an umbrella over my head, barely able to keep it upright in the pounding rain, but he walked bareheaded next to me down the path, holding my arm and helping me over the mud patches. Out of the corner of my eye, I saw Kai Hui's white face, watching from the door.

"It's a pity that we don't all see each other regularly, like we used to at the old man's study group," Mao shouted over the noise of the storm.

"Because everyone went to France," I yelled in his ear.

He guffawed. "Well, I plan a new study group. We will study only Marxism-Leninism. Will you join?"

I hesitated.

"Think about it," he urged. "Think seriously. The more women comrades, the better."

"I'll consider it!"

"What?"

"I said I'll consider it!"

Mao let me out of the gate with several other guests, one of whom offered me a ride in his rickshaw. But when I saw the rickshaw puller, standing in the rain and raging darkness of the storm as patiently as a horse, but without even a horse's blanket to cover him, I shook my head.

Mao, bidding farewell to the others and ignoring their pleas that he go back inside, followed the direction of my eyes and so, also, of my thoughts. He nodded at me gravely and approvingly.

"My good comrade," he said, and touched my shoulder in a manner so fine and direct that my heart felt an instant kinship to him. I understood then why even those who cared little for his ideas were so moved by him. Then his boisterous manner returned and he clapped me on the shoulder. "At least for now, eh?" He grinned.

I ran all the way home in the night.

When I arrived at the house, it was already very late, and only one light burned in a single window on the second floor. I stepped quietly into the hall and left my soaking shoes and wraps on the floor there. As I crept upstairs, I heard Wang Mang's low cough from the bedroom where the candle burned.

I opened the bedroom door very quietly. Wang Mang lay on the bed, his face worn and waxy from illness. Yong Li, who had been sitting in a chair in a dark corner, stood up, rubbing her eyes sleepily.

"He hasn't been too bad tonight," she whispered.

"Go to bed, Yong Li," I told her. "You look very tired."

She shook her head. "No, Elder Sister. You have such a big ceremony tomorrow; you need to rest. I'll stay up with him, and you go to sleep in my room. Please. Tomorrow I'll make you some lunch to bring for the ceremony."

I went to bed in my bare skin in the maid's little bedroom down the hall, leaving my wet clothes on a broken chair in the hallway. I shivered under her thin blankets. I should have bought her another blanket long ago, I thought. I wished she had said something to me about it.

19

The next morning, when I returned to my own room to find clothes for the day, Yong Li had left, although Wang Mang remained sleeping. I put on my best black gown and a light black spring coat with a little bit of squirrel fur at the collar that had once been Jin Yu's and which her parents had sent me at her written directions. I wore my everyday shoes for the walk to school, carrying my good shoes in a cloth sack.

In the kitchen, Yong Li was busy at the stove. She put a cup of tea and some rolls on the table for me.

"Here is your lunch box, full of noodles," she said, putting it down before me.

I nodded, my mouth filled with tea and bread. When I looked up over the rim of my cup, I found Yong Li looking at me.

"What is it?" I asked. "Do I have a loose thread?" I looked at my coat.

"You go every year to graduation ceremonies," Yong Li murmured. "What are they like?" She seemed embarrassed by her question, because she brushed the crumbs off the table into her hand and threw them in the stove.

The question surprised me very much. It had never occurred to me to wonder what Yong Li thought about all day, caged in this old house with the Pans.

"You mean the graduation? Well, the girls wear black gowns and get their diplomas, which means they have finished in this school. Then the valedictorian of the class—who is the best talker—gives a speech. And this year we have five young ladies going on to university, the most ever. Including Miss Patience, whom you have met." Yong Li nodded eagerly. "Then we serve cakes and tea. The teachers aren't allowed to have any. We all have to go back to the faculty room afterward and eat noodles, which is why I rely on your lunch."

Yong Li laughed at this. She brushed my coat with an old hairbrush dipped in boiling water, fussed at my hair a little, and put the lunch box in my hand.

As I started down the path to the gate, I felt as if I were being watched. I looked back and saw Yong Li at the window, her face pressed against the glass. I hesitated a moment on the path; then I turned and walked back to her. She opened the casement quickly and leaned out with a concerned expression.

"Yong Li, the master and the old ones won't be up for hours," I said. "Would you like to come to the graduation with me?"

Yong Li's face filled up like a cup with happiness. She shut the window and pulled off her apron; in a moment, she was outside with me, carefully closing the door. She gestured toward the inside of the house.

"Will they be all right?" she asked.

"Of course. You'll be back by lunchtime. Just tell them that I needed you to help serve tea."

Yong Li nodded, her face glowing at the prospect of a morning away from the Pan house. I was very sorry I had not taken her to school before.

At the graduation, I sat with the other teachers on the dais that had been set up in the courtyard of the school. The parents sat before us, a motley bunch, ranging from the noble-blooded Changs, who counted several dukes in their ancestry, to Fat Sung and his wife, who ran a prosperous shellfish stall in the market and paid their daughter's tuition with multiple bags of small coins every semester. Fat Sung, with his earring and his huge, meathook hands covered with tattoos, looked nothing like the slender and lordly Chang, yet their daughters were equal in learning, equal in all things really, except that Fat Sung's daughter was fat too.

The girls filed past us and took their diplomas, rolled up like small bolts of silk, from the hand of Principal Chen. Patience gave me a surreptitious grin as she passed, and I had to frown as hard as I could at her.

Yong Li helped serve tea; I could see her smiling face as she moved about the courtyard. Afterwards, I sent her home to see to the Pans, and I sat down in the faculty sitting room, where the other teachers were gathered, already slurping hungrily from their tin lunch boxes. Wheat-flour noodles and leftover rice and salt fish brought from home, and bruised apples picked up cheaply at the fruit stands. But we were all in a good humor and laughed loudly as we ate. I went home slowly in the afternoon, lingering in the warmth of the day and the clarity of the air, thinking about the girls who were leaving, perhaps forever.

But when I got to the Pan house, I found the gate wide open and the doctor's rickshaw standing outside. Alarmed, I quickened my steps. The front door flew open and Yong Li gestured wildly to me. I saw a scrape on her cheekbone.

"Elder Sister, thank heaven you are here," she cried. "Come quickly. The master was taken very badly this morning, while you and I were away. The old Pans didn't know what to do and there was no one to go for the doctor. When I got home the master was coughing blood into a basin, and the old ones wringing their hands and cursing heaven. I ran to the doctor right away. He's upstairs now, but I think it's too late." Yong Li started to cry. "I'm sorry, I'm sorry," she wept. "I've neglected my duty!"

"Stop it!" I snapped, then added, more gently, "It's not your fault. It is mine." I threw off my coat and ran upstairs, Yong Li at my heels. I burst into the bedroom where Wang Mang lay, the doctor leaning over him and holding his shoulders while he coughed. Wang Mang looked up from the basin Madame Pan held and, surprisingly, gave me a crooked, bloodstained grin.

"Was it a nice ceremony?" he asked, then he laughed until he began coughing again, convulsively.

I took the basin from Madame Pan's hands, ignoring her glare, and gave it to Yong Li. I sat down on the bed beside Wang Mang and held his thin shoulders. Madame Pan did not leave the room, but stood nearby like an angry ghost, her face on fire with her fury.

Wang Mang finally turned over and fell asleep when it was near nightfall. Madame Pan had not moved the entire time, as if she were afraid I would escape from her. I put my finger to my lips for her silence.

"If you have something to say, then come into the hall," I said coldly. "He is finally sleeping."

We shut the door behind us, closing out the doctor's amused and curious stare.

In the hall, we spoke in hoarse and furious whispers.

"You left for your damned school and took that useless serving girl. You left us alone here to die. Old Pan was so frightened he's in bed now. You want us all to die. It's a plot to murder us. I curse you. With all my breath I curse you." Madame Pan was hissing like a snake, and drops of her spittle stung my face like a viper's venom.

"If I had known he would get worse today, I would have stayed home," I snarled back. "There was no reason to hit the maid, you terrible old woman—I ordered her to come with me. How was anyone to know this would happen? You are useless—why didn't you take your delicate self outside onto the street and find a neighbor to go for the doctor?"

Madame Pan struck me, surprisingly hard. My nose began to bleed. Without wiping the blood away, I pushed the old woman away from me. She struck out again at my arms.

"Stop it!" I hissed. "I'm going back inside. Go eat your heart out somewhere else."

"I curse you!" she whispered. "I curse every day of your existence."

I went into the bedroom and shut the door in her face. The physician was taking vials and bottles out of his leather bag at a table under the window, his back to me. I glanced at the bed and saw that Wang Mang's eyes were open now, alive with speculation. He could hardly move the muscles on his face, but he lifted his eyebrows sardonically. Looking at the glint in his eye, I realized he had heard everything his mother and I had said in the hall, and inside his skin he was laughing very hard indeed.

I stayed awake by my husband's bedside for three weeks, smoothing his brow with a wet cloth, changing his shirt for fresh clothes, helping him to the chamber pot. When he clawed at my hands in his delirium, I commanded myself not to pull away. I slept in a hard chair.

The doctor was a former minor physician in the imperial household and highly regarded in Changsha as a result. He was, of course, expensive, yet I spared nothing in the way of money to pay him. The physician bled Wang Mang and took his temperature and his pulse. As he bustled about the bedroom, mixing powders and ordering Yong Li about, he chatted about his days in the imperial palace.

"It's a good thing your husband isn't a royal princess, madame."

"Oh, yes?" I said politely.

"When the imperial physicians were called to attend the princesses, we were not allowed to set eyes on them. I attended the Emperor's younger sister. She sat behind a screen. Her maids laid a thin silk thread across her wrist, and I felt her pulse through the vibrations of the thread."

But in spite of the doctor's efforts, Wang Mang sank closer and closer to death, and finally hovered on its very tooth's edge.

"There isn't much I can do," the physician said. "Too much opium. His body is a rotten reed. The very next pipe will be his end."

"What if he asks for his pipe?" I asked, looking over my shoulder at the sick man in the bed, sweating in spite of the thinness of his silk covers.

The physician shrugged. "It doesn't matter," he said. "Not anymore. It is the difference between today and tomorrow."

In the early hours of the morning, when the cold night air began to soften with daylight, Pan Wang Mang awoke. He saw his wife sitting by the bed, staring intently at him. He saw that she had his opium pipe in her hand, already prepared. There was no one else in the room. He moved his fingers weakly.

"My pipe," he croaked. He looked a hundred years old, his skin seamed and yellowed from sickness and opium, his thin beard scraggly and unkempt. Barbarian dust had turned his dark hair white. His fingers picked nervelessly at the covers.

Hesitating just a little, Pan Wang Mang's wife leaned over him and inserted the pipe gently into his mouth. She held the pipe for him as he smoked, and with her other hand she smoothed his forehead, brushing his hair back softly and massaging his scalp. He grimaced in concentration, and put his efforts into puffing on the pipe. After a few moments, he lifted his dreamy eyes to hers and let his gaze walk over her features. He frowned slightly, as if he were surprised, or as if he had just remembered something he had forgotten long ago.

He leaned back onto the pillow, his face blurred in the sweet smoke of the pipe. He drifted away like an unmoored boat, into the fog of the Perfume River.

20

I borrowed money from my mother, and from Jin Yu's mother and father, to pay for the funeral. I hired twenty professional mourners and dressed the Pans in new suits of white clothes. I had a daguerreotype made of Wang Mang's dead visage and had it carried at the head of the procession. I marched behind his picture, to the elaborate stone tomb of his ancestors squatting on the hills outside the city, where we laid him to rest under the earth. I was thirty-five years old.

I was surprised at how sad and lonely I felt at the death of my husband, for I had disliked and feared him while he was alive. The heart is perverse, I thought, wiping away the tears as they lowered his wrapped and bundled corpse into the tomb, because now I wish him back again. Perhaps he was better than no one at all.

A few days later, I made a bonfire of Wang Mang's clothes. Yong Li carried the garments and cloth shoes from the house to where I stood in the front garden. I looked at the expensive silks ruined with wear, with grease, with holes from the dropped burning ashes of his pipe. I burned every last scrap, every shirt, every gown, even his shoes and the bed quilt that had covered him when he died. When all the clothes were on the fire, I stirred them with a stick, poking sleeves and laces into the flames. Thick billows of white smoke curled from the pile of cloth, perfumed with the scraps of opium left in the seams, and I rubbed my eyes. When I looked up, I saw Madame Pan, standing in the doorway, on the other side of the smoke. We stared at each other a moment. Smoke obscured her tiny figure. Then she was gone.

That night, the three of us sat at dinner in a silence so complete I could hear the cicadas outside and the rustle of the trees. The Pans clicked their chopsticks against their teeth. I kept my face in my rice bowl. I felt like death. Then Madame Pan stood up and left the room. She came back with a dish of mushrooms, which she placed on the table.

"Yong Li picked these today," she said gruffly. "I thought we should have some nourishment, after these last few days."

I was pleased at her gesture. "You are right," I said. "Please, let me serve you." The Pans watched me as I served them mushrooms from the side of the dish closest to them, as good manners dictated. I sat down again and was about to reach for some mushrooms myself, when Madame Pan stopped me.

"Let me serve you," she said, picking some mushrooms from the side of the dish closest to me. I looked up in surprise at this attention. She seemed to think that her courtesy needed explanation, for then she said, in a choking voice, "The picture of my son you made for the funeral was beautiful." She wept into her napkin.

Old Pan put down his chopsticks and patted her arm. "Stop now," he mumbled. "Just eat. Let the girl eat."

"Eat, eat the mushrooms," Madame Pan gasped, waving her hand toward the dish. "Leave me alone, and I will be all right."

"Of course, Mama, I will," I said. I was all she had left in the world besides Old Pan. "My, what delicious mushrooms they look."

"Yong Li is a good cook," mumbled Old Pan, putting his head down to eat again.

The mushrooms did taste good, and I had eaten very little since Wang Mang had died. But as I ate, I began to feel a slight numbness about the lips. I smacked them together to get rid of the feeling, but the numbness persisted and grew. The room began to swim, and the lamp swung its light about in great arcing circles. I put my hand to my head. The Pans looked up with surprise in their faces.

"What is it?" asked Madame Pan. "You look ill."

I dared not open my saliva-flooded mouth, for fear of vomiting. I struggled to my feet, and the room spun like a Buddhist's prayer wheel. I blinked, trying to focus my vision. The Pans stared at me, openmouthed.

"Yong Li," I croaked, clinging to the edge of the table. "Yong Li!"

I felt Yong Li's hands grabbing my arms and dragging me away from the table. I heard her murmuring faintly. She took me to the back garden. I bent over and vomited in the grass, with such heaving violence that my ribs ached. I leaned, exhausted, against the western wall of the house, sweat running down my face. The night sky flashed and jumped above my head.

Yong Li lit a candle and looked at the ground where I had left the remains of my dinner. She moved the candle back and forth, searching.

"What did you eat?" she asked. "It looks like the mushrooms."

I nodded weakly.

"But I picked and cooked them myself," she said, frowning. "Then I left them on the kitchen table to take in to you all, but Madame Pan came and got them instead."

Madame Pan's voice was heard in the hall. "What is it? What's the matter?" The old lady sounded very frightened. Behind her, I heard the shabby shuffling of Old Pan's cloth shoes, and his querulous voice.

Yong Li turned to them. "Go back inside, madame, the night air isn't good for you. Go back in. She's all right. Just an upset stomach. Too much grief and too little food these days. I'll take her up to bed."

I heard the Pans move away behind me. Then Yong Li's voice was in my ear, as she put her arm around me and dragged me up the stairs.

"Leave this house, Elder Sister," she whispered. "Leave it tomorrow, or you will leave it like the master did."

I looked at her in horror and tried to shake my head. Yong Li supported me on a slow walk back inside.

"Do as I say," she whispered. "I will stay up and watch you tonight. But tomorrow you must do as I say."

I did not leave the next day, because I could not arrange to have a man with a wheelbarrow come for my books until the day after, and I was afraid that if I moved out without them, I would not be let back in the house. Instead, I visited my mother and ate a large meal there. I told her what happened.

"Yong Li had a beating this morning from Old Pan, because she told them she picked some bad mushrooms. She doesn't want them to know we suspect." I sat exhausted and still queasy, sipping tea and rubbing my eyes, which were circled with giant blue rings of fatigue. My mother sat beside me, her brows drawn together with concern. "I want to report the matter to the magistrates."

"You can't," my mother said calmly, rubbing my cold hands between hers.

"What do you mean?"

"Do you know for a fact what happened? Bringing a false accusation is a crime. In my youth, it was a capital offense. Yong Li would just get blamed for picking bad mushrooms, since she has already confessed to that."

"Oh no, Mother," I gasped.

"Indeed. This was badly managed. You should have come to me first. In any case, you are leaving their home, and you need not think of it again. When will you need your old room ready?"

I put my cup down.

"Mother, I'm not moving back here," I said hesitantly. "I rented a room at the Society of Silk Fans. It's much closer to school."

The Society of Silk Fans was an association of women who offered lodgings to younger women on the condition that they be unmarried. Some of the older society members had been active in the anti-foot-binding campaign at the turn of the century; the younger ones were suffragists. Jin Yu's friend, the lady teacher who wore the watch on her dress front, was the society's recording secretary. The lodgings were in a large communal house in the new silk-weavers district—the house itself owned by a family of twelve widows spanning three generations, all of them society members. Recently, a woman had left to marry, and the secretary had offered her room to me.

My mother looked at me in silence. I drank quickly from my cup.

"As you wish," she said. "Perhaps it's better. It is always shameful to crawl home after being widowed. This way, we can blame your being a modern woman."

"You . . . you live too far from school," I faltered, squirming under her measured gaze. "It would take me an hour to walk there, every morning and evening."

"Of course," my mother said. She leaned back in her chair and pushed a strand of gray hair out of her eyes.

"Here, let me," I said, and stood up to rearrange her bun. When I put my hands on her hair, she turned her face around and looked up at me kindly.

"I know you have suffered," she said. "There was no alternative, you understand. And the greatest test for you is what you do when there is no alternative."

She turned away again, and I finished pinning her hair.

"Mother," I said.

"Mmm?"

"Am I behaving wrongly by leaving the Pans there alone? Shouldn't I continue to live with them, now that their son is dead? I would have thought that you of all people would tell me to stay."

"Why? You bore no grandsons. You have done enough of your duty. In any case . . ."—she stood up and fixed the last hairpin herself—"there is no point to endangering your life. You must, of course, find a way to support them."

She stood up. "Have you hired the man with the wheelbarrow for your things?"

"Yes, we go tomorrow."

"I'll come too."

"It isn't necessary. Yong Li will help me carry things."

My mother leveled a curious glance at me. "I think I will definitely go."

"We don't want you here, you beggar!" said Old Pan in his croaking crow's voice. "You barren wife!"

I said nothing, but stood in the middle of the floor in the central hall, averting my eyes in anger, but still assuming the humble stance of the daughter-in-law, my hands folded like birds' wings before me.

"I know why she is leaving!" shouted Madame Pan. "She is afraid of us! She is afraid—one little stomachache, and she is afraid! She is making a false accusation, she is libeling our name!"

"I'm not making any accusation," I cried, shocked at the gravity of what my mother-in-law was saying. I opened my mouth to say more, but my mother interrupted me, stepping forward swiftly.

"Your own mouth accuses you, old woman," my mother snapped, more sharply than I had ever heard her. "Be careful of what you say. The viper you take by the tail will turn to bite you. Take heed."

My mother turned her back on the Pans and drew me aside to the door.

"Get the hired man," she murmured. "The maid and I will pack your clothes." She glanced back at the Pans. "You see why I didn't want you to come alone? You needed a witness, just in case the old lady tried to lay the groundwork for an accusation. This was going to be her strategy—to turn their crime into your crime. Old women are tough and cunning because they have lived so long. You young ones are no match for us."

"I'm glad you are leaving," Madame Pan was hissing. "You brought down the entire house. You closed the doors to all our friends, and kept them from visiting us. You made us look poor and ashamed."

My mother left to go upstairs, ignoring Madame Pan's cries of fury. I looked back at my old mother-in-law. Madame Pan was holding Old Pan's arm, as if fusing her own strength into his weak and aged flesh. She stood very straight and looked right at me as hard as she could. Her black eyes had a mineral glitter. Old Pan put his hand to his forehead. And I felt a sudden aching pity for them, for whatever was left of their souls, under the choking layers of self-delusion and pride. I felt as if I had come upon two trees in the forest, buried beneath springing vines, vines that had killed the lives within and held up the empty shells. The changes in the world had ambushed them. I turned my face away in pity, unwilling to witness any longer this slow, smothering death.

My mother and Yong Li brought my books down and stacked them in the wheelbarrow that stood in the muddy street outside. The hired man hopped from one foot to the other to pass the time. Yong Li decided to carry my few dresses over her arm all the way to the House of Silk Fans to prevent wrinkling, and my mother put my shoes and hand mirror into cloth bags. When my goods were all assembled, they looked pitifully meager.

The entire time we were packing, the Pans sat in the main hall, face-to-face, in their large carved wooden chairs, in utter silence. They did not stir even as we passed them, stalking back and forth, carrying my things outside. But they had one last thing to do that day. When everything was in the barrow and my mother and I stood ready to leave, Yong Li came out of the house in tears, still clutching my dresses.

"What is it?" I asked, alarmed.

"The old ones have thrown me out of the house," she sobbed. She began weeping into my clothes. "They said I was your spy and told me to leave."

"But that's good!" I exclaimed. "You are free of the bond, now that they have thrown you away!"

But Yong Li wept even harder. "Elder Sister, I have no place to go. I am an orphan. No matter how bad it is here, I have my bowl of rice. Now there is only the street for me."

My mother glanced at me reproachfully. "How foolish you are," she said to me. "Do you think that being free is always a good thing?"

She turned to Yong Li. "Don't cry, you silly girl. You come to my house, and I will employ you. I already have a cook, and she is bad-tempered . . ."

"Yes, indeed," I said fervently.

". . . so you must obey her in all things," my mother finished, glaring at me.

Yong Li dropped to her knees in the road, kneeling on my dresses and crushing them into the soil, and clasped my mother's hand and wept some more, while my mother and I tried to raise her and comfort her. The wheelbarrow man sighed ostentatiously and stamped his feet, until finally we left. I turned as we all made our way down the narrow street, looking up at the great Pan manor, once my home, and now with its windows shrouded in mourning and its doors barred forever against me. In that whole great empty house, which a century ago sheltered four generations and a hundred servants under its curving tile roofs, there remained only two proud and jealous ghosts, living at the center of its secretive heart.

That night, my first in the new lodgings, I surveyed my situation. The room was tiny and overlooked the back alley, the outhouse was communal, and the only running water was a tap in the courtyard. The distempered walls and bare wood floors trapped and intensified both cold and heat; the walls would sweat in the summer and be icy to the touch in the winter. But the sounds of the other women in the house crowded the room like benign spirits, emerging from behind makeshift curtains of bed quilts, swirling around the iron charcoal braziers set in heaps of sand, mingling with the clang of cook pots and the snapping of wet laundry on the lines stretching from each window. The one water tap in the yard gurgled. I set out my books on the rickety table, thinking happily that Li Shi must have lived this way when he went away to university.

Later, I sat at the window and looked out on the narrow, dirty alley below. I leaned out the window into the cool night air and craned my neck to see the stars. There were a few faint glitters in the velvety distance, and the edge of an enormous yellow moon showing behind the chimney pots. I'm free, I thought. As free as I ever can be. I sat on a chair and put my elbows on the edge. I fell asleep that night on the windowsill, the back of my neck exposed to the slow-burning light of the planets.

I went to the market the next day and bought a large tin cooking pot with a cover and a basketful of eggplants and garlic. That afternoon after classes, I stewed the eggplants in the pot over the tiny fire in the school kitchen, reading by candlelight as I waited for it to finish cooking. I left it on the step outside the gates of the Pan manor on my way home that night and banged loudly on the gates. In the morning, on my way back to school, I stopped by the gates again and collected the pot, now empty.

I left food every day. I left charcoal in the winter, to burn in the stoves. Once a year, I left two new suits of clothes for them on the step, wrapped in red paper to show my good intentions. Other people left food for the ancestors at the graveside, and paper clothes for the spirits to wear. I left real food and real clothes, and my ghosts actually made use of them all. I did these things for many more years than I had expected when I first began, but then pride and anger are a sort of nourishment too, and can keep people alive much longer than love.

METAL

21

The neighborhood where the House of Silk Fans stood was in one of the oldest parts of Changsha, a neighborhood known as the Birdcage. The Birdcage had been for more than one thousand years the quarter of the salt merchants. Now the salt merchants were long gone, their profits folded into a state monopoly. The Birdcage, in the days I lived there, was filled instead with workers from the newly constructed silk and cotton mills, whose stacked chimneys and metal roofs now glowered ill-temperedly beyond the unrepaired gaps in the ancient stone walls of the city. The gray walls and graying wooden beams of the large, aged houses—these days divided and divided again inside to house many workers like rooks in multistory nests—shouldered each other with familiarity, if not friendship, and the sky above was only a thin blue line weaving between the eaves. The streets were so narrow that on rainy days drips fell onto my umbrella from the roofs of the houses on both sides of the way. Blankets hung out to air on the windowsills, and the smell of garlic drifted down the alleys.

The house itself sat on the foundations of a Sung dynasty house, which in turn sat on the foundations of a Tang dynasty house. One of the women who lived there with me had found old queerly shaped coins in the root cellar. The children of the neighborhood would sometimes find shards of pottery and oracle bones, scratched with old words of prophecy. Carelessly, the children would put them in their dirty pockets for a few days at a time, and when they were tired of these little pieces, would throw them away again, into the dustheap, into the public lavatories, into the river or the ponds. This distressed me at first, because I felt that these bones and shards had survived thousands of years, carrying their messages faithfully from the dim and shrouded past into the glaring light of the present day. So I made some of the children give me the pieces that they found and laid them out on my table. But the scratched prophecies were too old and long ago, and I could not read them. I traced the scratches with my fingers, as if their shapes could be stored in my hands. At last I sighed and put them all away in the bottom of my drawer.

At night, the aged wooden building creaked in all its bones, and its old ghosts whispered to us. Every woman who came to live there, escaping some part of her life or her intended life, brought her own new ghosts too. The women all lived in separate rooms inside the house, but we shared the courtyard. Coming home from school, my chief pleasure was to fold up my sleeves and sit outside on the tile step, watching the others wash their clothes under the tap, or boil tea on a little outdoor stove, or gossip in the fading sunshine. The twelve widows who owned the house—ranging in age from eighty-six to twenty-six, the surviving wives of twelve soldiers of the surname Chang, all of whom were too brave or luckless to survive past the age of thirty—lived together in the same wing and emerged together every evening to take the air. They sat as companionably as cats in the sunshine. When I sat in the courtyard, among these affable and undemanding strangers, I felt comforted, and the recurring loneliness that often plagued me would dissipate in the warm air.

Since there were few literate people in the province in those days, schoolteachers were often called upon to read letters and messages for entire villages. One holiday in 1926, when there was no school, I was asked to a farming hamlet a number of miles outside Changsha, to read a letter from someone's brother who had left for America. I rode out on the buckboard of a very rough wagon, driven by the lucky recipient of the letter. The trip took more than an hour, through the wet green fields, through the smells of earth and water and vegetable life that spread into the air. But irritably, I wished this farmer had just brought the letter to me, instead of bringing me to the letter.

When we arrived in the middle of the hamlet—a muddy lane with a few houses straggling into the earth on either side—all the residents who lived there came running out of their houses. They maintained a respectful distance of two feet or so, and no one touched my person, but they stared openly at me. The women rubbed their hands on their grubby aprons; the children wiped their runny noses on their naked wrists. My escort ran into his own hut and came out with the letter pinched tenderly between thumb and forefinger. I took it from him carefully, with both hands, nodding my head soberly to do justice to his honor, although in fact I was wondering why people who lived in the midst of open fields had to build their houses so unsanitarily close together.

"How long ago did it arrive?" I asked before spreading open the folds.

"A week ago." The recipient bowed. "I recognized my brother's name of course, but I can't read anything else. My family can all read our own names."

"Very commendable." I nodded. "Well, the letter is from San Francisco, America."

The crowd was excited immediately. "The gold mountain!" they all cried.

The letter itself was short, explaining that the brother was working as a laundryman in California, after having been a sharecropper and a laborer. The brother explained that another China man, a former scholar now turned cook, had been kind enough to write the letter for him, in return for a free bath in his copper clothes-washing tub. He also apologized for some hasty words said on the morning of his departure, four years ago. But I had to read the letter eleven times to the rapt villagers and explain where America was and where San Francisco was inside America, and I was made to guess how much money he made as a laundryman.

The villagers clustered around me in the road, some of them perched on the roofs of the surrounding huts for a better view of the tiny square of powdery paper I held in my hand. Each time I got to the part of the letter about the apology, everyone sighed and smiled at everyone else. Tears of pride glistened in the eyes of the correspondent's brother. The man's wife and sisters hung on each other and laughed embarrassedly into each other's shoulders. I thought I saw some jealous glares from neighbors who had never received a letter and who did not have a brother getting rich scrubbing clothes on the gold mountain.

After a time, with the skies growing dark and no one making any move to leave, I finally called an end to the letter reading. The man who owned the letter immediately bowed deeply, and his womenfolk bowed deeply. They gave me some oranges, apologizing for their poor quality, and the man helped me back into the wagon.

Sitting in the back on the way home, with my legs dangling from the rear board, watching the silent twilight countryside pass me slowly in reverse and slapping at the mosquitoes, I thought about the man's brother in San Francisco. I thought that maybe it would be years before another letter came. This one had already been six months old—was the brother still a laundryman? Still in San Francisco? Still above ground? I hoped the brother would always write. I had a momentary vision of my white-haired self, years from now, reading the eighth or ninth letter in the sequence to the same villagers, now all bent with age, and to young men who had been born since the brother's departure and knew of him only through his adventures as a laundryman in California. The vision did not displease me.

It was late by the time I hopped out of the wagon at the House of Silk Fans. I stumbled with fatigue up the stairs, setting the oranges down on the steps for the other women to find in the morning and trying to keep the stair boards from creaking too loudly.

On my landing, I paused in alarm at the door to my room. The door was open, very slightly. Through the crack, a light shone, and I heard a faint rustle. I thumped the heel of my hand against the door, and it shot open into the room.

Jin Yu was sitting at my table, all her long shining black hair cropped off close to her head. Her fine dark eyes, their expression as imperial as ever, looked up from a foreign newspaper she had spread out on the table underneath my tiny oil lamp.

"It's about time you got home," she said. "I've been waiting for hours."

Jin Yu had returned from France after several years, with her husband and two children. The new family had moved into one of the wings of the Xiang family manor. I held her hands between mine and looked into her face with such gladness and affection that her stern expression relaxed.

I fanned the embers of my charcoal brazier with a shred of rush matting while she talked, and prepared to make some food for her, since she remarked that she was faint with hunger. I had some steamed bread left over, which I began to toast on a flat pan over the coals. She watched me from her seat on my only chair and spoke to me of Paris, France, which was even further away than San Francisco, America. Her husky voice shaped the foreign city for me brightly and sharply, unspooling the great tree-lined avenues and fine buildings and the cool bite of air from the river that ran between, so far from the damp heat and distant clanging of cooking pots in my street in the Birdcage.

Jin Yu propped her feet up on the table, and I noticed for the first time that she was wearing men's trousers.

"Why on earth . . . ?" I exclaimed. "Are you wearing Hesen's clothes?"

"No, these are mine. I had them tailored in Shanghai when our boat docked there, before we caught the train to Changsha. I started wearing men's clothes in Paris. With my hair this short I can pass for a young man in the street."

"Jin Yu, you amaze me. Why would you want to pass as a man?"

"I can go where I please as a man. No gossip, no robbers. Besides, I am a spy now."

I glanced up at her, but she grinned crookedly and agreeably at me, and I laughed in relief.

"Don't talk so wildly," I reproached her.

"You are right. Spying is supposed to be secret anyway."

When I put the bread in front of her and poured her some tea, I leaned forward, my elbows on the table, and watched her eat. She seemed a little thinner, but even more flamelike than before. She had the same quality Mao had had when he came back from Beijing to marry Kai Hui—she gave the same impression of having gained strength and of having concentrated that strength in a single direction. But where the gathering of power had made Mao broad and thick as a stone wall, it had sharpened Jin Yu into an elegant sword. I thought she looked more beautiful than ever.

"I'll miss your hair," I said, touching the ends gently.

"I don't," she replied. "Of course, I look exactly like my son."

"Tell me about the children," I begged. "I haven't even seen them."

"Well, you will, all in good time." Jin Yu seemed reluctant to discuss them. "I wasn't very pleased, getting pregnant one after the other so quickly. But they're sweet babies. You must come tomorrow to our house, Auntie, just like old times."

I folded my arms on the tabletop. I felt a rushing thrill in Jin Yu's familiar presence; I felt that some part of me, bolder and fairer than the rest, had come home again.

Jin Yu put down the bread she was eating and put her hand on my arm. "By the way, I heard everything from my mother. I'm glad Wang Mang is dead."

"I'm not always sure I am," I said softly. My eyes trembled. "It's strange, after all this time."

"Don't have regrets. Now you are a free woman." She was watching me closely. She put her arm around my shoulders.

"I'm lonely sometimes." I shrugged, wiping my eyes with the back of my hands, to keep the charcoal on my fingers from getting on my face. I wasn't really sure what I was crying about. Freedom was a strange thing.

"I'm back," Jin Yu said. "And I won't leave again."

"My husband is on the Central Committee, and I am not," Jin Yu complained to me several days later, as we sat huddled together in the window seat of her old study in the Xiang house. Cai Hesen was in Changde visiting his sister Cai Chang in prison, where she had recently tried to hang herself, and Jin Yu's children were with their grandparents, playing with the presents I had brought. "The comrades direct all their policies to men. I don't know if there was a single woman at the founding conference in Shanghai. Those idiots. Did Mao Zedong tell you what happened? No, of course not. Someone informed on them to the Shanghai police while they were meeting at the girls' school in the French concession. They had to pretend they were leaving the city on a pleasure excursion, and finished forming the Party on a boat in the middle of the pleasure lake in Hangzhou. They would take turns walking around the deck, admiring the scenic views loudly, all the while muttering under their breaths about the organization of the cells."

I leaned against Jin Yu's shoulder and laughed until my stomach hurt.

"Yes, you may well laugh," snorted Jin Yu. "Go ahead, have a good time. But imagine what I have to put up with. It wasn't like this in Paris. In Paris, the women really were equal. We ran the student newspaper, our voices were loudest at the theory meetings. We heard about the Bolshevik women who were leaders in their movement."

"I thought a number of the Bolshevik women were executed afterward."

"Betrayal of the Party." Jin Yu shrugged. "Disagreements in the Party cause strife and dissension. It can't be allowed, not when all of us have our lives in danger."

I frowned in disapproval. "All you ever talk about now is the Party."

"It's my life."

"But you have children."

"Some women comrades and I have formed our own group—the Group of Seven." She leaned a little closer. "Listen, Jade Virtue, do you want to join the Party?"

"No," I said slowly, after some hesitation. "I don't."

She rolled her eyes derisively. "You will never join any movement," she pronounced. "If you won't be in the vanguard, then you will end up in the masses. Remember that I warned you."

"I don't wish to be in the Party," I said firmly. "But any worthwhile thing that you do, any work or demonstration, I will help you. You can rely upon me."

"I know you can be trusted. I know you'll die rather than give us away. But why are you against Party membership? It's important to be part of the larger group."

This was a very good question. All my friends belonged, or at least sympathized. And I would certainly protect them at the cost of my own life. Yet I held back. I had distinct reservations. I didn't think I feared the consequences of joining—at least, not the consequences from outside the Party, although those could be frightening.

"I think," I said, still speaking slowly, "I think I am uncomfortable with the level of devotion displayed by the membership."

"Because we all passionately believe in it," Jin Yu cried. "We have no skeptics, no doubters. Every one of us would live and die for the Party."

"I think you've put your finger on the problem," I said.

Jin Yu leaned back against the cushion and pulled her sleeves and her skirt in, away from me. She was wearing an old black sweater and skirt that looked a little like a school uniform, very different from the expensive silk dresses she had worn when we were girls.

"It's difficult for you to understand, I know," she said carefully, as if explaining to a child. "But before I was a member of the Party, I was nothing. I had ideas, but I didn't know how to put them into action. I had passion, but I didn't know where to direct it. I never had a true purpose; I felt strangled by my lack of true purpose. You look doubtful—I can see your face—but I ask you, do you have a true purpose?"

"Of course," I responded with assurance. "The comfort of my mother and brother and sister. The honor of my father's memory. The happiness of my friends, which includes you. The good of my country, which I try daily to accomplish in the education of my pupils."

Jin Yu shook her head impatiently. "Your benevolence speaks well of you, Jade Virtue," she said. "But I speak of a true purpose that burns your heart." Her eyes gleamed with a fierce exultant light. "It makes you feel as if you are passionately in love. It makes you feel strong enough to run a thousand leagues through the fields, and defy death. It makes you feel as if you matter in history, that you can make great things happen, that you can perfect the world."

Her passion haunted my imagination, as it always did. But my rational mind—my sense of proportion, the cursed thing—could not agree with her. "A true purpose," I observed a little coolly, "isn't just to make yourself feel important."

Jin Yu looked at me with an imperious gaze I had not felt on me for a long time.

"It is a triumph of being over nothingness," she said. "You don't understand. Because you have never had any emptiness in your heart. Not like me."

I put my hand on her shoulder with a surprised sort of tenderness. "Don't say your heart is empty. It's the ordinary human condition. We all feel it. But it always passes, if you let it."

Jin Yu's mouth curved into her half smile. "The emptiness in my heart is my weapon," she said.

22

Soon, Jin Yu was using my room as a meeting place in the evenings, for all the cotton-mill workers who lived in the Birdcage. The situation developed almost without my noticing. At first, she would arrive alone, bringing cakes, and I would sit and talk to her like the old days. She told me she spent a great deal of her time waiting outside the mills and factories, waiting for the workers to leave so she could speak to them. Then she began to arrive with a friend or two, and they would talk politics while I set out cups of tea. Then, groups of strange women would come and cluster in my small room, and their words were hot and angry. Many of these women were mill workers, and I was fascinated, for I had never really spoken to such women before.

I noticed that her husband Cai Hesen and their children frequently stayed at his parents' house in Shaoshan now. Cai published an underground theoretical journal, but it seemed as if Jin Yu kept him firmly away from her work organizing women workers.

"This task is mine alone," she once told me. "It's historical inevitability."

"Why don't you let Hesen help you?"

"If a man from the Party helps me in this work, then I will end up reporting to him," she snapped, suddenly angry again. "Now I am the commander." Then she shrugged. "Perhaps it's best. The children will need their father if I am hanged."

Those were days of confusion and chaos in every direction. Li Shi was often closeted in his office now, sending out and receiving a steady stream of telegrams and messengers, unwilling to come out even to greet my mother. Rumblings of war came from the south, and I heard Li Shi and Li Shi's subcommanders and even the people in the markets speak of the great Northern Expedition Army, led by the Guomindang's young officers, an army that was even now marching on Canton.

One night, I kept watch by my door, listening for sounds on the stairs, while Jin Yu organized a demonstration by cotton-mill workers. More than a dozen women crowded into my room, sitting on the windowsills, gathered around the table, squatting on the floor. The women were all middle-aged and strong like men, with huge arms like knotted oaks, powerful legs, and scarred or missing fingers. The candles I had lit spilled shadows into their eye sockets and across their broad, pocked faces, seamed with dark lines like deposits of coal. Standing in their midst, Jin Yu looked very delicate, but her pale face was passionate.

Jin Yu spoke to the women in a low voice that rasped with conviction. "Set a day for the demonstration," she told them, "and I will be with you to protest. The dog rapist overseer must be removed and punished, and reparations paid to the woman's family."

"They won't take the money," grunted one enormous woman named Big Li, whom I privately referred to as the "warhorse." So many of her earrings had been torn away in fights in the marketplace that her earlobes were ripped and shredded like lace. "They don't want to be publicly identified as the family of a woman who got herself raped in the mill and cut her own throat behind the looms. Ruined a whole day's work with her blood, the mill director said."

"All the more reason we should seek justice for her," Jin Yu snapped. "And this is just the opening. We work for the day when you will own the mill. Own the means of production one day, and you will have your own justice."

The women looked at each other. Some of them began to laugh, shaking their heads with disbelief. Some of them looked worried and afraid. One woman, whose eyes crossed slightly, looked foolish and pleased. "Will I then ride in my own sedan chair?" she asked another woman sitting beside her, speaking in a soft, teetering voice. The other woman took her hand with absentminded affection, but did not reply or look at her.

"Own the mill? That's for you to worry about, you Reds," Big Li said. Her tone was carefully indifferent, but her voice rumbled like thunder. "What we think about is Chang-O, lying between the warp and the weft, her life's juice spilled out all over the floor. I found her body myself. I knew her mother. She was a good woman." Big Li glanced away a moment, but when she turned her face to the candlelight again, her eyes were dry as dust. "Whether we ever own the mill or not, we will have our own justice today."

The women nodded to one another, and for a moment, I felt the curious understanding that surged between them, even between the ones who clearly disliked each other. I felt Jin Yu and I were like foreigners to them, coming as we did from so very far away. How pale and slender we must look to them, how weak and young and thin and dainty.

Another woman spoke, tugging at her worn sweater. "The mill as you know is owned by the Dog-Meat General, Feng. The Japanese pay good money for his cloth. There is no limit to his cruelty and avarice. He will behead us all."

Jin Yu shook her head. "Then who would work his mill?" she asked. Some of the women nodded in agreement. "Even the Dog-Meat General cannot kill hundreds of you."

Big Li spoke again. "He will kill the leader, of course. Do you doubt that?"

"Yes, he will," Jin Yu admitted. "It must be a mass movement, so no one stands out."

"Not possible," said Big Li. "A strike is like a fight. As you, fine lady, may or may not know. It's always easy to spot the leader."

Big Li was testing Jin Yu. The group fell silent, and awaited the outcome with an air of inevitability.

"Then I'll lead," Jin Yu said firmly. "I'll stand in front of the march line. You all follow me. It will be a peaceful strike. But if Feng wants anyone, it will be me."

The other women looked at the warhorse, seeing what she would do. Big Li stood where she was, leaning on the edge of the table, her arms crossed on her imposing chest. Then she grasped Jin Yu's shoulder in her iron grip. "Good enough," she grunted, unsmiling. "Good enough."

After the women had left, creeping out in twos and threes to avoid too much attention in the street, Jin Yu turned to me.

"Are you together with me?" she asked.

"Of course," I said quickly, surprising myself a little. But Jin Yu was always what was bravest in me. "You know better than to ask. But remember, Feng is mad."

"Yes, well, they're all mad, all these warlords. Feng is always risky, but don't worry. Our demand is reasonable, and our protest will be peaceful."

"It makes me wonder why you bother, if you really intend to be peaceful."

Jin Yu threw me a look. "You have to start somewhere. The workers aren't used to action. But they feel Chang-O's death keenly. It's real grief, not an abstract idea. Grievances become action. A demonstration will start to teach them what they can accomplish. And it will accustom them to work under leadership. Consider it to be the beginning of their training as an army. Besides, I have no weapons just yet."

"Well, I stand with you," I said. "With you and your unarmed army."

On a day in the grimmest, hottest part of August, we assembled twenty women in the small stretch of open land on the other side of the road that lay beneath the walls of Feng's fortified compound. We passed out some banners and flags Jin Yu had made from tearing up her grandmother's old silk dresses. Jin Yu stood to the front of the line to draw fire, with Big Li close behind and me in the middle to keep an eye on everyone. The woman with crossed eyes had been allowed to carry a small drum that someone had picked up somewhere, and she beat it slowly in time to our chanting, smiling with pleasure at the noise she was making. The friend who had taken her hand in my room kept close to her even now, one hand protectively on her back. "Chang-O, Chang-O," the women wailed in their deep voices. "Your death was unjust!"

We chanted Chang-O's name so often that it began to lose its meaning for my ears and became a pattern of mouth formations. I kept glancing up at the walls, but I could not see even a lone sentry. That made me nervous. I heard some of the women murmur that Feng intended to ignore us, but I thought Feng was not the type to ignore anyone. We were in the road perhaps an hour or so when the enormous log gates swung open, and General Feng appeared.

He rode across the road and directly up to us on his enormous chestnut horse, which was breathing heavily as if it had been galloping. From the waist up, Feng was almost as large as his horse, towering in the saddle, his eyes red with fury and wine, his teeth bared like a wolf. His huge shaven head gleamed in the light. His fine woolen uniform was decorated with bundles of tarnished gold braid and ribbons, simply massed together without any sense. He belonged to no army save his own, and the meaning of his decorations was known only to him.

Feng pulled up his horse immediately in front of us; we shifted anxiously and glanced about. There was no one else on the roads nearby, but surely even Feng would not cut down twenty women? We stood our ground, but the women around me were beginning to quiver with fear, and I could see, even standing where I was, that Feng's pupils had shrunk to pinpoints. But he said nothing, only looked at all of us as if he were memorizing our faces.

Jin Yu stepped forward. I struggled to the front as well and stood at her side, clasping her elbow.

"General Feng," Jin Yu began. Feng looked down at her and, to my immense surprise, cocked his head to one side like a bird and seemed to listen.

"General Feng," Jin Yu said, heartened by this moderate response. "The workers of your mill are gathered to protest the death of the woman Chang-O in your cotton mill. You have heard the circumstances of her death. We wish only to show our desire for justice. Punish the overseer who raped her and give a pension to Chang-O's old father. Then they will all return happily to work."

Feng looked at Jin Yu a long time. He twisted his head to the other side and stared at her more. Then he turned on his horse and glanced behind him briefly. With that small movement, fifteen or so soldiers with pikestaffs, dressed in a motley collection of uniform pieces, ran out from the shadowy shelter of the walls and took up positions across from us. The women murmured in alarm and looked at one another. My eyes swept to both sides and saw that the ends of the road on either side of us were blocked. I began frantically to think of a way to back down, because I saw that my flippant remark about Feng being mad was precisely the truth. He was not mad in any comical sense, but seriously, critically. Then Feng turned to us again. He looked over our heads at the worker women clustering close together. He seemed a long way away, up on his horse, on the other side of the abyss that separates the sane and the insane.

"I heard you gathering out here," Feng said finally. His raspy voice hissed down at us from behind the horse's head. He ran a hand across his sweating brow. "I heard you all the way inside my house. But strife leads to strife. I can't have any strife in my mill. So I can't allow any strife to start. Not at all."

He nodded at the soldiers, who came closer.

"By the way," Feng said, twisting his head back and forth and cracking the vertebrae in his thick neck, "you don't know anything about Chang-O."

Jin Yu and I stared up at him. Feng leaned down from his horse, leaning one forearm on his knee. I saw that his legs were as thick and as long as cannon, and his near boot was dusty and cracked.

"The overseer didn't rape her," Feng whispered. "He just held her down."

The sun blazed overhead.

"I slit her throat." He sat up on his horse. "I slit Chang-O's throat." His voice exploded. "I did! Did you hear that, friends of Chang-O?" His face was a sneering mask as he turned on his horse. "I am her killer! I cut her throat, for no other reason than because it was my will!"

A stunned silence. My stomach rolled with nausea. Then a howl of anguish came from behind me.

"You bastard!" roared Big Li, bursting from the crowd.

"Get back!" cried Jin Yu and I, almost together.

Big Li drew a knife from her sleeve and ran at Feng's horse.

"Stop her!" I shouted to the other women. "Stop her!" I flung myself at Big Li and wrapped my arms around her, but she tossed me off with her huge shoulders.

The soldiers burst upon us in a fury, dashing in from the ends of the road, leading with the wicked steel blades of the pikestaffs. They descended with high-pitched wails, like the barbarian women of the north.

"Run!" shouted Jin Yu to the other women. "Run for your lives!"

Panic came upon us like a plague. Jin Yu and I scrambled away from Feng, making for the open field beyond the road, yelling to the women to run, only to find the way blocked by a forest of spears. We spun around, my eyes searching frantically for a path. Feng's beast went down with a scream and a spray of blood under Big Li's knife, but then I saw the knife spinning through the air, glinting at me on its way, landing many feet away from the scarred hand that needed it most. Then Feng was back on his wounded horse, which plunged wildly about in the road, the general sawing with his reins at its foaming mouth. Feng's mount reared up and down, and its hooves came down on Big Li's outstretched arms and on the empty, soundless caverns that had once been her forehead and her chest. Screams came from all directions.

In the wild terror and panic of that moment, the cross-eyed woman ran past me, going in the wrong direction, not toward the fields but toward Feng's fort. I watched in horror as she ran blindly through the gates. "No!" I shouted. "Not that way!" I ran after her without thinking and followed her into the courtyard. She was only a few feet ahead of me and almost within reach. She held up her little drum in front of her protectively, but the pikestaff thrust through the fragile skin covering. I fell beside her and held her in my arms, to hear her last words. "My drum, my poor drum," she said sadly. I looked up in time to see the gates closing on me; my last sight was of Jin Yu running toward me, toward the gates, her mouth shouting. Then Feng kicked her away viciously, and she fell. I saw Big Li's body on the ground and, beyond her, the women running like lunatics through the fields. Feng rode into the yard, and the gates were shut slowly behind him, leaving us in the unkind embrace of the stockaded walls.

Feng dismounted and hit me in the face in an entirely businesslike and detached manner. I fell to the ground.

While I remained unconscious, dull and sharp intermittent sensations disturbed the black pool into which I had fallen. I had many terrible dreams, in which my teeth were all loose or falling out.

When I awoke finally, I was lying on a rough pallet of straw, in a dank chamber. I opened my eyes, and the ceiling was so low that for a second I had the terrifying sensation that it was descending to crush me. My head throbbed. I felt dried blood on my face, which was very sore. The window was set high up in the wall, a position that told me that my chamber was underground. When I sat up—a movement that almost made me vomit—I saw that I was alone. I ran my tongue over my teeth, checking to see if they were all still there. A small wizened man entered through the heavy ironbound doors and was now pushing a pot of water toward me.

"Drink it," he said, in a squeak of a voice. "You've been asleep for two days and a half." He nodded toward the light streaming in from the window. "It's afternoon now."

I picked up the water and gulped it down eagerly. The little old man got up to leave.

"Wait," I croaked. "Am I in Feng's fortress?"

The little man nodded. "It's called the Palace of Heavenly Prosperity."

"I demand to be released. This is kidnapping. It is an outrage."

The man shook his head. "Not possible. The Dog-Meat General will wait until your brother comes to rescue you."

"My brother?" Inwardly, I cursed my situation, a trap for Li Shi. "You better not let Feng hear you call him the Dog-Meat General."

"He likes the title," the little man replied. Well, I thought drearily, Feng certainly is further removed from human nature than I had thought, to take pride in such a name.

"Where is the body of that poor cross-eyed woman?" I asked.

"I put it outside the gates myself. Someone came and got it in the night. I didn't think it was right to leave it lying in the hot sun in the yard."

"Thank you," I said. I didn't know what else to say.

The little man was leaving again.

"Wait," I cried.

"What now?"

"Can I have something to eat?"

"Have patience. You are to be a guest at dinner tonight. Then you can eat your fill."

Two hours later, during which time my stomach ached with hunger, the little man came again. He set another pot of water in front of me.

"Don't drink that! It's to wash your face." He tugged from his pocket a comb of tortoiseshell set with expensive stones, but with a few teeth missing. I patted some water on my face, very carefully. In the liquid reflection, I could see that an enormous bruise covered one entire cheek and eye. I dragged the comb through my hair and staggered to my feet.

"All right. Ready," I said, coughing a little.

The little man led the way. "Are you afraid?" he asked.

"No."

"Why not?"

"Whether I live or die is not in my control. And no matter what happens to me, my brother will put Feng to the sword. And all Feng's men with him." I glared meaningfully at the little old man, who looked away. I wondered why I was not frightened, and decided that it was because I was furious.

We walked down a long corridor lined with tall windows, where soldiers lounged or stood, dressed in their strange, fragmentary, made-up uniforms and odd pretend decorations, their pikes leaning on the wall. One soldier was pissing out a window. One picked his teeth with a great knife. In the alternating light and darkness of the corridor windows, I saw that several of them had bare feet.

The little old man pushed open a large door at the end of the corridor, and we entered the remains of what had once clearly been a very grand audience chamber. A thick fog of tobacco smoke mixed with opium fumes. I grimaced at that familiar sweet scent and felt a painful rush of memory at the fragrance, remembering Pan Wang Mang. Pale afternoon light seeped in through the panes of a large square window that overlooked the courtyard. Through the smoke I saw blurry rows of men, reclining on cushions on the floor, laughing loudly and drunkenly over their wine cups and water pipes, their feet in the dishes of food that had been strewn haphazardly before them. Their shouts were deafening.

Scattered among the men like chaff were a number of women, with faces painted white and lips painted red, half-dressed in the stained elegance of dirty silk dresses. Every one of the women was bent over, eating leftovers from the dishes with speed and concentration, and hardly glanced up when I came in.

My escort led me to Feng, who alone of the entire company sat in a chair. A girl lolled drunkenly at his feet, her mouth open. As I approached, he kicked her, and her coarsened form rolled away from him on the carpet.

Feng looked up as I limped toward him. His forehead was beaded with sweat, and his mouth was wet. His strange eyes seemed clouded, but then gradually cleared as he looked at me.

"Liang Li Shi has not yet come to rescue you," Feng said.

"He may not bother," I replied, really hoping this would not be the case.

"I will kill him when he gets here," Feng said. Again, the curious sideways tilt of the head. "I can't wait. Of course he'll come. He's efficient. All these educated boys are efficient. Modern and efficient."

I desperately wanted to look around the room, to assess my situation, but I did not dare. Feng might be mad, and at this moment he might be drunk, but he had not lived so long for nothing and would spot my eyes moving in my head. So I simply stared back at him.

He drank deeply from a metal cup. He looked at my little old man. "You can go," Feng said softly. My companion ducked away and left me all alone.

"Sit," Feng said to me. I glanced around me. There was only the floor.

Feng saw my hesitation. "Is my floor too good for you?" he shouted. He jumped to his feet and pushed me down. I fell against the drunken girl nearby. Her skin was ice-cold, her limbs were stiff, and I recoiled in horror.

"This girl is dead!" I cried.

Feng sat down. "I know," he said, twisting his neck and cracking the vertebrae one after another. "She has been for several hours now. Are you so sheltered, then, that you can't tell a drunk from a corpse?"

"Why don't you have her body taken away?" I blurted out, unable to restrain myself.

"Sooner or later. For now, it's still pretty."

I huddled on the floor, cringing from the girl's body. She bore no marks of violence that I could see, but she had bruises under all her pale fingernails, and I couldn't think how they got there. The loud, smoky room seemed like a chamber of hell, and Feng's huge shaven head hung in the thick air like an apparition of a demon. Any moment, I thought, and the gongs will sound, and the great judges of hell will enter. Perhaps I have died after all. My head ached and spun. Around me, the whores continued to eat with purpose, paying no attention to me or Feng.

An hour, several hours passed, in the same misery as before. I hunched on the floor and rubbed my damp hands together to stay awake. My legs were stiff, my stomach hollowed out with hunger and fatigue. The dead girl continued to lie nearby, and sometimes when I looked over at her, I imagined her eyelashes fluttering. I finally produced my sweat-stained handkerchief and covered her face. Feng sat broodily on his chair and drank an unimaginable amount of wine, cup after brimming cup. There was one fight among the men, and a finger cut off in the course of it. The darkness of night fell, and the only light in the room came from a long series of tapers set into a floor stand. In the midst of the heat and the turbulence in my mind, I almost fell asleep.

"We have entertainment for our guest." Feng's loud voice came to me from the smoke. "An itinerant musician has shown up at the door. He has been here since the morning. Men, what shall we do if we do not like his music?"

A chorus of shouts rang through the great room. But one man spoke more loudly than the rest.

"What instrument does he play?" the henchman shouted.

"The lute!" someone else replied.

"Then we'll cut off his hands." Everyone roared. The whores continued to eat with purpose, paying no attention.

I remembered that I had heard some stories of unexplained disappearances in Feng's quarter of the city, of jugglers or dancing girls, heard the stories from the lowly workers of the Birdcage, and I had dismissed them as tales of malcontents who had run away. Now I wondered, as I sat next to the dead girl, whose blood had cooled so rapidly in her veins, if the vanished ones had made their very last appearance on earth in this hall. The thought made me shiver.

Then Feng called for the musician. There was a great deal of stamping of feet and shouting for the poor lute-player, and presently a slender, willowy young man appeared. His head was shaven bald, like Feng's, and his face entirely painted in red and black, like a character from the Chinese opera. He wore billowing old-fashioned robes and carried his lute in his soft young hands. He bowed before Feng in silence.

"Play," Feng grunted. I was surprised to see an approving look pass his face, and I realized that he liked the musician's old-style theatrical makeup and costume. His face wore an almost childish expression of pleasure. I wondered what kind of boy Feng could possibly have been.

The musician sat cross-legged on the floor near Feng and began to play his lute. He played a familiar song, "The Horse Soldier's Air," which all the men knew, and they all began to sing.

I had not bothered to look at the musician very closely when he entered—I was too preoccupied with my own situation and had no interest in this traveling showman. But when he began to play merrily, I looked up in spite of myself. I could barely discern his features through the smoke and the thick colored opera paints on his face, but I began to think he looked familiar. Then the musician, pausing briefly between notes, looked directly at me and touched his face with his fingertips. Our eyes met. I realized with a shock that the musician was Jin Yu, and she had shaved her head completely.

I looked down again immediately, fixing my gaze on the floor to hide my nervousness and alarm. I thought Jin Yu was as mad as Feng himself. I was relieved she had not been hurt. I was so nervous I wanted to laugh, and then I was afraid I might be getting hysterical. I could tell my face wore a startled expression I was anxious to hide, so I yawned very widely.

When Jin Yu finished playing, she gave a winsome bow, and the armed men all around us cheered, although to tell the truth their cheers sounded like threats to me. Without speaking, she started to play another song, a rough ditty from the streets about a pirate from Shanghai. Where had she learned these songs? I wondered.

In the midst of the third or fourth song, the large window facing the courtyard exploded into the room, spraying thousands of shards of glass all over the assembled company. Feng leaped to his feet and ran to look out, his more sober men crowding around him. I stood up, noticing out of the corner of my eye one of the whores holding her bleeding face, which had been cut by the flying glass. A deafening boom rolled through the room, followed by the quick crackle of gunfire.

"We're being attacked! The gates are open!" The men were shouting, some pushing toward the broken window to see and others pushing the other way toward the door. Everyone was buckling on swords, grasping bows and quivers of arrows, stamping the porcelain plates into powder beneath their feet. The whores screamed and flung themselves to the ground on their faces.

I craned my neck to see out the window. The darkness was now bristling with torch flames, and I saw by their light that the great gates of the compound were indeed open. Gunpowder flames leaped and flickered from the dark beyond the gates, where a number of khaki-clad men were standing and kneeling in the opening, firing rifles—one round after another, more rapidly than I thought rifles could fire—at Feng's men as they dashed outside.

Then a hand grabbed my arm. It was Jin Yu. She had flung off her billowing outer robes and stood in trousers and boots like a man, the opera paint still on her face.

"Come now!" she shouted, and dragged me away. "They will fire in the window!" I glanced one more time through the shattered opening and saw with amazement that a cannon was being rolled up to the gate, to fire directly into the compound.

We sprang for the door into the corridor. I heard a snarl of fury behind me, and I saw Feng leaping after us, the muscles rolling in his neck like a tiger's. I grasped a stand of tapers and sent it crashing to the floor behind us, and Feng leaped back with a yell. Then Jin Yu and I ran out the door into the corridor.

The corridor was empty—all the men were in the courtyard, where horrible yells could be heard along with the eerie tin whistle of bullets and the light twang of bows and arrows. Jin Yu ran down the corridor until she reached one of the tall windows furthest from the room we had just left. She climbed up on the low sill and put her boot through the glass, kicking out three panes.

"Get through!" she shouted. I clambered out immediately, narrowly avoiding taking an arrow in the top of my head. Jin Yu climbed out after me, and we ran across the crowded courtyard. I had always pictured a battleground as looking like an ancient painting, with men in armor fighting each other, hand to hand, on an open field. But this was much more confusing. Bullets cracked past; arrows landed nearby. A man would run in front of us carrying a pikestaff and disappear into the darkness. Then another would appear, screaming and holding an arm blasted like a tree trunk struck by lightning, and run in the opposite direction. There was a great deal of noise, but I couldn't really see anything happening, except the glare of light from the bobbing torches or the occasional flicker of gunpowder catching fire. The cannon fired, and I heard the crash of bricks and mortar behind me.

I saw now that the compound was a dirt square surrounded by the high wooden stockade, with a squat two-story watchtower at each corner, a torch burning on top. Jin Yu and I ducked into the doorway of one watchtower and crouched down, listening to the battle raging in the dark.

"What is happening?" I panted.

Jin Yu slouched down into a squat and leaned back against the wall. The dull golden light from the courtyard fell in a block on the ground and illuminated her boots. She looked very strange, in her opera-painted face and her shaven head and her military trousers and boots.

"I was disguised as the lute player, as you can see. Li Shi had his own barber shave my head." She was gasping for breath, and her words were labored. "Everyone knows that Feng likes this kind of rough country music-making. So I came and offered to play, and I got into the fortress that way."

"Yes, but how did they get into the fortress?" I cried, pointing to the cannon in the open gate. As I pointed, the mouth of the cannon roared again, and I flinched.

"Li Shi told me that the guard would be relaxed at night, because Feng thinks no one fights at night, because no one ever fought at night in the old days. I went to each guard tower on the pretense of playing for the guards while they were on duty, and gave them each drugged wine. Then I threw their bows and arrows over the wall and opened the latch on the gate."

She breathed heavily.

Men ran past our doorway, back and forth, in confusion. The acrid smell of the guns filled our throats.

"Come back from the door, here, under the stairs," Jin Yu whispered to me. I had only just shifted into the darkness with her when an enormous shadow filled the opening. It was Feng.

I steeled myself for his onslaught. Jin Yu's hand was a vise on my wrist. But Feng ran up the winding staircase to the top of the tower, without seeing us.

All at once, a crowd of khaki-clad men gathered beneath the tower, filling up the doorway.

"Don't go up!" I heard my brother's voice shout. "He's too danger-ous!"

"Li Shi!" I cried, leaping up and running out, with Jin Yu on my heels.

Li Shi, standing in the midst of his troops, turned his face to me. He blinked in surprise. I flung myself at him and embraced him, wiping my eyes on his epaulet. He put his hands on my shoulders and held me away from him.

"Did you see Feng?" he shouted to me, over the noise of the soldiers.

"He ran up the stairs, right past us," answered Jin Yu behind me. "He's headed for the top of the tower."

"Look!" many men shouted. We looked up to the top of the tower. Feng was silhouetted against the blaze of the great torch he kept burning there. The light shone on his brown skin and on his heavy shaved head. We could just see the dim outline of the unconscious guard at his feet. We all stared at him, openmouthed, and gradually we all fell silent.

Feng waved his sword. "Liang Li Shi! Are you there?" he roared.

My brother shouted up. "Surrender, Feng! You are finished!"

"Are you a man, Liang Li Shi?" Feng cried out to us. "If you are a man, come up the stairs with your sword! Fight me to the end! I will wait hon-orably until you are well-positioned before I strike at you! But fight me like a man! Fight until one of us dies by the sword!"

My eye barely followed what happened next. My brother barked out a word I could not discern. The young soldiers around him instantly raised their rifles to their shoulders and fired up to the top of the tower, all of them together in one smooth motion, like the gears turning in a machine. I felt my gaze jerked upward, following the shots.

At the tower's edge, Feng staggered back a half step. In the glow of the torch, even from the bottom of the tower, I could see his eyes widen in sur-prise and a kind of disgust. Then he stepped forward, into emptiness, and fell through the unreceiving air, slowly, slowly, tumbling reluctantly like a descending hawk, his huge arms and legs spread like sails. When he was al-most upon us, we leaped back. He landed very hard on the cold earth. His long sword, falling with him, plunged into the earth blade first and stood quivering.

Li Shi turned over Feng's great corpse with a disdainful foot.

"Poor old Feng," my brother said dryly. "Did he really think I was go-ing to fight him by hand?"

·   ·   ·

Jin Yu and I huddled near one of the towers during the following dawn while Li Shi organized his army in securing Feng's fort. Feng's men were bound with shackles on their wrists and ankles, and seated in long rows in the center of the yard. The dead had been stacked like wood in the corners. The whores had been turned out of the fortress, and I watched them in the pale light of dawn as they stumbled away across the fields, their bright silken sleeves drifting uncertainly in the morning air. The building itself was thoroughly searched, and a fair amount of gold was uncovered, which to my surprise was simply stacked in a wagon under guard instead of being divided up by the victors. The cannon was rolled away by horses.

The little old man who had brought me water emerged among the prisoners, a welt on his forehead. He squatted on the ground and clutched his old hands together convulsively. I left Jin Yu and found Li Shi where he was standing in the yard.

"Li Shi, release that one," I told my brother. "He's harmless."

Li Shi gestured briefly, and the old man was unshackled.

"Get out," Li Shi told him, without any rancor in his voice.

The old man shook his bowed head. He was crying. I looked at Li Shi, who only shrugged.

"You are free to leave," I said, stepping in front of the old man. "My brother has ordered it."

The old man raised a tear-streaked face. "Where will I go, now that my son is dead?" he wept.

"Your son?"

The old man pointed to Feng's body, still lying where it had fallen, but now covered with a sheet.

I looked back at Li Shi in confusion. Now what could I do? Li Shi came up quickly.

"Did he say he was Feng's father?" Li Shi hissed to me. I nodded. "Then get him out of here, or I can't answer for the number of days he has left." Li Shi looked around him in concern. There were some soldiers only a few feet away. His conduct surprised me—were these not his own men?

"Sir, please leave," I whispered. "These are your son's enemies." I dragged him to his feet and pushed him toward the empty gate. He stumbled toward the opening, weeping the entire time.

"Let him go," Li Shi called to the soldiers at the gate. "He's just a harmless old servant."

The old man passed them safely. But I watched him as he wandered out the gate and into the dirt road beyond, still crying, his steps uncertain and wavering, lost now, without his strange son. I thought of the half-witted factory woman who had died clutching her drum. Was it only a short while ago that her life had been quenched? Then the old man passed from my view forever.

Later in the day, Li Shi led us out of the fort and down the dirt road a short distance, toward a small house that sat by itself near a cistern.

"You'll have to wash your face, Jin Yu," he said as we approached the house. "A brave and clever warrior like you have turned out to be cannot walk about painted like a singer."

Jin Yu only laughed, but I heard pride and excitement in her voice. Her arm, which I was leaning on, trembled.

The stretch of ground around the little house was being used as a sort of field hospital, and several wounded soldiers in khaki lay about in the grass, being tended assiduously by their comrades. I noticed they had all been wounded with arrows or blades.

We picked our way carefully. "Li Shi," I said in a low voice. "I don't recognize these soldiers of yours."

"They aren't mine. I mean most of them aren't mine. I didn't have enough troops to attack Feng. These are Guomindang troops. This is a regiment of the Northern Expedition Army."

"These are the ones you were waiting for!" I exclaimed. "How lucky they have come just now!"

Li Shi said nothing, but led us into the house and into a room in the back. Even before we had stepped through the door, I smelled the sharp metallic tang of blood. Now, as I walked in behind Li Shi, I saw before me a bare-walled room with wooden floors and a single window of oiled paper. A table stood in the middle of the room. On one side of the table stood a man who was clearly a surgeon, with the surgeon's green badge stitched to his old-fashioned gown. He was in the very bloody process of removing an arrow from the forearm of a prematurely gray-haired man who sat across the table from him. The surgeon was digging the arrow out of the live flesh with a long, shining steel bodkin, and rivulets of blood ran out of either side of the wound. The gray-haired man sat with his wounded arm stretched out across some gore-soaked cloths.

With his other hand, he was playing chess.

"How are you doing, General Zhao?" my brother asked. I shuddered as the surgeon rocked his instrument back and forth. But the gray-haired man addressed as Zhao only grimaced mildly when he looked up from the chessboard.

"As well as can be," Zhao said, in a voice remarkable for its steadiness. "But it's taking a long time. I'll be finished with the game"—he nodded at the chessboard—"before this quack is done."

"I'm doing my best," snorted the surgeon. "But Feng's arrows have six barbs instead of two, barbs as long and skinny as fishhooks. Now steady yourself, this will hurt most." He yanked at the arrow, and it came roughly away from Zhao's arm, spilling yet more blood. Zhao only tightened his lips. Then the surgeon poured a liquid into the open wound that bubbled like acid. Zhao moved several pieces on the chessboard. I noticed he played very well.

"Are these the two ladies you mentioned?" Zhao asked finally, when the surgeon was binding up his arm with fresh cloths.

"My sister, Mrs. Pan. This is Mrs. Cai. This is General Zhao Han Ren, commander of the Northern Expedition Army in Hunan."

Zhao bowed courteously to each of us in turn. Jin Yu bowed, just as I did, but her face was shuttered and a speculative expression sat in her eyes. Behind the gaudy opera makeup, now streaked with grime and sweat, a darkness gathered.

"So you have finally come," Jin Yu murmured. "We've all been waiting for you."

"Indeed?" replied Zhao with a silky smile. "It warms my heart to feel so welcome in Hunan."

It was almost nightfall again by the time I reached Li Shi's compound and sank down exhaustedly onto his camp cot. His coat slid off my shoulders. Li Shi stood and stretched his neck in a manner so reminiscent of Feng that I felt a momentary lurch of fear. Then he rubbed the dark circles under his eyes, and my fear subsided.

"Li Shi," I said suddenly, remembering. "Where are Mother and Graceful Virtue?"

"In the south. I sent them away the very hour I learned you had been taken by Feng. I feared he might widen his circle of bloodshed to all the members of my family. I'll send for them to return tomorrow. I took care of the old Pans as well."

"Oh, no, the Pans!" I cried. "I didn't think of them at all!"

"I said I fed them. Army rations, I'm afraid."

He sank down onto the bed next to me and leaned forward, his elbows on his knees. He looked very fatigued.

"I'm glad you are safe," he said. "On the day you were taken, I received intelligence that the Northern Expedition was one day's march away. But they had some skirmishes coming upriver and took three days to come. I was very worried that Feng would kill you before they arrived."

"Did this army come at your bidding?"

Li Shi laughed at this. "Certainly not. They are making their way through the entire nation, south to north, rooting out the warlords and hanging them all from telegraph poles. I just happened to be in their path. They consolidated the southern provinces in just a few months. They were already on their way here to do the same, when as it happened, Feng kidnapped you." He took out a package of cigarettes and lit one, striking the match on the sole of his boot. "Directing them to Feng's stronghold was simple enough. I had already arranged by secret messenger to go over to them with all my men and to be made a colonel in their army. The other Hunan warlords have all fled across the Miluo River."

"My heaven, my brother," I said. "Are you Guomindang now? I wish I could say I was surprised at this sudden turn of events, but I think I am not."

Li Shi merely smoked.

"Is this it, then?" I demanded. "Is General Zhao the leader you've been waiting for?"

Li Shi blew out a mouthful of fumes. "Chiang Kai Shek is seizing power all over the country. We'll have a real national government, not this collection of crazed battle gods that have been ruling these past few years. As for Zhao"—he shrugged—"he'll do for now. Zhao Han Ren is what fate has presented to me."

"Well, I admit he's a remarkable man, this Zhao," I said. My voice was hoarse with fatigue. "Although Jin Yu behaved very strangely with him."

"I saw that too."

"I don't know why."

"I know," Li Shi said. "Zhao knows too." I opened my mouth to ask more, but Li Shi turned his face away decisively, and I knew he would not explain any further.

"Jin Yu is very brave, isn't she?" I asked, feeling a little eager to make up for Jin Yu's unpredictable behavior, and uncomfortable at Li Shi's silence.

Li Shi nodded. "Very brave. Very cunning. She is the one who thought of disguising herself to get in. Ruthless too. The way she dealt with the guards in the four towers. Although I can't say that I'm really surprised. It's a quality I always sensed in her."

A tiny tooth of doubt gnawed at me. "You mean the way she drugged the guards in the towers?"

Li Shi looked at me, his eyebrows raised.

"Is that what you mean?" I asked, more insistently. "She put them to sleep with drugged wine?"

Li Shi stubbed out his cigarette.

"Jade Virtue," he said, "Jin Yu cut the throats of all four guards in the towers."

23

General Zhao's troops overran the entire province in days, with the help of Li Shi's men. Zhao himself became the governor late in the year 1926, and appointed Li Shi the garrison commander. Zhao disdained to live in the governor's palace, and instead insisted on moving into an old mansion close to Li Shi's compound.

From that time onward our lives in the provincial backwater of Changsha changed very quickly. Women in short skirts, close-fitting cloche hats, and high heels strode past the armless and legless beggars on the streets. The wives of rich men called each other on their new telephones, raising their fluting voices above the clicks and the static. Shiny motorcars slid through the streets, breasting the waves of pedestrians with their chrome fenders, pushing aside the mud-encrusted ox-drawn wagon of the fruit vendor and the blackened figure of the coal hauler, who strained his meager muscles against the struts of his two-wheeled cart. The criminal brotherhoods of the Triads opened elaborate gambling houses and dance halls; by early morning, the streets nearby were littered with discarded dice and playing cards.

The swaggering bands of fighters in mismatched armor, holding pikestaffs, had been replaced by neat columns of soldiers in khaki battle-dress and carrying new rifles, who patrolled the streets at regular intervals and arrested many criminals. The new young officials rushed about importantly with their stacks of documents, their leather document cases, their Western suits and fedoras. The cobbles of the main roads were paved over with tar, and several new buildings of concrete went up overnight, including a new Telephone and Telegraph Station where any member of the public could pay to have his messages sent the fastest possible way. The merchants could not keep up with the demand for foreign cigarettes, foreign cloth, gadgets, and novelties.

Because of my brother, I saw Governor Zhao frequently. He played chess with Li Shi and the more junior officers and practiced archery in his spare time, hampered a little by the recurring soreness of the wound in his forearm. Yet he moved about comfortably in this emerging new world, using the telephone easily and driving his own Pierce Arrow convertible from America. The first time I ever used the telephone was in Zhao's office—he let me listen to Li Shi's voice at the other end, tinny-sounding and distant, and I began to cry.

My feelings toward Zhao were very admiring, in part as a reaction against Jin Yu. I was angry with her for lying to me about killing Feng's soldiers in the guard towers. In my innermost heart, I was afraid of her now too, now that she had shown herself capable of killing four men rapidly and without remorse. But I tried to tell myself that the incident at Feng's fortress was in the heat of battle, when all things are permitted, and I never mentioned my newborn fear to her. To relieve my anguished feelings, I shouted at her for lying to me about what she had done.

"I lied to you then because I didn't want to distract you while the battle was going on," she snapped back. "You would have spent precious moments feeling compassion for the poor dead boys—as you would have thought of them. We were in a dangerous position, and I couldn't afford your ethics just then."

These statements infuriated me, in part because I recognized their truth. Jin Yu was, without doubt, far more efficient than I was, because she never dwelt on such matters. I didn't know if I could have bluffed my way into Feng's fortress with such daring and skill. I had only my superior morality to comfort me.

Mao and Jin Yu were dismayed by Zhao's advent, since he filled the power vacuum that had existed for so long.

"The masses are sinking back into their sheeplike state," complained Mao, at their usual meeting at Teacher Yang's house. "They see the shiny cars of the rich new officials, and instead of being goaded to anger, they are merely impressed! They don't understand that everyone in China should own such a car."

"Well, that would be hard to accomplish," Jin Yu's husband Cai Hesen pointed out. Jin Yu's face twitched in irritation at the reasonable tone of his voice.

"Then no one should own a car!" Mao cried, and everyone nodded in agreement.

•   •   •

Worst of all, Zhao made fun of them and of their Party. On a single day in winter, Mao led two separate march demonstrations to the governor's mansion. The first marchers, who came in the morning, were factory workers from the cotton mills. Mao made a long and very loud speech, in which he shouted again and again, "We workers demand our rights!" Zhao opened his window on the second floor and listened to the speech while he worked at his desk.

The second group of demonstrators, who came in the afternoon, were students from the First Normal School, and again Mao spoke. "We students demand our rights!"

At this Zhao actually came out of the governor's mansion, with only a young aide-de-camp behind him. He walked through the crowd of demonstrators, which parted anxiously at his approach. His gray hair was visible above all the bobbing young heads. He stopped some feet away from where Mao stood on an upended box. Everyone stared, open-mouthed.

"I thought you said this morning that you were a worker," Zhao called up to him. "Now here you are, you are a student. Which one of these things are you, in truth?"

"I am both!" boomed Mao angrily.

Zhao considered him a moment. Then he snorted a laugh. "No such merchandise," he said, his voice edged with amusement. "One works for rice to eat; the other spends his parents' money on novels and candy." He turned on his heel and headed back toward the mansion. He called back over his shoulder, grinning, "If you are a worker, Mao Zedong, go work. If you are a student, go study. But it seems to me that all you are is a talker. So please continue with what you were doing."

From that moment on, Mao Zedong hated Zhao with passion, to a degree that I found verged on insanity. Jin Yu observed that all of Zhao's policies and politics did not stir as much anger in Mao as the one sneering remark, made in front of the students who were Mao's chief admirers. And for all his surface amusement, I saw that Zhao truly despised Mao, referring to him as the "rich peasant."

"The rich peasant was supposed to be our ally, albeit a rather compromised one. He certainly has a flexible notion of what that means," Zhao said to Li Shi in my presence. "Ah, well. One must be philosophical. Those who used to have power want a restoration. Those who have power are in

favor of the status quo. Those who want to have power clamor for re-
form."

"Surely it isn't merely about power?" I protested. "Surely it is a combat
of ideas as well?"

Zhao and Li Shi laughed very hard. I was ashamed of my lack of
worldliness in front of their cynicism. But I also thought that they might
be missing something very crucial about Mao Zedong.

My invitation to supper at the governor's mansion came in the hand of
a young soldier, who blushed when he handed it to me. It was a single
piece of fragile rice paper, on which Zhao Han Ren had brushed, with a
very slender and elegant brush, the following words: "Will you be my
guest at the evening meal? I will send someone to escort you." I was surprised and hesitant, but I consented to attend. My escort, as it turned out,
was the same young soldier, who blushed whenever I spoke to him, all the
way from the House of Silk Fans to Zhao's mansion.

The mansion was a large old-fashioned building with sloping tile roofs
and latticed windows. It sat just outside the concrete wall of the garrison,
across from the square concrete buildings of the barracks. In contrast to
the garrison, the mansion exuded a deceptive air of mildness.

When I entered, I was led immediately to the upstairs dining table,
where Zhao already sat. The windows of the room opened out onto a
weedy canal, where the green, vine-laden waters moved slowly. He rose to
greet me, bowing politely, smiling in welcome, his watchful eyes unchanging. His lean form was clothed in a silk gown instead of a uniform. He gestured me to a seat, and a servant immediately set before me a small white
ceramic cup and a jug of wine. Zhao raised his own cup, holding it with
both hands to show the finer courtesy.

"Your house has quite a history," I told him, as we set our cups down.

"Please tell me. I'm originally from around here, but I've been away
from Hunan for many years. If I ever knew this story, perhaps I've forgotten it."

"Years ago," I began, "a man left Changsha to go to California, America, during the gold strike of 1849. He worked as a coolie laborer and
panned for gold. He saw many hard things, surviving lynch mobs, high-
waymen, starvation, and several days lost in the desert. He wrote about
everything in letters home to his mother, and his mother told all her neighbors her son's stories."

"Of course." Zhao smiled. The servingman placed several small dishes on the table, with pickled cabbage and cold slices of duck and beef.

"But the coolie got rich, not through gold prospecting, which was for dreamers and fools, but by opening a restaurant and feeding vast numbers of miners in the mining camp. He learned to shoot and used a shotgun to keep away bad men. He sent home money to his mother and had her build a house for him at the edge of the canal, where the houses of other prosperous men stood. She did as she was instructed, and after twenty years, the former coolie came home to retire, hoping to marry, to live well, and to be a comfort to his mother in her waning years."

"All understandable desires," Zhao murmured politely, placing food on my plate.

"But the former coolie did not prosper at home in China. His energy and resourcefulness simply irritated people, for he no longer knew his place. He had, after all, only been a coal carrier's son. His success made others jealous. He no longer fit the eternal patterns of Chinese life, but had become another man."

Zhao watched me, his eyes opaque.

"This man married and had several children. But then in his old age, after his ancient mother had finally died, he left once again for California, deserting his wife and sons. He said that he had left his shotgun behind under the bed in his old shack where he had lived in the mining camp, and was going now to get it back again. No one ever heard from him again."

"Now, Mrs. Pan. Why did you tell me that?" Zhao asked, smiling slightly.

I was genuinely surprised. "Why, I thought you would find the story of your own house interesting. I heard from Li Shi that you love history. Of course, this is only a story. I don't actually know how true it is. I heard it from the Number Four Widow of the Silk Fans Society."

"It's entirely true," Zhao said.

"You've heard of it before?"

"Yes. I've heard it before. I think in my youth I may even have met one of the man's sons. It is true in every detail." But he said no more on the subject, and merely served me graciously from the various dishes.

During the rest of dinner, Zhao displayed great curiosity about my life. He asked numerous questions about the school, my students, about what I did with myself in the evenings and on my holidays.

"I read, write letters, visit with my friends," I said in response to the last question. "Up until recently, until you became the governor, I was active in demonstrations and union organization. I explore the city, walk in the fields, speak to the farmers. I plant flowers and vegetables in the borders of the courtyard at the House of Silk Fans."

Zhao picked up his wine cup. "And is that enough for you?" he asked.

I looked at my food, to cover my feelings of surprise and embarrassment. "Often it is enough. But sometimes I feel the lack of human companionship." Something impelled me to say more, for Zhao was very still, very watchful, and listening carefully. He was dangerously attractive to confidences.

"I have never expected love from this world," I faltered. "But sometimes I would like some company."

He smiled. "Your expectations are humble ones. Tell me, how old are you?"

I looked up. His face was perfectly serious. "I am now thirty-seven years old," I replied.

"And are you surprised to find yourself having reached that age so quickly?"

He did not seem to be joking with me.

"Yes. Very surprised, to tell the truth. I can hardly believe it. I was a girl, and then I was a wife, and then I was a teacher and then a widow. And now, here I am, eating dinner with you, and wondering why you are asking me these questions."

Zhao laughed at this. "Idle curiosity. I have not met very many women like you. You conduct your life almost like a man's, interested in books and politics and matters that usually don't concern women."

"Do women like me trouble you?"

"No."

We ate a little more food, and for a while, the only sound in the evening was the click of our chopsticks and the gentle buzzing of the insects from the open windows. The lamp on the table burned steadily, a small reflection of the yellow half-moon that rose above the roofs along the old canal.

"I hear rumors among the people," I said. "I heard that you are planning to have the province of Hunan secede from China, to be its own country, with you as the king. I heard that you are conspiring with Li Shi to accomplish this. I heard also that you and the authorities in Nanjing are conspiring to place the south under military rule. And I heard that there is a general conspiracy among the warlords that are still left in the north to install one of their own as the new emperor, to combat the Guomindang army that even now makes its way toward them. I heard that Generalissimo Chiang is part of a conspiracy to bring in the Japanese to assist him in his unification of China. Which one of these rumors can be true?"

Zhao regarded the lamp in front of him.

"Everyone these days sees a conspiracy behind everything that happens," he said. "They suspect giant webs of conspiracy, thousands of conspirators planning, scheming, executing intricate, deliberate moves on the great chessboard. These suspicions are a sign of the times. The world is overcome with changes, and if you read the sutras, you know that suffering comes from resistance to change. Everyone now is terrified and resistant. Everyone wants to think that someone, somewhere, is in charge. They see conspiracies because they want to see them. So much more comfortable to think that some omnipotent power is in control, even if that power is sinister, than to look at the reality of the situation. Which is that no one at all is in control."

"You terrify me," I said quietly.

"I doubt it." He smiled.

"What about Li Shi? Does my brother think as you do?"

Zhao shrugged. "Li Shi is an anomaly of sorts. He knows no one is in control, but he wishes ardently that someone could be. He wants to follow an admirable man. He wants to believe. But fate, and his own strong character, have placed him in the position of a leader. I've never really seen anyone like him, a born leader who wishes only to follow. He's an idealist, your brother."

"An idealist?" I exclaimed. "Li Shi is the most realistic, practical man in the world. Everyone says so. He's an opportunist. Look how quickly he leaped from the side of the Emperor to the side of the republicans to your side. Even I see him for what he is."

"No one understands Li Shi. Except me. Because when I was younger, I was just like him. But in the roughness and exertions of life, I found that I liked being without anyone I truly admired and wanted to follow. Because then I could do as I wished. I could always break free of entanglements. But the freedom and clarity of mind that comes with that realization is very frightening. I am a bird flying over a flooded valley. I can stay above the waters indefinitely, on the strength of my own wing, but there is no branch for me to set my foot on and rest secure. Such a place would in any case only be a delusion. Li Shi knows what I know, but he yearns for a resting place nevertheless."

Zhao picked up his ceramic wine cup and turned it gently in his hands, rubbing its warmth between his palms. He looked down the length of the table, and I wondered what he was thinking.

"Surely," I began hesitantly, "we are not as alone as all that? Do we not have our friends, our blood relatives? Can the ties between these people change?"

"Indeed, we have others," Zhao agreed, looking again at me. "But even those who care for us the most can have a change of heart."

"What leads you to such a hard view?" I asked, distressed in my heart and surprised to find myself so anxious to pull this strange man back from the desert he had wandered into. "Look about you. There are mothers who care for children, husbands who care for wives. Friends who die for each other."

"All true. But let me tell you about something." He poured more wine for both of us. "We are both a little drunk, and it is very late, so I will tell you this in the nature of a secret, and you will see my innermost self."

"I'm not afraid of it," I said.

"When I was a boy, I was my father's favorite. He taught me to read and write poetry. He taught me to ride and shoot a bow. He took me to hunt with him, on a fine black mare. I was his confidant in all matters. He loved me far more than he loved my sisters and, of course, more than he loved my mother. I spent every waking moment with him. And he made me promise him that we two would have an unbreakable bond, no matter what happened. He would often laugh that if bandits came, we two would fight back to back and never desert each other. And I was a romantic boy; I thought nothing would be finer than to fight and die by my father's side.

"But my father became very ill. He began to look upon me with suspicion, and accused me of turning against him. But I had done nothing to betray him, I had only been loyal, endlessly loyal. My mother begged him to see doctors, and one day when he became violent, she locked him in his study. But he crashed his fist through the glass window and came, blood dripping from his arm, into the hall, where we all stood in fear and irresolution. We clung to one another when we saw he had a knife in his hand. My father walked past every servant, past my sisters, past my mother, straight to me. He grabbed my arm and brought me close to his face, and held the knife right under my eye, with the point touching the skin.

" 'I will kill you for your betrayal, my disloyal son,' he breathed."

Zhao paused a second to empty his cup.

"But he didn't kill me. He cut his own throat, as he stood above me, and my father's blood spurted onto my face. And at the very moment he slid the knife across his jugular, I realized that I indeed had abandoned him, because I was glad he was killing himself instead of me."

I covered my eyes with my hand. Zhao's voice came again, with a final, calm inflection. "Nothing on this earth frightens me now."

When we finally rose from the table, it was almost midnight. A night mist had settled on the canal outside the window, partially obscuring the yellow half-moon, which now lay perilously close to the dim horizon. The plates had been cleaned away long before, and the servant stood in a corner of the room, suppressing his yawns. I felt dizzy with the wine, and drifted slowly into the central hall, where I sat down carefully on a divan. Zhao followed me, and took a large armchair nearby.

"Have you ever thought of remarrying?" he asked.

"It isn't really done among widows of my class," I replied, sinking back among the cushions.

Zhao began peeling an apple he took from a small yellow pile in a bowl on the table. "I think you should remarry," he said, wielding his knife.

"Whom shall I marry?" I smiled.

Zhao set the peeled and cored apple in front of me, and gestured that I should take it. "You might think of marrying me, for example."

I regarded him over the apple. "I see you are serious," I said.

He was silent.

I leaned forward and placed my hand on his wrist. "I think highly of you. But I can't marry you."

"I didn't think so. Please, don't look so devastated. I understand you completely."

"I feel that you do. But why did you wish to marry me? I thought, judging from what you said at dinner . . ."

Zhao smiled at me as he peeled a second apple for himself. "You are not very much like other women I have known," he said. "I feel as if change does not frighten you."

I sat in my chair, looking away out the window, and thought about what he had said. Zhao sat peacefully, eating his apple, as if waiting for me to answer was as pleasurable a way to pass the time as any other.

"I don't fear change," I said finally. "My life, once I married, was without hope or tenderness. My days were bitter. Any change could only be better than what I had before."

Zhao finished his apple and placed the core delicately at the edge of the plate. He wiped his hands on a linen towel. "I think you will remarry, Mrs. Pan," he said, as he did these things. "Your heart is tender. You will marry a man you admire and respect. Then one day you will perhaps realize that you love him as well. On that day, you will begin to fear change."

My voice when I spoke again had a tremor in it. "Will I also then cease to be lonely?" I asked.

"No. Love doesn't do that. Strangely enough."

I tried to laugh, ashamed of my fears. "Then what good is love?" I asked.

"I don't know." Zhao smiled. "But everyone seems to want it anyway."

It was one o'clock in the morning when I left Zhao's house, escorted by the same young soldier, who had fallen asleep in the hallway waiting for me. The cool mist that I had observed from the window lying on the canal was spreading through the streets slowly, shadowing corners, blurring outlines. I thanked the young soldier at my door, and tried to give him a coin, which he refused. He ran off into the fog, his form disappearing long before the last of his footsteps had echoed away.

24

*I*t was now late winter, and the air was cold, a welcome change from the damp oven-heat of Hunan summers. On my way to school, I stopped at the Pan mansion in the morning to pick up the pot I had left full of food on the step the night before. I rounded the corner and started down the narrow old street to the familiar stone doorstep, now the only portion of the mansion that still welcomed me. For years, I had walked to the gate every morning, trailing my fingers along the rain-faded wall, awaited patiently by the familiar squat shape and dull gleam of the cook pot resting on the paving stone. But today, even from a hundred feet away with the glare of the early sun in my eyes, I saw that there was nothing on the doorstep. I broke into a run.

I pounded on the gate with my fist, shouting for the Pans—calling them Mama and Baba still, even though those endearments had not passed my lips for years. I scrabbled desperately at the door, but it was an old-fashioned kind without a handle or lock on the outside, a relic of those far-gone days when houses were never empty, when there would always be some servant or other at home. I threw my shoulder against the gate again and again, shouting for help all along. People began looking out their windows. Finally the rusty latch gave way, and I fell to the ground inside. I ran through the front courtyard, my rushing feet kicking up the dead leaves on the walk, and burst through the rotting front door into the central hall.

A thick blanket of dust lay on the floor and blew up into the air as I ran past, mingling with the dull stink of staleness. The Pans sat dead in their great carved wooden chairs, their bodies and their chairs the only furniture left in the hall except for the altar to the ancestors. Old Pan slumped against the back of his chair like a sack of meal, his body inside his ragged gray gown limp and yielding and empty. Madame Pan sat rigid in her seat, her dead fingers clutching the arms like the claws of a bird, her face turned up to the ceiling as if she were straining even then to rise. The cook pot—with the barest scrap remains of the rice and chicken I had cooked for them yesterday littering the bottom and sides—sat between them on the floor, two large old spoons sticking out. They must have squatted on the floor to eat out of the pot and then painfully straightened their old legs to sit again in the chairs. I clutched my stomach, which suddenly ached with the acid feeling that had I stayed, their deaths would not have been so pitiful and so undignified. I should have kept their clothes clean, should have fed them gently from the pot like newborns, should have washed them tenderly. I was afraid that they might have felt great pain as they died. I am cursed forever, I thought, and I deserve to be.

I began to bawl like a child. As I stood with tears running down my cheeks, I heard the running footsteps of the alarmed neighbors, brought finally into the house by my cries and the crashing of the gate. I heard them gasp in horror at the sight of the dead. I sensed them clinging to each other with fear, trying to avoid the bad luck that spread through the musty air. Their eyes burned into my bent back, searching my grief for an explanation.

The local constables took the bodies away for examination by the coroner. I stood nearby with my mother and sister, who had both arrived within the hour. Graceful Virtue held my hand. My mother stood in front of me, barring the gazes of the curious and preventing the constables from speaking to me.

"Not now. Have you no shame?" she told one of them imperiously, holding out her arm to block him.

"It will have to go the examining magistrate," the chief constable muttered. "No one saw them die. If anything strange is going on, she will have to answer to the authorities."

"Let the magistrate himself speak to her, then. I do not allow it for now." My mother turned and led me and Graceful Virtue through an archway into the adjoining room, closing the shabby red curtain firmly behind us with a great clatter of curtain rings.

"Shh," my mother whispered. "Or all the bumpkins outside will hear you."

I smothered my sobs, and wiped my eyes on the kerchief my sister held out.

"Listen to me," my mother said softly, leaning closer. "There will be an investigation. I do not doubt there will be an autopsy."

"Why?" I whispered. "They were both old. Their deaths would come some day."

"At exactly the same hour?" She shook her head and came even closer to whisper in our ears. "My child, do you have any idea why the old Pans might have died in the night? Any idea at all?" Her black eyes scrutinized me from the delicate web of wrinkles that surrounded them.

"No, I don't. I really don't." My voice was hoarse with anxiety and a kind of lurking disbelief.

Graceful Virtue frowned with worry. My mother's voice sounded hollow like a drum. They took my arms, and we walked out of the house. The bodies lay in the weak winter sunlight, wrapped in undyed rough cloth and laid on the back of a wagon. Faces stared from every window and door and gate and alleyway. The driver whipped up his sagging mule, and the wagon rumbled off down the lane, taking the Pans away from their great house.

We went to Zhao Han Ren's office later the same day. He held in his hands a preliminary report from the constables. A scribe sat behind Zhao, writing down everything we said on a tablet of lined paper, using a steel pen whose scratching nib wore on my nerves. As I sat down across from him, Zhao tapped a document on the desk with his forefinger.

"The coroner's memorial of first impression. He diagnoses poison; he thinks it was the red poison. He will conduct an autopsy to be certain. Normally, family members protest the autopsy. As you know, they are afraid dismemberment of the body will keep the spirit on the earth as a ghost. But there are no family members in this case. Unless you, of course, wish to register an official complaint." He blew out a cloud of cigarette smoke.

The scribe scribbled industriously. Zhao's face was unreadable, his eyes curiously shuttered, as they had been the first time I met him.

"I don't wish to obstruct any investigation," I murmured.

"No? Good. Then we'll get on with it. No, keep your mouth closed. Say nothing to me. Li Shi and your brother-in-law Mo Chi have been sent for. They are coming in from the field now. Magistrate Sung and his new deputy magistrate, Wu Guai Er, will handle the investigation. You understand that I must stay apart from the case myself, in light of my friendship with your brother. I can't allow any allegations of favoritism to taint the

Guomindang Party. But Magistrate Sung and his deputy are just and intelligent men. And neither of them come from Changsha. They do not owe their appointments here to me. If you have done nothing"—he paused to clear his throat—"then you have nothing to fear."

I nodded, my eyes on the floor. "Thank you," I murmured. "Thank you, sir."

The attending officer escorted me away. As I left the room, I could not help looking over my shoulder at Zhao, searching for some sign from him that he believed me to be innocent. But he had already turned his back on me, his head bent over the black and red markings on the report in his hand. His dark outline against the light from the window looked like that of a great bird of prey. I thought about what Zhao had said, about resting places being only delusions.

A crowd was assembled in the street outside Zhao's office, behind a row of Zhao's soldiers. How I yearned for them to hoot and jeer at me! I even yearned for them to throw rocks. Anything was better than the avid curiosity that met me, the sly, cynical, or horrified looks arranged all around. A band of them followed us all the way home, murmuring among themselves. We could not shake off their closeness, not until the gate of my mother's house closed on their faces.

A strong wind sprang up just as I arrived home and grew throughout the evening in blind fury, rattling the branches on the trees and driving the dust and encrusted snow of the roads before it with the force of arrowheads. That night I sat on the cold floor and wept into my mother's lap. Yong Li crouched nearby, squatting on her hams like a countrywoman. Occasionally she reached out and touched my foot in sympathy.

"This is what comes of not having done my duty to the Pans," I cried bitterly. "Had I stayed with them, they would have had someone nearby at the end. And I would not now be in this position. Heaven punishes me, and I will pay for this with my life."

My mother raised my face, her hand under my chin. "Listen," she said. "The Pans would have done this thing one day, whether you stayed or not. To be candid, your presence was not a comfort to them. You galled them like a sore. And I could see in their faces when I came to take you away that day that they were already dying of their own pride and fury. If you lived there, they might have found some way to do you an injury. And when the end came, you would be involved much more deeply than you are even now. Because, as it is, the old ones deliberately set you a trap."

I gasped in disbelief; I heard Yong Li behind me murmur in anger. The wind howled outside in the darkness, clamoring at the windows, hurling itself against the sturdy walls of my mother's small house.

My mother nodded with great assurance. "Yes, I accuse them. I accuse them to you, and to you, Yong Li, and to all the ghost spirits that surround us. They knew you would be blamed, my daughter. They are doing their best—even now, from the next world—to kill you along with their own selves. As it is, you may yet be well. But had you lived in that house with them, with so many opportunities to frame you more surely, there would now be no escape for you."

"But Mother," I whispered, chilled, "if this is a trap, why not leave a message blaming me directly?"

The wind suddenly groaned so loudly that my mother did not bother to answer immediately, and the three of us huddled together, listening to the raucous sounds of the world, until the noise fell a little. My mother cocked her head, listening with great attention.

My mother spoke again. "Because I know these old ones. I remember such ancestors from the world of my youth. They cannot go before the chief judges of hell having made an actual false accusation—they would be condemned forever. They simply committed suicide, but in such a manner that it could only point to you. That is both the strength and the weakness of their plan. I'm sure they realized that too"—and here the wind raged—"but there was nothing they could do about it."

She looked up at the ceiling, at the creaking rafters, her eyes watchful as if she expected the roof to fall in at any moment. We heard a great branch from the elm tree in the garden break with a tearing sound like cloth, and heard the dull noise of its crash. A flurry of leaves leaped against the window, startling us.

"What a strange storm," she remarked after a moment. "No rain, no thunder or lightning. Just this terrible wind."

Yong Li crept closer to my mother's skirts. "Madame, this wind is like a live thing," she said softly, shaking her head.

I expected my mother to reprove Yong Li for being a superstitious fool, but she only nodded slowly. "Yes," she said. "I think you may be right." She looked at the ceiling again, then all around the room.

"It's very cold," my mother said. "Listen. I have some little paper images of the Amita Buddha. The younger Mrs. Luo gave them to me at last New Year. She's become devout, and who can blame her, married to

Young Luo. Get them from my desk, Yong Li. We'll put them in all the windows and stick them on all the doors."

Yong Li ran out of the room, hurrying through the darkened house with a small lantern whose tiny flame I could just see glimmering at the end of the hall before it disappeared upstairs. While she was gone, the wind roared so loudly that the walls shook as if they were paper and we heard the crash of a roof tile as it was ripped off the top of the house and dashed to the ground. A strong draft blew in through the chimney, and I shivered. Then the lantern glowed again in the hall, and Yong Li was back with a sheaf of little paper Buddhas in red and gold.

"Mother, why are we doing this?" I asked.

She took a long time answering. She handed us both paper Buddhas to hang.

"It's an evil night," she said finally, getting up without looking at us. "I feel as if ghosts are near." She put one of the images in the nearest window, propping it up so Amita Buddha could look outside and repel the bad forces. She walked across the room and propped up another little Buddha at the opposing window. In the main window that looked toward the garden gate, she set up a small hand mirror, the most powerful repellent force of all, which, like tai chi, turns the attacker's own strength against him. She faced us again, her face very somber and her eyes dark with some strange emotion.

"They are miserable, angry, jealous ghosts," she said.

The windows rattled as if someone were trying to force their way inside.

"Their own bad deeds drive them mad with rage."

We stood uneasily in the center of the center room, our Buddhas on guard at every window, and looked all around, as if the walls might buckle.

"I hear their voices in the wind," my mother said. Her voice trembled, I realized with a faint surprise, not with fear but with pity.

All night long we sat awake, a single lamp throwing its jerking shadows on the whitewashed walls. Listening, listening, listening, to the screaming of my demons outside.

Graceful Virtue went to school to tell them that I was taking a leave of absence to put on mourning for the Pans. Li Shi and Mo Chi arrived from their regiments in the field and posted a guard at my mother's gate. Li Shi came several times to see me, but mostly he was closeted with Zhao Han

Ren. Jin Yu visited me every day and once pushed a gawker outside the gates so hard he fell to the frozen ground.

A week after the Pans' bodies had been found, I received a notice to be interviewed by Deputy Magistrate Wu. My hands shook as I read the official letter, and I covered my face with them. The strain of waiting for the magistrate's summons had turned a small streak of my hair white overnight, which my mother dyed darker with tea and carefully combed under, so no one could guess I was worried. Now that the summons had finally arrived, I felt no relief, but only a new and greater pressure.

My mother took my hands away from my face. "Exclude useless emotion," she said firmly. "You will need all your strength."

I walked alone into the hall where the magistrate's court was held. A constable on duty alone there waved me down a long hallway with a polished wood floor, on which my cloth shoes slipped. At the end was a moderate-sized office with a desk and a scribe sitting behind the door. The deputy magistrate rose from the desk as I entered.

I stood before him, my eyes downcast. "This person is surnamed Liang," I began mumbling nervously.

"There's no need to refer to yourself in such an outmoded way. Just use the personal pronoun," Wu Guai Er said. I looked up at him.

"Are you Mrs. Pan?" he asked.

"Yes," I said. "I am."

"Mrs. Pan," said Wu Guai Er, "we've never met before, have we?"

I shook my head. "No, we haven't."

He turned to the scribe. "Make sure you note that fact in the official minutes of this interview." I sat down in the chair across from him and looked at him curiously. He was in his early thirties, his boyish face clean-shaven, and he wore wire-rimmed spectacles. His dark eyes had a steady and resolute gaze, and shone with eagerness. For the first time, I saw that he wore the white armband of mourning around his arm, a sign of recent personal loss. I knew the white band was not for me, but it seemed like a bad omen.

"Governor Zhao has given me all the reports," he said quietly. "I wish to inform you that the coroner has finished his autopsies of the bodies and has concluded very definitely that they were poisoned." Beneath the table, I could see his legs in black trousers, and his polished black English shoes. Behind him stood the newly designed national flag.

"Wait," I said heavily. Deputy Wu looked at me in surprise. "I hate suspense," I continued. "Please do me the courtesy of telling me now if you think me guilty or innocent. I am not strong enough to wait until the end of this conversation to find out."

Deputy Wu looked surprised. "I found the poison bottle myself three nights ago at the Pan house, Mrs. Pan. Constables Liu and Hsin were with me. It was an earthenware jar, and it had been smashed into pieces in the garden, and leaves raked over the pieces. The coroner tells me that he has found traces of arsenic on the shards. Indeed, the jar was one of those old-style pharmacist's jars from twenty or thirty years ago, and the contents probably just as old. I believe the Pans killed themselves."

I leaned forward on the desk with relief. "How did you find the jar, if it was smashed into a thousand pieces?" I asked.

"Because I was looking for it. Although I admit the remains of the jar weren't easy to find. For one thing, the wind kept blowing out our lanterns. We must have used up two boxes of matches. But if you had murdered them, I could not see why you would do it in a way which would point directly to you. You and you alone brought food to them every day. You are an educated woman. Why should you do away with them in such an obvious fashion? Why wait years to do it? And why not just take the jar away with you, instead of smashing it on the grounds of the house? Their deaths did not benefit you. They had no money to leave you, is that not correct? Yes, I thought so. And then of course, I had many testimonials as to your character. I did not think you had killed them."

"Then everything is now all right?" I breathed.

"Well, Mrs. Pan. I did wonder at first how a jar of arsenic got into the house. I wondered if they had asked you to bring it to them."

"No. They never communicated with me. And I certainly would not have allowed them to kill themselves."

"Yes, I know that now," Wu Guai Er said. "As I said, the appearance of the jar was quite old-fashioned. I had the archives of the Pharmacists' Guild searched. You know they are required to maintain records on all poisons sold for a period of one hundred years. You didn't know? Well, eight secretaries for four days went looking, and they found that several years before you married the young master, a woman from the Pan household purchased a jar of arsenic to kill the wasps in the eaves."

"My goodness," I said, suddenly remembering. "That must be right. We always were plagued by wasps under the roof. They had built their nests there."

"So your maid Yong Li tells me."

I was surprised. "You spoke to her?"

"Yesterday. But I swore her to silence, so don't blame her. I didn't want you to know anything until I had finalized my conclusions."

"In case I was guilty?"

Wu Guai Er bowed his head, slightly abashed. "Yes. I questioned her at length, without telling her what I was trying to find out, in case she wanted to lie for you. She is younger than you, is she not? She was a child in the Pan household when you went there as a bride. She remembered a jar of the same description appearing one day in the mistress's private cabinet. She was spanked and told to stay away by Old Lady Pan herself. Yong Li forgot all about it until I questioned her. She didn't know it had contained poison."

I lowered my head in fatigue and gratitude.

"You've been cleared, Mrs. Pan," Wu Guai Er said. "I'll put everything into an official report to Magistrate Sung. You won't have further problems."

"I owe you my life, Deputy Magistrate Wu," I murmured.

Wu Guai Er simply shook his head and smiled. His smile seemed tender to me.

When I entered the gate at my mother's house, I could hear the sounds of my family speaking quietly in the main hall. I could distinguish Jin Yu's voice, as clearly as a temple gong. But I didn't go inside right away. I found Yong Li in the rear near the kitchen. As soon as she saw my face, she jumped up and threw her arms around me with relief.

"Elder Sister, I'm sorry I didn't tell you about my interview with Deputy Wu," she sighed, "but he made me promise to keep quiet. He said it would hurt your interests to be told until everything was settled."

"I'm not angry," I said. "You were right to obey him." I drew her down to sit next to me on the stoop. "Listen, Yong Li. Did you tell him the truth about the jar? About remembering finding it as a child?"

Yong Li nodded. "Yes, it was the truth. I hardly remembered it because I was so small. But it was two or three years before you married the master. I used to be able to get into every cupboard, and I would look inside them all regularly. You know how children are. I liked the old lady's cabinet best, because she had all her perfumes and rouges in there. I found the jar there one day. I was trying to open it when Old Lady Pan came in and found me. She really walloped me that day, and told me that thing was dangerous and could kill me. So I never touched it again."

I leaned back on my elbow. "I believe you, Yong Li. I have never known you to lie, and I don't think you would do it even for me. But I can't help wondering. What was arsenic to kill wasps doing in the old lady's makeup cabinet? Why didn't the gardener have it? And why did we still have wasps when I got there?"

Yong Li looked down at her hands and twisted the cloth she held into a tight screw.

I looked at her closely. The sky was growing dark, and the wintry air bit at my hands and cheeks. "Yong Li?" I asked. "What is it?"

She turned to me with a desperate movement. "Elder Sister, last night, after I spoke to Deputy Wu, I came home and I was very troubled. Because recounting it all to him made me start to remember something else. You must never tell anyone this."

"What is it?"

She twisted her hands again and drew close, her voice dropping until it was barely audible. "I saw that jar twice. Once was in the old mistress's cabinet, like I told you."

I listened with all my strength.

"The second time"—Yong Li looked around fearfully and put her mouth to my ear—"I saw it at the bedside of the young mistress the night we found she had disappeared."

"Young mistress?" I whispered, momentarily confused. "Wait, do you mean Wang Mang's sister? The one who went away? The one who was married in Kunming?"

Yong Li was struggling with her memories. "The one they said went away," she choked. "We in the house always thought she ran away, because one night she disappeared. The old ones put it out that she had eloped, that they were displeased but everything had turned out for the best because she married the lover. But no one ever saw her again, she never came to visit. The young master never mentioned her name again, but it was after she left that he started to drink so much. He was different before."

"Yong Li, do you know what you are saying? How did you see the jar?"

"Her personal maid heard a noise and came in unexpectedly. She found the young lady's bed empty that night and raised the alarm. I ran in, and now I'm sure I saw the jar on the table. Just for a second. Then someone took it away."

"Yong Li, this is very important. Did you see the jar at her bedside before or after you saw it in the old lady's cabinet? Think, now. When the poison jar came into the house, whose hands held it first? Yong Li, who bought the poison?"

Yong Li was crying now. "I don't remember, Elder Sister. I really don't. I guess I forgot about it completely because I thought it was a dream. Because someone told me it was a dream."

"Who? Who told you it was a dream?"

"The old master. He told me I was not to worry about anything I had seen in the young lady's bedroom, because it was all a dream. I must have believed him, because I forgot everything." Yong Li was sobbing now, muffling the noise by biting down on the dishcloth.

"What else did you see in the bedroom that night?" I asked fearfully. "Did you see anyone in the bed? Maybe under the covers?"

But Yong Li shook her head. "I don't remember anything else, Elder Sister. I thought it was all a dream, so I forgot about it."

I sat on the steps with her for a while, with my arm around her while she cried. I thought of a hundred different explanations, and none of them made me happy. I knew this was a secret locked away in the past, that everyone who knew it was dead. Only Yong Li and I remained now, and we could only wonder.

When I went inside the house, I found my family and Jin Yu waiting for me, and I told them what had happened at the deputy magistrate's office. Li Shi put his arm around my shoulders with a great laugh. Graceful Virtue embraced me tenderly, and my mother held hands with Jin Yu. As we stood together in the middle of the room, our voices rising with laughter and relief, the wooden shutters on one of the windows blew open with a bang. We turned around to stare. The gust of icy air blew sand into our eyes and snapped at our clothes. We all blinked. Then the window shutter crashed back into place again, and the window was shut once more. I heard their angry voices for the last time in my life. Then the voices faded away.

25

"*I* wanted to thank you," I said to Wu Guai Er.

The deputy magistrate sat across the desk from me. He was wearing a gray Western suit, with the white armband of mourning I had seen before. His hair was brushed straight back from his boyish face, and his wire-rim spectacles glinted. His desk was next to an open window; from the court-yard outside, the earliest spring leaves from the cassia trees drifted in softly, scattering themselves on the wooden writing surface. His bicycle sat out-side on the paving stones, its metal handlebar digging a small indentation into the crumbling old wall. I was surprised at myself for coming back to him so soon. As I sat there, I began to think I wanted to come every day, to see his calm face.

"No thanks are necessary," he said, shaking his head. "Justice is done."

"Well, I give thanks for justice."

"Justice is the least that we should all expect. I don't give thanks for that which should be done in the ordinary course. I have done you no favors."

"How idealistic you are!"

Guai laughed at this. "I'm not idealistic at all. It's curious, I always think. Everyone else expects to be kicked like a dog. I expect to be treated as a man. Yet I am supposed to be the one who is eccentric."

"We stayed away from you for your own good," Teacher Yang said, standing in his hallway and holding my hand firmly. Jin Yu, at his left shoul-der, and Mao Zedong, standing to the right of him, both nodded vigor-ously. All the people in the room nodded also. "I don't want you to think that the comrades in this room didn't care about you. But we didn't want to muddy the waters by introducing a political element, which would maybe have given the authorities an excuse to hurt us through you, or in-deed, hurt you because of us."

"I know," I said, returning the pressure of his hand gladly. "I knew that was the case even then. I didn't wonder for a moment. I want you to know that I never doubted your loyalty, or Jin Yu's. In fact, I was afraid Mao might come anyway, to my detriment, just to embarrass the new officials or make a point about the feudal oppression of daughters-in-law."

Mao and everyone else laughed heartily at this, but Jin Yu and Teacher Yang glanced at each other. Later, the others crowded into the dining room to eat, standing up around the table, holding bowls and chopsticks in their hands and picking up food from the platters. Jin Yu's husband, Cai Hesen, whispered to me then, "Mao did want to make an example of some sort with your case. Anyway, an opportunity to show the officials in a bad light. Jin Yu and Teacher and I prevented him, because we were afraid it would affect you adversely."

I put my hand on his arm, my skin warm with gratitude. I had always liked Hesen, from the first time I met him.

"You are her childhood friend," he went on. "She would not have missed such a political opportunity for anyone else." He glanced up to make sure she was not nearby. "Not even for me."

"I was a student in Japan for a few years," Guai said. "I know all your Communist friends went to France. Strangely enough, all the colleagues in my party went to Japan. Anyway, when I came back, I gave my portion of the land inheritance from my grandfather to my brothers. Then I joined the Guomindang. Chiang Kai Shek will unify the country, I knew even then. So my place was to try to make that unification mean something, with the just administration of government. Unification by itself would just be an extension of tyranny."

"You gave away property?" I asked incredulously.

"I didn't want any distractions. I can't let considerations of personal gain stand in the way of doing what is right."

"What if you are not appointed to permanent office, when that day comes?"

"I'm not afraid. I can live on very little. The problem with today is that too many Chinese think of money only. They are not patriotic. They want land and gold. People in my own party are like that."

"It's human to not want to be poor," I said.

"Well, the easiest way to stop fearing poverty is not to crave wealth."

"And if you have wealth, you can have more influence. You can change things for the better." I was surprised at how anxious I was to persuade him.

"Maybe. But there are a lot of wealthy people with influence. And they are my friends. I don't need money to have influence. I just need moral authority."

I looked at him with an expression of mingled exasperation and admiration. "Then you will be the only man in five thousand years to retire from the imperial service a poor man. There has only ever been one river of gold in the nation."

"What imperial service? We have a democracy now," Guai said firmly. "Or at least, the beginnings of one. I hope the people can accept democracy, if we bring it to them."

"No one is against democracy."

"Well, not in principle. But the problem with democracy is that it's petty and boring. People's tastes are constantly jaded by the pleasures of both flesh and intellect. So they always want excitement. And the leaders always want glory, fame, and adulation. Democracy is unsatisfactory to them, because its business is very ordinary, and often rather halfway and compromised. People prefer grand schemes, violent revolutions, red banners, marching armies, pure motives. All these things are much more picturesque, more artistic, more thrilling, than dull old democracy. It takes a very strong mind to be a real democrat. You have to resist a desire for perfection, which can't exist in reality. The perfect is the enemy of the good."

He moved various objects around on his desk, shifting the positions of the inkstone, the brushes, and the brush rest, in a manner reminiscent of a chess game. The wind blew hard enough outside that I could hear the rushes along the ditch outside the wall, sweeping the air with their gentle stems.

"I hope everything comes out as you hope," I said. I wanted him to look at me again.

He glanced up, his face warm with pleasure. "I'm so glad you understand what I am saying." His gaze held mine, and I suddenly found myself deeply moved by the great and steady faith with which he addressed the world.

Wu Guai Er, I thought to myself, I saw from the beginning you were a just and honest man. But now I see that you are extraordinary.

"May I ask about the white armband?" I murmured, on another day, after I had run into him at the fruit market and he had invited me to his office to sit down.

He looked at me as if surprised, but only nodded.

"Who is it that you mourn?" I asked.

He looked away, as if embarrassed. "My wife died in childbirth years ago. She was still just a teenager then, I myself barely older than that. The child died also."

"You must really mourn her, to wear the armband all these years." I felt a curious knot in my stomach, which I could barely recognize as jealousy. Would anyone mourn me in this way?

"Well, we had only an arranged marriage. But she was a kindhearted girl, and she was very young. I felt very badly at her death. In some very painful way, I felt that her death was also the death of my own childhood." He touched the armband gently with his fingertips. "I don't know why I still wear it. Well, I do know. It keeps my parents from arranging another marriage for me. But I think I also wear it because it marks my state. Have you seen the line the water makes at the edge of a pond? This"—he touched the armband—"is my watermark."

"You are very solemn, to mark your state in life. The rest of us never think to do it."

"Solemnity is my worst flaw," he said, laughing. "It's a great temptation to be solemn, but it is almost the opposite of being serious."

"So what is your state?"

"I am between lives. I am no longer a student, really no longer a youth. I have buried my wife. But I feel as if I have not yet fully reached a man's estate. I look like one, and I fill the position of one, and I make decisions every day like one. Yet there is a part of my heart still childish and undeveloped, and which I wish to see fully unfold. Then I'll take off my armband."

"What . . . what part would that be?" I mumbled, in an agony of trepidation, but desperate to know.

He shook his head. "I'm too embarrassed to say."

He piled the tangerines we had bought into a painted tin bowl on his desk, carefully balancing one on top of the other. Standing there, he peeled one open tenderly with his slim fingers.

"Here," he said, handing me the peeled fruit. "You must be hungry, so late in the day."

My hands shook slightly as I put a sweet slice into my mouth.

"Good, yes?" he asked. He smiled at me, his white teeth gleaming, and handed me another piece. "Go on, eat it." I obeyed in silence. I was shocked to feel tears running down my face, but looking at him and his steady smile, I started to laugh as well, hiccuping a little from the tears. Guai only kept smiling, and handed me more fruit, one slice after another, the sweet of the fruit and the salt of my tears mingling in my mouth. He ate some himself, until the entire tangerine was gone. He took out his handkerchief, a large cotton square, and blotted the tears from my cheeks. Taking my hand in his, he wiped my hand clean.

"Sweet, but messy," he said, then immediately blushed to the roots of his hair. He stuffed his kerchief into his sleeve. He took his glasses off and polished them vigorously on the end of his scarf. "I mean, of course, the tangerine."

"I feel it's my duty to warn you about him," Jin Yu snapped. We were standing in the hall of her parents' house, where she and Hesen were staying on one of their periodic fleeting trips to Changsha. Upstairs, her children played—they sounded very distant, as if they were several miles away.

"About Guai? Why warn me?" I said, trying not to get angry.

"Jin Yu," said Hesen warningly. "I thought you said you weren't going to say anything."

She turned on him, an expression of angry frustration on her pale face. "I suppose you expect me to keep my mouth shut and say nothing, while my friend here simply leaps off a cliff?"

Hesen looked away.

"What do you mean, warn me?" I shouted.

"Guai is a Guomindang official," said Jin Yu through gritted teeth, in a tone of voice that sounded like a sneer. "If he is truly as good a man as you say, then he must be a tool or a puppet of the evil masters at the head of his party."

"He is neither a tool nor a puppet!" I cried. "How can you speak this way? Am I not your dearest friend? Would I say such things to you?"

Before Jin Yu could answer, Hesen intervened, this time more firmly. "Stop, stop, you two. Jin Yu, maybe you should ask your mother when we eat." Jin Yu stormed away and slammed the door behind her. The hostile sound echoed through the halls.

Hesen took me out to sit with him in the garden. We sat next to each other in silence for a while, our heads bowed in the sunshine. I tossed a pebble into the carp pond, which made Hesen turn to me.

"Don't be angry at Jin Yu, Little Sister. If you knew what was in her heart, you would be more forgiving."

"She dislikes Guai."

Hesen shook his head. "No, no. She doesn't. It would be more accurate to say she dislikes me."

I looked at him in surprise.

"It's true," he said. "Jin Yu is jealous, Jade Virtue. You are her oldest friend. From the time you were girls, you shared your thoughts with each other. But now you have a new person, whom you will marry, and he will be the recipient of your confidences. Jin Yu is angry because she is losing you."

"Jin Yu and I haven't shared our innermost thoughts in a while," I said. "She hasn't noticed that."

"She shares her thoughts now with Mao. I have been jealous of him for the same reason."

"Were you ever jealous of me, for that reason?" Hesen asked.

I did not answer.

"Exactly." He sighed. "That is the other half of the equation. She is also jealous of you because you admire Guai so much and have so many good things to say about him. She does not feel the same way about me. Maybe she did once, when she first knew me as Cai Chang's brother. Little Sister, I think she is tired of me."

"No!" I whispered. "You know Jin Yu, her attention wanders around like a mayfly. But you are her husband."

"You know that the latest thing from the theorists of the Party is free love," Hesen said sadly. "I mean, Jin Yu has taken up the concept. Over and over again, she has told me that we should only be together for as long as we feel like it. The minute there is any change in our feelings, we should part."

"She is so idealistic!" I exclaimed, then realized that I had said the same thing to Guai not long before. But it was true of Jin Yu in a way that was different from Guai.

"I used to be also, just as she is," said Hesen. "But I learned that idealism can be a very useful tool. You don't always suffer for your ideals. Sometimes ideals can be used to justify doing what you want to do anyway. What she wants, I think, is to leave me. And the theory of free love fits that desire."

"Is there someone else for her now? Not Mao?"

"No, not Mao, curiously enough. I don't think there is some other man, not in the way you mean. But her devotion to Mao's cause is complete. And I can't blame her. All the women in the Party are in love with him. Jin Yu is actually rather sardonic about him personally. But whatever else he may be, he is a true leader, which I am not. If I break with Mao, I break with Jin Yu. And we have two children."

"Do you want to break with her, Hesen?"

"No, I don't. Upon my life, I don't." He turned to me shyly. "You know, I love her. She has many flaws, she is selfish. Sometimes she is cruel. Often she makes me angry. She is very beautiful, but I love her not because of her beauty, but almost in spite of it. I see you nodding, you know what I mean." Hesen gazed out over the pond as if it were a vast ocean, brimming with salt and rough waves. "I knew when I married her that my heart would be pierced one day. But I also knew that with her, I would do things I would not otherwise have dared. And so I have done. I have fomented revolution in my country. I have spoken with the poor. I have shared my meals with enemies of the state. I have set myself against the eternal order of things."

"You have been a hero," I said, touching his arm. "You are all that is best in men."

We both looked down at the carp in the pool at our feet, watched their gaping mouths sucking at the surface, gulping air and insects and the thin green algae that lay at the edges on the water. The sun was setting, rolling along the top of the garden wall like a golden fruit.

"Perhaps I should have sought ordinary happiness," Hesen said. "But I am an ordinary man. I thought that in my life, I should try to grasp something exceptional."

The sun fell below the edge of the wall, and a gentle blue twilight spread through the garden. We heard footsteps on the gravel behind us, and turned to look. It was Jin Yu, holding a ceramic cup in her hand. She wore a penitent look on her face. She sat down on the bench between us, but with her body turned the other way, facing the gate that stood between her and the remaining imperfect world. She turned her pale face between us.

"I thought my two loved ones would share this cup of wine with me," she said. She smiled her heartbreaking smile at us. Hesen and I smiled back at her, and touched our lips in turn to the warm spot on the clay where her mouth had been.

.   .   .

"I've come to visit you, to tell you I am going to be married."

Zhao looked at me with an expression of polite but detached atten-tiveness.

"I am marrying the deputy magistrate, Wu Guai Er. I thought you should hear it from me personally."

"Well," he said, leaning back in his chair. "That was quick."

I said nothing, not wanting my irritation at this particular remark to register in my voice.

"He's a good man," Zhao said. "Genuinely good." His inflection was disconcerting.

"I think you believe that the world will be hard on Guai," I said. "Is that what you believe? He's been very successful so far, as you may know."

Zhao leaned back with a smile. "It's hard on everyone. But goodness can be just as tough as evil or self-interest. Look at you."

I bowed my head in embarrassment. "I'm not good," I murmured. "And anyway, if what you say is true, then why should anyone bother to be evil?"

"Because being good hurts more."

Zhao glanced away for a moment, and I felt a huge sense of relief, as if the weight of his eyes had been lifted off me. But his eyes came back to me.

"Why did you say you were marrying him?" he asked.

"I sincerely admire him, and I value his friendship," I said, stiffly. "I very much wanted to have him as my companion in life." As Zhao still didn't say anything, but simply kept looking at me, I said, "I'm sorry I didn't come to you sooner, but we didn't formally arrange it until just a day or so ago."

"Don't apologize. I admire your sense. Guai, you know, is one of these young men who confide in their wives. And so you have shifted your posi-tion, from the outside to the inside of someone's mind. Women always know what will make them happy. Please accept my sincerest congratula-tions."

For a brief moment, I felt a pang of regret about Zhao. I understood Guai. Zhao understood me. But these qualities were destined to be found in separate men. I tried to think a little about what Guai had said, about the perfect being the enemy of the good.

Zhao stood up and saw me to the garden gate, something he had never done before. Along the way he showed me the peonies he grew in profusion, fenced in with wooden stakes, the tamarind trees wreathed in vines, the giant old oak looming like an aging soldier by the tile-topped wall, stretching its limbs out into the lane, its leaves grieved by the wind.

"Guai thinks Chiang Kai Shek will unify China," I said, to break the odd silence. "Do you?"

"Someone will unify us," Zhao replied. "I wonder if we will like it."

I left him on the garden walk. When I looked back at him from the open gate, he was staring into the distance, holding his left arm in his right, stiffly, as if he still felt the old wound of the warlord's arrow.

The wedding announcement caused a scandal I had not anticipated. Widows of my social class did not remarry in those days. For many years, there had been talk of building a little gate in honor of my mother, somewhere not too close to her house so that she need not look immodest by passing her own monument every day. In the last year, a small subscription had been taken up among our neighbors and among wealthy do-gooders in the town. But when my impending marriage became known, the donations were withdrawn mysteriously within days, and the subscription canceled.

When I heard this, I was devastated. I rushed to my mother in tears to beg forgiveness. She was sitting calmly in her garden, arranging some flowers in a small jar. I flung myself on my knees at her side.

"Why are you sorry? Sorry for what?" My mother was alarmed at my reaction. "Get up, you'll get dirt on your skirt."

"The gate," I sobbed. "They won't build you the gate because of me. You deserve a gate. It's my fault."

My mother raised her eyebrows, genuinely surprised. "Why are you worried about the gate? Listen, Jade Virtue, I hope you do not let this gate foolishness keep you from marrying Guai. Guai is an excellent man. He has a good education, a good family background. He doesn't drink to excess. He will never beat you. I entirely approve. As for the gate . . ." She waved her hand. "Don't think about these external things. The gate is nothing."

"It is a tribute to your worthiness," I continued stubbornly.

"And with it I have purchased my child's happiness." She picked up a few more blossoms and began arranging them in the jar, tucking bits of leaf here and there. "Mrs. Lin is coming soon to show me her new grandson, so I have to hurry. You should wash your face, or she'll see you've been crying. Then she'll think something is wrong between you and Guai, and it will be too complicated to explain. Still so emotional, at your age." She plucked a leaf from the stem of the rose she was holding and inserted the bloom gently into the jar. But I still knelt there, and she looked at me again.

"I love him," I blurted out. "I'm marrying him for love." And it seemed that as I said it, it became true.

"Fine," my mother said. "Love is no more unreliable than any other reason for choosing a husband."

Fifty friends and relatives came to the wedding dinner, set up in Li Shi's hall on the hottest day of July. Everyone was fanning themselves with rice paper and silk fans, and the gentle rushing sound all the fans made moving together filled the hall like the distant sound of a brook. Zhao sat with Li Shi, as usual, and to my surprise, Teacher Yang insisted on sitting with them. They all seemed very at ease with each other, like old comrades who had gone their separate ways long ago, but who were meeting once more by chance and were happy for it. I put all the Communists at a table on the far side of the hall, from where they glowered at Zhao. Guai passed out packs of cigarettes to the guests. We posed for a photograph, paid for by Zhao as a wedding present. The photograph, which I had to leave behind in Changsha when I left China on one of the last boats from Canton, showed a scholarly young gentleman in steel-rimmed glasses and a woman—slightly plump and maybe still a little pretty—looking at the camera. We did not smile of course, but I thought that my eyes wore a look of serenity. There was no sedan chair; I walked to our new flat after the dinner, in a dark red dress.

After the guests had left, we found ourselves standing in the largest of the two little rooms we had rented in the rear courtyard of a shopfront. Neither of us had any property to bring to the marriage except what was now stacked in front of us—a carton of books and a cardboard suitcase each. The rooms were otherwise almost bare and echoed slightly to our voices; with each sound, a little dust shifted from the ceilings and settled gracefully onto the floor.

I sat down on my carton of books and smiled at my new husband.

"Well," Guai said. "Isn't this good."

"Very good," I agreed.

He gestured around at the empty space, at the empty whitewashed walls, innocent of paintings or pictures, at the last of the sunlight from the curtainless windows. A single red strip of paper, promising long life and happiness, had been pasted to the glass pane.

"I feel so free," he said, spinning in a circle in a comic way. I laughed at his playfulness, but suddenly felt an enormous sense of protectiveness. I grasped his cotton robe as he spun near me.

"Don't worry," I said earnestly. "I'll make a fortune for you. You'll accomplish everything you want."

"Material things aren't important," he assured me.

"You only think that because you grew up rich."

That night, as we prepared to go to bed, I felt nervous, like a young girl. Not the nervous dread I had felt when I married Wang Mang, a sensation that came from the sure realization that everything with Wang Mang would be just as terrible as I had feared. This anxiety seemed almost the opposite—the fear that perhaps nothing could possibly be so good without being self-deception. I can't turn a blind eye to the realities, I told myself sternly, as I sat on the edge of the bed, putting my fingers to my throat in a vain effort to still the throbbing vein there. He is younger than I am; we have no money; we differ politically; we both have strong characters and will certainly have many disagreements. There will be times when I will look at Guai and wonder why I was foolish enough to marry him. But I married Wang Mang because he seemed like the kind of man who was right for me to marry, and I had to turn myself into a block of wood just to survive. Guai was really all wrong, and no one approved of the match except my mother. Can it really be that this was not a question settled by reason, intellect, or willpower—that those things were a positive danger under the circumstances? That it was simply a matter of courage, of throwing all caution aside and flinging myself off the edge and into the air, and hoping for the best? Perhaps when it comes to love, the unwise course is the one that leads to life, with all its gladness and heartbreak, and the wise course leads only to a sort of living death, where neither success nor failure comes to remind you that you are a human being.

Guai stood before me and took my hand. I smiled up at him.

"Now, I know you are not a virgin," he said—blushing at having said this to me, even though I was his wife—"so I'm not sure why your hands are shaking,"

"It's been a long time since I've shared my room with anyone. It's strange getting ready for bed with you here."

He sat down next to me. "It will be just as it was before. The only difference will be that when you finally get under the quilt, I'll be there too."

26

My wedding to Guai was the last time that all of us would ever be together, for two months later, in September 1927, Mao Zedong led an armed revolt in the countryside. Jin Yu told me later that Mao had been ordered by the leaders of the Soviet Communist Party to prepare for such a thing, and even as he sat at my marriage banquet table, he was trying to raise support among the peasants and assemble weapons to assassinate landlords. Zhao Han Ren, for his part, sat at the same banquet while his soldiers were busy raiding Communist organizations, destroying their presses and their documents, and summarily executing the captured men in the streets. Apparently, some men can enjoy themselves at a feast under any circumstances.

This uprising by Mao's peasants—with an army of about two thousand men—was later written about in all the history books as the Autumn Harvest Uprising. He never reached Changsha; the army was swiftly suppressed by Zhao and Li Shi, and fell apart. Mao could no longer return to his home, and in October he took the remaining thousand or so men into the Jinggang Mountains south of the city. I never saw him again in person. He passed into history, into myth, into hero worship. I received one or two letters from him in the years to come, secretly passed on to me by Jin Yu, and it was always strange, as if the gods had written me. This guerilla-king, my friend, was eventually the cause of my own downfall, but I will come to that later.

Jin Yu had adamantly opposed the uprising. "They were too few, they had hoes and rakes as weapons. What did they expect? Mao would never have done it on his own, but the Soviets made him."

"Why take orders from Russians?" I asked. Since I had become Guai's wife, my conversations about these matters with Jin Yu now made me uncomfortable. But I did not want to say so, because it felt too much like making a choice between the two of them. I will straddle this fence while I can, I thought.

"Because Communism is a global movement, and they are in charge of it," Jin Yu answered wearily. "I tell you, nothing they instruct us to do will work in China. They just get us into trouble. We are going to have to break with them someday and find our own way."

Although Jin Yu never told me directly, I knew she was a spy for the Communists in Changsha. She continued her work organizing industrial workers and took me to see a Japanese-owned silk factory, where twelve-year-old girls plucked the silkworm cocoons from boiling water with their bare hands. I knew she used this work as a cover to organize cells for the Party. I never told her anything about Guai's work, and she seemed anxious to keep things from me in order to protect me. But I knew that she often traveled to Jinggang and took messages back and forth. Curiously enough, Governor Zhao and my brother knew it as well. Jin Yu's position was not secure in Changsha; she was often followed, and her mail opened. Li Shi's soldiers summarily shot Communists who were her comrades. But as yet, she had done nothing to cause them to act against her personally—she had not, for example, taken part in the Autumn Harvest Uprising—and she came from a prominent family. She conversed with Li Shi and Guai and even Zhao politely when I was present, displaying her usual charm. But they all averted their eyes from each other in the meanwhile, and avoided each other in the street. We carried on in this fashion for some time, pretending that all that existed between us—Jin Yu, myself, Guai, Zhao Han Ren, and Li Shi—were our private bonds of friendship, love, and blood relationship. All the violent revolutionary deeds and plans that separated us were left outside, like shoes at the door.

After Mao made his escape to Jinggang, Yang Kai Hui, Mao's wife, had to return to her father's house to live. Teacher Yang, fearful for her safety and that of her two sons, forbade her to leave for the mountains. He kept her very short on money so that she would have a harder time running away. She was further hindered by the fact that Mao never sent word as to exactly where he was at any time. She took to weeping hysterically, and Teacher Yang often had to lock her in his house. The children were sent to Mao's family in Shaoshan. When I visited Teacher Yang at his house, I could hear her sobs from the back. He himself seemed to have become a very old man overnight, his face suddenly fallen in, his teeth loose.

"Do you hear her?" he groaned to me. "I've lost my appetite listening to her. I won't have her die in the mountains. What will happen to my grandchildren if their mother is killed? But the only thing that terrifies her is that Mao will leave her forever."

I led Teacher Yang into the kitchen and seated him on a stool. I took out the pots and pans and began to prepare the food I had brought him. "I'm listening," I said. "But you must eat this soup when I'm done making it. I'll bring some to Kai Hui. Maybe she'll eat it from my hands."

Teacher Yang leaned his head against the wall. I could hardly bear to look at him, he seemed so wizened and so aged. I kept my eyes on the soup, and chopped up vegetables to throw into the pot.

"She says if she is away from him too long, he will get tired of being alone and he will leave her," he sighed. "I've told her she is his legal wife. It's better for her here in Changsha if everyone thinks he has abandoned her. And anyway, what other women can there be, in the Jinggang Mountains? Surely it is too difficult for any woman to survive up there with the male revolutionaries?"

I didn't say anything, although it seemed to me that any number of women of my acquaintance could survive in the mountains. I fed him the soup almost by force, pushing his shaking hand whenever the soup spoon had stayed still too long. Then I took a bowl into Kai Hui's darkened room. The shutters were closed, and the lamp unlit.

"Kai Hui, it's me. Jade Virtue." I spoke with a softness born out of my devotion to her father. "I made soup. You must eat some." I sat down next to her, and almost dropped the soup in amazement. If I had ever once thought of Kai Hui's face as being shuttered like an empty house, then it had changed completely. The most naked of emotions—fear, anger, impotence, and dreadful yearning—raged in her features, so that her face looked as if it had been skinned. She was terrible to see.

"Where is my husband?" she wept. "Do you have news of him? Does Jin Yu know where he is? I must join him!" She threw herself back down onto the bed and cried feverishly into the pillow. "He won't tell me where he is, he keeps me deliberately in the dark!"

"Kai Hui, stop," I snapped at her. I shook her shoulder roughly. "Of course Mao can't tell you where he is. He is trying to protect you. Eat this. You must stay healthy and strong, for the sake of your children."

She looked up with loathing for me in her eyes. "My children? My children? I want to know, where is my husband? Why won't he send for me? I'll escape to him in the middle of the night if I have to!"

Finally, I left the soup for her, pleading with her to finish it. I went and found Teacher Yang in his study. He was sitting behind his desk, his head leaning against the cool whitewashed wall, listening to her cries. His eyes were closed.

"She cares nothing for her children," he said, without opening his eyes. "It is unnatural."

"No, sir, that can't be. She's just hysterical. She cares for them, she must. All mothers love their children."

"Still the idealist, eh, Jade Virtue?" Teacher Yang shook his head slowly, his eyes still closed. "The children were things which tied Mao Zedong to her. But now they apparently do not serve their purpose, and so she cares nothing for them."

I sat with him awhile, although he did not open his eyes. I held his hands and talked to divert him. When he seemed to be asleep in his chair, I stole from the room. Outside in the garden, I looked up at Kai Hui's window. She had opened the shutters and was leaning her forehead and both her palms against the glass. Her eyes were closed as well. I went home and lay down for a while in the dim coolness of my bedroom, dizzy and sickened from what I had seen of our infinite capacity for desperation.

The following year, the Guomindang Party established a national government in Nanjing, with Chiang Kai Shek as the president. In Hunan, Zhao was still governor, Li Shi was the garrison commander, and Guai was offered the position of chief provincial magistrate. He accepted immediately.

"I'm a little worried," I said. "A government in power is very different from one trying to get into power. I'm afraid you might find it frustrating."

"I'm supposed to appoint village headmen and councils for now," Guai said, ignoring what I had just said. "Later, we're supposed to have elections. What I want more than anything for China is elections, so I have to be the magistrate. I'm afraid to leave it in anyone else's hands."

He did not say that he was afraid that Zhao and Li Shi between the two of them would run Hunan as they pleased, and that they both thought elections a foolish luxury when the country was in such a confused and violent state, threatened by Communists and the growing power of Japan.

He did not say that we both knew many officials who, once they were in office, would have to be taken out again feet first. But I was by now used to knowing what was in Guai's mind. I decorated Guai's new office for him with photographs of Generalissimo Chiang and other dignitaries of the new government.

"If you all mean so well, why not hold elections right away?" I asked Li Shi one morning, when I had visited him to pick up papers for Guai. He had not been expecting me and appeared annoyed. He was still wearing the silk bathrobe he had ordered from Paris. Li Shi had been a very early riser since boyhood, always waking in the dark to study or, later, to drill his soldiers. But lately, you could go to his house after breakfast and find him still unshaven.

"How?" he said angrily, pulling the robe around him. "Answer me how. Do you think any of the men in this province have the slightest idea of what it takes to conduct elections? Does any Chinese man? We haven't done this before. You don't give a sword to a child and push him into battle before teaching him to fight. An election now would be like taking a girl from the countryside with bound feet and giving her high-heeled shoes to wear."

"Ones like these?" I snorted, nudging a red pair with my toe. They peeped out from under the divan.

Li Shi flushed, more with irritation than shame I'm afraid. Then he shrugged. "You ask too much of me. And you certainly ask too much of these provincial Hunanese."

"I think—and Guai thinks too—that they have just as much ability to be good and wise as we do."

"Well, they don't," Li Shi said. He rubbed his face, which looked a little puffy. "Wisdom and goodness are taught. These are men practically in their natural state, especially after years of the warlords like Feng, may his soul be in turmoil. Men in their natural state are grasping and fearful. Remember that, when you have your democracy."

In 1928 also, one year after I married Guai, when I was thirty-eight years old, I became pregnant with our first child. I'm afraid that my first reaction when I found out was to feel annoyed, because now I would have to give up teaching. And as my belly grew, I realized that I was gradually becoming more fearful, more anxious, less daring. I refused to attend demonstrations, I refused to attend mass meetings, in case I was jostled or pushed or injured. Jin Yu was unsympathetic; her pregnancies had never affected her that way. But for the first time, I felt the need to preserve that which was mine. Once, the world was light in weight, containing little of importance, and the few important things were not in my power to protect. My mother and Li Shi had always been beyond my poor abilities. Mo Chi took care of Graceful Virtue. Those things that had at first seemed weighty had turned out to be empty. Until now, I had only myself to guard, and I did not view myself as a valuable treasure that required much care.

Now, I had a husband who was a reforming do-gooder and a baby in my stomach, and I was overcome with the desire to protect them both, and eager to grasp at any chance to do so. My relatively advanced age made this sensation even more powerful. Which I think may explain why I became such a money-grubber. But then, people often use their children as an excuse for greed and selfishness that would be unjustifiable if only for themselves.

While still in the early days of my pregnancy, I took a small amount of money—comprised of my small savings and a grudging amount that Guai's parents had sent us when we married—and attended the bankruptcy sale of a large, cavernous house on the outskirts of the city. I bought the house, and then paid the previous owner—who needed the money and would have sold me all his blood if I had asked—to divide it into several apartments with the labor of his own hands. I rented the apartments to various families who had moved to Changsha in an attempt to escape the violence in Wuhan. They were pleased to live among their own folk in the strange city of Changsha, and I was pleased to begin with the first of several buildings that I would own, although Guai would always be after me to give people more time to pay rent.

The bankrupt previous house-owner took the money I gave him to divide the house and gambled it away in the fan-tan games in the Street of Painted Houses, just as he had gambled away his house, his inheritance, and all his daughters. And he was pleased, at least for as long as his gambling lasted, which was approximately seven hours, for he was a heavy bettor. Then he drowned himself in the river. I had a plasterer insert fragments of mirror in the walls of the house to keep his feckless spirit away. But I was disturbed at night by dreams about him, so I woke early one morning and went to the riverbank, to the dock from which he had flung himself. I lit some incense and pressed the fragrant sticks between my palms as I bowed. I poured out a cup of rice wine and watched it mingle mistily with the river. Then, leaning out over the dock, I opened up a new box of dice and let them tumble from the box into the green waters, so that he might play in hell.

"Good winnings, sir," I murmured. After that, I ceased to dream of him, and I felt his ghost had turned its attention solely to ghostly games of chance.

27

"*H*ow do you feel?" Jin Yu asked, throwing herself into a chair at my bedside.

"Very tired. And I'm not supposed to wash my hair for thirty days!"

"Old superstition. I'll help you wash it in secret. The only reason for that rule is to keep husbands away from your bed until you've had time to recover from the birth. And I'm sure it works."

Laughing made my body hurt, so I muffled my face in a pillow.

"I spoke to Guai outside," Jin Yu said. I looked at her gratefully, for she rarely spoke to Guai directly. "He took me in to see the baby. She looks healthy. You've named her what?"

"Jueh. A nice simple name."

Jin Yu propped her feet up on my bed, and I reached out to take off her shoes. "You'll make the quilt dirty," I murmured, tossing the shoes onto the floor. She reached into the pocket of her skirt and brought out some tiny gold earrings in a silk purse. "For the baby," she said, putting the purse on my bedside table. "When you get her ears pierced, you'll have some real gold to put in them."

I smiled and patted her ankle. "Your feet are soaked," I told her. "Go put them by the brazier."

"It's started to snow outside, and I didn't have the right shoes. A terrible January day, auspicious only for the birth of Wu Jueh, future empress of China!"

"You have lost your mind, you strange woman. What puts you in such a giddy mood?"

"Despair, old friend, and nothing but." Jin Yu slouched down in her chair. I turned a corner of the quilt over her feet. The room I lay in was not our usual bedroom, but a separate chamber in the back of our rented house. The midwife's wraps still lay on a chair, and a basin of bloody water had been pushed neatly under the bed. My mother and sister were somewhere in the house—I had heard their voices through a fog of agony—and Guai had only been allowed in to see me about an hour ago. He said only that my mother had cooked lunch for the midwife, and he had paid her already and she was now napping on the divan in his study and snored dreadfully. I smelled wine on his breath and teased him about it. "I couldn't help it," he said. "I got so nervous waiting for the birth I thought I would die."

"Guai doesn't seem to be upset it's a girl," I said, picking at the sheets with my fingers.

Jin Yu looked at me severely. "Why should he be?"

"Well, I am."

"That again. If your man doesn't care, why should you?"

"His father and mother care. They hate me because I'm older than he is, and they think I'm some terrible radical. And they sent a messenger all the way from Yueyang to ask if it was a boy. We haven't sent him back yet. They have twelve grandsons already."

Jin Yu simply shrugged and put her head back on the headrest.

"The new baby makes me think of my first two," I continued sadly. Jin Yu looked up again, with more sympathy in her eyes. "I wonder what they would be like now." I laughed to make sure I didn't cry on such a lucky day. "Anyway, everyone said that childbirth grows easier each time. But it's not true. It hurt as much this time as the first time!"

"You aren't supposed to wait twenty years in between," Jin Yu snorted.

Yong Li brought tea for Jin Yu and red sugar dissolved in hot water for me.

"Does the new father want to join us?" Jin Yu asked.

Yong Li shook her head shyly—she had always been a little afraid of Jin Yu. "The master says the ladies should enjoy their gossip together," she said, curtsying slightly. We waited in silence until the door shut behind her. I turned to Jin Yu.

"So," I murmured into the steam of my drink. "Any ladylike gossip?"

Jin Yu's voice dropped. "Mao is withdrawing his troops from the Jing-gang Mountains. Your brother's campaigns against him have been much too successful. Mao has also killed too many landlords in Jinggang, and the lineage societies have turned against him. I told him that would happen. He is going to establish his base in Jiangxi, in the mountains between Jiangxi and Fujian."

I tried to hide an expression of pride in Li Shi. To outfox Mao!

"In fact," Jin Yu said between sips, "I just came from Teacher Yang's house. I'm very worried for him; he looks a hundred years old. I had to break the news to Yang Kai Hui."

"That's terrible. How did she take it?"

"What you would expect. She thinks he's going farther away from her, and now she wants more than ever to go to him. This past year and a half while he's been in the mountains . . ." Jin Yu did not finish, but shook her head.

"Has she gone mad, do you think?"

"I know that's what you think. I think it would be a relief if she did go mad. All this passionate misery is a torment to everyone."

"Jin Yu," I asked, "can you take her to him? Do you know where he is?"

Jin Yu glanced out the window at the wintry afternoon light before sipping her tea again. "No to the first question, yes to the second."

"Then why no to the first?"

"Because Mao has a new woman. He Zizhen. He calls her his second wife. She's quite a bit younger than all of us. Revolutionary love-mate type."

"Poor Kai Hui," I murmured.

"Kai Hui has no place in the Jiangxi Soviet now."

"Jin Yu." I struggled to sit up. "Do you? Are you leaving to join him in the mountains?"

Jin Yu rubbed her face in exasperation. "No, I am not. I have been instructed that I have things to do here. The great experiment in Jiangxi is taking place without me. I wanted Hesen to go, but he won't leave me or the children."

"I don't want you to go, Jin Yu. I'm afraid I'd never see you again."

"Please calm down. I'm clearly going nowhere for the moment." She stood up and looked out the window, pushing aside the half-open shutter with a familiar impatient gesture. As she stood with her back to me, I was suddenly reminded of the first time I visited her in her room at the Xiang mansion and of the storm that broke over our heads. She stood just as straight today as she did then, and her head, if anything, was held even higher. But then she had been the center of the house, and the center of the student movement, and she had gone to Beijing and Nanjing and Paris with all the other comrades. Now she had been ordered to stay in Changsha, while Mao and the others fought the real war in the hills. I suppose I might have felt some satisfaction at Jin Yu getting a taste of what it always felt like to be me, but it washed away in a rush of pity.

"Mao is unjust. You would be the best fighter of all. You are their wild falcon."

She turned and leaned back against the sill. With the light of day behind her, I could not read her face. But her low laugh came to me in the dimness. Then she walked back over to me and brushed my hair back.

"Get some rest," she said, taking my cup. I lay down and fell asleep.

When I awoke it was the middle of the night, and Guai was climbing into bed with me in all his clothes.

"Why aren't you in our bed?" I asked, making room for him under the cover.

"You are here," he mumbled sleepily. "But I had to wait until everyone went to bed, because all those tyrants wouldn't let me come here. Your mother, the midwife, Graceful Virtue, Yong Li." He counted them off on his fingers. "Women are always so bossy about women's matters." He went to sleep with his face in my shoulder.

The rains that spring splashed the red mud everywhere, under the doors, into the wagon wheels, in great streaks along the sides of the buildings. The laborers in the field looked like terra-cotta statues when they stood still. From the upper windows of the house we had rented for the last year or so, I could see the gray moss on the roof tiles of the neighboring buildings grow bright and green with the rain, glistening with wetness. I stayed at home with my new daughter. I concentrated my whole attention on her while she was in the room with me. But when Yong Li came to take her away to be bathed or put to sleep in her crib, I often opened the shutters—closed against the early spring chill, for fear the baby would get sick—and put my face out into the falling water, catching it on my tongue and feeling it slide down my face.

In those days, a woman of my class did not breast-feed her own baby, and so I did not either. Nor did we spend all day caring for children, for the servants raised them. But now that I was a magistrate's wife, I was expected to spend my time on housewifely duties, and that I could not do, for I worried about money all the time. In 1929, the whole world was poor, and China was even poorer. As I sat in my room, I received reports from my agents, and wrote dunning letters to the shopkeepers who leased my two storefronts, and calculated the mortgage payments I could make. I wrung my hands over the taxes I owed, which apparently increased daily. I cooed over the first of my children to live past her first month, then turned almost in the same breath to upbraid a lazy bookkeeper. In my free moments, which were more numerous now that I did not go out to conduct business myself, I reflected on the swiftly dropping rain and on all the desires I had now for worldly things, like money in the bank and gold under the floorboards, desires that I had never had before.

Before the spring was over, my former student Patience visited me. Her round face was as merry as ever, and when I saw her in my hall, I thought that Patience, more than anyone else I knew, had a talent for happiness.

"I am so proud of you," I told her, when we sat down in my sitting room. "To be honest, I never thought you would do so well. But here you are, you are a doctor in Nanjing."

"I'm just starting out," Patience said, with a becoming show of modesty. "But I have my first job. I am treating opium addicts."

"That's not the way to become rich," I said. Good heavens, I thought, I have become completely soulless. "But I'm glad you are working for the good of the nation," I added quickly. "Are you working in some hospital?"

Patience's face glowed. "I am a new resident at the Opium Suppression Bureau, Nanjing Office. I really wanted to do this, although it is sordid, working with these addicts all the time. But opium has eaten up our country, and I know I am helping to put things right. Things haven't gone right for China since the British forced opium down our throats a century ago. But the bureau does excellent work. We register all the addicts, and we force them to come for treatment."

"Is your treatment successful? Here, eat more." I pushed two more steamed buns onto her plate.

"No, don't, I am getting so fat. Well, whether the treatment is successful remains to be seen. Some of them get released from hospital and go directly to the nearest opium parlor. Some of them last a few days, then go directly to the nearest opium parlor." She giggled helplessly. "I haven't yet hit upon a way of making treatment last. Do you think that men can ever overcome such a hideous yearning for opium?"

I sat back and considered this. "I think," I said slowly, "that people always end up with exactly what they want."

"But addicts are powerless to resist the drug." Patience pursed her lips in a manner that told me she thought me rather a mean middle-aged woman. "I think you are not very sympathetic to their plight."

"Perhaps I should be more sympathetic," I relented. "You know more about their medical conditions than I do." I fed her more steamed buns.

"Do you have a young man?" I asked. I had to stifle a momentary qualm. How I had hated it as a young girl when the older women asked me such questions! I felt as if their merely asking implied that I would do nothing with my life.

"Oh, boys." Patience sniffed. "I certainly don't intend to have any time for them. I don't wish to marry."

"Then you should not."

She smiled. "I'm glad you react that way. Whenever I tell any woman your age, she always says in an awful warning tone that I'm still young and I'll change my mind, and then it will be too late, I'll be an old maid. I always say I would rather be an old maid than a regretful wife."

I leaned forward and took her hand. "People always say you will be sorry when you don't want to do things exactly as they do. You always made me proud, Patience, and you still do. You will do great things as a doctor."

I took Patience inside to see the new baby, who lay on my bed swathed in silk wrappings. She tickled Jueh under her fat little chin and leaned over her. "What will you do, now that you've had the baby?" she asked. "What more could you want?" Patience and Jueh gurgled and laughed together.

I opened my mouth, and the following words came out of it. "I want to build a house," I said, and then blinked in surprise.

Patience glanced up. "Well, that's a good idea."

"I just thought of it. I know what's missing now, Patience." I turned to her. "I was sitting here all spring, looking at my lovely daughter, and welcoming my husband home at night . . ."

"Your lovely husband." Patience giggled.

I blushed and went on. "And I have been wondering what I am missing. I want to build a house. I want to live in my own house. I lived in my father's house, in my mother's house, in the Pans' house, in the House of Silk Fans. Guai and I have lived in rented rooms, and here we are, still in some other landlord's house. Whenever I buy property, I look at it and think how I can improve it. But I can never make it wholly satisfactory, because it already exists and I can't change it all unless I tear it down and start over. Always, the past and other people's ghosts weigh on me. Now, I want to begin from the beginning."

I started by looking for land. I searched all spring, circumnavigating the city, thinking that the only place I could find empty land in Changsha—as ancient and overbuilt as it was—would be in the newer suburbs. But the suburbs were dotted with factories, or flooded with cheap new slums or lavish brothels. As the weather got hotter, my hopes began to dry up.

In the midsummer, when the air was absolutely still and thick, I was walking through one of the older quarters of Changsha, not too far from the bridge over the Xiang River, when I saw a few men, their faces blackened with smoke and bare arms shining with sweat, come out of a narrow street and pass me.

"What happened?" I asked, looking at the buckets they carried in their hands.

"A small fire. An old house burned down."

"Was anyone hurt?"

"No one has lived there for years. Old Cho owns the property, but never lived in it."

The name was familiar. "The landlord Old Cho, who used to be a barber?"

The men nodded indifferently as they passed. Old Cho had also bought the orchard when I was still young Mrs. Pan, I remembered. When Old Pan and his wife had died, he had bought their old mansion, where he now lived, and which I had sold to him for basically a basket of pigeon eggs, in return for which he paid off many of the Pans' debts.

A few small, oily clouds of smoke rose above the tile-topped walls. I turned down the narrow street from which they had emerged. The street was old, winding and narrow, paved with square cobblestones the size of gold ingots and lined with tall shadowy whitewashed walls. The brutal sun-soaked heat of the day seemed far above me, and I walked down the center of a cool well. Trees in the gardens on the other side of the walls leaned gently out into the street. I paused at a crossing to stand aside for a horse and cart carrying more firefighters and accidentally leaned against the street name, set in raised red letters on the corner of the wall. "White Crane Street," my fingers read.

The gates stood wide open, and the rubble of the burned house was still smoking slightly. Acrid puffs of smoke floated vertically up into the blank skies before dispersing. A last few men were picking up buckets as I looked inside, and they warned me away from the hot embers. Even from the gate, I could see that the property was a good size, and the walls were strong and high. The house, before it burned, had taken up only a third of the property, and now I skirted the edges, where the grass was trampled but still green in spots. The trees planted along the walls were sooty but in good condition. In the back, I found the remains of an old pond, undrained but thick with moss and algae. It was half empty, its water spent to quench the flames.

Standing by the pond, I felt a slight rise in the air, a shift, as if a breeze were starting to blow, and it ruffled the surface of the pond. I looked up, and saw that the smoke above me was drifting sideways instead of straight up. A wisp of hair blew into my face, and I put up a dirty hand to push it back. Far above me, as high up as the hawks that flew down from the hills, I saw a gleam of silver, flashing with sun. A distant whirring roar reached my ears. I stared in awestruck silence. I had heard such things described by my brother and Zhao Han Ren, but I had never seen one before, and I could hardly credit its existence. I was not used to thinking that anything could be directly above me in the sky, unconnected to some pole or mountain peak or outstretched hand. But on that summer day, an airplane crossed above the place where I would build my house, and the force of its passing had blown all the smoke away.

28

The summer of 1930 was a strange one, cooler than usual, damp and gray from lack of sun. The air was thicker than porridge, weighted down with humidity, smoke, and the bad smells of the city—urine, old food, and tar. The air and its smells seemed to collect on my skin, pooling in the hollows of my eyes and the insides of my elbows and knees. The river was very low and did not move as strongly as usual, and the water stank as if it were stagnant. The tame fishing cormorants of the fishermen on the river sat very still on the bows of the rowboats, red scarves knotted around their necks to prevent them from swallowing their catch before the fishermen could extract the fish from their beaks. But the fish they caught were small and few, and the birds seemed almost to spit them out in disgust. Each simmering dusk brought with it the cries of an itinerant apothecary, who hawked his wares. "White powder to cure fever! Invented by Western doctors! All Westerners take it! Three yuan a bottle!"

Guai and I got up every morning before dark, in part to eat breakfast in the relative coolness of the dawn, and in part because we could not stand more than a few hours in our swampy bed. Yong Li, who lived with us now, had suggested that we sleep apart for comfort, but Guai flatly refused, and I was glad for his reaction. If he had wanted to sleep apart, I would not have wished to seem unreasonable by insisting on staying in the same bed with him. But I slept better when Guai was with me. When he was away from home on government business, my old sleeplessness reasserted itself, and I paced my room in exhaustion until very early in the morning. When he was there in the bed with me, I slept in complete serenity.

Yong Li placed a bowl of tepid rice gruel in front of me and several small dishes of pickled vegetables. I passed the bowl to Guai, who ate absentmindedly, reading his dispatches in the mingled light of a candle flame and the faint pink of day. I drank tea and looked out onto the veranda, thinking that I would visit my new house again today, to see how the builders had gotten on. I sketched the outlines of the second courtyard on the dusty sill with my finger.

We all looked up at the distant popping sound. The sounds of gunfire were instantly recognizable, and we all ran to the windows. Then Guai turned and sprang up the stairs, to gain a better vantage point from the second-story windows. "Stay here!" he shouted as he ran.

"I see gunfire in the distance!" he cried from upstairs. "I can see the flares from their muzzles!"

"Whose guns, master?" shouted Yong Li, clinging to my hand. We heard distant yelling, emanating down to us like waves.

"I can't tell," Guai said grimly as he came back down. "But I'm going to find out."

"No, you are not," I snapped, angry and fearful. I grasped his arm—it was damp with perspiration. "What if you were shot? What would happen to me and to Jueh?"

"Let go of me, wife. I am the chief magistrate, I can't cower in my house if the city is in trouble." He yanked his arm out of my grip and started for the door, pausing only to snatch up his umbrella.

"Guai, stop!" I cried. "Think of your family, if you won't think of yourself!"

"I must think of my duty to the country," he said firmly, and tried to shut the door behind him. I pulled it open and ran out into the garden behind him pleading furiously, but nothing I said would make him turn back.

"Lock the gate behind me," he ordered, and I watched him run down the lane toward the main streets.

All day I sat inside, listening to the constant gunfire, the sound of running footsteps, wishing with all my heart that Guai would come home safely. I was angry at him too, and I considered taking Jueh and leaving him if he was always going to put the nation's welfare before ours. Then I struggled with the injustice of my feelings. Did I not love him because he was selfless and brave? It felt better to think about my own feelings than to think about the terrors of the world outside, which I could neither control nor make sense of.

Guai came home after nightfall, with Mo Chi and some soldiers. "Let me make your men something to eat, Little Brother," I said to Mo Chi, but he shook his head.

"We can't stay," he said. Without another word, he and his men ran out of the courtyard, and I heard the sound of their truck starting in the lane. The headlights flickered over the top of my garden wall and surged away into the darkness.

"Tell me what's happened," I demanded of my husband.

"Let me eat something first," he croaked, his voice as hoarse as a raven's. "But something small. I don't know when we can go buy food again. How much do we have in the house to eat?"

He sent the servants around to close all the shutters, and ordered them to push furniture against the doors and windows. Then he gathered all of us in the central hall.

"The city has been attacked by Communists," he said, turning over his words carefully, like a man choosing pearls. "Aided by their comrades inside the city walls, they have actually succeeded to some extent. In fact, it is safe to say that they hold large portions of the city. You can say, even, that they hold the city."

We were all too astonished to reply.

"It is troubling because Governor Zhao is away, with a large armed retinue. Your brother, wife, has already sent for him, and he is trying to hurry back. But communications are unclear, since the Communists have seized the Telephone and Telegraph Building. Apparently, such an attack was considered so absurd that we have not been sufficiently on our guard, and so it has succeeded out of its very absurdity."

For ten days we never stood up straight, but crawled on the floor. The cook refused to use the stove standing up, and we let her build a small fire on the stone floor of the kitchen, hedged about with bits of brick, where she cooked squatting on her hams. The baby slept in the stone washbasin by the water tap, partly covered over by a wooden washboard. Guai and I wrote letters lying on the floor, propped up by our elbows. It was as if the world had reduced itself to a level three feet off the ground, and we ourselves were like small children, seeing only the legs of the furniture. My hands blistered and callused from crawling about, and the knees of my trousers wore through.

We ate sparingly to conserve food, but our household had grown from the first days of our marriage, and we had many hungry stomachs. Guai, the baby, myself, Yong Li, the cook, the wet nurse, two maids, the outside workman and his wife, all lived in our house. We pulled up vegetables from the garden and picked oranges from the ornamental trees. At night, the workman and his wife hunted for frogs along the old canal. Sometimes Yong Li, who displayed a soldierly disregard for her own physical safety, would scuttle out before dawn to buy food. Amazingly, she reported, some of the stall-keepers in the market were conducting business, although they kept their shutters down. Yong Li would join several other women dodging through the market alleys in the predawn darkness, ducking into the stalls and running home again with their scraps of food under their jackets. There was no newsprint to wrap the things, so Yong Li often had animal blood dripping down her side when I took the pieces of pork stomach or sheep tripe from her. The sight never failed to disturb me, for it always looked as if she had been wounded. Of course, the stall-holders doubled and tripled their prices every day during the ten days, but that was to be expected.

Other than our furtive, anxious dashes to get food, which could not be helped, I allowed no one out of the house. I felt then that we could be safe, if only we stayed within its walls. At night, we all gathered in the hallway that ran through the center of the house, which had no windows, and slept there on the cool floors, our heads pillowed on our hands. The wet nurse cried incessantly because she was trapped with us and could not go home to see her own baby in the countryside; her soft sobbing kept me awake most nights. Lying there, I thought guiltily of her child, eating gruel so that mine might have breast milk, and I decided never to hire a wet nurse again. But then I remembered how poor she was and how the money I paid her kept her children from starving, and I could only pull my hair in frustration and wonder if there was such a thing in this world as an action without endless complications.

Bursts of gunfire punctured the atmosphere, and we would try to judge from its loudness how far away it was, as if it were thunder. Flashes of light would intrude on our sleep, spilling into the hallway from around the edges of the closed shutters and shut doors. Occasionally, I would hear the ping of a bullet, fired from the top of the Telephone and Telegraph Building, or from the windows of the post office or the Nakagawa Silk factory tower, thudding into a wall nearby. I could always hear the sliding crunch of the bullet as it burrowed into plaster or brick, as if slowed down to the pace of a heartbeat, and then the sifting sounds of the brick dust crumbling out. Guai denied that I could hear such a small sound so precisely, but I could. The heat of the summer, damp and thick as mud, brought on a condition like drunkenness.

"How could such a thing happen? We have an army." I was whispering to Guai one night, when everyone else had fallen asleep. A single candle still burned, because he was still reading.

"It's not so simple," he said, without looking up. "Our army is not very big, it is underpaid and untrained. And the Big Four families eat up all the money in China. The soldiers' feet are coming out of their boots because the Chen family got the boot contract and cheated the army. All that money we paid them, and we get boots made of cardboard."

"Don't read anymore," I begged. "You will only hurt your eyes, and you are nearsighted as it is."

Guai took off his glasses and rubbed his eyes. Then he leaned over to me and kissed my ear.

"Don't do that either," I snickered. "We are lying in a hallway with so many other people." He lay on his side, his head on my shoulder, staring into the candle flame. The floor was cool against my stomach.

"I can't believe this battle is delaying the building of my house," I said finally. Guai and I immediately burst into giggles, which we tried to suppress as the rest of the household stirred uneasily in their sleep.

"Well, since you are determined to be so selfish, how is the house coming?" he asked finally, snorting his laughter through his nose. He lay on his back and polished his glasses on his sleeve.

"Very well. I wish you would take more of an interest. I'm putting glass shards in the tops of the walls, barbed wire over that, to keep out intruders. Double-barred main doors and gate. Your study overlooks the fishpond, and I'm putting your new desk in the bay window, with trees right outside to shade you."

"When it's finished, I'll move in and be perfectly satisfied. But I feel sorry for the builders, since you are harrying them so much."

"You feel sorry for everyone," I said.

"It's funny. That's what Jin Yu said about you."

"When did she tell you such a thing?" I sat up to look at him.

"I ran into her in the street a few months ago. You know, usually we try to get by with just a polite nod. But I literally came around the corner and bumped into her, and we had no choice but to speak."

"What else did she say to you?"

"I think that was all."

"I don't believe you."

Guai only smiled and shook his head. "Everything else is between me and her."

"I hate it when you have secrets from me."

"I myself have no secrets from you. I have certain confidences which I must preserve, just as I preserve your confidences. It's only fair."

"But I'm your wife. You shouldn't treat me like everyone else. What's fair to me is different from what's fair to other people."

"Do you ever think of Wang Mang?" he asked, a little later that night, still staring into the candle flame.

I stroked the back of his head. "Not really," I said. "I thought of him a great deal in the years after he died. There was a blackness around my heart then, so black and deep that even now, the mere memory of it seems like a shadow in itself."

He turned his head to look at me. "Don't think of it, then. There are no shadows now."

"No, none. Except the ones cast by the outside world."

"Well, there's nothing we can do about those. Those shadows are there all the time."

I did not ask him if he ever thought of his first wife. I believed she rarely crossed his mind, but there was always a chance that he might tell me otherwise if asked, and I had no desire to feel like an afterthought.

On the tenth day, we were awakened by a great roar nearby. We sat up from where we lay in the hallway, rubbing our eyes. The window shutters glowed red around the edges. Another roar followed, and we all cried out in terror.

We heard and felt an earth-shaking rumble from the street outside our house. Guai, kneeling by the window, cracked open the shutters to peek. I watched the sunlight fall on his face and the motes of dust settle on his eyeglasses. Then his mouth opened in a shout of surprise. He fell back on the floor in time to avoid being banged in the head as the shutters flew open and the windows were broken. Three, four, five soldiers in shabby Guomindang uniforms leaped into the house through the windows. I staggered to my feet. Behind them, I could see the garden wall crumbling and the back of an army truck emerging through it, driving up into my garden, leaving deep tire tracks in the flowerbeds. More soldiers jumped out of the truck, and they all ran past me up the stairs to the roof. I heard firing from the roof, and chunks of roof tile sailed down into the garden.

I flew to Guai and wrapped my arms around him. "Are you all right?" I cried. "Are you hurt?"

"Stay out of the way!" he shouted, and pulled me back into the shelter of the wall. The rest of the household had disappeared.

"I don't know where Jueh is!" I screamed, and started to get up, but Guai dragged me back down again.

"Don't! Stay down! You can't do any good running around in the middle of this!" The ceiling rocked to the tread of many feet, flakes of paint floated down. Several of my tables and chairs were broken as the soldiers made their way to the upper story. Guai put his arms around me, and we stared above us.

As we cowered in the corner of our own living room, we heard the thunder of boots, and the soldiers ran downstairs again, this time clearly in pursuit. I heard many shots, in rapid succession, yelling and curses in the streets outside, trailing off into the network of alleys that surrounded us. Then the noises gradually died away, and I heard the soldiers shuffling back. There was a moment of quiet. Then three more shots, this time fired—it seemed—with deliberation, evenly spaced, with the kind of pause before each one that told me that someone was taking careful aim. I could almost sense the reflexive straightening of the elbow before each one.

I jumped up and ran through the house, shouting for Yong Li and the baby.

"Elder Sister, we are here!" came her muffled voice. I ran into the kitchen and found everyone crouched against the walls near the clay oven. Jueh was screaming lustily in Yong Li's arms. I dropped into a squat next to them and put my arms around them both.

"Don't cry, Elder Sister," Yong Li ordered. "We are all safe." She glared at the other servants. "Useless, all of you, running about like geese."

"Stay here," I said. "Don't anyone move." I crept back to the front of the house. Out of my window, I saw Guai standing next to the truck in the great hole that had been made in my garden wall, looking out into the street. I went out to him and looked over his shoulder. Two men and a woman in simple peasant clothes lay on their faces in the street. They had been shot in the head.

"Don't look," my husband said.

"It's all right," I murmured.

The truck started, and we shifted out of the way. It bumped over the rubble of my destroyed garden wall and pulled out into the street. The soldiers got inside and drove away. The three bodies lay where they had been left.

Guai stepped carefully over the broken brick. "Don't go near them," I called out, but he walked up to the bodies and turned over one of the men. He looked at the dead man's face for a moment and came back.

"Did he look familiar to you?" Guai asked.

I nodded.

"Me too. Where do we know him from?"

"Patience's older cousin," I sighed. "The young watercolor artist. Remember? He came to tea with us last week."

"Ah. Of course." His voice was weary. "Rather a nice young man, I thought."

I followed Guai into the house. He picked up his umbrella. This time I did not try to stop him.

"I'll send a message if I'm not coming home tonight," he said. "Don't cover up the bodies. I don't think we should look as if we are expressing . . . anything like respect or sympathy for these dead rebels."

I watched from the gate as he hurried down the street, and it seemed to me that for the first time his shoulders stooped a little. I went back inside and shut the windows, even though the glass had been broken, and closed the shutters, even though the lattices were in splinters. I tacked up a quilt to shield us from the gaze of the street, since the wall was now partly gone. The servants and I spent the rest of the morning cleaning up the house, picking up broken sticks of furniture and mopping the floors where the soldiers' boots had left rubber tread marks like the tire of a car.

In the early afternoon, when all was silent in the midday heat, I went outside into the garden simply to breathe. But I heard a noise behind the shed at the rear of the garden, near the fishpond. I looked around the corner of the shed, but saw nothing. I tiptoed and looked inside the shed's little window, rubbing the dirt from the pane with my sleeve. I saw Jin Yu sitting on the floor of the shed, her arms around her legs and a bloody rag wrapped around her arm. When Jin Yu looked up, I saw that her face was badly bruised and her lips thickened by blows.

I sent the servants in all four directions on various errands, to town, to the canal, to buy rice, to buy lumber for repairs, barking orders with impatience. After they left, I dragged Jin Yu inside, more dead than alive, and laid her down on my own bed. I extracted some scattered shot from her arm with a pair of embroidery scissors and some kitchen tongs. Yong Li, the only member of the household who could keep a secret, stood by with towels and a steaming basin of boiling water. She caught all the blood neatly in the towels, and burned them in the kitchen stove. A black smoke rose up from the burning cloth.

Jin Yu was breathing quickly, but made no other sound. Her white face was motionless, her dark eyes like cold pools. The usual storms of feeling that crossed her face had withdrawn, leaving an eerie expressionlessness. I had once seen a man who had been struck and badly injured in his head by a falling roof tile; he lay in a trance, still alive, but the outline of his physical body was filled with absence and incomprehension. I knew little of trances, but I was afraid Jin Yu might be entering one. I shook her gently to make her speak to me.

"Jin Yu, say something. Say something to me." I sat down on the bed next to her and stroked her shoulder. "I take it you led one of the attacks."

"I held the Telephone and Telegraph Building for nine days, with only thirteen men."

"You're very brave."

"Not nearly brave enough. For they are all dead, and here I am, alive."

"Jin Yu, how did you think you could take Changsha for good?"

"I followed orders." She shrugged and sat up, wincing in pain. "Mao was supposed to come with reinforcements from Nanchang. But he didn't think he could prevail, so he withdrew instead. I suppose he's gone back to depose the Party secretary who ordered the attack. Very convenient."

"Jin Yu, they'll be after you."

"You must get me to the river by dawn tomorrow."

"You're too badly hurt."

"The river by dawn." For the first time, her dark eyes met mine. "There is no other path left now. For either of us."

In the evening, a message came from Guai that he would have to stay all night at the governor's office. I waited until midnight and then got Jin Yu out from under Yong Li's bed, where she had lain for the entire afternoon. I took Jin Yu out the gate into the side alley. She leaned heavily on my arm, and her panting came thickly; the slowness of our progress was making me fearful. We crept through the streets in silence until we reached the river. The rustling of the trees made me look over my shoulder again and again, but no one was outside tonight except us. Crickets sat in the grass nearby, and the night air smelled very fresh, although an occasional drift of sulfur would make me wrinkle my nose.

"Find out what happened to Hesen," she whispered to me. "Find out, and find a way to let me know."

We sat in the bushes by the water margin until a faint gray light showed on the eastern horizon behind us. The river water looked leaden. A boat drifted up to the bank and halted. A single man stood in the stern by the rudder, the pole in his hands. The center of the boat was covered with a large oilcloth.

"This is for me," Jin Yu whispered. "Stay back." I saw a hand emerge from under the oilcloth and lift up the corner slightly. I saw a pale blur of a face underneath, and realized that several people were hiding there.

She stumbled once on the pebbly shore, and I ran to her, but she pushed me firmly back. "Don't come nearer, Jade Virtue." I watched her slosh through the wavelets at the shore, and then climb into the boat and lie down. She glanced at me before they put the oilcloth down, and gave me her half smile. She lifted her hand in an unfinished gesture, and it fluttered like a lost bird. I watched the boat until it was swallowed up in the mists downriver, and then I hurried back home.

It was still very early as I approached my street, and no one was awake yet. But I saw a gathering of large birds, some circling overhead, some dropping out of the air to land somewhere beyond my line of sight. I stared curiously. When I came around the corner, I realized that the birds were vultures, and that they were clustering on top of my house. I broke into a run. I ran into the house and up the stairs, and threw open the trapdoor that led to my roof. The vultures were on the other side of the hipped roof, and I climbed cautiously toward them. When I looked over the ridge of the rooftop, I saw the vultures had gathered around the body of a young Guomindang soldier, who lay sprawled across the tiles on his stomach. His face, twisted to one side, had already suffered much damage from the carrion birds, and I shut my eyes. For a moment I could not imagine what had led to this body being here, but then I realized that the soldiers yesterday morning had used my roof as a vantage point to flush out the nest of Communist snipers firing from the next street. One soldier had been killed, but he had fallen onto the side of the roof, and his comrades had rushed away without seeing him. In the confusion that followed the three executions on the street and the dash to the next skirmish, he had been forgotten.

I opened my eyes. I could see the boy was very young. I shouted at the birds. Then I hauled up roof tiles with my bare hands and threw them at their heads, striking them. They beat their wings like thunder. My shouts roused the house, and I heard the cook's voice below.

"Madame, what are you doing? Come down! Help, someone, she's gone mad!"

I paid no attention, but clambered over the ridge and kicked at the birds, flinging the tiles with all my strength. Finally, they all flew away, cawing angrily and glaring at me with their pink eyes. Not as angry as I am, I thought. The workman climbed onto the roof with me, and we maneuvered the body down through the trapdoor.

"Get a wagon to take him to the garrison," I gasped. "And cover his poor face."

But I remained on the roof, watching the sun come up and fill the city of Changsha with its virulent heat. Above me, the vultures sailed the breezes from the river. From a distance, they seemed oddly graceful, floating lazily above the sleeping world. But I knew them for what they were.

Li Shi's soldiers arrested Yang Kai Hui. They took her away almost unconscious with shock, leaving her aged father standing in the doorway. She was taken to the army garrison and imprisoned in a small cell under heavy guard.

"Will Mao give himself up for her?" Li Shi asked me. "I am willing to promote this plan to Governor Zhao. She is the mother of his children. I would much rather have that bastard in front of my rifles than this foolish woman."

"Please ask Zhao to at least try to make the trade with Mao," I begged him. But even as my lips moved, I knew Mao would never give himself in return for Kai Hui's life. Mao was impervious to the ordinary pathetic motivations of other men. He had He Zizhen in the mountains with him, and I kept hearing persistent rumors that she was pregnant now. Most of all, Mao had a great destiny to fulfill, which I knew even then, and Kai Hui did not. Those who are born without great destinies, it seems, must always be the ones to sacrifice. There was nothing left for poor Kai Hui except to die for her cause.

Teacher Yang was not allowed to see his daughter on the eve of her execution. Instead of being able to embrace his only child, Teacher Yang paced his house all night long like an anguished tiger, howling with grief, weeping freely. About ten of us who had been his students—but not Xiang Jin Yu, not Cai Hesen, not Mao Zedong, for they were now missing forever—clustered like frightened children around him. Several times he rushed to bang his head against the wall, and we pulled him away frantically, with bloody smudges on his white hair and beard. I was terrified to the depths of my heart, because I had never seen Teacher Yang devoid of reason before, and the sight had the force of an earthquake. The family maids screamed and wept in the hallway, the students clutched Teacher Yang's arms and begged him to bear up under his misery. The entire house seemed shaken to its foundations by this typhoon of grief.

On the misty, iron-gray morning she was executed, I huddled outside the wall of the garrison with Teacher Yang and my fellow students. We were not allowed inside the garrison, and Teacher Yang had run to the spot we calculated would be closest to where Kai Hui was to be shot. A small ring of armed soldiers watched us carefully from a short distance, placed there to keep us from trying to rush into the gate, but even they could see that we were nothing but a bunch of helpless, unarmed scholars, and did not bother to approach. Above us, the sky was lowering with gray clouds, pressing down on all of Hunan. Swirls of hot and cold air mingled around our limbs. I was sweating and chilly at the same time.

My teacher pressed his face against the wall of the garrison, on the other side of which was the yard where the firing squad was assembling. He was straining to hear her footsteps. The old stone wall that had surrounded the garrison yard when I was a girl, and which had a million colluding cracks to peer through, had been replaced by one of smooth gray concrete, thick and neutral and seamless in all its places. Even so, we heard the crunch of footsteps in the gravel on the other side, and the chink of rifle butts set down on the ground.

When these sounds came to our ears, Teacher Yang threw back his head and howled at the sky. "Kai Hui!" he cried. "Kai Hui! My child! Your father is here! Your father is here!"

One of the other students tried to shush him, fearful lest the soldiers come and arrest the old man. But Teacher Yang pushed him away and continued shouting his daughter's name. The soldiers remained at a distance.

There was some confused shuffling inside, and then suddenly we heard Kai Hui's voice from inside the walls.

"Baba!" she bleated, her voice high like a child's. "Baba, help me!" Then immediately her voice was shut off.

Teacher Yang clawed at the concrete wall. "Kai Hui, Kai Hui, my poor girl," he cried out. "Listen to the voice of your father. Be brave. Close your eyes and think of your father and your children, and how you have our love!"

"Baba, help me!" came her voice again, once again quickly muffled. I clung to Teacher Yang desperately.

"My child, there is no help I can give you!" Teacher Yang's voice was strained and cracking with grief, and with the long hours of the night that he had spent weeping. "Close your eyes. Don't look at them."

From over the top of the wall, the sounds of Kai Hui's sobbing reached us. To this day I can hear the sounds of her cries, to this day it brings an ache to my stomach, and I remember that what chilled me then as it chills me now was that her voice was unhinged, not with sadness or despair or fear, but with a terrible yearning, which was blindly unceasing, even at that moment, when its object had left her behind forever. In the last minutes of her life, even as she was being hurried out of this world, Kai Hui was being eaten alive by frustrated desire, a desire that knew no comfort or resignation or even exhaustion, but that leaped and bounded in her mind like a cannibal.

Teacher Yang gritted his teeth and ground his forehead into the wall. Then he flung back his head and shouted to her again.

"Kai Hui! Don't look." His voice ebbed a little, as if at the poverty of the comfort he had to offer her. "Don't look. Don't be afraid. Be brave. It will all be over soon."

Kai Hui began to scream, short sharp bursts of sound, and every cry was her husband's name. On the other side of the wall, there were sounds of a struggle. My blood was thundering in my ears, and the sounds of the officer's orders to the firing squad came to me curiously muffled, as if the officer had a scarf around his mouth. There was the relentless snicking of metal on metal. I clung to Teacher Yang until my knuckles were white.

There was a roar of ordnance. Then there was the smell of sulfur. Then there was silence, broken only by the crunch of boots on the gravel on the far, far side of the wall.

The other students sobbed beside me. Teacher Yang slowly pushed himself away from the wall to which he had clung in such desperation, staggered away a few steps, and abruptly began walking away, making his way stiff-jointedly down the street back toward his house. The rest of us stared at him fearfully, then scuttled after him. We stumbled at his side, afraid to draw too near, swimming at his outskirts like small fish. He stared straight ahead, unblinking, tearless. We went on in this fashion all the way to his front gate. He entered, and after a moment's hesitation, we followed.

When the maids saw his face, they burst into wails. But he held up his hand for silence with such grim authority that they stopped immediately, their mouths open in bewilderment.

"We have guests. And I am hungry. I didn't eat all night. Go prepare a good meal and serve it."

The maids fled the room for the kitchen. The rest of us all sat down, very quietly. Teacher Yang took his usual chair by the window and looked out on the heavy gray day.

When the meal was served, Teacher Yang rose immediately and sat down to eat. He ate steadily, not with any appetite, but with purpose. I picked at my food, pushing it into my unwilling mouth. When Teacher Yang had finished two helpings of rice, he drank several cups of tea in rapid succession and then returned to his chair in the window. The rest of us looked around at each other, although some eyes avoided mine. One of the women wiped away tears with her sleeve. After a little while, several of the men left to return to the garrison, to try to recover Kai Hui's body for her father.

I went to Teacher Yang and knelt on the floor next to him.

"Teacher," I said softly. He looked at me attentively. "Your strange conduct worries us. If you have grief in your heart, then don't be afraid to show it before your friends. If you go on this way, you will become mad."

Teacher Yang looked at me steadily. "After Mao left for the mountains," he said, his voice firm, "I grieved because I knew Kai Hui was terrified that he would abandon her. When Kai Hui was arrested, I grieved because I knew she was afraid of her enemies. When she was brought out into the garrison yard to be executed, I grieved because I knew she feared death."

He turned his head to look out the window once more. "But now she is dead. She is no longer afraid. And I have no more grief. There is nothing in my heart now."

When I left, hours later, to go to my own home, he had not changed position or spoken any other words. He did not look at me as I shut the door gently behind me. I turned in the garden to look at my old teacher sitting in the window, and I knew I was looking at a man purged of all desires, even of the desire to die. Merely waiting, waiting for the end of his obligation to remain on earth.

I stood by the gate in the twilight. The yellow candlelight from wax tapers burned through the slits and cracks in the shuttered second-story windows of the neighboring houses. From the other side of the garden wall, there was a distant anguished cry, the sound of cloth tearing, as if someone had ripped a sleeve out of a clutching hand, and then the bang of a wooden window shutter. The dogs in the alley were howling.

FIRE

The building of my house was completed right before the lunar New Year of 1931. It was a plain house of red brick, whitewashed with lime, with an old-fashioned garden where I had cream and violet tiles laid out in the shape of a five-petaled plum flower. It was south-facing, symmetrical on an east-west axis, with an outer courtyard for the kitchen and servants, connected by a moon gate to an inner courtyard planted with ginkgo trees and wisteria, where we would live. The river wound nearby, to the west, and its silver shimmer could be seen easily from the upstairs windows.

At this point, early in 1931, I was expecting my second child with Guai, and it was my intention to move into the new house right after the lunar New Year, one month before the birth. I had consulted all the astrologers and had taken the auguries at the city temple. I brought in blue-clad Taoist priests to perform their rites, and they assured me that I was pregnant with a son. If all this seems silly now, remember that I was then forty-one years old. I knew it was my last chance. I was not very much a believer in the gods, but I prayed to them for a boy child. Three girls I have birthed already, I think to myself as I pray and light the incense. Just once, I say to the lords of heaven, grant me my heart's desire. I have never asked for anything from you before, and I will never impose on you again.

I set about drawing all the good luck in the universe to my new house. With my own hands I carried in fruit and incense and packets of vermilion dye, and spirit money made of silver paper. I set off firecrackers in the street, and sprinkled chicken blood in the corners of the garden to expel demons. I had charms written on slips of peachwood, and cakes of rice and tea leaves broken up in the stoves. I hired an artist to paint the symbols of long life on each of the pillars—the crane, the tortoise, rocks, peaches, deer, evergreen trees. I myself brushed the characters for wealth, good fortune, longevity, and natural death from old age in discreet corners all over the house, inside doorjambs and window shutters. I filled the small fish-pond with lucky carp. On the day we moved in, in the late winter of 1931, just after the lunar New Year, I pasted up strips of paper on the gates declaring the arrival of the five good fortunes. I put a kitchen god in the niche above the stove and two door gods in battle array above the front door. In an upstairs window I placed a mirror to ward off ghosts.

It seemed that the more I prayed to the gods, the more I believed in them. The more tasks I fulfilled to placate the gods and to please them, the more I began to feel sure that they would hear me and satisfy my longings. I bought a statue of Kuan Yin, the goddess of compassion, who watches over women in childbirth, and I burned incense to her in the front hall. I bought the most expensive and sweetest-smelling incense, so that she could not refuse me.

But Guai was angry and ill at ease at all my attempts to flatter and extort from heaven. "Peasant superstition," he snorted. "You are too intelligent for this."

Even my mother raised her eyebrows slightly. "There is danger," she said, "that comes from trying to force the gods to your will. They will see through your tricks."

But Guai's mother in Yueyang entered eagerly into my plans, seeing, perhaps for the first time, something that she might have in common with me. She sent me a fortune-teller of great fame, who arrived at my door, his face covered with a red veil draped from the top of a tall conical hat that only sorcerers wear. He drew a great circle in the dirt of the unfinished kitchen courtyard. He danced there in a prophetic trance for hours, watched with fearful fascination by my servants. Guai retreated into his study in fury, and only glanced out the window from time to time to glare at me. I myself pasted a cynical smirk on my face and leaned against the walls with my arms crossed. It's your mother, I mouthed at him. The magician flapped his gilt paper fan like a giant bird's wing. He swung a censer of sweet woodsmoke into all corners of the yard. He chanted long strings of syllables, sifting them together like grains of sand. He wrote a character on a strip of red paper and gave it to me. Then I paid him and he left. The character was "heir." In front of the servants, I shrugged. But when I got inside, I immediately wrote a letter to Guai's mother to tell her, sealing up the note in an envelope with a red border, to signal to her that only good news lay within. I felt as if, for the first time, Guai's mother and I felt something together.

In March of that year, the Xiang River is high and its jade-green waters very brown with mud. Two small junks make their way down from the shores of Tung Ting Lake. Their sails are red—red for luck, red for happiness, red for good fortune—cracking in the wind, brilliant and sharp against the pale skies of early spring. The junks have been sent by Guai's parents, and are bursting with things to eat, things to wear. Chickens and fish and candy and sugar and bolts of silk and little silk shoes and hats for the new son. Big porcelain jars of Chinese medicines—powdered deer horn and tiger's rib and a whole forest of different kinds of bark to stew in soups. The junks come to rest at the dock a few streets away from my new house. I can see the sails through the window from my bed on the second story, jutting mysteriously above the low-lying roofs of the dockyards. Like looking at a Japanese woodprint, I think, where only the sails are visible, only hinting at the boats that lie beneath the frame of the picture, out of the viewer's eye. As I feel my labor pains, I keep my eyes fixed on the red sails, my reward.

The maids rush back and forth. The midwife, a figure of awesome authority—even my mother is a little afraid of her—speaks in low sharp tones. She has me drink bitter broth. She rubs my temples. I am old, I am old, I think. Pains are sharper now, and dig deeper, and matter more.

My daughter Zhen is born at midday. She is the twin of a boy, born dead. I am shown the living baby, and I look at her for a long time. There has been a horrible mistake, I think. I feel the weight of my years. I think about how now I have fewer years to live than I have already lived. For the first time in my life, perhaps, I truly understand the nature of my mortality, that human life is a road that does not turn back, that never passes again the places it has passed already. You might wind through the mountains, you might turn at the bridges, you might even pause in the shade of the trees. But you will never have again the chances you had before. The sights that met your eyes once will not meet them again. I think about my dead son, the only one I will ever have. Lying back on my pillow, sweat-soaked, my tangled hair spread out over the pillow, I think that death is inevitable and always very near, and the gods are usually silent.

I hear the cracking of sails on the wind. I look out the window, and see the red sails fill with the breeze, billowing above the rooftops. The man from the boats, waiting in the courtyard for news of the new son, has already run down to the docks and told the captain. The captain, without unloading one grain of sugar, one stick of candy, or one inch of silk cloth, sets sail again. The junks move slowly back up the river, back to the givers of the gifts. I watch the mysterious sails drift past the curving tile roofs of the neighborhood, and I think that I never did see the ships themselves. Perhaps they were not sails at all, but only banners, borne aloft by men, pretending to be sails.

Guai is anxious about me. He tells me, "It's a nice baby. Very pretty." But he cannot hide his disappointment. With my eyes fixed on the masts retreating into the river mist, I vow never again to pray to the gods. From now on, I will make my own luck.

Not being able to give birth to a male child is unlucky in more ways than one. The effects are widespread, far-reaching, although not entirely unexpected. Guai's mother ceased placing her faith in sorcerors and now took more practical action.

"I have begun to look for a small wife for Guai. I am sure you understand that since we consider a son unlikely at your age and state of health, we must take some sort of action. Of course, the girl will be respectful and subservient to you at all times. You will always be Guai's intellectual companion. We intend to acquire a girl of education, so she can take over some duties from you and you can rest. I am sure that you want Guai's happiness as much as we do. I will write again soon, dear daughter-in-law."

After I read this letter, I sat back in my hard chair in despair. I rarely cried these days, it seemed, but I had tears in my eyes now. I was sure that I could make a concubine subservient to me, but I had no wish for such an existence, always being the villainess in the house, oppressing the younger woman. The servants would pity the girl and turn against me. Worse yet, what if Guai came to have feelings for her? Guai was coming into his middle years, and men were even more fickle and foolish at that time than at any other. A lovely young girl—and I knew that my mother-in-law would find a girl both lovely and clever—could well establish herself in Guai's heart.

I took the letter and trudged to my husband's study. Guai was hearing complaints at the governor's palace, and the study was empty. I sat, not in his chair, as I sometimes did when he was absent, but on a low stool by the window, and waited for my husband to come up the garden walk. I saw my face reflected in the glass pane of the window. I imagined myself growing older by the minute, until my white hair hung down to my ankles and my eyes disappeared in a nest of wrinkles. I glanced down and surveyed my body. I had always been a little plump, and when I was young my plumpness had been pretty and feminine. Now, I thought, I was merely getting fat. The weight of my body hid its infertility—all this flesh, and no son. I sat by the window as the day turned into dusk, and the sky darkened.

When Guai came into the study, it was almost twilight. The house was bustling with dinner preparations. He found me crouched on a low stool, staring out the window with a face like a mask.

"What's the matter? Are you ill?" he asked. I turned my head to him slowly, and saw the shock in his expression when he saw my eyes filling with tears at the sound of his voice.

"Wife, what is wrong? Did one of the children get sick?" He hastened to me, and placed his hand on my shoulder gently. Without a word, I handed him the letter, crumpled and damp from the long hours that I had held it. He read the letter soundlessly, and looked at me in dismay.

"A small wife?" he exclaimed. "Do people even have them anymore?"

"I guess they think it's necessary."

He began to stride up and down. We stayed in silence for a moment. Then I spoke again.

"You had better write your mother and welcome the girl. You have no choice. She is your mother, and I can't give you a son. I'm sorry. I'm sorry, I'm sorry, I'm sorry . . ." I wrapped my arms around my knees and began to rock back and forth in an agony of self-sacrifice.

Guai was alarmed. "Here, stop this, wife." He patted my shoulder kindly. "Even if we had to have one, you would be the big wife. The house is yours."

I stared at him for a long time before answering. Does his willingness to consider a concubine come as a surprise? Guai always tried to be perfect, but it was Chinese perfection he strove for, and the bedrock of Chinese perfection was filial obedience. Your desire to be a perfect man will be the death of me, I thought.

"A big wife with no son is not a match for a small wife with a son. A big wife with no son is not a big wife. I would have to scold her all the time. I have no wish to be so hard all the time, in my own house. Besides . . ."

"What?"

I blurted out, "What if you decide you like her? And she gives you a son? If I scolded her, one day you might take her side. And then I would hang myself from the ceiling beam above your bed." I buried my face in my hands and sobbed furiously.

Guai raised his eyebrows. "Is that what you are afraid of? That I will take her side?"

"You will, you will!" I gasped wildly from between my fingers.

"I will not!" said Guai sternly, shocked at the accusation. "I would never do such a thing." But I only sobbed more wildly still. He sat down in the chair a few feet from me and watched me for a while. I wept until my voice was hoarse.

"Wife. Wife, listen to me. Listen."

I raised my head a little, and said in a muffled voice, "I'm listening."

"I won't have a small wife. Do you understand? I don't want one. I will die without a son before I take a concubine."

"Don't you want a son?" I asked.

"Of course. But I cannot compromise my principles. What kind of principles would they be, if I gave them up the moment they conflicted with my own desires? A concubine is just too old-regime degenerate. And"—here he turned to his desk and began tracing his finger along the edges—"I don't want you to be unhappy."

I was surprised and touched. "Do you think that's enough of a reason?"

"Yes," Guai replied calmly. "I mean, we did not have an arranged marriage." He paused, and the enormity of this simple statement of fact made us both suddenly very serious and very shy. "I will see what we can do to refuse this small wife."

He began to take papers out of his leather case and spread them out in front of him. "I have a little work to do. Will supper be ready soon?"

I stood up and put my hand on my husband's shoulder. He glanced up briefly, but looked back down at his work again immediately. He opened his bottle of ink and picked up his English fountain pen and began to write. I looked down and watched the flow of words from his pen from above, much as one would watch the flow of a river in a ravine far below. I felt sudden confidence in those words, rippling out onto the paper in a fine stream of black ink. I knew that every word would be just and good. My hand was still on Guai's shoulder. I moved my forefinger just a little, and brushed his cheek as lightly as an insect. Guai's writing hand faltered almost imperceptibly, but he kept writing. I stole from the room, shutting the door quietly behind me so he would not be disturbed.

.   .   .

"You can't leave it up to men," my mother said. "I am sure Guai thinks he means what he says, but men are famously weak and foolish. They always think they mean what they say."

"But he said he didn't want one."

"Yes, of course. But the old lady and gentleman will make his life a misery to him. Their ideas are ancient and very strongly rooted. They don't want his blood to die out, you see. And he won't want to make their old age bitter by disobeying them. So you will have to try to fend them off some other way. You will have to do something else."

"What? What can I do?"

My mother was lying in her bed in the middle of the day, since she had not been feeling well. She was embroidering a bird on a piece of silk.

"First stop crying," she ordered me. "Still so emotional."

"Why do you always say that?" I muttered.

"Since you are now over forty years of age, you might try to think instead. What exactly will satisfy them?"

"Guai's son," I sniffed, rubbing my nose.

"And what will satisfy you?"

"No concubine."

"There. You must obtain a son without a mother."

"I don't understand."

"Find a boy to adopt. Hint to Guai's parents that the boy is the child of Guai's mistress."

"He doesn't have a mistress."

It seemed my mother gave me a skeptical glance, as if to say that wives never really know what their husbands get up to, and that only foolish wives insist they know. But she said only, "The old ones don't know that. Just find a healthy little boy. Tell the old ones whatever story you want."

"Am I being selfish?" I pleaded.

"Yes. You would rather Guai's line die out than just put up with another woman in the house. To keep you happy, he must be a willing participant in extinguishing his own line of descent. Take care of him, Jade Virtue. He is making a terrible sacrifice for you."

This made me irrationally angry. "Then why are you helping me?"

My mother smiled very slightly, and looked over her embroidery. "Well, you are my daughter. Guai is not my son. Whether his line continues is not, strictly speaking, my concern." Now she looked at me. "Daughter, the substitution of sons—one way or another—is not so very uncommon, not in my day nor this one. As long as everyone thinks a man has a son, it is usually good enough. The only one who is never fooled is the woman. In a way, that's a pity, because we can never take refuge in the illusion."

In China, spare girl children are easy to come by, very cheap or often even free. Had we decided to adopt a daughter, that would have been as simple as walking out into the countryside, to any farm family with a girl's mouth to feed. But no one to my knowledge ever gave up boys. I had to be secretive about my search, which made it more difficult. Li Shi looked among his soldiers, and my mother made quiet inquiries in the poor neighborhoods, but I could find no one willing to give up a son. Autumn faded into winter, and still I had not been able to find a boy without a mother.

But in January 1932, something terrible happened that gave me my chance. There was a skirmish between Guomindang soldiers and Japanese marines in Shanghai, in the poor Chinese neighborhood of Chapei. The Japanese bombed Chapei—which was only an area of wooden houses, lived in by coolies, barbers, and laundresses—into the dirt, and then threw three full divisions at the city itself. Many, many civilians were slaughtered. The Guomindang commander—who had been a classmate of Li Shi's at university—fought with great bravery, and in May, the Japanese arranged an armistice. But the Generalissimo did not trust his commander's loyalty, and did not enjoy the reputation the commander's heroism had won for him in the eyes of the outside world, and transferred him from Shanghai all the way down to Fujian. I believe worse would have befallen him than merely a transfer, but Li Shi and Zhao Han Ren interceded for him and got him out of harm's way. Of course, this transfer of the hero of the defense of Shanghai encouraged the Japanese to renew their aggression.

My main reaction to the bombing of Chapei was to feel horror for the victims, but I did not think beyond this pity to the greater ramifications of such an action by the Japanese in China. At this stage in my life, I followed politics very little, being too concerned with family matters and the need to make more money. I was not interested in politics anymore, I thought. I worked only to preserve my home, and see to the comforts of my family. But Chapei affected me nevertheless, because Li Shi informed me that he had heard that a number of infants had been orphaned by the bombing. Boy children as well as girls had been left without homes.

One month after the armistice, Guai and I took the train to Shanghai, accompanied only by Yong Li. I had never traveled out of Hunan before, and I spent the three days on the train trying to imagine what Shanghai would look like. Guai and Jin Yu and my other friends had often described its size to me, its jostling crowds, its tall buildings along the waterfront, and the thick smoke that lay on it, eating into the masonry and stinging the eye. The train pulled into the Shanghai North Station in the evening, when it was already dark in the surrounding countryside. But even in the nighttime, the sky glowed red over Shanghai, a dark, smoky red, a color thrown up from a thousand festive lanterns, from the streetlights in the foreign concessions, from the lighted windows of the restaurants, cafés, tea shops, gambling halls, and brothels. The streets and alleys brimmed with light and noise in a way I had never seen, not even in the Street of Painted Houses in Changsha. All around the edges of the sprawling city, the rest of China was sunk in darkness and silence.

Guai impatiently tugged me along through the streets, much hampered because I kept staring up at the height of the buildings, which were built with thick stone and looked like the buildings in pictures I had seen of Paris and London. I was more composed than Yong Li, anyway, who held my hand tightly and gaped with her mouth open at the feathered hats and horribly short dresses of the women in the streets, apparently unmarried yet walking unaccompanied, swinging their hips and smiling at the young dandies strolling past.

"Close your mouth," I hissed to Yong Li. "You look like a bumpkin."

"How do you think you look," she grumbled back, "with the hem of your dress down around your ankles?"

Our hotel was a small wooden house in a small street off the main thoroughfare of Yan'an Zhong Lu, not too far from the racecourse and the Bird and Flower Market. We had to take a pedicab there, with Guai and I sitting behind the driver and Yong Li perched on the rear axle, clutching her bundle fearfully. I had to keep turning to look at her, in case she fell off or was snatched away by some Shanghai gangster. Guai actually ordered the pedicab driver to take the long way, in a big circle from the train station to the hotel, so we could see the famous Bund along the Huangpu River. The streets were so crowded that people passing by leaned into our cab, and bumped us with their elbows and baggage. I had never seen so many Western faces—Russians, Frenchmen, Englishmen, Germans. The smell of strange foods, of wine spilled in the gutters, of perfumes and incense, filled my nostrils and made my eyes tear with their pungency. I had often heard Shanghai referred to as an evil place, but it seemed no more evil than anywhere else where men lived. It was just brighter and louder, and I thought I had to be careful or I might grow to like it too much, and have a hard time going back home to Changsha.

"Well, I haven't been to the city since I was a student," Guai sighed when we were safely in our room, throwing his hat on the bed. "I must say, it is even more decadent now, and I thought it was pretty hazardous even then." He chuckled in a way that made me feel jealous.

"Really?" I said. "What did you do then that was so decadent?"

"Oh, nothing really," he said, concentrating for a moment on unbuttoning his coat and not meeting my eye. "You know how students are. Smoking cigarettes was considered decadent then."

"You must confess everything to me," I said menacingly, approaching him with my hands in the shape of claws.

"Never," he laughed, backing away behind the bed. "You can't frighten me with your threats. Stay away now, or I'll call for the police."

"You can't afford to, since you yourself are such a criminal." I grabbed at the lapels of his coat, and he put his arms around me. I clung to him a moment, and let my eyes wander over his face.

"What is it?" he asked.

"I was just thinking how happy I am, more than I've been in a while," I murmured. "But I shouldn't say things like that."

"That's right. The gods are jealous." He turned his face up to the ceiling. "Do you hear that, you gods? We are very unhappy!"

"Miserable, in fact!" I shouted.

"I am a misshapen dwarf, my wife here is a leper"—at this point Yong Li came in the room, cross at all the noise—"and our maidservant is angry at us all the time!" I buried my face in his shoulder and laughed so hard I thought my heart would burst.

"Enough now," I gasped. "Even the gods won't believe such blatant lies as that."

"Jade Virtue," Guai said, "I don't think we should stay in tonight. Let's spend some money."

"You always want to spend money."

"Yes, but we are in Shanghai. We'll eat dinner in a fancy restaurant on the waterfront, and go to the opera. All three of us."

"Master, I can't go," protested Yong Li, who had her hands on her hips. "How can I go?"

"It's different here," Guai said. "Everyone mixes together more. We'll all go. But Yong Li will have to stop frowning."

When people think back on their lives, they can think of only a handful of days or nights that seem perfect to them, which require nothing more in the way of happiness. My night in Shanghai was my perfect time, and I think of it to this day. I knew the city was dangerous, crime-ridden, in the thrall of warlords and opium gangs. I knew that addicts and whores filled its alleys. There were bomb craters in some streets, and many of the buildings bore the blackened damage of battle. And yet, even knowing all those things, and perhaps especially knowing all those things, I had never felt so free and so happy. I had never eaten dinner outside my own home at anything other than a private banquet or a noodle stand, but we ate thirteen courses at a restaurant overlooking the river, hung with red lanterns. We went to the opera and ate peanuts and oranges in the stand and cheered the good singers and hooted lustily at the bad ones. Yong Li went home with a headache from too much wine, and Guai and I watched the sun rise from the bar of the Cathay Hotel, where Englishmen and their wives danced to a jazz band of amazingly black men imported from America. Walking home in the dawn, I did something I had never done in public before, and took my husband's arm.

"Everything feels so new here," I murmured, just before falling asleep.

"That's the remarkable thing about big cities," Guai answered.

"Do you think we could ever live here, in the present, instead of where we live now, in the past?" But I fell asleep before I heard his reply.

We slept only three hours, and then got up to dress hurriedly and take a hired taxi car to the French Concession. All of us were bleary-eyed from lack of sleep and the wine from the night before, and I couldn't help giggling at how we all looked. Guai leaned his head against the window, and Yong Li fell asleep on the short ride.

Our destination was a Christian orphanage in the Concession, run by French nuns, women who vowed to remain virgins and wore long black and white gowns as a sign of their status. The orphanage was immaculately clean and free from any odor, which was unusual in China. A number of children of all ages lived there, the infants lying in cribs and the older ones running in the yard or sweeping floors. The rooms were very quiet compared to the cacophony outside, so quiet that my ears rang for a while after entering its doors.

We went first to the director's office and spoke to him briefly. We were guided by one of the nuns to a waiting room, and it was there that my son was brought to us. The nun holding him stood next to me for some time, but my hands were shaking too hard to take him from her, and Yong Li had to take him instead. He looked a little less than a year old, perfectly healthy and even unusually alert.

"Poor thing," said the nun, looking at him fondly and touching his foot. Her Chinese was surprisingly good, and I stared at her. I had never heard Chinese come out of a non-Chinese mouth before, and I could hardly fit the face with the language. It was almost as if she had broken a code to which I had been privy. "He was left an orphan after Chapei. A Chinese Christian heard a baby crying in the wreckage of a house that had been demolished by the bomb. He found three dead women in the rubble, and lying under the body of one of them, this baby. There was nothing left standing, and no other person left alive, for many streets around." She looked at me with her strange blue eyes. "He has come to you by the grace of God, my dear lady."

"Yes, yes," I said, transfixed by the blue of her gaze. "Yes." I bowed to her again and again, and bowed until she had left the room. "Thank you," Guai called after her in broken English, and that sounded strange to me too. Everyone has changed places, I thought. They are speaking with strange tongues.

Guai felt in his pocket and took out a little black silk hat with a red tassel, such as firstborn sons wear. He fitted the cap on the baby's head. The baby looked curiously at him. I began to sniffle, and Guai gave me his handkerchief.

"We should go, if we are to catch the train," he said. I nodded, and allowed myself to be herded outside by him. I never took my eyes off the baby.

In the train, waiting to leave and listening to all the steam whistles, I came back to life a little and took the baby from Yong Li's arms. Guai, sitting next to me, met my eyes and we both smiled.

"What an ugly baby!" he exclaimed, and we both began laughing.

"What will we tell your mother and father?"

"I'll write to them and hint that my mistress had a child by me, and we have taken it into the house as a legitimate son. Just like we planned."

"I feel a little funny. Like I've been shamed by the fact that you have a mistress."

"What are you saying? I don't really have one."

"I know that. But everyone else will think you do, and so I'll be shamed anyway."

"Women's logic. I'm not listening. We have a son, and no concubine, exactly as you wanted, and still you are unsatisfied."

"No, no." I started to laugh again. "I'm perfectly satisfied. Do you think your family will be satisfied?"

"Well, my eldest brother, that whore hound, will certainly write me to congratulate me, not on having a son, but on having had a mistress."

The steam whistle went off again in a piercing shriek, drowning out our voices.

"Wait, I have a joke," I said.

Guai and Yong Li waited expectantly.

"What is the Soviet idea of poetry?"

Guai and Yong Li shook their heads.

"O Steam Whistle," I chanted sonorously. "O Lenin."

Guai laughed until he had to wipe his eyes. Yong Li sighed and took the baby again. "An intellectual's jokes are hardly even jokes," she muttered. "I feel sorry for this baby."

When the train was picking up passengers in Jingdezhen, I asked Guai about names for the boy. "Something auspicious."

"You know, I thought of calling him Jiao Ren."

"After Song Jiao Ren?" I asked.

Guai nodded, and his face was suddenly somber. "You know, I was only twenty-one when Song Jiao Ren was assassinated. At the Shanghai North Station, the one we just left. I thought about him when we arrived, and again when we were leaving. He was my hero, the political hero of all the young men of my era. If he had lived, surely our country would now be the democracy we all wished for. You know, they never really found out what happened. The main conspirators disappeared or were assassinated in their turn. I heard about his death just before I got on the boat to Japan to study, and it was like the death of an older brother. He himself was only thirty or so. I thought to turn back, but then I tried to imagine what Song would want, and I believed he would want me to study in Japan and learn things to help our country. So I went, with a terrible emptiness in my heart. No leader has yet appeared who can fill that hole completely."

"You sound like Li Shi. Why do men always wish for great leaders? You have a family. Isn't that enough?" My voice sounded querulous and irritated, even to me.

Guai did not answer, but only looked out the window. I do not deserve the sacrifice he has made for me, I thought. And proving myself worthy, every day for the rest of my life, will be a burden on both of us. The train began to move, and I watched for an hour or so while the landscape ran past my window.

"Guai, if you want to name our son Wu Jiao Ren, I have no objection."

He shook his head. "No. Fifty miles ago, I thought that was what I wanted. But I think a name like that is too great a burden for such a small person." He was smiling again. "We should think of something luckier."

"Wan Li," said Yong Li.

"We're naming him after you?" I asked.

"Not my 'Li.' My 'Li' is the plum tree. 'Wan' which means 'ten thousand' and 'Li' which means 'miles.' Wan Li. Because I hope this child will go far."

Guai and I looked at each other.

"I think we have a name," he said.

"We have no choice. She'll just call him that until we give in."

30

1 planted aromatic trees in the garden, cassia and camphor and rose mallow. With my own hands, I planted a dozen varieties of roses, thorny and sweet against the walls of the house, with a rambler rose beginning to climb over the front gate, and a wisteria vine on the back wall. Rooted in the mud of the fishpond were yellow and white lotuses, and the sleeping lotus from the far south, which retracts below the water at night and emerges again into the air during daytime. Although I frequently hired men or boys to dig up the beds or to plant trees, I mostly tended to the garden myself, going out in the cool of the early morning or in the waning heat of dusk. I wanted to build a gazebo, but there was not quite enough room, so I built out a covered porch from the back of the house instead, leading it in a zigzagging curve to the edge of the pond. I put a chessboard there for Guai to play, which he did most often with Zhao Han Ren at twilight.

"Zhao, you've left me in a position where, no matter which way I move, I must lose."

From the flowerbed where I was digging below, I heard Zhao's dry laugh.

"Doesn't that happen sometimes?" he replied.

I grew a bed of sweet basil and other grasses under the chess-playing porch, for no other reason than to see their tender stems waving in the breeze. To protect them from the harshness of the elements, and the running feet of my children, I placed them very close to the wall, and thought they seemed like tiny creatures nestled there.

"I think you should oppose the founding of such a bureau in the national council," Guai said.

"I'm not going to. There's no point in asking me."

"A Bureau of Investigation and Statistics? Can you imagine what that will be like? A secret police, nothing less."

"You know our policy. We must crush the Communists quickly so we can turn our unified attention to the Japanese problem. You and I can both quote from the Generalissimo's latest speech. 'Internal pacification before resistance to attack.' Must I remind you?"

"The Japanese are already at our gates! Have they not built up a puppet country on our northern border, and called it the Manchu Kingdom, and put the Emperor there as king?"

"Yes, yes, I know. We should have killed Puyi when we deposed him."

"Zhao, that's terrible. He was just a boy then."

"That is always your problem, Guai. Always you refuse to do what needs to be done. Had we killed Puyi then, he would not be the head of Manchukuo today. You wring your hands at the outcome, but you do not take the necessary steps to influence that outcome."

I had written many letters to a dealer in rare plants in Canton, searching for the saffron crocus, a fragrant autumn-blooming purple flower that had been imported from Persia during the Tang dynasty. It was my intention to extract the red-gold saffron from the dried stigmas of the flower and use it to flavor the sweet wine Yong Li made in the winter. Thus far, the Canton dealer's prices had been too high, but I hoped to bargain him down.

"If you objected so much to our arrangement with the Triads . . ."

"They are criminals, Zhao! Murderers and thieves and opium smugglers. How can we ally with them against the Communists?"

"They have enough men, enough arms, enough money, and they are everywhere. The advantages of a criminal organization over a mere government are obvious. You should have spoken then. Now it is too late. Although I did wonder why you did not object more strenuously at the time. You could have gone to Nanjing to the council."

Guai was silent for a long moment. "Because I doubted my own judgment. I thought perhaps everyone else was right. That it was the only way. Perhaps it still is. But I feel now as if our government has put itself against the people. We've given the crime lords the run of the country, and the people will never forgive us."

I fetched my new watering can filled with water and hoisted it over the earthenware pots where the peppers grew. The leaves of the miniature orange trees looked a little brown, but when I felt them between my fingers they seemed moist and flexible.

When Zhao left, Guai came out to where I squatted weeding in the flowerbeds.

"Did you hear?"

"Yes, of course. Don't worry. Everything will be fine." I turned the earth over forcefully with my fork. "We are all well. The children are healthy, and I am making money. Everything will be fine."

"Jade Virtue, do you think what Zhao said was true? About my never doing what is necessary to ensure the outcome? Are you listening?"

Jueh ran around the corner of the house, shouting for Yong Li.

"She's in the kitchen courtyard," I called back. "Go there and find her, precious." I went back to digging.

"Did you hear what I said?"

"Yes, yes, I'm listening," I said hurriedly, straightening up. "Do *you* think it's true?"

Guai hung his head. "I don't know. We can't govern unless the people see that we act morally. But it seems that if we act morally, we can't stay in power, and so we can't govern." He looked up at me, his face stiff with confusion and worry. "Perhaps I'm just not the man for these times."

"Guai," I said, dusting off my hands. "I'd like you to consider taking the position as head of the Soong family bank." He spun away in anger, but I seized his sleeve. "Please consider it! Being the magistrate gains you nothing except criticism. As the head of the bank, you would have everything, prestige and influence and rewards. You could use them to accomplish what you want. You could have your own foundation for the poor, if you wanted." I looked at him pleadingly, but for the first time since I had known him, I saw a look of disdain cross his face.

"Do you wish to buy more gold, wife, to bury in your floor?"

"Guai, that's unfair. All my concern is for you and the children. That's all I care about."

He pulled his sleeve out of my grasp. "Yes, I know," he said. "You are not the woman you used to be." He walked away in the failing light.

"Well, and whose fault is that?" I hissed after him, not daring to raise my voice too much in case the servants should hear. "I must concern myself with keeping this family secure and in comfort, since you will not!" I heard the door shut in the middle of my sentence. I threw down the weeding fork in anger.

My children grew as quickly as my garden, as if the damp heat of Changsha affected them as well. As they emerged from infancy, they were more interesting to me, more like humans and less like vulnerable kittens.

Then I often found myself looking at Wan Li, and wondering where he came from. Jueh looked like me, and Zhen looked like Guai, but of course, Wan Li did not look like either of us. Indeed, his appearance was so foreign to me that I wondered if he was not quite Chinese, if he did not have some Mongolian or other outlander blood. In idle moments, I thought he might be the descendant of a Mongol prince, or perhaps he had simply been one in his previous life.

Jueh, by the time she was four or five, was old enough to accompany me on my business in town. She held my hand when I went to meet with my rent collection agent, and sat quietly in a chair waiting for me. Indeed, I often waited to leave the house until she had awoken from her nap or finished her bath, since I preferred her company to simply going alone. She was from the first very well behaved, but I noticed with concern a tendency to play on her charm with adults. She would tilt her head to one side and smile like an opera star. When she interlaced her fingers under her chin, I pushed her hands down. "Only silly women do that kind of playacting," I said solemnly. But she always did it again. All very well while you are young, I thought, but those kinds of flirts never seem to age gracefully.

One day in the early summer, while Jueh was standing by my side in the street in front of the bank, she saw what must have been for her a very strange creature. A Buddhist monk in his saffron robe walked by with his alms bowl, his prayer beads swinging at his waist. He was a startling flash of color among the tradesmen who crowded the surrounding streets, all of whom were big-muscled men with roughened hands and greasy clothes, smelling of garlic and onions, accompanied by underfed-looking apprentices. "He's a monk," I said, letting her have a coin to put in his begging bowl. The monk winked at her in the friendliest manner. She opened her mouth with surprise, and then stared at him all the way down the street. As I concluded my business, I realized that she had begun to follow the monk, and without saying anything, I followed after.

We came to the end of the alleyway, where it joined a much larger street, a bustling thoroughfare filled with bright sunlight and hundreds of people and shops. A great water buffalo, muddied to its knees in the grayish drying soil of the fields, lumbered by, pulling a two-wheeled wooden cart loaded with baskets of grain. A boy trundled next to the beast in a bored sort of way, occasionally flicking his switch and squinting in the sun. Little bells hung from the cart with red yarn tinkled merrily.

I looked around for the monk, but Jueh saw his saffron robe first. She

darted after him, and I walked more quickly to keep up with her. I followed her little form up some steps to the great red gates of a temple complex, which closed before she could squeeze through. But when I got there
and pushed open the gates, we were both dismayed. The courtyard was
filled with saffron robes and shaved heads, hundreds of them, walking
about in the courtyard and along the wooden galleries that surrounded it,
in and out of the various temples and pavilions.

"Where is our monk?" she whispered.

"I don't really know," I said. "They all look exactly alike."

We entered the nearest temple. It was warm and dark and smoky, and
I wondered how long it had been since I had stepped inside one of these. In
front of us were three tall gilt statues of Buddha, side by side. There were
four other large statues, two on each side, painted in bright colors—the
guardian gods of rain, thunder, lightning, and wind. These guardians were
fierce, with bristling mustaches, brandishing weapons or banners, a
marked contrast to the preternatural serenity of the ascetic Buddhas.
Sticks of incense thrust into a large metal urn in the center crumbled under their flames, making tiny pinpoints of light in the gloom.

There were a number of smaller statues too, of the Twelve Immortals
and the Eighteen Wise Men, and a host of other figures and deities. Before
the statue of Kuan Yin, the bodhisattva of compassion, a pregnant woman
knelt and bowed, a stick of incense between her supplicating palms. The
silence was broken only by the hushed grind of several large spinning
prayer wheels, with prayers and petitions written on slips of paper stuffed
inside. Each revolution of the wheel was one prayer sent up to heaven, and
there were monks who did no more than squat before them all day, spinning the wheels with the palms of their hands, spinning thousands of
prayers to heaven every day, millions and millions of prayers in a lifetime
of spinning, building a great fortune of virtue in heaven. Were prayers
more likely to be answered if they were repeated?

I could see Jueh was attracted by the flashing quickness of the wheels,
but was afraid to approach the monks, who chanted as they spun. Instead,
I followed her to a wall of bright embroidered banners. There were hundreds of them, completely covering the walls of this temple. Each banner
was at least six feet square, and every inch of the great squares of cloth
were covered by tiny, perfect stitches, and the whole made up a brilliant,
detailed picture. The banners were the finest embroidery I had ever seen,
even finer than Graceful Virtue's. There were scenes from Buddha's life—

his birth as a prince in India, his Enlightenment under a pipal tree, and his preaching to disciples. One inventive embroiderer showed the arrival of the first monks in China, teaching at the emperor's court, surrounded by court ladies, gay and charming and playful in their graceful hairdos and silk dresses. One court lady held up her sleeve to hide the fact that she was laughing at the poor barefoot monks, so skillfully rendered that I felt a surge of indignation with her. And every picture was done in the most beautifully colored silks—burnt orange, bright pink, jade green, and a shiny, glossy black for the court ladies' hair.

Jueh reached out to touch them, but I prevented her, for I could see they were very old, and I was afraid they might crumble under her fingers.

A young monk approached us.

"Do you like them?" he asked my child in a serious tone.

Jueh turned to look at him, and was suddenly shy. She only nodded, and then partly hid behind my skirt.

"Each one takes fifteen years to sew." The monk stepped forward, and examined the corner of one banner before dropping it.

"Who sews them?" I asked. "Surely not the monks themselves?"

"Oh no." The young monk touched away traces of a smile with his fingers. "We sometimes have to repair our own clothes, but we don't do fine needlework. They are embroidered by unmarried girls from respectable families. Many of the temples in China have them. We ourselves have thousands—there are some in every building in the complex. They have been made for hundreds of years."

"Family honor, that kind of thing?"

The monk nodded politely.

"Fifteen years to sew a single one? My heaven," I said, properly appreciative. "What happens when they finish? Do they get married then?"

"No," the monk sighed. "At the end of the fifteen years of embroidery, the girl is usually blind. Then she has to live on the charity of her father or brothers. But they are happy to care for her, because she has honored the family with her sacrifice."

I took my daughter home. Yong Li was waiting for us.

"Where have you been? You are too big to spank, but I should have a try at it."

"We went to look at monks," I said, suddenly exhausted and upset.

"Look at monks? Have you turned Buddhist?"

Later, Yong Li told me that Jueh had sat down with her little embroidery hoop and announced that she would sew a banner. "But she got tired of it in a short while and wanted to eat dumplings instead. I had to clean up all the threads. It's a good thing, Elder Sister, that she isn't taking up embroidery. The only woman in this family who can really embroider is your sister."

"What did you do with her little piece of work?" I asked.

"I picked out the stitches and put the cloth away," she called over her shoulder as she left the room. I sat for a while, thinking about the maidens sewing, their needles skimming like birds over the bright silk, sewing in the service of a religion of impermanence. I seemed to imagine them wearing blindfolds over their eyes as they sewed, and before I went to eat dinner, I meditated just a little on the nature of those who go blind on purpose.

Sitting in my garden one summer evening shortly afterward, I heard the distant roar of a low-flying airplane, a sound that was becoming more and more familiar to me. Once, I had found the noise thrilling, and I always jumped up from what I was doing, or leaned out the window, to see the airplane. In those days, many of the planes could not fly very high, and you could see the pilot inside very clearly, his goggles glinting in the sun like the cloud dew on the nose of his metal bird. But the sounds came more often now, and had begun to take on an ominous groan, hidden inside the exultant thrust of the engines.

The plane flew over my head, and I turned my face with it steadily, watching it until it was out of sight, not shifting my gaze even as it released a snowstorm of fluttering white papers over the entire area. Dozens of them landed in my garden, flopping into the pond, sticking in the trees, coming to land with a whisper among my flowers. One impaled itself on the rosebush nearest me, and I plucked it off carelessly. I was familiar with its contents, since I had seen them before. "Greater East Asia Co-Prosperity Sphere," it said. "The Empire of Japan desires peace, but will not accept dishonor," it said. "The duty of Japan is to protect its neighbors from disorder," it said. All the usual things. I stood in the dusk with the leaflet in my fist and looked around my garden, and wondered how I could possibly build these walls up any higher.

31

*I*n January 1935, in the midst of a very cold winter, I traveled to a shrine in the Xuefeng Mountains, the White Horse Mountain shrine. I told everyone I was visiting the shrine to offer sacrifices for Guai's father, whose lungs were weakening every day. The prayers of the priests at the White Horse Shrine were widely reputed to be very effective. I took only Yong Li with me. I had a bad cold, and coughed in great shudders in the train station. At the station, I averted my eyes from a small band of Blueshirts, who were on their way to a party rally somewhere.

We went by train on a small branch line from Changsha as far as we could go toward the mountains, the steam engine chugging and groaning through the empty rice fields, where bare browned stalks were all that remained of the harvest. Several hundred miles of winter landscape rolled away from us. But the transportation minister had embezzled some of the money to lay more track, so the train tracks ended in the middle of nowhere, with no station or platform to receive us. We simply climbed out and set foot on the hard frozen ground, our skirts and trouser legs whipped by the winter wind. A number of sedan chairs waiting for custom were ranged around in the mud, their carriers swilling tea in their mouths, or chewing betel, or pissing on the ground. Steam rose from their unwashed bodies, and I wrinkled my nose. Yong Li hired a sedan chair for me, and pulled my fur-lined jacket more closely around my neck before I climbed in.

"There's room for two," I said, but she shook her head. She pulled down the dirty sateen curtain and walked alongside, her hand on the inner rail to comfort me with her presence. The inside of the chair smelled sour and musty. I heard Yong Li's voice scolding the carriers in the coarsest country dialect, telling them I was over forty years old and they should take care not to jostle me. From time to time, she put her head in under the curtain and said she didn't know why I was bothering with the priests, I would find out soon enough if Old Wu were meant to live through his latest illness.

It took two days to reach the White Horse Shrine. The first night I spent in a flea-ridden inn at the side of the road, like a Tang dynasty traveling merchant. I felt I had stepped back several centuries, a far distance from my modern house in Changsha. I got up in the middle of night to find lice in my bed. Yong Li shouted for a kettle of boiling water and poured it all over the thin straw mattress, killing the lice, whose white bodies—like rice kernels—flooded out onto the dirt floor. She laid our coats on top of the damp mattress, but my old problem of sleeplessness reasserted itself, and I simply sat up in a chair and watched for the dawn. Yong Li slept soundly, though, and I listened to her funny little snores in the breaking light of day. I was sick, and could not eat the white rice for breakfast.

All through the second day, my chair wound slowly up through the karst hills, the bare rocks and evergreens starting to show patches of snow. I asked for some snow, and Yong Li handed me a little through the curtain. I held it to the back of my flushed neck until it melted down my spine. The air smelled spicy with cold, and I put on gloves. The bare-chested sedan chair carriers seemed impervious to the chill, however, and talked loudly the entire time. I wished they would stop, because the silence I would hear in the breaks in their conversation sat sweetly on my ears. It occurred to me that in Changsha, I almost always heard constant noise, background or foreground, nearby or far away, man or machine, and always, underlaid by the rushing of the river. But the mountains made no sound, they looked down on me with a sort of mysterious stoicism.

We reached the shrine at nightfall, and I was exhausted. Yong Li wasted no time scolding me, but got me into a bed in the pilgrim's dormitory and pulled a mound of old quilts over me. A few other travelers were already sleeping in beds, dotted here and there in the gloom of the dormitory room, which was so large I could not see the far end. I shut my eyes, every muscle aching. My stomach was rumbling with hunger, but I was too nauseated to eat anything. I thought Yong Li was right, and that I had lost my mind in coming here.

The following morning, I saw through the greased-paper window that peculiar brightness of light that is present when there is snow on the ground. I walked out to the common hall where the priests served noodles and steamed bread to the pilgrims, in the shadow of the gigantic statues of the temple guardian deities, fierce in their armor and mustaches. I drank only tea, and watched my breath come out in white puffs. Over the top of the temple walls, the evergreens exhaled their sweet scent. The sun was bright, and I had to shade my eyes against the shining snow.

"Let's go now," I told Yong Li. "I want to get this done with."

"You travel for days, Elder Sister, being sick as you are, just to make some prayers, and now you want it all done quickly." But she took me across the courtyards into the main temple. A gust of incense wrapped around us at the door, and I took a few seconds to become accustomed to the dimness, after the white-enameled brilliance of the world outside. Ranged all around the room on shelves were jars filled with exorcised spirits, held imprisoned there by the priests' spells.

The blue-clad Taoist priests received me kindly, and took from my hands my offering of silk and coins. They sat me next to a charcoal brazier, and arranged themselves to pray. They murmured the Taoist rites, a series of paradoxes. They wished Old Wu a long life, and praised me as a dutiful daughter-in-law.

"Ask them how to get to the Little White Horse Temple," I told Yong Li. "I intend to spend tonight there to meditate."

"That's abandoned now," she said.

"I'm aware of that. Just ask."

By late morning, Yong Li was following me along a path of pine needles toward the smaller, older abandoned temple, five miles from the main compound. My coughs sounded hollowly in the thin air.

"No one goes here now," she was complaining. "And you want me to leave you there? There are bandits in these mountains."

"What bandit would go to a ruined temple?"

"What if you fall while you are alone there?"

"I don't intend to perform exercises while I'm there. I'm only going to meditate."

It took us more than an hour of walking to get there, but finally I spotted it through the trees, a small temple with plaster walls built into the slope, and vines climbing through the wooden lattices. Although abandoned, the thatched roof was still reasonably solid, and there were no holes in any of the walls.

"It looks well enough," Yong Li conceded, gathering up sticks to make up a fire in the single room. "I'm building this fire, which you will feed all night long. When you go to sleep, the embers will keep the room warm until morning; then you must blow on them to bring the flames up again."

I stood outside and gazed around me at the mountains, fading in and out of the mist.

"Do you know why no one comes here anymore?" Yong Li grumbled as she spread out a cloth on a stone block in the sun, sheltered from the wind by a retaining wall.

"Why?" I asked, sitting down heavily on the block, and rubbing my face in the sunshine.

"Ghosts. This temple is haunted. You will probably see a ghost, and it will be bad luck."

"I'll be fine. Come back for me after daylight tomorrow. Now go."

Yong Li walked away reluctantly, calling back to me that I should not forget to eat food from the bundle she had placed at my feet. I waved to her and called out not to worry, that all the friendly spirits of the forest would protect me until she came back to look after me herself.

I sat at the Little White Horse Temple by myself for almost an hour. The sun was climbing toward the middle of the sky, and the warmth, reflected off snow and stone, was beginning to make me sleepy. The silence was absolute. But then I heard a step behind me.

"Did you have a boy or a girl after I left?"

"A girl," I replied, without turning. "I heard you coming. I thought you were able to move through the mountains like deer."

"I did it deliberately, so I wouldn't startle you." Jin Yu's low laugh circled around to my front, and I saw her face again. She was wearing trousers and a heavy leather belt and a thick quilted jacket, with dirty woolen wadding sticking out of the burst shoulder seam. She had leather boots on her feet and a revolver stuck in her waistband.

"Your hair has gray in it now," I said.

"Yours too." She sat down on the ground across from me and leaned back against a fallen tree. "Do you have anything to eat?"

"Yes, yes," I said anxiously, hurrying to open my bundle. "I brought you all kinds of things. See here, steamed buns, stuffed pastries, winter melon, sesame biscuits. All the things you like."

Jin Yu smiled apologetically as she began to wolf down the food. "The winter is a hard one," she said between bites. "I have to save some of this for the comrades."

I touched her face tenderly. "You are so thin," I murmured. I handed her my flask of tea.

"You certainly picked a strange way to get a message to me," I said. "Come inside by the fire, and I'll sew up your sleeve for you. I brought needles and thread, as you asked, and I'll leave them with you."

"Later we'll go inside. Let's just enjoy the sun for now."

I watched her eat for a time. Then she sat back and put her feet up on my block of stone and put her head back. I watched the sunlight fill her face like a golden bowl.

"Do you want to sleep a little?" I asked. "I'll keep watch for you."

"I won't wake up surrounded by Li Shi's men?"

I must have looked devastated, because she said quickly, "I'll sleep a little. Almost all our operations take place at night now, and I can only sleep in the day."

"Go ahead." I sat quietly in the sunshine, and listened to the soft rustling of the trees, while she slept. My eyes swept over the dusting of white snow, which lay in patches in the lee of the rocks. When she awoke, she ate more, and I boiled a little tea over the fire in a metal cup.

"How is your family?" she asked, as if she were sitting down to tea with me on my veranda. She lit a cigarette, which I found rather shocking.

"Very well."

"And your new house?" She adjusted the gun in her belt to sit more comfortably.

"Finished. It's beautiful. Inner and outer courtyards, a garden with a fishpond, which I restored, a higher wall for security with broken glass embedded in the top. And rosebushes all along the sides of the veranda."

"Well, roses of course. Always your favorite." She nodded in a distracted way, her eyes elsewhere, on the trees of the forest around us, on the sun glinting on the pine needles and patches of moss.

"I gave birth to Zhen there, my second daughter," I said. "But we also adopted a little boy, Wan Li. He was orphaned at Chapei."

"Raise him to fight the Japanese."

"I will. Although I hope by the time he is old enough, they will have gone away."

She turned her head away and back again, a movement of sudden disgust and impatience. "You hope they will have gone away?" Her voice was hissing. Her anger had blazed up so quickly that it must have been there all along, barely disguised by her civilities. "Do you think the Japanese will take it into their heads to simply go away? With the way your husband's government serves and flatters them? So you can continue in your comfortable life? Riding on the backs of the poor, like the rest of your kind?" She stood up and flicked her cigarette away, her lips pressed together, pale with fury.

"Stop it, Jin Yu!" I snapped, getting just as angry. "Guai is an honorable man, and he is doing his best!"

"You can't travel with jackals unless you are one yourself!"

"How dare you?" I jumped to my feet and took a step closer to her, my fists clenched. All my own doubts about Guai's position and the constant strain of my friendship with Jin Yu only fueled my defiance. "What are you, other than a wolf, killing men you don't even know?"

"What difference does it make if I know them or not?" Her face twisted into cold disdain. "They represent landlords and wealth and oppression. Whoever they may be as men, they deserve to die because of the cruelty they serve. How can you live with yourself, seeing brutal injustice every day in the fields and streets, and still be married to a government man?"

"Because I don't care about Guai's government!" I was shouting now. "I only love Guai! Just as I don't care about the Communists and their murders, because I only love you!" We stared at each other a moment. More quietly, I said, "For me, there is only you and Guai. I don't care about the rest of them."

"Well, there is a limit to that," she said, her normal voice returning. She lit another cigarette. "At some point, you can no longer divide the person from their actions. Then you must choose."

"Yes. And for today I choose you. Tomorrow I will go back down the mountain, and I will choose Guai."

We looked at each other in silence for a long time, and then sat down again, wary and exhausted. Jin Yu inhaled a deep breath of tobacco smoke, and blew it out elegantly through both her nostrils, like a particularly beautiful dragon.

"Well, do you do anything at all now?" she asked. "Do you teach? Do you write?"

"No. I have to think of Guai's position. And I have three small children. I have to mind my own business."

"Everyone has that disease, and it's killing the nation."

"I can't help it. I'm only interested in my family, anyway."

"What a perfect little woman you are," Jin Yu sneered, folding her arms over her chest. "Perfectly content in the domestic sphere, now that we have a man and infants to call our own."

"I'm more like a human being than you ever were," I said, my voice tight. "My feelings are natural. Hesen and your children never had that effect on you."

She raised her eyebrows. "What do you mean? Of course they did." I looked at her in surprised silence. "Do you think I was never tempted to withdraw into the woman's world? Into its safety? Into the perfect peace of mind that comes from having no choices? When my son was born, I remember thinking that all I wanted was to nurse him and to cook Hesen's dinner and wash his socks."

"I never expected that of you." I was stuttering in surprise.

"But I steeled myself to do more." She leaned forward in her intensity. "Because the world must change, and that change must go in the way Mao directs. Because there had to be a part of my life which did not concern men or children or family, but which concerned my thoughts and my will. Because having a husband or having children does not answer the question."

"What question?" I burst out anxiously.

"What we exist for. Do we live just to eat, drink, shit, and copulate? Or can we make a new world, here, within the physical boundaries of the old one? What are you here for, Jade Virtue? What do you want to say about your existence?"

I hesitated a moment before answering, even though I had considered this question before. "I want to say that at the end of my life, I understood more than I did at the beginning."

Jin Yu suddenly threw herself back with a hearty laugh. "Well, now you are asking perhaps for too much!" Her ringing voice made me happy, and I laughed as well. "But at least," she said, getting serious again, "at least you know you are not here merely to breed, as everyone has bred since time began. Give up your fantasies of perfect safety, Jade Virtue. No one is safe. Not me in the mountains, not you in your fine new house. The tigers still come for us, wherever we may sleep."

"If none of us is safe, what can we do?"

"We can be fast. Clever. Fierce. Brave. All these things, all of which you can be."

"But never safe?" I poked the fire.

"No. The world itself is one unending revolutionary turmoil. And as Mao says, a revolution is not a dinner party."

"But it is hard for me. I'm not alone in the world. We are tied into a ten-thousand-strand spider's web that holds a person hostage. It demands that we betray precious things in order to preserve other precious things. You know about the execution of that newspaper editor in Hanzhou, don't you? His own sister informed on him, and so sealed his fate. But everyone knew that she had done it to shield her son from suspicion. In the uproar over the brother's execution, the son was sent quietly away to an industrial apprenticeship in the distant northwest. I heard he put on a head cloth and is passing for a Muslim. These are the kinds of choices our lives lead us to, if we have anyone we love."

Jin Yu shrugged. "Of course it's hard. I'm not alone in the world either."

I looked down at my hands.

"Jin Yu, I have news for you from Changsha," I said soberly.

She looked at me. "Tell me."

"Your children are doing well. Hesen's parents care for them, and they want for nothing. I'm making sure of that."

She said nothing, but continued to look at me.

"But Hesen." I stopped when my voice broke. "Hesen is dead. He was arrested in Hong Kong. The British handed him over to the Guomindang."

"He was executed?"

I nodded.

"Shot?"

"Yes. A firing squad, as usual."

She leaned her head back again, her eyes closed. "Poor Hesen," was all she said, and her voice was hoarse.

I hesitated a moment before going on, but I thought that the swiftest surgery was always the least painful. "Jin Yu, I've known you a long time. So I tell you everything at once, because I know that is what you would want. Your parents both died last year, within a few months of each other. They didn't suffer."

"Well," she said, "I really am alone in the world after all. But it's better this way."

After a while, I asked, "Do you ever cry, Jin Yu? I mean, cry tears?"

"I haven't wept since I was a child. Since before you knew me."

"I still cry tears."

"Yes. You have a soft heart, Jade Virtue. You feel sorry for everyone, whether they deserve it or not."

"It's not a question of what they deserve. It's just the way I am."

Throughout the afternoon, the sun grew pinker and sank lower in the sky. Even though it was winter, the daylight lasted longer here in the mountains than it did down in the valleys, where the rice fields and the cities lay. We picked up the things I had brought and moved them inside, and I spread out a few blankets on the floor.

"Wait, we can do better," Jin Yu said. She went back outside, and returned shortly with an armful of fragrant pine boughs, which she piled in a heap on the floor by the fire. She spread the blankets out on top.

"This will keep us off the ground, where it is coldest."

The room was small and soon warm from the fire, but the outer edges stayed very cold. Jin Yu and I kept shifting around, moving closer to the fire when we got cold and farther away when we became overheated.

I took out some wheat buns and put them in the ashes of the fire to warm. Jin Yu rubbed her reddened eyes.

"Tell me how it is in the mountains," I said.

"Not much to tell. It's very hard. When the Red Army broke out of Jiangxi in October, they left behind thousands of us, mostly wounded. Well, fewer wounded now, because they are dying like worms. They are scattered in camps throughout the mountains, but many have been captured and killed by Li Shi's soldiers."

I said nothing, but looked down at my hands.

"We're supposed to stay behind and go on fighting, and try to maintain the soviets here in the south. The main columns—well, they are trying to retreat to some safe place in the north. Only thirty-five women got to leave with them. He Zizhen of course, Mao's woman, although she's pregnant. And Zhu De's fourth wife."

"Fourth wife? What happened to his third?"

"Executed by government soldiers. He lost no time in remarrying. This new woman"—at this Jin Yu smiled wryly—"you would hate her, Jade Virtue. I invited her to be my deputy in the soviet women's bureau. She said she never concerns herself with women's problems, because she works only with men."

I stuck out my tongue.

"Yes, my feelings exactly," Jin Yu snorted. "Zhu De's Number Four wife rides horses and does one hundred push-ups every day with the male comrades. She says she will never have children because then she will get out of condition."

At this we laughed so hard that drifts of snow fell through the thatched roof and dusted our heads.

"How did you stand her?" I asked finally.

"I ignored her as much as I could. But now she's been put into command of a platoon of soldiers for the retreat. She's a real battle commander."

"You command soldiers too. You were the first woman to do it."

"Yes, but my soldiers are the *rear* guard." She smirked without humor as she emphasized the second to the last word.

"Jin Yu, why weren't you allowed to go too?"

"Well, there are a million reasons, aren't there? But I think the main one was Peng Shuzhi. I had a love affair with him in Jiangxi. For some reason that bothered everyone. Things were supposed to be free in the soviet, everyone was supposed to follow their own hearts in these matters. But it turns out that adultery is only for the male comrades. Sleeping with Peng got me purged as the chief of the women's bureau. And I think it was why I was left behind. He went on the march, though. I hear they just crossed the Wu River, going east."

I got up from my seat on the boughs and sat on the ground next to Jin Yu, leaning against the wall. "Don't, you are sick, I heard you cough," she demurred, but I shook my head.

"It feels better for my back to sit down low," I said. She leaned her cheek on my knee, and I suddenly felt a great rush of feeling, a desire to protect her, and pain at her gauntness. When I put my hand on her back, even through the quilted jacket, I could feel her bones. The drifts of gray hair on her head, once black and glossy as silk, made me touch my own hair and think about time passing, and the brevity and fragility of our lives.

"Did you love Hesen?" I asked, watching the fire.

"Yes, once I did, very much. But it didn't last."

"If love is real, doesn't it then last forever?"

"Why? Life is real, and it doesn't last either."

"I'll see you again," she said, picking up the bundle with what was left of the food I brought her.

"Yes," I said, through my tears. I tucked the little cloth packet of needles and thread into her jacket.

"Close your eyes. Then I will be gone."

I stood still and closed my eyes, feeling the salt tears on my cheeks freeze in the cold. I heard the crack of twigs. When I opened my eyes, I was alone in the midst of a ruined temple. Then far down the slope, I saw Jin Yu's back disappearing into the dark of the woods, a last flash of sunlight glinting off her hair. As I watched, a nugget from the past tumbled into my mind, some shred, some fragment, some ghost in the trees. But I could not remember the rest.

Six thousand miles and one year later, the Communist Army reached Yan'an, in the far northwest, as far from Changsha as one could go and still be within the Great Wall. And for some time thereafter, wild rumors about Jin Yu abounded. The government put a price on her head and put up posters in towns and villages. Twice the newspapers reported her death. There were frequent reports by people who claimed to have spotted her. I found a dispatch on Guai's desk once, which noted that a woman had been in command of a platoon that had fought a desperate skirmish several miles up into the mountains, running along the narrow trails and scrambling up the almost perpendicular slopes a bare hundred feet ahead of the pursuing Guomindang soldiers, hurling rocks onto the troops below. The dispatch noted that the female commander had seemed especially fearless and wild, hacking at the enemy with a curved threshing blade. "When last seen, the commander and the remains of her unit disappeared under cover of night, and we were unable to pursue. It is rumored among the informants that the commander is a woman of good family from Changsha." I ached when I heard about her having to fight armed men with a farmer's threshing blade. I wondered if she still carried her pistol, and if she had run out of bullets for it, up there in the hills, so far away from everything else.

That night, lying in the pilgrim's dormitory at the White Horse Mountain temple with Yong Li snoring quietly beside me, I dreamed that I was standing in the contorted rocky foothills of Jinggangshan, which spilled like mounds of grain into the borders of Hunan and Jiangxi. Above me loomed the narrow, angular mountains, wrapped about with mist and rain and gray sky, a monochrome brush painting composed of feverish strokes. Among the rocks the mountain cherry grew, a burst of brilliant pink among the wet black rocks. I dreamed I was waving to Jin Yu, a distant figure in a woolen cloak and a farmer's straw sandals, who was clambering over the rocks, ascending the mountains, traveling away from me, ever up-ward. Jin Yu's long black hair floated down her slender back, spreading out into the disturbed air, flowing silently over the rocks like the train of a silk dress. I called to her. But when she turned beneath the spreading branches of the cherry tree to wave back at me, I saw that the mountain climber's face was my own.

32

My brother Li Shi married in 1935, when he was forty-eight years old. His wife was twenty-two, freshly graduated from a woman's college in Nanjing, and carried the name Zao Zao, which is a child's nickname. However, since she was a child, it suited her well enough. She was slender and pretty, with a lipsticked pout. I did my best to be kind to her, and to tell the truth, I was relieved. Li Shi had many women in his later years, and I preferred to see him living with somebody in a regular way. So much the better if she was his legal wife, so my mother needn't be ashamed.

They moved into a large house in Changsha, not far from the army barracks. She held frequent tea parties there in the afternoon, to which I was often invited. Always, the conversation was about movies, or makeup, or love potions or astrologers. My new sister-in-law followed every fortune-teller in the province, now that it was no longer illegal to forecast the future. I am happy to report that all the fortune-tellers had nothing but good news for her.

On Li Shi's forty-ninth birthday, Zao Zao gave him a dinner party and invited all of his friends and all of hers, the two groups being separated by at least a generation. It was a shock to me to realize that she and her friends were the age that my first two daughters would have been if they had lived. The girls—for that is what they were—all wore tight satin dresses and much jewelry, given them by their rich fathers or rich husbands, although I remember thinking that none of them were as beautiful as Jin Yu. The men, imposing in uniforms or suave in expensive Western suits, lounged at the tables, basking in the pleasurable attention of the girls. Although I was well-dressed, and I had put up my hair rather fashionably, I had no desire to prop my chin in my hand and gaze breathlessly at the men at my table, bursting into peals of laughter or gasps of astonishment at everything they said. I took refuge in being extremely courteous.

Zao Zao presided over the dinner tables with an appearance of great pride and dignity, looking to me often for assurance. I always nodded and smiled to her, unlike Graceful Virtue, who rolled her eyes or looked away. My mother was unwell again and could not attend, so I took her place of honor, between Li Shi and Zao Zao's father, the millionaire Old Sui.

"My mother raised silkworms to survive," Old Sui told me over dinner. "But I have big deals with Mitsui, with Mitsubishi, with Taido Electronic and Asahi Glass. I even import guns from Germany."

Li Shi glanced up at this, but said nothing.

"Who buys the guns?" I asked without expression.

Old Sui shook his head and laughed heartily, holding out his hands in front of him as if to disclaim responsibility. Later, I heard him tell another tycoon at the table about his new country estate. "It's better to hire seasonal labor to pull the plow than to buy animals," Old Sui said. "Seasonal labor can be laid off out of season. I would have to feed an ox or a donkey all year round, even as it did nothing in the winter."

When Old Sui left the table, I leaned over to Li Shi, who was calmly eating the rest of the steamed fish. I put my ear next to his temple, where the hair was going gray.

"I'm glad your new father-in-law is a Japanese collaborator."

"He's not. We aren't at war. Not yet, anyway."

"The Reds declared war on Japan three years ago."

"I'm not impressed. There aren't any Japanese in Yan'an. They are all here, where I must deal with them. Japan is flooding China with opium and secret agents. Old Sui passes a lot of valuable information to me about them."

"Information goes back the other way too, I'll wager."

"Probably, but that can't be helped."

"Flexible as ever, eh? The Asahi Glass factory is where that ten-year-old worker girl was killed, when her braids caught in the machinery."

"I'm aware of that, thank you."

Zao Zao hurried up to me. "Elder Sister," she chirped, leaning on my shoulder.

"Yes?" I said, with a slight sigh, which made Li Shi smirk into his food.

"Please help me, since you are the oldest woman in our family here tonight. I have to gather all the women together to go to the drawing room for tea, while the men will stay here and have whiskey and cigars."

"Why must we be separated from the men?"

"This is how the English do it," she said reproachfully.

"We, of course, are not English," I said, getting up anyway and signaling to Graceful Virtue, who rolled her eyes again.

The summer night was very hot, and all the doors and windows were open. Still, I felt the atmosphere in the drawing room, as Zao Zao called it, to be oppressive, and I gestured to her that I would step out into the garden. She wiggled her fingers at me in a little wave. As I left, there was a burst of gasps, followed by a shriek of delight, and the teaspoons—we were drinking English tea—tinkled in the cups all at once in agitation.

When I had been in the garden a while, Zhao Han Ren joined me. His hair, always prematurely iron-gray, was now almost snow-white, although he still stood as straight as a young man. He sat next to me on the bench and rubbed his arm.

"Does your arm hurt?"

"Usually."

"Is it the arm with the arrow wound?"

"Yes."

We sat a moment in silence. The night was so warm that the moonlight felt like sunlight on the backs of my hands.

"Why don't you remarry, Han Ren? You could find a young wife like my brother did, to make your old age a comfortable one."

Zhao smiled, and I could see the tigerish flash of his teeth.

"I've never found anyone worth going to the trouble of divorcing my old wife. Except you, of course."

I flushed with embarrassment. "I thought you were a widower."

"In all but name. My wife entered a Buddhist convent many, many years ago, and I have not seen or spoken to her since. Since before I came to Hunan. In fact, one of the reasons I agreed to take the Hunan command was to get away from home. Not that she would object to a divorce. But now so many years have passed, I might have trouble finding her."

"If I had married you . . ."

"That was when I first came to the province. I still knew where she was and could ask for a divorce. For all I know, she might be dead now, and I might in fact be a widower in truth."

"Why did she become a nun?"

Zhao sat back and rubbed his arm, wincing as though it hurt him greatly, although he waved off my inquiries. He held his forearm in his hand and squinted at the stars above us.

"You know," he said, "I married when I was already a mature man, almost thirty years old. My wife was an heiress. She had been betrothed to me by her late father, who left her a fortune when he died. Her mother and the mother's new husband tried to pass off the new husband's daughter on me instead, who was prettier but not nearly so rich. My family held out for the heiress, and we got her. We got along quite well, you know, for some years. We had no children, but we weren't otherwise unhappy."

I watched him light a cigarette.

"But then we got a new maid into our home, and I took the maid as my concubine. At first my wife beat her, and the girl often ran away, but always I rode after her and brought her back. That was when my wife turned to Buddhism. So instead of being a bitter and jealous old wife, she became the household saint. An object of veneration for miles around, and also a subtle rebuke to me, her husband, who had not given up carnal desires as she had. Her virtue was a constant reproach to me and my imperfection. The Hunan command was offered, and I came here. My wife entered the convent."

"And the concubine?"

There was a long silence. "That was a long time ago," he finally said. "Besides, the girl is dead." A cloud passed over the white surface of the moon, and for a second I could not see his face.

He winced again and flexed his elbow. Ignoring his protests, I grabbed his arm and pushed up the light cotton sleeve of his gown. In the light of the moon, I saw many small dark marks inside his elbow, as if a small animal had gnawed on his skin.

"What's this?" I asked, touching the marks.

Zhao shrugged and pulled his sleeve back down. "I've been taking morphine injections for the pain," he said lightly.

"You must be careful with that!"

"Yes, yes. Don't worry. I'll never be addicted to anything. I'm too easily bored."

"Zhao, you never told me that the pain was so severe. Have you been to the doctor?"

He laughed. "I've been to many doctors. None of them can say why an arrow wound that is nine years old still hurts me. It's as if that old demon

Feng put poison on the barbs, a poison that acts very slowly, so that it weakens me only now."

I was very alarmed by the sound of his voice. Zhao's voice had always had a clarity of tone to it, like a deep bell ringing. But now for the first time I noticed a ragged quality, like the sound of cloth tearing. I disliked this new sound very much, and it frightened me.

"How does it weaken you?" I asked. "Are you otherwise in poor health?"

"No. But the fact that I can no longer merely endure the pain as I once did is certainly a sign of weakness. The relief brought me by the morphine is a delusion. It does not last, I require ever new and increasing doses. It does not cure the wound, but only masks the pain by deadening my nerves." He lit another cigarette. "Don't look so worried. I'll be all right. I've lived with it thus far. Tell me, how are things with you and Guai?"

"Um, we're fine," I said.

"Li Shi tells me that you would prefer Guai to leave government service?"

"I just think he could do so much better at the Soong bank. They have been trying to get him for a long time."

"But he doesn't want to go."

"He has a wife and children to consider."

"If he goes, what is left of his core will disappear."

"What do you mean, what is left?" I asked indignantly. "Guai is a successful and happy man, except for the part about what to do in the future."

"Haven't you noticed that all the successive compromises Guai has had to make, with me and Li Shi and others in the government and out of it, have worn him down? He is successful, and he might even be happy, but he is hardly Guai anymore. It is like watching someone drown. You are his wife, and I believe you love him. Don't let him disappear beneath the waves."

"I can't believe you want me to help him resist you more."

"Someone should always be on the side of pure goodness. I like to see it, even if I don't do it. Besides, if he doesn't stand up against us, we would go too far."

"Guai is always good," I said, watching Zhao's fine profile.

"Yes. Yes, he is. Isn't it ever tiresome? Don't you ever wish that he would simply crush your spirit and have done with it?"

"No. Don't be ridiculous," I snapped, very angry now. "How dare you say something like that? It is most unlike you."

"I'm sorry. I'm only joking. Come, come, don't be in such a passion with me. I'm tired tonight, and I don't watch my tongue." Zhao took my hand and held it before his face, turning it this way and that as if he were examining it. He blew smoke through my fingers, and I let him do it, even though I was shaking. Then he rested his face in my palm as if he were tired, and I let him do that as well. His skin was hot and damp.

"Let's go inside," he said, dropping my hand.

"You go first," I said. "I'll come along in a moment." I listened to his footsteps, crunching on the gravel of the garden path, and then the click of his boots on the flagstone porch. I sat and stared at the moon until my eyes hurt from its light.

"Zhao told me you were still out here," Guai said from behind me. I turned in eagerness to see him.

"Yes, my dear, here I am," I said. He sat next to me and put his arm along the back of the bench, behind me. I moved closer to him and took his other hand.

"Isn't the moonlight lovely?" I asked.

"Very beautiful," he agreed. He squeezed my hand affectionately. I could not help noticing that even in the heat of summer, Guai's hand was cool and dry. I clung to it nevertheless, as if I were the one who was drowning.

In December 1935, students all across China demonstrated against Japan's growing power in China, calling for an anti-Japanese boycott of goods. The central government decided to suppress such protests, fearing Japan and not wanting to be distracted from its battle with the Communists. In Changsha, Zhao and Li Shi, on orders from the central government, moved immediately to extinguish them, as their brother officers and officials did in Wuhan and Shanghai. Before he had to resort to gunfire, Li Shi turned fire hoses of water on them in the freezing winter weather and then hauled them off to the hospital, where they all had pneumonia.

In the midst of these brutal strikes and counterstrikes, I received a note at home from Li Shi, telling me in his abrupt way—for all his correspondence resembled military dispatches—that Teacher Yang was one of the demonstrators in the hospital with pneumonia. "I hear he's unwell, the old fool," my brother wrote. "You had best see to him."

On the morning I received this note, I was sitting in the kitchen, watching Yong Li bathe Jueh and Zhen in a tin tub. She always scrubbed them very hard with the washcloth, and I had just told her that she looked as if she were scrubbing turnips. But when I read the note, I leaped from my chair in the warm corner by the stove and ran down the hall to my bedroom for my coat and fur-lined boots.

The air was frosty, and the skies loomed very gray above the rooftops as I ran down White Crane Street to the main thoroughfare and hailed a pedicab. The streets were thronged with people in thick coats, brought out early because of the unseasonable chill. Between them struggled beggars and laborers without coats, wearing the same rags they wore in summer, their bare dirty limbs pimply with gooseflesh. I realized I had forgotten my gloves, and tucked my fingers into my sleeves. I urged the pedicab driver to go faster.

The hospital was a new building near the center of town, low and sprawling. I had been inside only once, to get some medication for Guai, who suffered from dry red skin on the backs of his hands, and I had been intimidated by the endless white corridors and the gleam of steel instruments. At the front entrance, I stepped on the hem of my coat and stumbled through the door.

A nurse directed me to a room at the far end of one of the endless corridors. I slunk along the wall, anxious not to be in the way, for everyone was rushing back and forth, pushing carts of medicine bottles, trays of sharp surgical knives, trolleys with patients on them. I wondered why it was so busy. When I finally found Teacher Yang's room, I was out of breath.

He was lying in bed behind a white curtain. No one else was in the room, and the other bed had been stripped of all its sheets and blankets. I approached cautiously and fearfully tugged the curtain aside. I felt a sudden lurch of shock. His face was very pale, like the curtain, and there were great dark circles under his eyes. I could see the outlines of his skull underneath his lined skin.

When I touched his hand, he awoke and looked at me. I smiled in relief and gratitude.

"Mrs. Wu, what a surprise," he said, very weakly.

"I came as soon as I heard," I said, pushing aside my surprise at hearing myself addressed so formally. "I can't believe the soldiers would turn a hose of water on an elderly person. I was horrified."

"Don't be too hard on your brother, Mrs. Wu. He could have easily used bullets instead. Ah, but I forget. At some point he did use bullets instead. There is a memorial protest tonight in the market, in honor of the dead students. But I don't think I will be able to attend."

I stood by his bed in uncomfortable silence.

"Teacher, I haven't seen you in a while. And the longer I stayed away, the harder it was to come. I never heard from you either."

"I thought perhaps in your new position you did not wish to know me."

"I would never feel that way. I thought you perhaps did not wish to know me."

He nodded slightly. "Perhaps that was indeed what I wished. But it is good to see the face of an old friend again." He coughed, but even his coughs seemed weak and halfhearted.

"When you get home, I will visit regularly," I said.

"Don't bother to make such plans. I am dying here. No, please don't shake your head. We have always been straight with each other, from the first. I know I am dying, and I am not sorry."

I pulled a chair to his bedside, wincing as the metal feet screeched on the tile floor.

"Everything is metal here," I muttered.

"Everything. Even the men." At this we both laughed a bit, and it felt a little more like old times. I took his hand in mine.

"Teacher, why do you say that you did not want to know me? Do you disapprove of me so very much?"

"Jade Virtue, you gave up being a teacher in order to turn into a landlord. So the answer is yes. I disapprove of what you have become."

"All my old friends do. But I have responsibilities. I have to earn money for my children. Guai is too busy in government service." I gestured helplessly. "I repeat myself over and over."

"Everyone always says the things you say. That is how lives drain away, into meaninglessness. You have many valuable things to teach your children besides how to collect the rent from those who cannot pay. I hear you are often engaged in litigation now, a sure sign of lowliness."

"Recently I have had doubts," I said, starting to cry.

Teacher Yang looked at me more softly. "What doubts, child?"

"When I was a child, you didn't call me child," I sniffed, smiling through my tears.

"Because now I think you will find it flattering," he chuckled, his voice rasping like a snake. "What doubts?"

"Everyone criticizes me. You, Jin Yu, why, even Guai . . ."

"Jin Yu?" he murmured. I looked around, but the hall outside the room was filled with the usual shouts and crashes, and I leaned close to him.

"I saw her last winter, Teacher Yang. In the mountains. Just after the rest of the Red Army left for Yan'an."

He closed his eyes a moment. "You know, I used to think of you two as being two halves of the same person."

I had no answer to that. I supposed I was the lesser half.

"And your doubts?" he asked.

"Just everything you said. About my life draining away into meaninglessness."

"You would not be upset at our criticisms, if you did not feel in your heart that they are true."

"Yes. Yes." I scrabbled in my purse for a handkerchief.

Teacher Yang opened his eyes again. "Jade Virtue, I would be unjust if I didn't tell you the truth now, now that I am dying. I have never given you delusions."

"What is it, Teacher?"

"I have struggled for a long time with my feelings. Because together with my affection for you, my respect for your abilities, my understanding of the difficulties of your position, I have also felt something else. For the last five years, part of me has hated you. I have struggled to put aside my feelings, because they are irrational. But I have them nevertheless."

My stomach tied up in knots, and my heart pounded wildly. "Hated me?" I sobbed, starting to cry again. "Why? What did I do wrong?"

Teacher Yang looked at me very somberly. "Because you did not save Kai Hui's life. And Liang Li Shi is your brother."

I groaned in pain, doubling over in my chair. "But Teacher," I wept, "I could have done nothing. Even Li Shi himself, had he wanted to save her—he could have done nothing. The head of state himself wanted Kai Hui's blood!"

I put my forehead against his hand, and was wretched when I felt him withdraw it. But then I felt him place it on the top of my head.

"I know you couldn't have done anything to prevent what happened. I know if there had been something you could have done, you would have done it, for my sake if not for Kai Hui's. I told you I know these feelings to be irrational. And yet I have them all the same."

"Teacher Yang," I wept. "Don't leave me now, with this hatred in your heart."

"My poor child, I hope to put it out of my heart, and greet the kings of hell with a perfectly serene countenance. That is why I told you about it. I thought it would be unfair to keep my thoughts from you, and keep you here by my bedside, under false pretenses, as it were. Because"—and at this he sighed, so I looked up at him—"because I feel my death is near, and I would like very much if you would stay until it is over. Because for the first time in my life, I feel a little fearful." He looked at me directly. "I would like you to stay of your own free will, in spite of what I told you just now."

I held his hand in both of mine. "I won't leave. Even if you hate me more than anyone, I will not leave until you have closed your eyes on this world."

"I do not merely hate you," he protested weakly. "I have also loved you like my own child, and I still feel that way as well. Strange, how a person can have six or seven emotions all at once. But all the clocks in my house ran down after Kai Hui was taken away, because there was no one to wind them."

I waited by his bedside all day. I watched over Teacher Yang as he faded in and out of consciousness. I held his hand so he would always know my presence at his side, and spoke to him occasionally. I could see him grow-ing weaker, almost as if he were sinking into the earth away from me. And I had a great deal of time to think about the nature of helplessness, and how one can be at fault even when one has no power.

That night, there was no wind at all, but it was still very cold, in that hard frozen way when it is too cold to either rain or snow. The ground rang like iron under my footsteps as I entered the central market square. There were hundreds of students there. The fiery glare of their torches made me blink, coming as I was from the darkened side street. The heat of the flames fell on my face. There was no moon and no stars, but only the resin-scented flames held aloft by the students. The memorial speeches had begun already, and a photograph of a young man had been propped against the locked door of one of the market stalls. Some of the students recognized me and called out surprised greetings.

"We were expecting Teacher Yang," someone said, a voice I did not recognize.

"I'm sorry," I said. "Teacher Yang died this afternoon." There were sor-rowful murmurings, and a girl student in a pleated skirt began to sob.

"But he sent me," I added. "I hope I will be enough for the occasion."

33

A small black-and-white dog lay dead in my kitchen courtyard. Cook was squatting over it, weeping, wiping her eyes and nose on the backs of her hands. She buried her face in her folded arms and sobbed loudly. Yong Li was kneeling beside her, murmuring words that I could not hear from where I stood in the kitchen doorway. From one of the internal windows, the crackling voice of our new radio could be heard, in urgent squawks like a wounded bird. But I did not listen to the voice on the radio. When I ran up to the two women and bent over in concern, Cook looked up at me with fury.

"Your evil son has poisoned my dog!" she screamed.

"What are you saying?" I had to raise my voice above the radio's.

Cook pointed a finger at a corner of the courtyard, where Wan Li stood. I could barely see his small form in the shadows.

"I found him with the wasp arsenic in his hand myself. Look at him, the killer!" Cook wailed. She fell to her side, and leaned on the bricks of the courtyard with one hand, as if she were suddenly overcome with dizziness.

I looked at Yong Li. She looked down, her eyelashes fluttering slightly against her cheek.

I flew at my son and grabbed his hand. "Is this true?" I shouted. "Did you do such a cruel, terrible thing?"

He stared back at me. His eyes and flat cheekbones made an unreadable map, a strange territory I could not penetrate.

"Answer me. Answer me now."

He nodded slowly. I slapped him. He opened his mouth with surprise, and for some reason the action galled me, and I slapped him again. Then I raised both my hands, and I found myself slapping at him mercilessly, while he screamed for me to stop and put his small hands above his head to fend off my blows. The radio announcer's panic-stricken voice shrieked behind me. Yong Li grabbed both my hands and pulled me away, begging at me to stop. Wan Li ran inside.

"Yong Li, what can I do?" I groaned softly to her. "Wasp arsenic. What kind of six-year-old boy poisons a pet dog? He knew that wasp poison was deadly."

"Don't think of it, Elder Sister," she murmured, with a glance over at Cook, who was still sobbing wildly by the little dog's body. "He's only a boy."

"Yong Li," I said, my voice breaking, "the other day the neighbor came, and told me that Wan Li put two cats inside his pigeon coop and closed the door." Yong Li leaned her forehead against my shoulder and pressed my hand. "Yong Li, whose son is he? Tell me. Whose son can he be?"

"Speak to Cook, Elder Sister. She's very upset. She's just a poor widow, and the dog was all she had."

Cook's weeping had subsided into an agonized moaning. I put my hand on her shoulder. "Cook, don't cry. I'll go today and buy you a new puppy in the market. A black-and-white dog, just like this one. You can name it today."

"Your son would only poison that one too," she spat, and some of her spittle struck my chin. I wiped it away, and took out my handkerchief to wipe her face.

"No, no," I said. "I'll let you keep it here, in the kitchen courtyard instead of the garden. Then you'll have it under your eye all the time. Go to your room now, and lie down. I'll buy something at market for lunch, and you won't have to cook." I eased her to her feet, calling to one of the maids to help her to her bed. I got my purse and put on my street shoes.

Yong Li clung to my hand all the way to market. "Don't be like this, Elder Sister. Many children are cruel. They don't know better. He'll grow up to be a good boy."

"That boy has an evil destiny," I said, my voice ragged and thin. "When he was a baby I loved him more than the girls. Much more, may heaven forgive me. But he is so alien to us all—a foreign body, like something trapped between my skin and my clothes—and nothing I do can make him belong to us. My heart is breaking."

The streets were uncommonly crowded, with corners so packed with heaving masses of men that we had to struggle into the middle of the street to pass. They were all shouting, and some were waving newspapers. The crowd was so numerous the cars could not pass, and so added their blaring horns to the din.

"What is happening?" Yong Li asked. "I can't hear what anyone is saying."

Every crowd has its mood, immediately apparent to all observers through some mysterious process of understanding. This one did not seem hostile or vengeful, but rather, frightened and expectant.

"What is it?" I asked a man in an old-fashioned gown and a bowler hat. He thrust his newspaper at me. Perspiration ran in rivulets down the furrows of his face, and he mopped his brow with a cotton kerchief.

"What does it say?" Yong Li asked, staring at the characters, black splashed liberally with red headlines. She touched the paper tentatively with her fingers.

"Wait, let me read," I snapped. I scanned the lines of text anxiously, looking for meaning, assembling bits of meaning from where it lay scattered in the lines. I pulled Yong Li out of the crowd, folding the newspaper under my arm. We pushed toward the market. When we got to a narrow doorway, we stopped and I looked at the newspaper again.

"We are at war," I said.

"War with who? Is it the Japanese finally?"

"Japan. Some soldiers had a skirmish at the Marco Polo Bridge, not too far from Beijing. Now Japan says we attacked them and they are at war with us." My voice sounded flat and disbelieving.

Yong Li looked frightened. "What will that mean?"

I did not reply, but only stared at the newspaper, as if answers could be found there. I had never in my own life experienced a foreign invasion, but the Japanese were very fearsome, and chewed at the nation like a savage beast. When I looked up at the rooftops, I realized that my heart, which had been pounding like a drum since I saw the dead dog, had slowed almost to stillness, sounding hollowly in my chest and skipping beats. I took slow, deep breaths, a faint fear crossing my mind that my heart might stop at this very moment. I am getting old, I thought, and my heart is weakening.

"What does this mean for us?" Yong Li asked again, her voice insistent.

I simply turned my steps toward the market and hurried along, Yong Li running alongside.

"I don't know, I don't know. I don't know anything," I kept repeating.

Dog meat was eaten very little in the summertime, but there were several cages of small puppies for sale in the street of butchers, a long, high-walled street on the western edge of the market, laid out so that the offal from the stalls could be swept into the sewers that ran next to the river and were flushed with river water. I picked out a small white dog with some black markings.

"It's not as pretty as the old one," I said, holding up the puppy to show Yong Li.

"It's all right. It has a lucky patch over its eye," she said consolingly. "Good fortune, then."

I paid the dog meat butcher—who was very surprised that we wanted a live dog, and seemed to think he made out well on the transaction, getting full price and not having to slit its throat for us—and we ran home, holding the puppy in the fold of the newspaper. It was very young, and too frightened to bark. I could feel it shivering in my hands. It seemed incomparably frail.

When we got home, the house was utterly silent. But then we heard the radio announcer's voice coming from the back. All the servants, even Cook, were clustered around the radio, staring at it as if their eyes would pop from their heads. All I heard clearly was the word Japan, repeated over and over again, almost every other word. I realized that they had heard the news before I did, even though they had all been at home and I was the only one who could read, and the thought was strange to me. I handed the puppy to Cook, who took it silently. She petted it softly and cradled it, rocking it in her arms like a baby and whispering in its floppy ear, but continued to stare at the radio. My children huddled in the doorway, their eyes enormous with incomprehension. I remembered that I had forgotten to buy anything for lunch at the market.

Yong Li came to me that evening in the main hall, where I was waiting for Guai to come home with the latest news.

"I meant to tell you this morning, Elder Sister, but what with the dog and the war, I didn't have a moment."

"What is it?" I asked, surprised, wondering what Yong Li could possibly have to tell me.

"I am going to be leaving your service. I am going to marry."

I stared at her, a surge of hurt feelings rising.

She continued, a little nervously now, since I had said nothing. "A matchmaker came to this neighborhood a few weeks ago, acting on behalf of a grocer in the western suburbs. He is a widower, with five children, the eldest nearly grown. We met last week. Your mother came with me as my representative. We found each other satisfactory, and I've accepted the proposal."

My mother, the traitor. I wiped away the tears in my eyes. "Have you been unhappy with us, Yong Li? I never thought you were unhappy. You have been as our own blood."

"Don't cry, Elder Sister," she said, drawing close and patting my arm. "Nothing in this house has ever made my heart grieve. I have loved you and the master as if you were my own blood, and the children too."

"Then why leave?" I was sniffling like a child. "Why leave me?"

"Elder Sister, my entire life I have lived in the houses of others. When my father first sold me to the Pans as a girl of all work, when I followed you to be your mother's maid and then yours. Now I am getting old. I will be forty in a few years. I dream of my own house, with my own children."

"Will this grocer satisfy you? It will be his house and his children."

"But I can make them into mine. I could never make your house and your children into mine. Because I would always be your maid."

"I have never thought of you as my maid."

"Yes, but I am." She nodded, looking up into my eyes in her clear and sober way. "I am. That would always be my fate with you, no matter how hard you tried to treat me differently. It is not your fault, or the master's. It is the way things are."

I searched for my handkerchief before remembering that I had given it to Cook that morning. I put my arm up and wiped my eyes on my bare skin. After she left me, I opened a window onto the courtyard, and looked up at the narrow strip of dark blue sky, serrated at the edges by the jutting roof tiles. The radio voice was beginning to sound familiar now, as if it were someone who lived with us. July 8, 1937, I thought. I must remember this day, because my life has broken in half.

I gave Yong Li's wedding banquet in my own house, in spite of her embarrassed demurrals. As it happened, she could not be married until the early winter, since the astrologers could find no auspicious days. Finally, I held a small party in the main hall for her in early December of that year. She wore a blue silk dress that I had given to her. Her bridegroom, smiling shyly, was a portly, hearty man with red cheeks and a broad smile and work-roughened hands. He seemed overcome at having his wedding in a great house, and bowed to Guai and me again and again. His children, the oldest of whom was quite big and the youngest still very small, gathered like mice—mice with pained expressions—in the corner and would only speak to my daughters, who were six and eight years old. The servants were all invited to drink rice wine and eat a small cold supper. I would willingly have given Yong Li an enormous banquet, but she refused, saying that it was not proper to give a servant such a fine wedding, and that I had already stretched the bounds of propriety very badly as it was, and she did not want me gossiped about in the other houses as if I were a fool. I could only shrug my shoulders, since I had observed that servants were often contemptuous of masters who were too kind or familiar. The phenomenon is, of course, not limited to servants, but frequently finds expression in the way subjects view their kings, and women view their men. The object of worship must be worthy of worship, and cannot be deemed worthy unless it behaves like a tyrant.

Inside my hall on that winter's day, we celebrated Yong Li's wedding in a quiet but contented way, as if everything in the world were just as it always had been. And in a way that was true, if one realizes that the world is always in turmoil. If I had been a god, and could look down on the roof tiles of my house in White Crane Street, I would have seen a tiny, temporary island of ordinary human endeavor, in the midst of a hurricane of history's making. The Japanese had invaded and occupied the north of China during that summer. By November of that year, the Chinese army was retreating, stumbling backward on Nanjing, the old southern capital of the Chinese empire. Streaming backward in disorder because the Japanese had set up radio stations in Chinese frequencies and beamed fake orders to the troops, leading them into traps, into swamps, into the empty fields, where they were cut down as if they were not human. Finally, on December 13, 1937, the Japanese entered Nanjing. We did not know all the details of that until later.

All this I did not know at the time of Yong Li's wedding. I did know however that even as we lifted our cups of rice wine, there was outside my house, in the winter streets, the first waters of a flood, the flood of men and women and beasts, fleeing the war in the north, looking in vain for safety in the south, finding only starvation and sickness and banditry. Through my upstairs windows I could have seen these first escapees that December day, dressed in rags, with quilts tied across their shoulders with string, carrying piglets or chickens or more often nothing at all, begging from the strangers at the side of the road, trying in vain to sell their hungry children. I saw their hollow eyes and blue lips when I went out from White Crane Street to the large avenue to bid the bridal party farewell. The new clothes of Yong Li and her husband and children shone momentarily among these strangers, and then disappeared. The refugees were specters at the feast, and signs of things to come.

In the following month or two, we heard many things about Nanjing, whose sacking by the enemy lasted seven weeks. Her orphans continued to crawl into the southern provinces, beaten, starving, and horribly wounded. For the details about Nanjing, you will have to consult the history books, if they are truthful ones, and not ones written by the Japanese, because I cannot bear to write them down. Some rough beast had taken possession of the Southern Capital, and its black presence brooded over the land. Every time I looked north, toward Nanjing, I thought the horizon looked darker there, as if a great cloud roosted low in the skies. Every day I looked north, the cloud seemed to have grown, and to have spread closer to us.

"There's a woman outside in the street, madame," the maid said to me. "She's been standing outside in the snow for ever so long."

"What does she want?" I asked.

"I don't know. She doesn't speak or approach the house. But she gazes up at your windows as if hoping to see you. Cook says she was there yesterday too, although you didn't go out all day yesterday."

I threw a shawl over my shoulders and went to the garden gate. The snow had muffled the sounds of traffic in the distance, and the air was very quiet. The icy dampness of the flagstones seeped into my shoes. When I opened the gate, I saw a woman on the other side of the street. She was some years older than me, and fairly well-dressed in an old black coat, but she was shivering with cold. Her face was turned up to the second story of the house, as if she expected to see someone come to the window. There was something about her that looked familiar.

"Missus," I called out. She looked at me, startled. "Missus, it's very cold outside. Are you looking for someone in particular?"

She crossed the street slowly, her hands clenched together. "Are you Teacher Liang?" she whispered.

"No one has called me that in a long time," I sighed.

The woman stood very close to me and put up her hands to clutch my shawl. "I'm sorry, forgive me. I am Mrs. Yu." I looked uncomprehendingly at her. "I am the mother of Patience Yu. And I have waited here for you, · because I don't know anyone else who can help."

"Come with me," I said. She followed me through the white garden without a word, but inside the hall she clutched me again.

"I can't stay. But I beg you to help me. Patience spoke of you so often. She said you could do anything, that you could walk through walls."

"Please, Mrs. Yu. Come in and let me change your clothes for you."

"I can't stay, I can't stay. I don't wish to bother you. But Patience said you could do anything."

"What is it you wish me to do?" I demanded impatiently. "Where is Patience?"

"Oh Teacher Liang"—the woman began to break down—"I'm afraid she's still in Nanjing."

I felt sick with fear. "Was she in the city when the Japanese entered?" I asked.

Mrs. Yu could only nod, her eyes on my face and her hands on her breast as if she had been stricken. "The last I heard, she had fled the city with everyone else. I know she'll come home to Changsha. Every night I dream of her, I see her walking down the main trunk road. But I don't know how to find her among all these people running away. Please, Teacher Liang. She wanted to be just like you. You can find her."

"Mrs. Yu, how can I find her? How is it possible? I can make some inquiries for you, I'll ask my brother or Governor Zhao, but . . ."

"Please, Teacher Liang, please. Her father has been an invalid for years. Her brother is away in the army. I have no one but you." She took a small package wrapped in cloth from the pocket of her coat.

"It's not much I know, but if you will accept it . . ." She pulled aside the cloth to reveal a small silver necklace.

I shook my head. "Mrs. Yu, it is not necessary to bribe me. I will not accept this." I pushed her offering hand away. "I'll see what I can do. Save the necklace for Patience to wear when she comes back."

After Mrs. Yu left, I stood in the hallway. The white trees outside shivered in the wintry breezes, and fluttered their bare branches uncertainly. I felt a kind of anger, which came when people asked me to do things for them that I feared I would fail at. Where could I find Patience, in the midst of this terrible upheaval? She could be dead in Nanjing, or anywhere in China. I sat down on the floor of the hall and thought for a long time. At the end of an hour, I had come to a decision, which was something like this—that I would not be able to find Patience, and yet I would have to try.

Li Shi flatly refused to use his radio and telephone lines to help me. When I went to see him in his headquarters, he was busy raising troops, trying to reassemble the remnants of the Nanjing army from among the refugees, and drafting farm boys who had no shoes.

"You have two minutes to tell me what you are here for," he snapped when I appeared and insisted on seeing him. I needed only ten seconds, but he shook his head anyway. "No, absolutely not. I barely have any telephone lines, and all the radio traffic is compromised. I'm sending messages by Morse code and mirrors, as if I lived fifty years ago. We'll be fighting with swords next. Even if I wanted to help you, what could I do? Broadcast to all the Japanese listening to my radio messages and ask them if they've seen Patience Yu?"

"Li Shi, there's no need to speak so harshly to me. I know we are in terrible trouble, but I thought if you knew anyone . . ."

"I don't." Then his voice softened slightly. "Listen, Jade Virtue. Have you heard the reports of what happened in Nanjing to all the women there? Women from seven to eighty-seven, raped by gangs of enemy soldiers. And then killed, bayoneted in the head or machine-gunned or any which way. I don't wish to upset you more, but if Patience Yu has a good destiny, then she is now dead. Only an evil destiny would leave her alive after that."

When I left Li Shi, I went to Zhao Han Ren. I was rather shocked at his appearance, but I smoothed away the surprise on my face with my fingers. He was very thin, and his silvery hair was completely white. His hands shook as he smoked his cigarette.

"Have you been feeling all right?" I asked.

"Never mind me," he replied. "I am the least of the nation's worries." Then a ghost of his familiar grin reasserted itself, and I felt oddly comforted, as if I had just found out that an old friend was still alive after all. "Unfortunately," he said, "I don't know how to help you. Everything is in chaos right now, the entire army in retreat, all the Nanjing battalions who surrendered executed down to the last man. Can you imagine? Thousands of soldiers, dead and gone overnight. How can I find one girl for you? Besides, all that is in Li Shi's hands now."

"I know," I sighed. "But her mother asked me. She said she dreams every night of Patience walking home to Changsha."

Then I thought about that. And I thought about the great trunk road.

The trunk road ran from north to south some miles east of the Xiang River. It ran through Shanghai and Nanjing and then curved in from the coast to run through Kaifeng and the three cities that made up Wuhan. The earliest road was quite ancient, built in the time of the first Qin emperor two thousand years before. Somewhere between building the Great Wall and burning all the books that predated his reign, that ambitious lord found time to band his new empire with roads, set with way stations where his messengers would change horses. Since the rail lines had been laid down, the trunk road was used less, but it still held the empire together in its ramshackle ghostly fashion, with narrow stretches of dirt road occasionally giving way to cobblestones and, very rarely, in only a few overgrown places, to a paving stone or two carved with the seal of the first emperor, appearing suddenly in the dust, where least expected.

It was now this road, as well as the river and the rail lines, that the refugees used. I began to walk out every day and stand a few hours at the side of the trunk road, watching for familiar faces among the tide of humanity that swept past. Some days, I would stand there by the side of the road for nine or ten hours. On other days, I would only be able to spare forty minutes from home. I never dared miss a day entirely. When the sun shone, I sometimes brought my children. I knew that I would never find her this way, because I did not know if she would use this road, or if she would use this road during the few hours of the day that I stood there, assuming she was trying to get back to Changsha, assuming she was alive. And yet that winter I went every day and stood in the snow or the rain, under an oiled paper umbrella, and anxiously searched the tragic faces that paraded before me. When I saw someone who looked like an educated person, I would ask if he or she knew Patience Yu, but I never received an answer. Except for the tramp of their feet, the cries of infants, and the groans of the wounded, the crowds were silent and unspeaking, as if words could not do justice to what they had seen.

On one day, I saw an enormously fat man in very dirty yellow silk, riding in the back of a broken-down wooden cart like a Buddha of prosperity, the cart being pulled by his two middle-aged concubines. On another day,

I saw an old lady in gray silk pulling herself along the road by her elbows, since her bound feet were too tiny and useless to support her. She paused in the shadow of a low retaining wall near me and propped herself up against the stones. The front of her dress was very dirty and torn, since she had pulled herself a thousand miles on it. I ran over to her, but she was angry at my interference.

"Leave me alone, you beggar," she snapped. "I have nothing to give you."

I hesitated, wondering how to convince her that I wanted nothing at all from her, but then I saw her take off her three-inch slippers. She dug inside the seams and produced a small ball of sticky opium paste, which she proceeded to tuck inside the bowl of a brass pipe she had in her sleeve. She leaned her head back against the wall, lying in the snow as she was, and smoked the pipe. There would be nothing I could do now, and I went away. I saw her there the next day, still lying against the retaining wall, but not the day after that.

In early March, the sun was already growing stronger. And on a day in that month, as I stood peering into the distance as I had for the many weeks before that, I thought I saw, far down the road, amidst all the milling and groaning, the sudden outlines of a familiar face emerge from the crowd. Refusing to believe my own eyes, afraid to allow the slightest hope to penetrate my heart, I began to walk up the road, against the tide of refugees, jostling them as I went by in the wrong direction. There, in a confused blur of eyes and noses and foreheads, was the round young face of Patience, coming toward me, gaining in definition as she drew closer. I put my hand to my throat, which had started to ache, and waited for her in the middle of the road, stumbling back a step or two when someone bumped into me. She was being led by the hand by an old man who looked like a very poor peasant, and her face was completely without expression, which made it the face of a stranger.

I stepped in front of them. The peasant stopped and looked at me, putting his head to one side in a sort of friendly curiosity, still holding his charge's hand. But he said nothing, which was unsettling. Patience stared straight ahead, blinking softly against the sunlight, but she showed no signs of greeting me or recognizing me. Looking into her pupils, which held no feeling or responsive warmth, I thought suddenly of Wang Mang's dream, so many years ago, of a girl child with empty white eyes, and I realized that my poor Patience could not see me. I waved my hand in front of her face just in case, but she merely stared ahead.

"Patience, it's me. Teacher Liang."

She turned her face up, as if looking into the sky. "Teacher Liang," she repeated slowly, as if she were repeating her lessons at school.

I turned to the peasant. "Where did you find her?" I asked. He said nothing, but only smiled at me, a toothless grin. "Where did you find her?" I asked again. He only put his head to the other side.

Patience laughed. "He cannot hear you, Teacher Liang. He is deaf. It seems we have all lost our senses."

34

*P*atience's hand was warm and sweaty in mine as I led her across the city to Li Shi's headquarters. She said very little, but occasionally asked me where we were. When I told her what street we were on, or what temple we were passing, or what bridge lay ahead of us, she would fall silent again. But she followed me without resistance. I did not tell her as we crossed the bridge over the Xiang River that the river was choked with the drowned bodies of men and cattle, or that in the north there had been dead bodies taken down from the forks in tall trees. It was now June 1938, and the Generalissimo had blown up the dikes that held the Yellow River in its course to keep the Japanese from advancing to Wuhan, north of Changsha. The Yellow River's insulted waters had poured down angrily into China, swamping Japanese and Chinese alike, but mostly Chinese, destroying thousands of villages, and spreading its destruction over the fields and through all the Chinese waterways as if coursing through a bloodstream. Every canal, stream, river, and lake brimmed with death. South of Kaifeng, where the Japanese would now be stalled for the next three months, a dead body or two even bobbed up in the country wells. No one denies that war brings death. But I had never realized before just how much death war brings, and in what unexpected ways. The inhabitants of a village standing landlocked in the center of the country, far from the tidal waves of the sea, men who tilled the soil and never ventured out onto boats, probably never expected to meet their death by drowning, and would have bet money against that possibility in the games of chance. And yet that is precisely what happened, to them and hundreds of thousands like them. I saw Patience wrinkle her nose as we crossed the bridge, but she asked no questions.

The army doctor who was going to examine Patience had his clinic on the first floor of the east wing of the army headquarters. I steered Patience carefully through the jostling soldiers and servants who filled the yard and placed her before the doctor carefully, as if she were made of glass.

At the end of an hour, the doctor shook his head. "There is nothing physically wrong with her eyes. I don't know why she can't see."

I glanced furtively at the other room, where Patience sat quietly awaiting our return.

"The other doctors I have taken her to—even the missionary doctor at the Yale clinic—have all said the same thing, sir," I said. "Do you think she is malingering?"

The doctor snorted and shook his head. "Why should she pretend to be blind? What benefit does she get from this?"

"That's what I can't understand."

"By the way, I don't think she is playacting. It's as if her eyes think they can't see, even though they can. She believes she is blind, so she is."

I sighed and looked over again at Patience. "The other doctors didn't think she was pretending either. It's strange. She's so different now from the way she was. She used to be so talkative, so spirited. Maybe a little bit of a braggart. But endearing, do you know?"

The doctor said nothing.

"Now she says very little. And her words are dry and cutting. I would never have used those words to describe anything about the old Patience. Well, I shouldn't say the old Patience. It is not as if she has been replaced by someone new."

The doctor lit a cigarette and waved the smoke around to dispel mosquitoes. "Perhaps she has been," he said.

All that summer, we had strange weather. Hailstones fell in June, followed by torrential rains and then plagues of locusts out of season. The birds migrated early, flying south in July in great airborne wedges, beating their wings against the steamy heat of midsummer. Guai went away to his ancestral home in Yueyang, to make sure his widowed mother and brothers were safe following all the flooding. I was reluctant for him to go, because Yueyang was north of us, and closer to the front, but he insisted and in the end I simply patted the front of his coat with my hand and said nothing.

While he was gone, I often had Patience brought to my house during the day, and let her sit in the courtyard or on the veranda while I gardened or read over accounts. She seemed neither willing nor unwilling to be there. She held yarn for me while I rolled it, or listened to me talk to myself while I added and subtracted sums of money. She said very little, and her smooth round face, which I once thought of as the face of an especially merry sparrow, now seemed like a hard mask.

It rained like a monsoon for part of that summer, as I said, and then we would sit indoors. The one thing that seemed to give Patience pleasure was the feeling of the raindrops, so I would leave a window open and sit by it with her, letting the rain fall into her face. The drops seemed to melt the hardness of her mask a little, and I saw faint glimmerings of expressiveness and softness at the corners of her mouth and her empty eyes.

"Is someone in the garden?" she asked me on such a day, when the early evening sky was still bright, but fading.

I looked. "No one is there."

"I thought I heard someone."

"There is no one. There is only us. It is raining too hard for anyone to be out in the garden."

"Still, I sense a presence," she insisted. We sat in silence a moment. "Perhaps it is a ghost," she said.

I had been staring out into the rain-darkened garden so hard that I almost began to imagine I did see someone. And something in the evening air compelled me to tell her that I had once seen a ghost.

"Really?" Patience asked, the slightest animation in her voice.

"Years ago. When I still lived in the House of Silk Fans."

Patience fixed her unseeing eyes on me. "Tell me, Teacher Liang. I want to hear about the ghost."

"You know I lived in the House of Silk Fans for a number of years, while I was teaching. I can't remember if you were my student at the time or not. But one night I was sitting in the courtyard with a candle and a wooden board across my lap, correcting school papers. The heat and damp of the summer night had made it impossible to stay in my room. My candle, set in its own wax at the corner of the board, threw a tiny yellow light onto my pages, and glimmered gently in the humidity. I sat with my back against the water tap and enjoyed the lukewarm drop of water that leaked onto my neck every few seconds or so, mingling with my perspiration and then trickling down my back. By the time I heard the distant city clock chime midnight and folded up my papers, my bottom was quite wet. I got up, clumsily wedging the papers under my sweaty arm, and clutching the candle and pen and ink bottle, and trying to pull my wet skirt away from me, all at once. Then I groped my way across the pitch-black courtyard.

When I raised my candle at the door, its light shone upon a young woman in an old-fashioned white shift, just coming down the stairs. Her hair was dressed elaborately on top of her head.

" 'Excuse me,' I murmured. She slipped past me without a word. I climbed the staircase. She must be new in the house, I thought. I haven't seen her before.

"At the bend in the stairs, I peered out a tiny casement window that overlooked the courtyard. The young woman was still there. She was kneeling at a corner of the yard and seemed to be trying to pry up a tile in the pavement. I put my head out the window.

" 'Hey,' I called down softly. 'What are you doing?'

"The young woman lifted her face to me. Her expression was stunning—I have never before or since seen anyone whose face was so contorted with anger. Her eyes seemed to glitter with her mad emotion, and she bared her teeth at me like a wolf. She stood up so quickly I drew back, half expecting her to fly up to the window and attack me. But she turned and ran into the shadows at the far end of the courtyard.

"I searched for her among the women of the house the next day, but no one who lived there resembled the woman I saw. I spoke to the oldest of the twelve widows who owned the house. I described the woman's elaborate hairdo.

" 'But, my dear,' the old lady exclaimed. 'No one has worn their hair like that for eighty years or more.' She lowered her voice. 'Be careful. This is a malignant ghost. She is angry. And she is still here in this courtyard. Did you say you saw her digging under a tile? We must examine it.'

"I followed the old woman out into the yard and pointed out the tile. The old lady tapped it powerfully with her cane. It resounded hollowly. When she jerked her withered chin at it, I bent down and laboriously pulled at it. It did not come loose.

" 'Take that hammer the workmen left,' the old woman ordered. 'Break the tile—it's only clay. Go ahead. I give you permission. This is my house.'

"I did as she told me. I picked up the ball-peen hammer and brought it with a single great crack down onto the center of the tile. The tile splintered apart at once, its pieces flying out and away. From underneath exploded a nest of scorpions.

"I jerked back with a cry. The old lady stood transfixed with horror. I ran to her and picked her up and carried her to the shelter of one of the pillars at the far side of the courtyard, gritting my teeth in the fear that the scorpions would sting me through my cloth shoes. We both shouted to the others in the house, and soon every window was filled with faces. A few of the more capable women came out from the kitchen with torches of fire and ran among the scorpions, stabbing at them with the torches. The scorpions scuttled about and set fire to one another, burning themselves and their nest-mates to death. I counted over one hundred of them afterward.

"'Call a Taoist priest,' ordered the redoubtable old widow. 'We need an exorcism.'

"The workmen came back and dug up the scorpions' nest, which proved to be enormous. They stopped it up with poison and filled it with cement and earth, before laying more tiles on it. The Taoist priest came and performed a long series of chants, and tied a white scarf around the water tap. Midway through, he seemed to fall into a trance of sorts, and choked and cried out in a terrible voice. But he returned to himself after a few minutes and burned purifying incense in every corner of the house. He graciously accepted the free meal we gave him and went on his way, but warned us to call him immediately if we saw the girl ghost again.

"'I hope I have cast her out,' he said as he left. 'But I am not sure. I could not quite locate her in the house. If any of you ladies sees the creature, do not speak to it, and do not listen if it speaks to you. Send for me, and I will come at once. The dead are not to be trifled with when they are angry.'"

Patience sat listening, her face immobile.

"But none of us ever saw the woman with the elaborate hairdress again," I said. "I was glad of that."

Patience turned her unseeing eyes out to the garden. "I have a ghost story of my own," she said.

"I would like to hear it," I said encouragingly. She spoke so little now that any conversation came as a relief from the gnawing sense I had that a stranger sat inside the familiar face and figure of Patience Yu. Patience began to speak in that stranger's voice, dry and expressionless, the muscles of her face never shifting, the focus of her unseeing eyes perfectly immobile. Her voice never once broke, but simply spoke as if she were reading from a book of accounts.

"You know I was trapped in Nanjing when the Japanese came. This other girl who worked at the clinic—she wasn't another doctor, she was actually my nurse—she and I hid in the cellar of the clinic for days, with no food and very little water. She was my closest friend in Nanjing, and I had visited her parents' home in the country with her once. From our hiding place, we heard the firing squads, the sounds of the mass beheadings. We were afraid that the Japanese would inevitably find us if we stayed. So we put on some clothes from the laundry and tried to leave the city by night. But we ran into a patrol of Japanese soldiers. There were twenty of them, exactly. I know, because I later had the opportunity to count them. One soldier pulled our scarves off our heads. Then they pushed us to the side of the road, and I watched while the twenty soldiers raped the nurse. She struggled against them. It seemed to last for hours. Then one of them took a pistol out of his belt and knocked out every one of her teeth with the butt end. She wept the entire time. Then he shot her in the head.

"They left her there on the ground and came over to me. They said nothing, and made no gesture. I unbuttoned my shirt willingly. I put my arms around each of them willingly, all twenty I embraced eagerly as if they were my lovers. That lasted for hours too. At the end, they were going to kill me, but some officer or other was shouting orders from far away, so they all pulled up their pants and ran. Except the last one with the pistol. He fired it at my head, but it must have misfired or something. I heard a roar, and my ear burned, and I lay still. When I looked up later, they were all gone. My willing embraces, I thought, had purchased my life in some strange way.

"I got up and pulled my clothes on and started walking south, which was the only direction I knew. I just got on the road and put one foot in front of the other. I think the only reason I got to Changsha was because I didn't care if I did. As I walked, my vision began to fade. The skies grew darker and never lightened again. The buildings sank into the ground. For days I walked in a half-light, which became the mere bare line of the horizon in the distance, which finally became night. It is the night that has stayed with me permanently. The last two weeks I was on the road, I could see nothing. I drifted in my own dreamland, simply walking where everyone else was heading. I never tripped, curiously enough. The crowds of other people bore me along gently, as if I were floating in the sea. I felt the snow in my shoes. The last two days, someone took me by the hand and led me on, until you found me. He was deaf, I could tell, by the way he muttered gibberish to me. I don't know where he thought he was taking me. You told me later it was a peasant, but I had no way of knowing that then. It could have been the Emperor himself leading me back to Changsha."

35

I held Zao Zao's hand when Li Shi took his army outside the city walls of Changsha in October. Guai had gone to Wuhan to join the government, presently in retreat before relentless Japanese assaults, and Zao Zao was supposed to stay with me.

"Why not stay inside the walls, Li Shi?" I asked. Zao Zao sobbed into her little lace handkerchief.

"I can't take the chance that the Japanese will trap me inside the city." Li Shi spoke over his shoulder, for his eyes were focused on the long convoy of mule wagons, troops and a few trucks that was winding slowly out of the gates. "They slaughtered the defenders of Tien-chia-chen fortress to the last man. It's better to be in the countryside—I'll have more mobility then."

"What will happen to us in the city if they attack?"

"I hope to be able to prevent that. But the key to this, as to all else, is superior flexibility."

"I thought more powerful guns."

"That's just one factor. And sometimes a strangely minor one."

He kissed Zao Zao, and she clung to his neck, weeping. He took my arm and gave it a light squeeze, the most affection he had ever shown me.

"Be careful," he said. "Look after Zao Zao and Mother. Look after Zhao Han Ren as well, since I'll be away."

My brother swung himself up into the front seat of one of the three trucks he had at his disposal and drove away. I watched anxiously as the ragged army marched out into the red fields, wondering how they could fight the enemy when most of them had no shoes.

I saw the fire from my second-story window on the afternoon of November 12. I climbed up to the rooftop and gazed in horror. It had begun in the eastern half of the city and seemed to be racing toward the river, gobbling up everything in its path. I heard its manic crackle, and the sharp smell of burning wood stung the air. I ran down the steps, shouting instructions to Zao Zao and the servants.

"The city's on fire!" I cried. I grabbed Zao Zao, who was holding her hand to her mouth. "I have to go for Mother!"

"Yes, yes, I'll come with you!" she gasped.

"No, stay here. I'll take the gardener. If the fire should come this way, abandon the house and everything in it except for Guai's strongbox on his study table and my jewel box in my bedroom. Take the children and flee to the river. Get in the water if you have to!"

As I ran through the city streets, where soft flakes of ash fell like black snow, the old gardener at my heels, I wished Yong Li were with me. I was always more capable when she was around.

My mother was lying in bed, her shutters open, watching the orange blaze of the fire flaming against the red sunset. She turned her eyes to me as I burst into the room.

"Mother, where is your serving girl?" I shouted, alarmed that the fire looked so close in the window, almost as if its tongues could lick at us through the opening.

"I ordered her away. She could not move me herself, and there is no one around to help."

The gardener wrapped my mother in her quilt and I helped to heave her onto his back. Her wrists were very thin, but her hands clung to his shoulders with wiry strength. I ran about her room, gathering up her jewel box and stuffing a few of her clothes into the cloth bag I had brought with me.

"Wait, Jade Virtue. Under my bed. Your father's scrolls."

"Mother, that doesn't matter!"

"Take it! I will not leave without it."

I flung myself to the floor and scrabbled under the bed, catching hold of a long, thin box made of some light fragrant wood, well-oiled and slippery with linseed, with a brass lock.

"The key dropped!" my mother cried.

"Never mind!" I was shouting above the roar of the fire, which could not be more than a few streets away now.

"Missus, we must go now!" The gardener hitched my mother more firmly onto his back, her foot bindings fluttering absurdly on either side of him. He heaved his way through the doorway. With my father's box of scrolls under my arm, I followed, banging my elbow on the doorjamb.

As we scrambled through the streets, we were overtaken by vast crowds fleeing the fire, by braying donkeys and crashing rickshaws and men straining to hold all their treasures in their arms, with silk quilts and clothing boxes spilling over into the muddy streets, and one old lady who tottered along on her tiny bound feet, coatless in the late autumn chill, carrying nothing but a single jade bracelet clenched in her fist.

The gardener pointed at the skyline of the city. "There may be nothing left when we get home!"

But all the houses on White Crane Street were still standing, although the fire was close by. The servants had covered the roofs with wet blankets, soaked with water from the fishpond in my garden. Zao Zao and the maids stood on the roof with brooms, sweeping the sparks off the roof before they could catch. Cook was squatting in the fishpond itself, holding her little dog above the waterline. My three children clustered around her, the water up to their chests and the drifty green weeds from the bottom clinging to their arms and shoulders.

"Don't go inside, Missus!" shouted my gardener, putting my mother down on a patch of muddy lawn near the fishpond. "You can't take a chance on being trapped inside if it goes up. Stay out here." He began running around the outside of the house, pulling up the rosebushes and other plants that I had painstakingly nurtured beneath the windows. He piled up the brush in the center of the garden and set it alight, so that nothing could feed the fire, should it arrive. The black ash fell all around us, and I thought of the first day I saw the house that stood there before, when it had just barely finished burning from the fire that time. For a moment, it seemed as if no time had passed between then and now, and one wall of flame connected past and present.

I got up on the roof with the last broom.

"How did you know what to do?" I yelled to Zao Zao, who was on the other side of the roof.

"My father's country house was threatened by fire once, and this is what the caretaker did!"

I looked at her with new respect.

All that night, and for several nights thereafter, we swept the roof free of sparks and kept the blankets soaked in water. By the third dawn of that terrible conflagration, the fish in the pond were barely swimming, flopping about in less than half a foot of water. The fire turned away from White Crane Street, leaving its houses mostly intact, but it continued to rage through the city, rising high in bright walls, eating up the narrow, crumbling wooden houses that filled the miles of streets and alleys on the eastern side of the river. Every bucket of river water or well water that the men of the city passed along in brigades simply made the flames recoil a moment, then they burned more brightly than ever. The refugees sheltering from the war in the north were now chased out again by this new danger, wearily escaping through the smoking streets, across the bridges to Orange Island and to the western banks, where thousands lay on the wet sand, damp cloths protecting their faces from the heat.

The fire was finally quenched four days later by early winter rains. Our faces smeared in soot, my entire household sat exhausted on the veranda, too tired to take shelter inside from the cold and damp.

"What you heard is true," said Zhao Han Ren, his fingers shakily lighting another cigarette. His thumb was stained yellow by nicotine. "I set the fire deliberately. Li Shi will be furious."

"But why?" I could scarcely comprehend it. "Han Ren, what have you done?"

"I received intelligence that the Japanese had overcome the national government at Wuhan and were on their way to sack Changsha. So I burned the city, rather than let it fall into their hands. I did not want it to become a stronghold for the enemy. Unfortunately, only the first half of my intelligence was correct. Which is to say, only the first half was intelligence. The second half, about the advance on Changsha, turned out to be merely rumor. And so the only conclusion can be that I panicked at a rumor."

I looked at him a long time, my eyes tracing the inside of his elbow. Then I reached out and pressed my fingers against the puncture marks in his arm. One fresh puncture spouted a tiny droplet of blood under my fingernail.

"Did you panic?" I asked.

"I did." He nodded, regarding his arm with a thoughtful air. "The dragons which haunt my sleep were upon me. They consume me with the pain of my old wound. I can only keep them at bay for short periods of time. And they have changed me. I have lost the ability to see similarities between disparate things, and distinctions between similar things. I am now overly decisive where inaction is called for, and paralyzed when action is needed."

He looked up at me, and for a brief moment there was in his eyes something of his old vigor and purpose, as if brought to the surface by his need to make me understand what he had done.

"You know Jade Virtue, five years ago I would have done the same thing. I would have burned the city down if I thought the Japanese were coming to attack."

I inclined my head slowly in assent.

"But five years ago I would have been right. Now I am always wrong. It is as if I am a clumsy stranger in my own body."

I looked up, startled, into the eyes of this stranger, one of many that I knew now.

36

I had grown up—all of us had grown up—thinking of China as being essentially immovable. However my own life might twist and turn, the civilization that gave birth to me seemed to endure unchanging. Drought and famine might come, birth and death, plagues of locusts or bursts of rain, but the Chinese people never moved. They remained and remained and remained, tilling the same land generation upon generation, with the same wooden ploughs that had been used for millennia, their subterranean sense of place rooted in the belief that all their ancestors' spirits continued to haunt those fields. The spirits built up over the centuries like coral. But in the first year of the war of Japanese aggression, all this changed, and in looking back on it now, I see it was a sign of all the drastic movements to come.

By early 1939, the country was controlled by three powers. The Japanese controlled Manchuria and the eastern half of the nation, including the rich coastal cities. The Guomindang had retreated to the other half, controlling—from the new capital at Chongqing, shrouded in unhealthy yellow mists and constant rainfall—the mountains and narrow passes and gorges of eastern China, which strung out brokenly westward until they reached the Himalayas and the Burma border. My province of Hunan lay barely inside the eastern edge of the Guomindang sphere of control. The main body of Communists controlled the north below Mongolia, an area of cold and desolation.

Between those three magnetic poles, rivers of black-haired people flowed, pouring out of the eastern half into the west and the north, people traveling in great streams, in waterfalls, in currents and eddies and tides. Farmers abandoned their fields to climb to the western border to build the Burma Road, to bring outside supplies to the government at Chongqing. I saw them as they passed through Changsha, the calloused skin of their shoulders and backs exposed to the snow and wind. Workers dismantled entire factories by night, carrying the machinery parts on their backs or on the backs of beasts across the land, poling the machinery on handmade bamboo rafts up the Yangtze River, then by rail to Hankow, or by steamer up the Yellow River and then by junk to the gorges of Szechwan, then by donkey and cart and man to Chongqing. I saw them as they passed through Changsha, their breath steaming in the winter cold. Students and professors abandoned their universities in Beijing and Nanjing and walked across the entire face of the nation, carrying their books and microscopes to the new national unified university at Kunming, in the far west. I saw them as they passed through Changsha, the mud of early spring staining their long scholars' robes in tiger stripes. Our people simply withdrew from the Japanese, withdrew into the vastness of China, and were swallowed up in her mountains and valleys. Watching them as they flowed past me, I felt the same dizzying sensation that I got when I leaned over to look into a rushing stream, as if the water was standing still and I was moving.

My brother-in-law Mo Chi was drawn into this great tide, sent to Chongqing because the capital needed senior military officers, and because Zhao and Li Shi thought it just as well to have one of their own men in the capital to report back to them, the political currents of the times being treacherous. My sister Graceful Virtue and her teenaged son and daughter moved into my house, where my mother and Li Shi's wife Zao Zao already lived. Graceful Virtue did not care for Zao Zao and treated her coolly, was critical of her frivolous interest in clothes and makeup, and haughtily dismissive of Zao Zao's prettiness. Zao Zao was often in tears at this treatment and also because, with Li Shi gone all the time, she could not get pregnant and therefore could not cement her place in our lineage. Her anxiety at this sort of ancestor-homelessness made her high-strung and weepy. When I spoke to Graceful Virtue about this, she would deny that anything was wrong. When I spoke to Zao Zao, she would stamp her foot crossly and tell me that Graceful Virtue was nothing but a block of ice, and dirty ice at that. My mother claimed to feel nothing at the loss of everything in her house, and yet I felt that since the fire, she had become an old woman overnight, her once-smooth face now a fine web of wrinkles, her eyes immeasurably tired. She always kept the box of my father's scrolls under her bed. My house, which I had built as my peaceful sanctuary, a stronghold for what I held dear, had turned into a noisy marketplace. If the war had made the world outside into a world of men, then it had

turned my house into a world of women, overcrowded and ridden with
squalls.

Guai was away often now, preoccupied with the war. When he was
home, he found the noise and fuss unbearable, and would demand to
know why I couldn't keep things more quiet. "You are never here in this
house," I wept one day, after he had lost his temper with me. "You know
nothing of what it is like to be here, without you, with all these quarrel-
some relatives who hate each other. You leave it to me to manage an impossible situation, and to feed you at all hours of the day and night,
whenever you choose to come home, and when I cannot perform like a
trained monkey you are angry." He came toward me then, to place a comforting hand on my shoulder, but I ran upstairs away from him. When I
came back down, he had left for the governor's palace, leaving his noon
meal uneaten on the table. I was sick with anger and misery all day, comforted only by the fact that when Guai came home late that night, I saw
that he had been miserable all day too.

My mother merely shook her head. "I'm glad I am not young," she
said.

"I'm not young either," I sniffed.

"Who could tell that, watching your conduct?"

The Japanese had attacked Changsha in late 1939, but Li Shi turned
back their troops in the field, far away enough from the city that the attack
itself had little effect. But it inaugurated a new world of danger, because
from that time on Changsha was bombed regularly by Japanese planes.
The planes would fly in over the horizon and circle over the city, as if they
were browsing for targets, dropping a load of bombs here and a load there,
leaving behind a mound of blackened brick and twisted beams. I felt as if a
new age had dawned, where one was vulnerable wherever one might be,
and where walls and distance gave no safety. After every bombing run,
there would always be a dead man or two in the streets who had been shot
by our own soldiers for smoking, for if soldiers saw a lighted window or a
burning cigarette tip after the bombing warnings had been sounded, they
would simply shoot at it.

The bombings, strangely enough, became boring, because they were
always the same, and so boredom mingled with terror in curious ways. We
would sit in the darkened room listening to the buzz of the planes overhead, and argue about dinner or clothes or movie stars, just as if we were

living a normal life. But how clearly I remember one summer evening, when the bombing run coincided with a total eclipse of the sun. The day grew black, and a cool breeze began to blow as if it were night. The stars began to emerge from the light in which they hid during the day, as if to remind us that they were always present, even if unseen. And in the midst of the awful roar of Japanese ordnance, I heard another kind of crash and clang—the common people of Changsha running out into the streets, superstitious and brave, banging pots and pans together, ignoring bombs and bullets just to frighten away the giant heavenly dog that was swallowing the sun. Leaning out of a second-story window, I could see them in the narrow alleys and courtyards of my neighborhood, their arms raised above their heads and shouting, oblivious for once to the red-orange explosions, to the angry orders and threatening rifles of our soldiers, oblivious to everything but the terrifying imperative to drive away that monstrous beast that could not be seen but whose voracious appetite was causing the darkness around us.

Several years before the war began, I had bought a large, rambling farmhouse several miles to the south of the city, near the banks of the river, with some vague idea of making it into a country house for us when Guai retired. Actually, I suppose my idea wasn't so very vague, because I raised oranges there and sold them, and the land turned a profit. But I always assured Guai that one day we would live there when we were old, and then the only oranges we would grow would be the ones we ourselves would eat. I did very little to the house other than to fix its red-tiled roof, and I let the orchard foreman live there.

But now, because the bombs were falling so thickly on the city of Changsha, Guai and I decided to move the entire family to the farm. The foreman would go on living there, in rooms off the kitchen courtyard. But Guai and I would remain mostly in the house on White Crane Street. Most of its rooms would have to be allotted to army officers, Guai told me, once our own family members moved out.

"It's our patriotic duty," he told me, pushing his spectacles higher on his nose. "We should be proud. A colonel will be living here with us. But I wish you would go out to the farm with the children and your mother and sister."

"I won't leave you," I said. We were standing in the kitchen courtyard, and a distant explosion burst upon our ears. A sudden fear came on me, unrelated to the falling bomb, shaking my heart in rhythm to the rocking waves of the explosion. "Guai, promise me we will never be separated."

"How silly you are. Suddenly you are sentimental, Mrs. Moneybags. You know I will have to travel from time to time in the war effort."

I clutched his sleeve in my fingers. "I know that. I don't mean that. I mean that we must never have our homes away from each other. Not like Mo Chi and Graceful Virtue. I couldn't bear it. Wherever you go I'll go. Will you promise me?"

"Of course, I promise. I would never willingly part from you."

I felt better then, and put my head on his shoulder. "I don't want to lose my home, and everything in it," I murmured into his coat.

"What did you say?" he asked a little absently, patting my back gently.

"Nothing," I said, afraid I would start to cry.

So I moved the family in the autumn of 1940. The cold weather came early that year, crowding angrily into the summer heat with frosts and sleet and icy rain. When I think of the war years, I think of winter. Zao Zao refused to leave Li Shi, but I took my mother and sister and my children and Graceful Virtue's children in hired carts, with bedding and pots and pans piled high in the back, out to the farm. The wooden wheels of the carts crunched the dead leaves on the country lanes into the mud, leaving a strange lacy pattern in the red earth.

When we got there, the children leaped out immediately and began to run about, prying into the outbuildings, bringing up water from the well, and running like tiny ghosts through the cords of morning mist that bound the wavering trunks of the orange trees. The farmhouse was chilly and damp, and I had the foreman build a fire in the main room. I stood at a window while the unpacking and unloading went on around me, and the servants ran back and forth with armloads of blankets and firewood and vegetables. Outside, the thick white mist began to lift under the heat of the autumn sunshine, and glimpses of a startlingly clear blue sky could be seen through the leaves.

I recognized guiltily that I moved the family as much to get away from their crowding and arguments as to safeguard them from the war. But the farmhouse seemed to attract people. I wrote to Yong Li, offering to let her family live there as well, for I heard that the eastern suburb where she and the grocer lived was also the location of several factories and often came under heavy bombing. She moved the children—including her own newborn twin boys—into one wing of the farmhouse within days of receiving my letter. Then she walked all the way into town to thank me, because, as she explained, she had never learned to write and so had to make all her courtesies in person.

"But I wish you and the master would come out to us to live, Elder Sister," she said, standing in the hall with me. Her cheerful, sensible face had changed very little; now she was frowning slightly, the brown skin above her eyebrows drawn into three parallel lines.

"I'll be out from time to time, but the master won't leave town, and I don't wish to leave him. Besides, with these soldiers living in the house now"—I dropped my voice and glanced around—"who knows what could happen to all my things? They might steal or break them."

"Who cares?" Yong Li asked, a genuine expression of suprise on her face. "This is a war. What matters what happens to a few tables and chairs?"

"It has nothing to do with the tables and chairs, Yong Li," I said, wondering how I could make her understand. "This house is where I live, where I belong. It weighs down my life, which would otherwise blow away. I can't let it go."

"What nonsense," Yong Li snorted. "Do you think this house is what keeps you from blowing away? Either you—you, Elder Sister—weigh something, or you do not. Outside things have nothing to do with it."

"Well, you are a perfect Buddhist then, Yong Li, since you need nothing other than yourself." I sighed, feeling misunderstood. "But every night I wake up with a start, because I have dreams of earthquakes."

My Changsha house became the residence of an army colonel, and it was filled daily with the comings and goings of his staff, their feet in polished Western boots gradually wearing out the shine on the wooden floors, a shine acquired over years of shuffling cloth-bound Chinese feet. They often did not step over the high wooden thresholds, but jumped up on them like playful boys, leaping off to land with a thud in the room, printing the outlines of the nails in their heels deep into my floors. When I slept in the house, I heard their talk and their shouts at all hours.

The colonel's young second wife lived there too, a tall, slender woman with a high-cheekboned, angular face and mysteriously slanting eyes. She brushed her long black hair straight back from her forehead, revealing a slightly crooked widow's peak. She was very unfriendly and rarely spoke to me, merely nodding when she passed in the halls. She spent most of her time shut up in her own room on the second floor, or walking in the garden. I noticed that she seemed to have a love of inclement weather, and frequented the garden most when it rained.

One winter's day, in a feather-soft snow like duck's down, I crossed the river, going from the farmhouse to the Changsha house. The snow fell continuously, at first fading quickly into the bricks and dirt of the pavement, but by the time I reached White Crane Street, it had begun to collect in the hollows at the foot of the trees, and in the upturned eaves of the tile roofs. I plodded through the streets in a nodding silence, moving slowly in my heavy boots and thick coat. I came to the familiar red gate, and I spoke to the sentry outside. He nodded without a word—he too in harmony with the silence of the day—and pushed open the gates for me.

I stumbled over the threshold of the gate. The tiles were now muddy. But in front of me was the moon gate, washed in red paint that had been faded by the weather into a rosy pink. In the moon gate the colonel's young wife stood, cupped in its circle, her thin body in a long, close-fitting black silk dress. She wore no coat. She was smoking a cigarette, which balanced delicately between the long slim fingers of her left hand. Her left elbow rested for support in the palm of her right hand, as if she were too tired to hold her arm upright. She stood perfectly still, except for the smoking. Then she blew a long, soft puff of white smoke out into the falling whiteness, and as if in response, a gust of winter wind raised a sudden flurry of snow from the floor of the courtyard and whirled it madly in the air. For a trembling moment, I stood blinking, thinking that it was a flock of cranes taking flight from the center of the courtyard.

That was long ago, and far away. I do not remember the woman's name, and did not like her when I did know it. She was never my friend, and when she and her husband left my house the following year, I was glad to be rid of them. But for a brief second of time, in the midst of everything interminable, she turned my moon gate into a magic circle, a globe, a planet, a cool lunar reflection. Like a sorceress, she blew out her visible breath, and I realized that the very snow on the ground could be turned into white cranes. The incident has no meaning, yet I remember it to this moment, after I have forgotten so much else. Perhaps we can keep only the fragile and ephemeral, and it is the massive and solid things that we always lose. I press my fingers to my lips and blow gently. But my breath is invisible, and cannot be seen here, in the bright sunlight of a different country. No moon gate. No snow. No wild birds.

37

My brother-in-law Mo Chi had been gone for almost two years. In the first few months he was in Chongqing, he wrote a burst of letters, short, quick, and dutiful. But almost immediately they shrank to a thin trickle, as if he just had been waiting for an opportunity to disappear from our lives and that opportunity had arrived sooner than he expected. Now his letters were very rare indeed, and were mostly about the children.

Guai and I blamed the war and all the ways in which it interrupted life. But Graceful Virtue did not believe us. For one thing, she knew that Mo Chi sent telegrams regularly to Li Shi and to Zhao Han Ren. She told me she did not understand why Mo Chi would not write to her. "I thought we were happy. He's never once raised his voice to me. He always protected me and handled everything for me, and never criticized me."

I was combing her hair for her when she said this, and I gave her locks an irritated yank, which made her wince. "Graceful Virtue, we are fighting a war," I said brusquely. "He has more important things on his mind."

"What could be more important than his family? I didn't think there was anything wrong. We have a comfortable life, we have everything we need. I produced a son and daughter. Why isn't that enough to make him happy?"

"What makes you think he's not happy?" I asked, a little surprised at this remark. I leaned over to look into her face, but as usual it told me almost nothing.

"Before he left, he spoke in vague terms. He said something about feeling as if he were dying inside. I couldn't understand what he was saying."

"Dying inside?" I said. "Graceful Virtue, there is nothing very vague about that." She did not have a single gray hair. Other than that, the top of her head told me no more than her face did.

"I think that's vague." She frowned in a preoccupied manner, and I wondered how she could live to this age and understand so little about men.

As the days crept by, dragging themselves along by their hands, it seemed, like the beggars with no legs, Graceful Virtue began to feel that she was the object of gossip among the neighbors. Every time someone asked about Mo Chi, she detected a hidden maliciousness, a probing and testing of her mettle. More and more, she felt that the questions of the neighbors amounted to a challenge to herself, to show herself as a person who could hold her husband. I was angry with her for her attitude.

"It seems to me," I told her, "that you don't really miss Mo Chi the man. You just want to make sure that your life keeps on looking the way it should. Do you love him?"

"How obsessed you and your friends have always been about romance," she snapped, angry in her turn. "True love, true love, true love, that's all I ever hear from you. That's not what makes marriages successful."

"Oh, really?" I said, trying not to lose my temper entirely. "Then what does? That you hold property in common? That his mother likes you? That you look good together in your best clothes?"

"All you care about is being modern and you always say that anything other than true love is feudal. Well, the rest of the world doesn't function that way. Family comfort and unity are the important things. You can criticize me all you like about that."

"Those things mean nothing and less than nothing if your presence is a burden to your husband."

"I think," my sister said tearfully, standing up and snatching the hairbrush from my hand in a decisive gesture, "that your interest in what you call true love is really rather nasty. It's just a vulgar preoccupation with sex." She hurried out of the room, glancing back at me for a moment as if she expected me to go after her, but I was too annoyed and confused, and I simply turned to the window to look out.

"I don't believe it," I told Li Shi later, when I consulted him, on one of the few occasions when I could find him in his office. I had pushed my way in, past his orderlies and aides. To hold his attention I walked around to his side of his desk and planted my bottom on the edge, where it interfered with his writing. "Please listen. I don't want to burden Mother, so you have to help me with this."

"What about all this surprises you?" my brother asked distractedly, stretching his arm around me to scribble on the documents on his desk.

"Why should Mo Chi feel he is dying inside?" I demanded, bewildered. I pushed Li Shi's shoulder. "Look at me, will you?"

My brother leaned back and lit a cigarette, considering. "Don't you think," he said, "that people that you can never shout at, never criticize, but must always praise and pity and protect—don't you think those people are tiresome? Is it possible to love such a person for very long?"

"They have a perfect life. He is perfect to her."

"Nothing is more sterile than perfection. Perfection is really—strange as this may sound—an entirely unsatisfactory state of affairs." He laughed. "I suppose because it can never really exist, and so its presence must always be in some way a sign of something false."

"Do you love Zao Zao?" I asked.

"As a matter of fact, I do."

"Why?"

"Because she is a bundle of problems, like a real human being. Because when she is angry with me, she gives me dagger looks and shouts at me the moment we are alone. I am bombarded day and night with her transparent feminine wiles. She does not simply swallow what I choose to dish out to her, or make me feel sorry for her. Because I could not survive on a steady diet of compliance."

"What nonsense. Men always want compliance in their wives."

"Yes, they do. Then they wonder why they do not love them. They fall in love instead with greedy courtesans who pout and cry and demand presents and insist on this thing or that thing. Why do you love Guai?"

"Because he is so good."

"Do you think of his goodness as a weakness?"

I thought a minute. "No. I think Guai's goodness is almost divine in nature. It is inconvenient in ordinary life, because he is so idealistic, but that's just because he's better than other men. He's larger than they are, more noble, more self-sacrificing. He's always willing to suffer for principle. Not remotely like you, of course."

"So you don't think that he's just a silly intellectual, an absentminded bookworm."

"Of course not," I said, a little indignant in case this reflected Li Shi's own opinion of my husband.

"And Guai loves you," Li Shi said, finishing his cigarette and tossing it over his shoulder out the window, "because he thinks you are very formidable. He doesn't approve of your money-grubbing—neither do I, for that matter—but your toughness and practicality draw his admiration. Have you ever wondered why you and I have always spoken of everything to each other, and never brought Graceful Virtue into our counsels?"

"She's the youngest. We had our duty to protect her."

"Graceful Virtue is now a middle-aged woman. Yet we still don't tell her anything, because we still have to protect her. Mo Chi has had to do the same thing their whole married life, and it killed his affectionate feelings for her. It's not possible to love the weak, Jade Virtue. And it's not possible for the weak to love you."

One night, my sister finally came to us in the room I had set aside in the farmhouse for Guai to use as a study and told us she was setting out herself to join her husband, without waiting for further word from him. When Guai tried to dissuade her, she only wept, "I will go. The sedan chair can take me, or I will walk. The train will carry me, or I will walk. But I will go."

When she left the study, Guai turned to me, his face troubled.

"We'll have to let her go," I sighed. "She won't live otherwise." I rubbed my face and the back of my neck, and looked at my husband.

"Do we know he's ready to take her back, now?" Guai asked, his voice soft with concern.

"Ready or not ready, she's going to go to him."

"How do we know . . . How do we know . . . Well, we don't know, do we, whether or not he still wishes to live with her?"

I sat up, irritated at myself. "Am I the only one who did not see this coming?" I asked, striving to keep my voice low.

"You aren't the only one. Graceful Virtue didn't either," Guai replied.

"You and Li Shi didn't bother to say anything to me."

"It wasn't like that. We never discussed it between ourselves either. But I could tell when we were with them that Li Shi could see what I saw. Graceful Virtue isn't a very emotional person. She is pleasant and obedient, but narrow in what she feels. Do you know what I mean by narrow? She is your sister, so you never had dealings with her beyond those of a certain family kind, and she is not your confidante, so perhaps you never realized it. You are very understanding with her. And you are nothing alike."

"She is Li Shi's sister too, and he seems to have realized it. She's not like him either."

"Li Shi"—Guai shrugged—"does not bother with being understanding. He just sees everything. His view is never fogged, not with pity or affection or anything else."

I remained sitting in the study after Guai had gone to bed. Could nothing ever stay the same? Even something I thought had stayed the same turned out to have been changing all along, in secret. I picked up a porcelain egg set in a little wooden stand on the table next to me and rubbed the egg over the glass surface of the table, making little scratches on the glass, over and over, until I had covered the small round surface with translucent scars.

The day Graceful Virtue left to join her husband marked the beginning of autumn, for it was very cool outside in the dawn air. The great round face of the harvest moon was still visible at this early hour and hung enormous and silvery, very close, filling up the eastern horizon just above the garden wall.

The sedan chair stood just inside the walls of the house, ready to be carried out by two stringy but muscular sedan carriers, who leaned against the wall smoking homemade cigarettes and spitting energetically into the dirt of the yard. Graceful Virtue's children, who were nearly grown, would walk behind the sedan chair to the train station.

The servants and family clustered at the door as my sister came out, followed by her son and daughter, who mumbled their thanks to Guai and me. The carriers shifted to their feet and pushed aside the curtain for her. On the steps she turned to Guai, who took her hand.

"Everything will be fine." He smiled at her. "Don't worry. If there is a problem, come home to us right away."

"Yes, of course. Thank you." She kept her eyes on the ground.

"Graceful Virtue," I said. "Guai is right. If you and Mo Chi should be unable to live together harmoniously, then it is better to live apart. There is no shame in that."

My sister made a slight movement of her head, which might have been taken for dismissal. She turned and stepped into the sedan chair. With a grunt of effort, the carriers hoisted her to their shoulders and set out through the gate, her children following after, whispering to one another and looking back at us.

My younger daughter Zhen, who was still less than ten years old, stood on the steps holding Yong Li's hand. She knitted up her face in confusion.

"Where is Auntie going?" she whispered to Yong Li.

Yong Li shushed her.

"But where is she going?" Zhen insisted.

"Be quiet, Zhen," I said to her, turning slightly. "Auntie has to make a journey. She's going to see Uncle."

"But where will she sleep? What will she eat?" Zhen asked, her voice rising in panic.

"Everything is already taken care of, Zhen," I told her, trying to take her other hand. But she pulled free of both Yong Li and me and ran down the steps to the gate.

"Auntie, where are you going?" she cried out in her small, weak voice. "Where are you going? Where will you sleep? What will you eat?"

The sedan chair moved out of the gate and slowly out onto the narrow dirt footpath that led across the rice fields. The sound of Zhen's childish voice rang alarmingly through the early silence. It was Yong Li who ran out to get her; I leaned against the wall, suddenly tired, and closed my eyes. The sedan carriers walked on, stepping out onto the footpath, retreating further and further into the stalks of rice. "Auntie!" I heard Zhen cry again. But the sheaves of rice closed behind the chair and its carriers, with a sound that my closed eyes could not keep away, a sound like calligraphy brushes on rice paper, filled with the whispers of water, delicacy, impermanence.

hen we were warned of a second Japanese advance on Changsha, in the winter of 1941, I brought everyone into the city from the farmhouse, and the families of the servants in from the countryside as well. Dozens of people now slept under my roof, in the hallways, next to the kitchen stove, and under the tables. My house is a refugee camp, I thought gloomily. And why did I dwell on the most trivial matters in the midst of the most titanic cataclysms? Because I would have gone mad if I had looked right into the face of the war. All the smallest tasks—embroidering handkerchiefs, repairing a broken porcelain cup, weeding a small vegetable bed by the kitchen door—came as an enormous relief to me. I thought about the disciple who asked a Zen master what the essence of Zen was. The master asked, "Have you had your breakfast?" "Yes," the disciple replied. "Then wash your bowl," the master told him. The lesson in that story, I suppose, is to do the very next thing that presents itself, but I began to see it as a way to control the world, an attitude, unfortunately, which is the very opposite of Zen. If one could put one's head down and do all the small repairs that needed to be done, one could survive the great deluges of history. This is how the peasant lives, I thought, century after century. I wondered about my brother, because Li Shi looked everything in the face.

Indeed, we had not heard anything from Li Shi for several days, and I went to look for him. He was placing troops all around the city walls, I was told, and I began the long walk around the inside perimeter, looking for him. I pushed past the soldiers who were marching to the walls, past the laborers who had been ordered to reinforce the walls with dirt and logs on both the inside and the outside. Whenever I saw an officer, I asked him for my brother, and he always pointed onward. When I finally found my brother, he was standing in the courtyard of an abandoned factory, on the railed walkway on the second story, watching several men on the dirt floor of the courtyard below stir great steaming cauldrons of human excrement.

"Li Shi, what is this?" I coughed, taking out my handkerchief to cover my face.

"What does it look like to you?"

"I mean, why have you collected all this?"

"We extract the nitrates to compound explosives. Otherwise I'll have none. I'm out of explosives, and no one is going to send me any more. There's only enough gasoline in the city for my car, a few motorcycles, and the two flamethrowers. Everything else is manpower. Do you know, I got a box of bullets the other day that was marked made in 1931? Where had it been all this time?" He gestured toward the dark brown poisonous pools. "Shit, at least, we have plenty of in China."

I followed him out of the factory and into his car, which was waiting outside. Li Shi rolled down the window.

"You smell terrible," he chuckled.

"Mother was worried," I said, ignoring his remark, "because she sent you a dozen messages and you haven't answered one."

"I haven't been back to headquarters in a couple of days and nights. I haven't slept in all that time either."

The car stopped in front of a troupe of ragged men, led by a uniformed sergeant. The sergeant held a long rope, which he trailed behind him. The ragged men followed him in a single file, holding on to the rope. When the sergeant saw Li Shi, he shouted to the men to stop, and they shuffled uncertainly to a halt. I stared fascinated at their queer, blue-filmed eyes. Li Shi looked out and nodded in approval.

"They'll do," he said, before tapping the driver's shoulder to go on and leaning back.

"Li Shi," I said, craning back in my seat to look at this ungainly herd through the rear window. "You can't have them fight. Why, they're all blind."

"I know. I'm afraid of the Japanese sapping and digging at the city walls. I have to fight them out in the fields and villages, but at least the walls are some kind of obstacle, however momentary. They either have to enter the city through the gates, which would narrow the front of their advance, or blow up the walls, or tunnel beneath them. So I've sunk wooden tubs all around at the base of the walls, and rounded up the city's entire population of blind beggars. One beggar to each tub. If the Japanese start weakening the walls, digging to place explosives or anything, they'll hear it."

"Why blind men only?"

"Their ears are sharper, of course."

"You are very inventive," I said.

"I have to be. I'm used to being abandoned in the field like this. You know, I even print money now. My very own Changsha currency, considerably more stable than the national kind, which is toilet paper." Again, the bitterness swelled in my brother's voice, only to fade away again. "Here, you have to get out at this corner. . . . No, go. I have work to do."

"What will I tell Mother and Zao Zao?" I called, stumbling out clutching my handbag. The driver took my hand and hauled me over a mud puddle onto the paving stones.

"Tell them I won't be back for dinner."

I leaned in the window. "Tell me the truth. Will they take the city? Will the Japanese take us this time?"

"Did you bring everyone into the town from your farmhouse?"

"Yes."

"Then there is nothing to do but wait. Don't venture out again. I've been hearing bad things about those the Japanese capture."

"I know. Will the Americans come to help us? Didn't the Japanese just bomb them? Aren't they in the war now?"

"Yes, but I doubt they will ever come to Hunan. Why should they? Just to save us? No one comes to save us."

My brother's car drove away, leaving me to find my way home under a leaden winter sky. It was not yet very cold, but the air was dank, as if in a cellar, and settled in humid streaks on all the windows and bricks, clinging to my skin and making it feel at once cold and greasy. The streets were filled with country people, who had fled into the city at the approach of the Japanese, and with the carts of the city people, who were rushing to leave for the same reason. They jostled against me endlessly, jolting me up against the walls, stepping on my feet. I would go anywhere there are no people, I thought, clenching my handbag under my arm. Some muddy pigs were driven past me, followed closely by a cart filled with red-lacquered furniture.

When I got home, I helped the gardener nail wooden boards over all the windows. I filled the fishpond with drinking water, and threw the ornamental carp out onto the grass to die.

Over the course of the next several nights, the sound of howling dogs came closer and closer. My mother observed that she had not heard wild dogs since the last famine, ages ago, and that she had never heard them so close to the city before. When the attack came, it was in the early morning. We lay on the floor of the house, listening to the deep roar of cannon in the distance grow louder and louder, the slicing roar of airplanes overhead, the heart-sickening shock of explosions hitting the earth. A glow of bright white light would flash through the crevices in the boards covering the windows. Guai lay with his head near mine.

"I wrote a poem," he said. "Do you want to hear it?"

"When did you find time?" I asked dully, worn out from the fatigue and boredom and anxiety.

"Do you want to hear it or not?"

"Please."

He cleared his throat and opened his mouth. A screeching air-raid siren silenced him. When it went off, he tried again.

> *A monk passes by our gate,*
> *His saffron robe a prayer flag in the winds,*
> *His bare feet safe in the dust of the road.*
> *His begging bowl rings with a few square coins;*
> *His bamboo staff is a planting stick for patience.*
> *He has come ten thousand miles*
> *From the gardens of Luoyang.*
> *He has ten thousand miles more to go.*
> *Neither he nor I know his destination.*

"Do you like it?" he asked shyly, for he did not think highly of his ability to write poems.

"It's lovely," I said, turning my head to look tenderly at him. "It sounds a little Western style. But so serene. So different from our life now. The monk has peace, and a place to go."

"He owns nothing," sighed Guai. He took off his glasses and polished them with his kerchief. "I sometimes wish we had nothing too. So we wouldn't have to worry so much about losing things."

"Do you want us all to turn monk? You and me and the children?" I smiled at him to keep any harshness out of my words.

"No, but the fear of losing everything is hanging over our heads always. I would like to be free of that fear."

Me too, I thought, but said nothing.

The Japanese decimated the villages in the province, but failed to take the city, their thrust turned aside by my brother's troops, many of whom ran into battle over the cold ground in their bare feet. Afterward, we found that the Japanese had slaughtered entire villages, down to the last man, woman, and child, down to the last ox and sow and chicken. They had robbed entire valleys of their population, taking away the men as laborers and the women as whores, none of whom ever needed to be paid or returned, since all were slaves. Wherever the Japanese had set foot, they left behind them a poisoned desert.

Li Shi finally came to my house to sleep and eat after surveying the damage to the city, which had been extensive. He looked the same, but spoke very little when he came in the door, pausing only to gently take Zao Zao's arms from around his neck and to wolf down several bowls of rice. I sat across the table from him and watched him eat. He raised his eyes to me over the rim of his porcelain bowl, and I was startled at the emptiness I saw in them.

While he was sleeping, I went into his room. He opened his eyes when he heard me, and pulled himself painfully into a sitting position—he was still dressed in his dusty uniform trousers, although his shirt and boots lay on the floor beside him. I knelt on the floor and touched my head to the wooden boards.

"What are you doing, Jade Virtue?" he said, sitting up in surprise.

"You have honored our father's name, Elder Brother," I murmured, using the old honorific, which I had not called him in many years. My brother was silent a moment. I could hear the crickets in the garden.

"Get up and sit next to me, Jade Virtue," Li Shi finally said, in a voice that sounded hollowed out with fatigue. I obeyed.

"You've won a great victory," I said.

He shook a cigarette out of the packet that lay on the table and looked out the window. "I had nothing, no resources, to win it with."

"That makes the victory greater."

"Then I wonder why it makes me so bitter. Ah, well. I've used up all my luck in one life, and I'll have none left over for my other lives."

He lit his cigarette.

"Two days ago," he said, "as the Japanese were retreating, a small knot of people approached the main gate of the city and shouted to the guards there. They refused to come any closer, and yet they would not go away. Instead they shouted for me, over and over. I went to the gate with binoculars, and through the glass I saw the face of a village headman I know well. He's a good man, he's been very useful to me a number of times. He was there with several men of his village, and I could see that they were all sick in some way, with purplish swollen limbs and boils on their faces. I walked out a very short way, to the crest of a little hill which lies just on the western side of the gate. Do you know the spot I am speaking of?"

I nodded.

"The headman came a little closer, so I could hear his voice. He told me that the Japanese had caught the entire village and injected them all with plague bacillus, so they could spread the disease into the city. He was crying when he told me that I must be certain to let no one from his village enter the city, or to even come near. He had killed his own wife and daughter—cut their throats in their sleep like beasts—rather than let them suffer as he was suffering. I asked him what I could do for him, if I could put out food or medicines for them. He cried out that he only wanted to die quickly, and anything that would delay that would be unmerciful. He and the others ran away into the fields. I don't know where they went. But they were all weeping like small children, the tears running down their cancerous faces."

I tried to take my brother's hand, but he brushed me aside, shaking his head. He put out his cigarette half smoked, but immediately lit another, his hand perfectly steady.

"Later in the day," he said, exhaling, "some people from the village did come to the gate and started running toward the city. I had all the guards equipped with binoculars so they could see them. The guards ordered them to stop, but these people were so very sick, so desperate and terrified, that they kept coming, kept heading for the gate. So on my orders, the guards shot them from the walls. After a day and a night, I sent a man with a flamethrower out to incinerate the bodies where they fell."

He tilted his head back against the pillows, still smoking.

"You know, I counted that village headman as a friend of mine. He was a good man. Always gave accurate information."

Li Shi swallowed—I could see his exposed throat contract. He smoked a little more in silence.

"I can't remember the last time I felt this way," he said. "Sometimes I think I'm dying."

39

The oddest thing about a war is the endless combination and recombination of people. Persons who would never meet or speak under ordinary circumstances—because they lived far apart, because one was rich and the other poor, because their families hated each other—were thrown together as close as lovers. Persons who would otherwise be together—husband and wife, mother and child, dear friends—separated and did not see each other for years. After the second Japanese attack on the city, in the winter of 1941, I sent most of my family away. I sent my aged mother and my children to Graceful Virtue and Mo Chi, who were now in Kunming. Zao Zao's father Old Sui took his daughter to Chongqing with him. My house in Changsha was one day an overcrowded barracks, the next day a desert. Guai wanted me to leave as well, since the Japanese were not far off. But I refused. I think I had an irrational fear that if I cut all my ties to the place of my birth, I would somehow be unable to return. I agreed to stay in the farmhouse with Yong Li and her family, and I saw my husband every few days. On rarer occasions, I saw my brother, who had moved into my city house, but I had the sense that he was casting off all personal ties, so that he could fight the war without any encumbrance on his concentration.

We lived like this for some time, wrapped in the strange rhythms of wartime. Boredom, tedium, and the sense of being severely circumscribed were our daily portion, alternating on certain sudden occasions with terror, panic, and despair. We had food shortages, which grew worse and worse, until the countryside was close to a famine state, and trying to obtain food became in itself a source of boredom and tedium, as if there were nothing we could not become bored with, given sufficient time and familiarity.

Later in the war, Guai went to Chongqing. I went to the airfield the Americans had been building near Hengyang to see the airplane take off. It was a cold, sunny day, the skies so bright I half shut my eyes against the light. I waved from the edge of the tarmac. Guai, blinking his eyes behind his spectacles, waved back to me from the top of the little movable staircase on which he had climbed to the door of the plane. I watched the plane take off, worried and anxious about Guai and already empty from missing him, but also thinking guiltily that I never tired of seeing airplanes fly. Then I went back to the farmhouse.

Yong Li still lived with me, together with her small twins and her five stepchildren. Her husband the grocer still had his stall in the suburbs of the city, and on the days he did not sleep in their old house in the town, he traveled back and forth with his loads of vegetables, which were frequently pathetically sparse. He took his two oldest sons with him. I helped Yong Li grow vegetables for the stall in the large garden she had laid out near the house—eggplants, cucumbers, cabbage. In fact, I had nothing else to do, since there were no rents to collect, and few tenants to pay them. Working like a laborer, I followed the seasons, planting in spring, weeding in summer, harvesting in fall, raising different crops for different times. My hands bled, then grew callused. Once, I found a maggot in my leg, and sat down on the edge of the well, crying from fear and self-loathing. Yong Li burned it off with an ember from the stove, biting her tongue in disgust, and gave me homemade whiskey to drink.

I don't think Yong Li found this country life much easier than I did. She herself had grown up in great houses in the city for her entire life, doing domestic work but not agricultural labor. Her husband was a city grocer and not a farmer either. Together, we made many mistakes, but every year we dragged some vegetables out of the ground.

"I've been thinking about the seasons," I panted to her one spring day, as I dug one hole after another for a row of turnips. "I hate turnips, I can't believe I am helping to bring more into this world."

Yong Li laughed. "What about the seasons?"

"Do you know why we have them?"

"No."

I pounded the hoe into the earth. "You know the earth goes around the sun, and the earth itself is round, and rotates as it revolves."

"I have heard such a thing," she said dubiously, covering up the seeds she had just dropped into the little hole I had dug, spreading the earth as smoothly as a blanket. Without getting up from her squat, she shifted herself along like a crab to the next section.

"We have seasons because the earth is tilted on its axis. It doesn't sit up straight. Like this." I picked up a pebble and tilted it. "So for part of the year the sun is stronger in our part of the world, when the part of the earth where China is—the northern part—is tilted toward the sun. That's summer, and the other time is winter. The solstice in summer is when the sun is closest to us, and the solstice in winter is when it is furthest away. The days are long in summer and short in winter."

I paused to wipe the sweat from my brow with my sleeve, leaving a streak of dirt along the back of my hand. I was wearing a straw farmer's hat, but the sun glared off the red earth as off a scarlet mirror, and shone the reflection under the brim. Yong Li had no hat, and I could see the shine of sweat in the part of her hair. She looked up at me a little impatiently, blinking into the sunshine.

"What are you trying to get at?" she asked.

"But imagine if the earth did not tilt. If it sat up perfectly straight, we would have no seasons. We would have light exactly half the time and darkness exactly half the time, and the weather would always be the same. Day after day, exactly the same."

Yong Li shifted along the turnip row again. "How horrible. Here." She pointed, showing where I should make the next hole.

"The ancient stories tell us that long ago, even before the days of the Yellow Emperor, there were still giants roaming the world. Men did not know the seasons, and they talked easily with the gods. The earth was perfectly flat. I mean, the ancients thought it was flat. And two giants fought a mighty battle to see who would dominate the world. During the battle, one of them stumbled and fell against the Great Northwestern Mountain, and crumbled it beneath his weight. Since the mountain was one of those which keeps heaven and earth apart, of course the earth immediately tilted up in the north and crashed into the sky. So the flat earth slanted forever afterward, being higher in the north and west and lower in the south and east. All of China's rivers flow south and east, every single one."

I had been digging holes all along, but now I stopped to sit down for a rest. Yong Li wiped her face and dragged a tin kettle toward us, and we both drank water from its rusty spout.

"That is why we have seasons?" she asked. I could tell she thought this story much more sensible than the first part, about the earth being round and revolving around the sun.

"Not just seasons," I said, pausing to drink water. I rubbed a few drops on the back of my dirty neck. "Because once we had seasons, then time began. With time came mortality for men. The giants disappeared. And we could no longer talk to the gods."

In the evenings, we were often alone with Yong Li's children and stepchildren. I told them stories from history, or Yong Li and I gossiped about the neighboring farmers. I also took to sharing a bed with her on the nights her husband was away. I often dreamed about my house in Changsha, where Li Shi now lived. One night I dreamed that I arrived at my house in the middle of the night, and none of the doors and windows could be opened, and I ran around the outside shouting for someone to let me in. The dream woke me in the middle of the night. I sat up in bed and stared out the window into the faint, faint light of the stars.

"What is it?" Yong Li whispered sleepily.

I told her. She sighed and sat up as well, propping her pillow behind her head. The rice husks with which it had been filled shifted, and made a sound like rain.

"Why are you so attached to a building, Elder Sister?" Yong Li asked. "You have a nice house, but a lot of rich people in Changsha have nice houses. I'm sure they don't dream of them."

I leaned back too. The starry gleam from the window made it possible to just make out the outlines of furniture in the room, but Yong Li's voice came out of the darkness.

"Haven't you ever wished to belong somewhere, Yong Li?" I asked, a question in response to a question.

"Where would I belong, but here?" she said, raising her hands in a gesture and letting them fall back onto the quilt.

"Maybe you don't suffer this. But I always felt like a guest in this world. We left my father's house when my father died. My mother's house we rented, it belonged to others. The Pan mansion really did too, but I didn't know it at the time, and at the end I had to sell it, and all the furniture inside. I lived in rented rooms, and other people's houses, until I built the house on White Crane Street. A moon gate, a garden, a goldfish pond, all my books and Guai's books on the shelves. A wall and a gate. For the first time, I was not a guest. I was the person who belonged to the house. The world stopped feeling like a roadside inn to me."

"Until now?"

"Until now." I sighed, and punched my pillow behind my head to make it more comfortable. I could smell the rice husks through the rough cotton cover. "It's not the luxury, you know, or the things I own. I don't think about my silk dresses or my French face powder or my shoes or my coat from America. I don't even think about my desk or my cook pots or my paintings. I just think about the empty walls and floors, and the ceiling beams. I think about the cool space between them."

I turned over on my side to face Yong Li. "Am I silly?"

Yong Li was silent a long time. I was beginning to think she had fallen asleep. Then her voice came to me.

"You know, when my old man dies, he will share a hilltop grave with his first wife."

"Why, where will you be?"

I could feel from the movement of the quilt that she shrugged. "I don't know. I have raised five children for this woman already, but she won't give up her grave site for me."

I waited.

"Her children will only burn incense at her grave, not at mine. The house we live in is hers too. When I moved in, all her things were still there. My old man wouldn't let me throw them out, what with ancestor veneration and all, so I had to use her pots and dishes and quilts. At least I didn't have to wear her clothes. I wanted to give them all to the oldest girl, but she didn't want them. Too old-fashioned, she said." Yong Li laughed. "So much for ancestor veneration."

"I would be so unhappy, living in some other woman's home."

"It is my home now, because she is gone, and I am here."

"But the dishes and quilts?"

"Those are mine now also."

I struggled to understand my thoughts, because there was something about all of this that would have been unbearably painful to me, had I been Yong Li. I was even jealous of Guai's first wife, who had died so long ago, and who had made no mark on my life, and hardly any on his. If everything I had, someone else had had before me, I would feel as if I were somehow just a shadow of the true thing. But Yong Li seemed to think of herself as the true thing, and the woman who had gone before as the shadow. Perhaps it was because I was the one who always felt like a guest, and Yong Li was simply at home wherever she was.

I said this to her.

"Elder Sister, there are people who are guests inside their own home.

They are alone in the middle of ten thousand people. But I just think, every breath of air I breathe has been breathed by someone else before. It makes no difference. I am the one who is breathing it now."

She yawned and slid down on the mattress until she was lying flat. "It's still too early to get up," she said. "Try to sleep more." In a moment, I heard her regular soft snores.

I lay awake. Outside, I could hear the wife from the neighboring farm half a mile away, walking through the night-blackened fields with her lantern, as she had done for many days now. She was calling her infant son's name, over and over again. I had heard the little boy was very sick, with a mysterious illness. But the spirits of men, and especially of infants, are often meek and biddable, and sometimes you can persuade them to change their minds about dying. If you call their name and beg them to stay, sometimes they can be persuaded to remain on earth, in their earthly form. "Little Red!" the woman cried, her voice hoarse from grief and begging. "Stay with me, stay with your mother!" The momentary gleam of her lantern passed my window, and then was quenched by the outer darkness. The child died a few days later, but for a long time afterward, his mother still wandered the night, calling for him to return.

40

*T*he summer of 1944 was very hot indeed, and the heat produced a kind of hush over Hunan. There had been fewer bombing runs by the Japanese, in part because the Hengyang airfield had been completed and American bombers roosted on its tarmac like watchful birds, and in part because the war had gone on for years, and even the Japanese can grow weary. I even started to stay in the city more often now, so I could keep house for Li Shi. It was easier for Guai to send me messages from Chongqing as well, since Li Shi had telephone and telegraph lines to the capital of resistance. I left the farm to Yong Li and acted as Li Shi's secretary instead.

The city was really no better than the farm—everything was shut down in Changsha. I had no servants and did all the cooking and cleaning myself. We always had to keep the windows closed at night so my brother and his men could light lamps to work by in the dark. I could not clean the entire house, so I closed off most of it and lived with my brother and his aides-de-camp in just a few rooms on the ground floor. Li Shi and I each slept in tiny rooms near the kitchen, and the other officers had bunk beds and desks in the main hall. My brother used Guai's study as his office, after I had carefully put away the fine carpets and paintings. When I closed up the rest of the house, I thought of the Pan mansion, and what I did there. My house is just sleeping, I thought, not dying. But I had to admit that those two states often look alike.

There came a week or two in midsummer when Changsha was almost breathless in the heat and silence. We still had blackouts at night, and it felt as if all the city and the surrounding fields were smothered in a hot dark blanket. I would sit at the dining table with Li Shi and his young officers, and we would eat in silence, too hot to talk. Only the clicking of chopsticks against the dishes would disturb the silence, like insect noises in the countryside. Strangely, I felt almost happy on those nights, without noise, without flashing lights, without the howl of sirens. Maybe not without worries, but without the power to do anything about my worries, which is a sort of peace also.

But it was that summer that the Japanese attacked a third and final time, and this time they succeeded. We had heard of the gathering enemy forces in the north, had seen those birds of ill omen, airplanes marked with the red Rising Sun. Zhao Han Ren, who was by now very ill, left for Chongqing on one of the last of our airplanes to beg the central government for reinforcements—he carried a letter from Li Shi and all the city magistrates, frantically asking for troops, each man signing his name in his own blood.

Then every day I sat in the central hall and waited for messages on the telegraph that Li Shi had in the study, for the one message that would tell us that troops were on their way to save the city, to save us. Every night we sat, with the windows closed in the stifling heat, the lamps lit, while my brother and his men received cables, pored over maps, exchanged mysterious remarks. Sweat poured down their faces, and they walked around in their shirtsleeves, with handkerchiefs in their hands to wipe their brows and upper lips. Someone would twist the dial on the wireless, and an electronic whine would alternate with furious voices speaking in Japanese. It seemed as if we never slept—we were awake all day and all night and never closed our eyes. Every hour I waited for something to happen, and a week later, around midnight, it did.

"Jade Virtue!" My brother's voice rang through the house. "Come quickly!"

I ran into the study. Li Shi stood in the middle of the room, his hand resting on the desk. Hunched over the telegraph was one of his young officers, who gazed in dismay at his own handwriting on the piece of paper in his hand. Papers lay all over the floor.

"What is it?" I asked, breathless with fear.

"The scouts report that the Japanese are almost here, and we can't keep them back. Pack a bag. I have to get you on the last train out of Changsha. Pack only what you can carry by yourself, Jade Virtue—you won't have anyone to help you. Take what's left of the rice."

He leaned out of the door and began shouting for the other aides, who came running. "Open the safe," he shouted at them. "Burn everything in it—maps, cables, all the documents. We can't leave a single piece of paper behind."

"Li Shi, what is it? Aren't our troops coming?" I clutched his arm.

"Of course they aren't coming!" he shouted at me. "When have they ever come? Zhao just cabled me—the central government isn't sending anyone, and Zhao tells me to get out of Changsha as fast as I can. There's a train left in the station—I'm holding it for you, but you have to move quickly!"

"I have to go get Yong Li—she has to come with me!" I cried.

"There's no time. What will you tell them that they don't know already? That the Japanese are coming? They'll know to run. There is no room on the train for anyone except you, and getting you on it will be quite a trick in itself. Go now!" He grabbed my arm and flung me in the direction of my room. I was sobbing as I tumbled some things into a small cloth bag. I poured what was left of the rice and corn in the kitchen into one of my old stockings and packed that away as well.

Li Shi was shouting to me from the courtyard, where he was making a bonfire of all his papers. His aides rushed back and forth, emptying out cabinets of documents and tossing them by the handful onto the flames. The orange glare against the night sky leaped out at me in all its strangeness—I had not seen a light out of doors at night in years, and I suddenly felt queasy with the sight. "Hurry!" Li Shi shouted, wiping his hand across his brow. The strain in his voice, bordering on panic, or as close to panic as Li Shi ever got, frightened me and made me fumble with my things. I heard them smashing the telegraph equipment onto the paving stones of the courtyard and then the radio as well, a dying whine rising from its broken wires. Then the aides were throwing things into their own bags—extra shirts, letters from their mothers, jars of candy. One of them strapped a black-and-green army radio-telephone on his back, and another was adjusting the frequencies. Li Shi himself appeared with a black leather bag.

"The car's outside. Let's go."

I looked around my house. All the windows were still closed and fastened.

"Come now!" Li Shi shouted from the gate.

I pulled out my key ring and locked the front door carefully behind me. I stepped through the gate in the garden wall, lifting my feet over the high threshold, built to keep out evil spirits, who can only travel in a straight line. I locked the front gate behind me as well, my hand shaking so hard that the key made little scratches in the paint around the lock.

We all climbed into the car, sitting almost on each other's legs. The driver pulled away with a screech of the balding rubber tires, none of which had been replaced in years. Li Shi was shouting on the army radio—I stared out the window and barely heard him, but I could guess what he was saying, for soon the sound of explosions rocked the night air. His soldiers had begun blowing up bridges, ammunition dumps, and food stores, and pulling down the telephone and telegraph wires. We passed ranks of soldiers, who were herding pigs before them and shouldering bags of grain, all to feed them in the mountains of the west, where they were evacuating. I watched the soldiers march away with tears of pity in my eyes. How could they fight the Japanese? I wondered. Many of them were provincial troops whose dialects no one could understand, and their attempts to talk to the citizens of Changsha had drawn only blank or hostile stares. Their eyes seemed bewildered to me. Their feet were swollen and puffy in their homemade straw sandals, and the only battle rations they had were socks stuffed with rice grains, swung around their necks like sausages. We passed an abandoned building, and I saw that a small group of soldiers had paused to make a meal before leaving the city, and I saw that they were boiling rice paper to eat, in a tin pot, over a small fire. I started to cry silently. My poor people, I thought. Always so pitiful, so weak, so hungry. Gobbling down things that the beasts would scorn to eat.

"Look." One of the younger aides breathed the word. We all looked in the direction of his pointing finger, even the driver. We had rounded a corner into an open square, from which we could see over the city walls onto the road beyond. For miles along the road shone the headlamps of the Japanese trucks, pair after pair of glowing golden eyes, one following another as far back as we could see until the lights farthest away were dimmed and swallowed by the night. "It's beautiful," the young aide said, wondering.

"Speed up," Li Shi said hoarsely.

It was hardly possible to drive faster than we could walk. The streets were clogged with a heaving, terrified human mass, marked by the black holes of open, crying mouths, by the squalls of terrified infants. I know we struck several people as we forced our way through the streets. I covered my ears, because it seemed as if everyone in the city were screaming in fear all at once. Then I covered my mouth, because I was overwhelmed by the fear that I would start screaming too.

The last train west out of Changsha was in the station, great clouds of white smoke bursting from its smokestacks, the entire train shivering and panting from the strain of the boilers. It looked like a creature that had been keyed to its highest pitch, stung until it was maddened, until it could barely be restrained, and which at any moment would burst its bonds and barrel out of the station. The train was surrounded with armed soldiers, who would allow no one to board until the order was given. They had already shot several people who had tried to board in defiance of their shouted orders, and the bodies lay on the tracks and the platform.

Li Shi and his men dragged me through the station. By this time I was openly crying. I was suddenly afraid of leaving my brother—he felt like the last person in the world that I knew. He was thrusting me away from him, into the dark strange world where I would be friendless, and the idea was unbearable to me. "Please let me stay with you!" I wept. "I'll go to the mountains with you!" He ignored my cries and held my arm so firmly that I later found bruises on my skin in which I could clearly discern my brother's fingerprints.

If I had not been surrounded by soldiers, it would have been impossible to move, because people pressed up against each other like spoons, knees curving into the knees in front, backs curving into the stomachs behind. An intellectual in a long black gown suddenly raised his umbrella and began raining blows on the heads of the people around him. The train let out a long whistle, and the crowd began to rock back and forth like a tidal wave. The soldiers waved us through a pair of doors that led to a deserted waiting room. Li Shi hurried me through the waiting room and out the other side, which gave onto the platform. We began to run down the platform toward the train. I recoiled in surprise—the train was already almost full, with weeping, white-faced refugees. Where did these people come from? I wondered. Then the whistle blew again. I was just climbing aboard the train when the soldiers raised their rifles and the crowd burst onto the platform. They stumbled down the tracks, they ran along the platform, they fell and bled on the concrete. Li Shi forced me into a seat in a compartment already filled with people. I clung to his hand. "Don't make me leave you." I wept like a child. "Please, I'm so afraid." Li Shi shook his head, and for a moment, through the veil of my tears, I thought I saw the ghost of a smile. Then he was gone, pushing his way out again, without another word to me. I saw him draw his pistol and force his way out past the oncoming flood by simply shooting into the crowd until they let him pass.

Then the entire train was choked with people, bulging through the doors, climbing over each other, trampling on each other. From the window I noticed with a twinge of horror that there was a dead woman crushed between the others at the door, her body swaying back and forth with the movement of the crowds, her face blue. Dead of fright, I thought, or suffocated in the mobs. I suddenly felt tired beyond all imagining.

The train began to move slowly, but there were still crowds pulling themselves on, swarming all over the roof of the train and clinging to the sides like bees in a hive. The noise they made was like that of bees too, an angry humming that rose and fell with the roar of the train. The train started to pull out of the station and still people were flinging themselves at the moving engine, flying down the platform and dragging at each other and falling under the wheels. Each time the train went over someone, there was a sickening little jolt.

I had a seat facing the back of the train, and I watched as the ground was pulled out from under me. I pressed my face against the side of the window and tried to peer out. On the platform, half the crowd was embroiled in an enormous fight. I had a momentary glimpse of bloodied faces like masks, before the train pulled away. As we steamed past the end of the station, I saw Li Shi, running back toward his motorcar with his men around him. One of them carried a flashlight, which he shone randomly here and there. The light briefly gleamed on Li Shi's white hair as he took off his hat. I shouted his name, again and again. But he could not hear me, and he disappeared into the big black car that would take him west.

Mashed into the crowded compartment, stifled by the heat, and nauseated by the press of bodies, we all leaned exhaustedly against each other. The lack of movement made my limbs stiff with pain. I had nothing to eat or drink, and my throat hurt with thirst. I fell asleep in fits and starts, and dreamed of the dead woman, who had almost gotten on the train, only to have her life snatched away within a few feet of its doors.

Several hours later, toward dawn, the train sped into a low tunnel. And with the onrushing darkness, a great collective scream rose that jerked my eyes to the ceiling, a cry that swelled from the front of the train to the back as the train went through the tunnel. Everyone's eyes followed the scream across the ceiling of the car, and listened to it fade away in the direction of the caboose. I sat there stupefied for several moments, until I realized that people—hundreds of them, from the sound of the cries—had climbed

onto the roof of the train at the Changsha station and had been riding
there all this time, and now all of them were dead.

The train on its way west passed the enormous crowds of refugees
fleeing the Japanese. They thronged the road that ran alongside the rails,
clambered over the fields and rice paddies farther out on either side,
pushed through patches of wilderness in the distance and flattened them.
They carried or towed their things—their bedsteads and quilts and bags of
seeds, their books and scrolls and winter clothing—dragging along their
children and oxen.

Then the train stopped in the middle of a vast plain, empty of settle-
ment and blasted by a stiff wind. There was what sounded like a riot on
the tracks ahead. I leaned out the window to listen, and I heard cries of joy
and exaltation.

"What is it?" I shouted to the crowd nearest me. "What is out there?"

"The Emperor!" a man cried back. "Someone saw the Emperor!"

Those of us in the train craned out the windows in disbelief. All along
the road, the women were bursting into tears. Men were falling to their
knees in the dust and knocking their heads on the bare earth. "Where is
the Emperor?" someone shouted. A woman came running back from the
front of the train, weeping. I reached out and grabbed the shoulder of her
tunic, with fingers made strong with a powerful desire.

"Stop!" I shouted. "Tell me what you saw!"

"The Emperor was walking on the road with us," she sobbed, wiping away her tears with her fingers and rubbing her runny nose on her
sleeve. "I saw him myself, just a young boy walking along, with a bundle
wrapped in imperial yellow silk. When we saw him I knew it was the
Son of Heaven. He's a refugee, just like us." She sat down in the dirt and
wept as if her heart were breaking. "Poor boy, poor boy," she kept murmuring.

I knew that Puyi, the deposed last Emperor, was a prisoner of the
Japanese in Manchuria. I knew too, that by now he was no longer a young
boy, but a man of middle age. I knew he would not be found walking on
this road, with a bundle wrapped in yellow silk. But I began to cry too, for
reasons that are still unclear to me, and then everyone in the train was crying. The train began to move again. I scanned the crowds as we passed,
looking for the boy with the yellow silk bundle. But I only saw the
tearstained faces of the people, their craning necks as they looked for him,

their confusion and desperation, and heard their desolate cries for that one man on earth who could speak to Heaven.

I lived the rest of the war in Kunming, with Graceful Virtue and Mo Chi and their children, and my mother and my children. A few months after my arrival, Guai came to join me. Kunming is famous for its salubrious climate and its fine fruit, and I hear it is now a big city, but at the time it was a muddy, tropical provincial town, filled with refugees. We lived in very crowded circumstances, but our year there was uneventful. When we had nothing to do—which is a curiously common condition in wartime— Guai and I would walk out of the city to a ravine pocked with caves and explore there, lighting torches to examine the remains of the brightly colored paintings that had once decorated the cave walls. No one else in Kunming seemed very interested in the cave paintings besides us, although someone had plucked out the eyes and mouths of the painted figures, to prevent them from coming to life at night. We asked each other about the ancient men who had made those pictures, asked why they had climbed up here to make them, asked how they had disappeared. Guai told me that he had heard of ancient cities that had been built in the desert and that had vanished with the passage of time, their ends mysterious and unknowable. I said I remembered reading, when I was a child, of an imperial army sent out to fight the great tribes of barbarians in the north and west. The army left the Middle Kingdom by the Jade Gate, the gate in the Great Wall that leads directly to the Gobi Desert. A great sandstorm descended on them, which was so quick and so fierce that the sand buried them even as they marched. So an entire army of men simply marched into oblivion.

We were up on the ravine on the day in August 1945 when the Americans dropped an atom bomb on Japan. Then they dropped another, and the Japanese finally surrendered. I imagined I could see the light of these new bombs all the way in China, and I rejoiced in the fiery death they brought. Whatever terrors the new age would hold, I thought, it was worth it just for this heaven-sent storm of fire, cascading down like burning water upon my enemies.

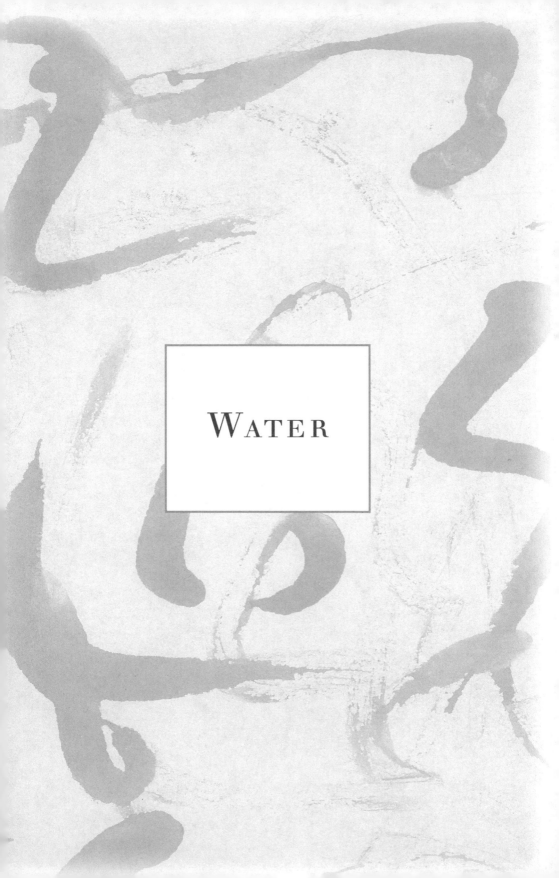

WATER

41

Sometimes I dreamed that I returned to White Crane Street and there was only a blackened hole in the ground where my house had been. Sometimes I dreamed that I returned and the house looked, from a distance, perfectly intact; yet when I approached, I saw that only the front remained standing, like a stage set, and the rest had fallen away into an untidy heap of bricks and mortar. Sometimes I dreamed that the four walls remained standing, but the roof and all the rooms inside, the floor that divided the first and second stories, all these had been crushed to the ground.

In the fall of 1945, after the Japanese surrender, Guai and I made plans to return to Changsha, and every night I dreamed one of these three dreams. In the daytime, I knew that one of these three possibilities was a reality, waiting for me to discover it. So there was a part of me that was reluctant to go home and find the devastation that would surely meet my eyes, even as the rest of me longed for Hunan. And even in my longing, there was as much curiosity as there was yearning for home.

The preparations for the return proceeded quickly enough. Li Shi had emerged from the mountains and had been promoted to brigadier general, commander of the Hunan and Jinggang garrisons. He had a new car, a former Japanese staff car, to replace his old one, which he had abandoned in a ravine in the mountains. Guai was to become deputy governor—he refused to unseat Zhao Han Ren, who would still remain governor, in spite of his increasing illness.

I started packing for our return home. I had thought all along that everyone in my family would return with us, but Graceful Virtue and Mo Chi seemed to drag their feet when it came to preparing to leave, and were noticeably silent at family discussions of the matter. I didn't know what to make of their entire situation. Mo Chi was always out of the house, and although he lived with Graceful Virtue in the same room, they rarely spoke beyond the most basic commonplaces, as if they were afraid to say more. Once, I came home unexpectedly early from the market to find everyone out except my mother asleep in her bed and Mo Chi sitting on the rickety wooden stairs, leaning against the wall and weeping like a child. He stood up immediately when I appeared, ran up the steps and into his room, shutting the door behind him. I knocked timidly and asked if he were sick, and he called out that he was feeling unwell and would lie down for a while. I said nothing about this to anyone and neither, as far as I know, did he.

Later, as we were in the midst of our preparations, I found Graceful Virtue in the room she shared with Mo Chi and their children. Their children were sprawled on the beds, reading. None of their belongings were packed. I beckoned to my sister to follow me, and she did, rather unwillingly. We walked outside and stood in the muddy little patch of vegetable garden that we kept on the side of the house. Kunming is southerly, and so winters are mild, but they are marked by great rainstorms, and one was even now forming on the horizon. The sky was blackening steadily in the south, where the monsoons came from.

"Are you and Mo Chi thinking of not coming back to Hunan?" I asked. "Please tell me if that is the case, so I can make arrangements without you." I spoke with some asperity, because I was angry at having the entire burden of our return home placed on my shoulders and on Guai's.

Graceful Virtue pulled her sweater around her shoulders—the building wind was making the air a little chilly. She looked away a long time, and then looked down. "I don't think we are coming, Elder Sister," she said rather formally.

"But why?"

"Mo Chi can have a good position here. He can be the deputy commander of the Kunming garrison."

"He can have a better position in Changsha, a more important one. Li Shi will see to that. If it is position you are after, then you would do best to come home with us."

She shook her head recalcitrantly. She still would not look at me, and finally I put my hand under her chin and raised her face to mine. But her eyes slid away to the side, like egg yolks on a tilted dish. "What is it? Tell me, Graceful Virtue. I am your sister."

"Mo Chi does not wish to leave Kunming, for personal reasons." Her voice was uncharacteristically intense.

"What do you mean, personal?" I asked, although I suddenly had a suspicion.

My sister now almost seemed to be grinding her teeth in fury. Her eyes darted around, and she tugged at her skirt with twitching fingers. I stared at her in amazement. "Because his mistress is here!" Graceful Virtue finally blurted out angrily. "He will not leave her, not even for me. Especially not for me." She hung her head.

I looked up anxiously at the sky. The storm clouds were now almost upon us, and I felt a few large drops of rain. I drew Graceful Virtue underneath the jutting eaves of the roof. "Will you stay here with him, then?"

"What else can I do?" she muttered bitterly. She still would not look at me.

"Come back without him."

"That is what he wants me to do!" she snapped. "That is exactly what he wants me to do. He offered . . . He said . . . He said I should return with the children if I wanted, and he would send me money."

"Wait, I'm confused," I said. "Return if you want? He is not sending you away, then?"

"He is not doing anything at all. He says I should stay if I wish or return to Changsha if I wish. His indifference makes me more angry than if he just sent me away. He is unhappy all the time—he cries in our bed at night. All this mess over that woman."

"Who is she?"

"I don't know. I found a love letter and accused him, and he admitted it. A general's secretary at the garrison headquarters. A young girl in a short skirt and high heels."

The rain began to fall more heavily, and the earth was growing marshy beneath our feet. Graceful Virtue and I huddled under the roof, leaning against the wooden wall of the house.

"Is he in love with her?" I asked.

For the first time since I began questioning my sister she turned her eyes to mine, and they burned with fury. "Always love, it's always love with you!" she shouted, while I tried to hush her. "I don't know, I don't care! But I won't leave, because then he can live with her openly!"

"You are ruining your own life just so you can ruin his," I hissed back at her. "Why on earth would you want to live with a man who loves someone else? Just to make them suffer? What about you? Aren't you better off living your own life with some dignity?"

"I will keep everything I have," Graceful Virtue snapped. "As long as I want Mo Chi to stay, he will stay, and so I'll make him stay."

I opened my mouth to say more, but Graceful Virtue struck me, balling up her fist and bringing it down on my shoulder, like a child cheated at games. "How can you be this way?" she wept. "Are you my sister or someone else's?"

"Be calm, be calm," I said in my most soothing tones, alarmed at how upset she was getting. "Fine, certainly don't leave if you don't wish to. Stay here and make him have to live with you, then he can only see her on the side. Maybe the difficulties of having you still in Kunming will break up the affair."

"Nothing will break up this affair," my sister groaned miserably. "Nothing. Only his sense of duty keeps him with me. He says he will never abandon me or stop supporting me."

By now it was raining heavily. I gazed out at the storm, the wind whipping my damp skirts. I thought again about how protective Mo Chi had been toward Graceful Virtue from the beginning, how at their wedding he had laid his hand on her shoulder as if to shelter her from all harshness. When their first child Suan-Suan had died, he said he did not blame her. Now he loved another, but he continued to protect my sister and for some reason that only made the whole thing worse.

I was startled when Graceful Virtue snatched my hand. "Elder Sister, go speak to her!" she said, her eyes widening in appeal.

"To whom?" I asked, surprised.

"To the mistress. Tell her to stay away. Mo Chi has no money to spend on her. We'll help her find a husband, and then she can get what she wants and I'll have Mo Chi back again."

I was very reluctant to do this, but Graceful Virtue begged and begged me, and clung to my hand with a kind of desperate strength. The storm was now so strong that the wind was making it hard for us to stand up straight, its buffetings making us stagger. But finally I agreed to go and see the mistress. We made our way inside then, soaked to the skin and already hoarse-voiced from the chill.

·　　　·　　　·

Guai located the woman for me. Her name was Xiao Li Li, and she had adopted the English name Lily. She was indeed the general's secretary. I went unannounced to the general's office the following day and found Lily at her desk outside his door. I stood in the hallway for several minutes, struggling with what I should do, and surveying her very carefully. Her appearance surprised me. I had thought she would be quite young, but this woman was over thirty. I had thought she would be pretty, in a red-lipsticked sort of way. This woman's prettiness derived solely from long, very clean hair and clear skin. She did wear a short skirt and high heels. But the skirt looked frayed, and the shoes were cheap. I spent a moment rearranging my expectations before going in.

"Are you Lily?" I asked.

"Yes?" She looked up in surprise from what she was writing. I noticed her handwriting was rather fine. I glanced at the general's open door. As I expected, he was out.

"I am Wu Guai Er's wife."

"Mrs. Wu," Lily said, standing up flustered. "I'm sorry I didn't recognize you."

"I believe you are a friend of my brother-in-law's."

The woman flushed a dark red and looked down.

"I would like to speak to you, now, while the general is away."

She nodded obediently, like a child, much to my relief. If she had refused to discuss matters, there would have been very little I could have done about it.

"Perhaps we could step outside. There is a tea shop down the road."

She picked up her handbag and followed me out the door and down the road to the tea shop. It was almost empty at this time of day, and we had a corner table to ourselves. The room was tiny and dark, with a floor covered in fruit peelings and peanut shells, the only light a faint glow from a small, deep window covered with oiled paper over my right shoulder. The wooden table wobbled on uneven legs, and I placed my foot against it to keep our little earthenware cups steady. The tea was very dark and strong, and tasted of earth. Lily sat looking into her teacup. I decided I was tired of looking at the tops of people's heads.

"Look at me please, Lily," I said evenly.

She looked up shyly.

"I'm not here to scold you. I'm not sure I would scold Mo Chi. Heaven knows, my sister is not such an easy person to live with, she's spoiled. But she is Mo Chi's wife. She will not leave him, and he will not leave her, however he feels about you."

She nodded, her eyes filling with tears. "He says that too. He says he must look after his wife. I understand, I really do."

"And Mo Chi has no money. He will not be able to keep you in any kind of style."

"I don't want his money."

Now here was a surprise. A mistress who didn't want money. She must be the only one in the world.

"Then what do you want?"

"I only want to be with him. I love him." She peered at my face, a little defiantly, as if daring me to find her reasons insufficient.

"Do you truly love him?"

She nodded, and gulped back more tears.

"Drink your tea, dear," I said. I am so kind to my sister's husband's mistress, I thought, sitting here discussing the situation with her like old friends. How worldly I've become, I thought. Like my mother.

"Do you have any family?" I asked.

"Just my old mother. I support her with my salary."

"I could help you find another husband," I said tentatively. "Someone who's been widowed or divorced, who won't mind if you've had a lover. I know my husband or my brother could find you a noncommissioned officer, a sergeant or something. Your life would be very comfortable. You would be a wife."

Lily sniffled into her handkerchief. "I would like to be a wife," she said, her voice muffled.

"Then take up my offer to help you. You don't have to break it off with Mo Chi until we find you a man."

"I can't accept, Mrs. Wu."

"My dear, why not? It's an excellent solution."

"I don't understand it myself." She stopped a moment to weep a little into her handkerchief, and swallowed tea to dampen the sobs in her throat. "But I have been so lonely my whole life, with only my mother, who is often very ill. Then Mo Chi came along, and it seemed as if he had been lonely his whole life too."

I felt a pang of pity for my sister.

"For me to marry another man, whom I do not love," she continued, "would only bring the loneliness back again."

I tapped her sunbrowned arm gently. "Lily, what did you do before the war?"

She covered her face with her hands.

"Were you a sing-song girl? A prostitute?" I was speaking very quietly now.

She nodded and replied without uncovering her face. "After my father died, our situation was very precarious. I had my mother to look after. I went away to the southern coast, to a city there, and I was a sing-song girl. When the war came, I escaped back home."

"I thought so," I said. Then she looked up in a sudden burst of anger.

"Mo Chi knows already, so don't think you can blackmail me to go away by threatening to tell him!"

"I thought he would know. If he didn't, I certainly wouldn't tell him." I said this firmly, looking into her eyes, and she seemed to relax a little. "Lily, if your background makes you think you are unfit to marry a respectable man, then we can come up with a plan. No one need ever know. I'll say you are a distant relative of mine."

"You are very kind. Why are you so kind to me? Another woman would simply beat me in the street because of this affair."

I sighed and leaned back. I thought that the world was a very equivocal kind of place. I thought that what we wanted, for the sake of keeping some part of our true souls alive, and what we felt duty-bound to do, to keep a different part of those same souls alive, were often at war. I thought that what looked to outsiders like a typical sordid sexual affair in fact involved the deepest of human emotions. I thought that the wronged wife, my sister, was also at fault, had contributed to the death of her husband's love with her own selfishness. I thought that I and everyone I loved had been guilty of so many sins, of so many different varieties, that I was in no position to judge this particular person. I thought I was now too old to be cruel for no reason.

"You seem like a nice girl," was all I said.

"I still cannot accept your offer," she said. Now she was crying outright, her head buried in her arms on the table. The proprietor chose that very moment to come over with a teapot, his eyes and ears avid to glean scandal. I took the pot from his hand.

"Clear off," I snapped. "We don't want your company." He retreated, and I turned to Lily again. "Because you only want to be with Mo Chi," I said. "Is that right?"

"Yes," she mumbled.

"Do you know what you are sentencing yourself to? You will always be in the shadow. You will never have your rightful place in a true home."

She sat up and wiped her face with her hands; her eyes were very red. "I don't deserve anything else," she said. "Mo Chi is already more than I deserve."

She hurried off down the street, back to her office, stumbling a little in her cheap high heels. I walked home slowly. The sun was setting early, and the dying light shone with strange effect on the great banks of black and gray storm clouds that clustered all over the sky. Here and there, an opening punctured the clouds, and the reddish-gold light poured down unobstructed, reflecting on the undersides of the clouds. I stepped around the puddles in the road, transient oval mirrors of the empty sky above.

When I got home, I saw Mo Chi in his uniform pants and boots, but with only an undershirt on top. He was watering the vegetables in the patch where I had yesterday stood with his wife, gingerly shifting the large tin watering can from spot to spot. I walked up behind him and waited until he turned around. He set down the can and wiped his hands on his trousers. For the first time, I thought, he seemed older to me.

"Do you know where I was?" I asked.

"Yes," he said, with a soldier's directness. He looked right at me. "I was dead for so long," he said simply.

"Do you wish to divorce my sister?" I asked, with a surge of guilt for my disloyalty. Well, so what, I thought. I'm not putting a new idea into his head. You can't force people to forgo their destinies. "Perhaps it is for the best. Then you can marry Lily."

"I can't," he said simply. "Graceful Virtue would be destroyed and shamed before everyone. I can't do that to her. All she cares about is if I stay. Then she feels as if she has triumphed. And I couldn't bear the shame of doing something like that. She is the mother of my children."

People, apparently, forgo their destinies all by themselves. "This way, you destroy everyone," I sighed.

He twisted his mouth into a mirthless smile. "But only a little at a time, this way. We are destroyed slowly, so slowly that we can all bear it."

I patted his shoulder and said nothing more on the subject to anyone ever again.

Graceful Virtue and Mo Chi came to the train station to see us off
when we went back to Changsha. We had a special sleeping car because of
Guai's new status as deputy governor. My mother and my children waved
from the windows. Guai and I stood on the platform with my sister and
her husband until the whistle blew, and then we boarded. Both Graceful
Virtue and Mo Chi lived for many years after that day, and we exchanged
letters often, but I never saw either of them again. In those days, distances
were much longer, but lives just as short as they are now and ever will be,
and history, as they say, intervened. I remember the two of them standing
on the platform waving, seemingly normal, like any other old married
couple. But they were acting, and would have to act for the rest of their
lives, and ultimately, perhaps, Graceful Virtue was comfortable with acting
and preferred it to being. Two years later, I wrote a letter to Lily, and she
sent me a photograph of an infant boy, with Mo Chi's down-turned eyes. I
sensed she lived in straitened circumstances, and I wrote her back warmly,
sending money and inviting her to visit. Her final note to me was brief,
begging me not to write again to so unworthy a person as herself.

42

*I*n the Xiang River, where the fisherman once used tame cormorants to catch fish, soldiers now caught fish with grenades, tossing the explosives into the water and blasting hundreds of pike and perch at a time onto the banks, where the leftover ones rotted uneaten. All around Changsha were vast piles of rubble, pocked with great blackened bomb craters and studded with lone chimneys and the staggered remains of walls. The houses left standing huddled like orphans, shy and impecunious. A few blasted shoots were all that was left of the trees, and the patterns of the streets had been obliterated, as if a dirty sponge had been rubbed across the entire neighborhood. I found White Crane Street easily, even though the entrance was largely blocked by rubble. Guai held my hand as we made our way down the street past heaps of broken masonry, the ox-drawn cart with all our luggage rumbling behind us, jolting in and out of the holes left in the road by the missing cobblestones. I was sick with apprehension, because in the year or so we had been gone, every house we passed, on either side of the street, had been damaged. Walls had fallen in, windows were broken, roofs had been bombed into the cellars, half-uprooted trees tilted at wild angles, black smears disfigured the plastered walls. Piles of brick lay in the yards, mingling with sticks of furniture and shards of pottery. The marks of bombs, of bullets, of fire, were everywhere.

I found my gate, which still stood, embedded in my garden wall, which also still stood. The flowering trees that put out their blooms above the wall blocked my view of the roofs from the street. My hand shook as I tried to unlock the gate, and Guai had to take the keys from me and turn the lock himself. The gate swung open slowly, and I saw before my eyes my own house, sitting peaceably in its flowering garden in early spring, seemingly unhurt.

Guai went ahead of me and unlocked the front door. "Jade Virtue, come and see," he said, in a neutral, quiet voice. I stumbled up behind him and looked. Everything was exactly as I had left it. The shutters were still closed on the unbroken glass of the windows. The porcelain vases stood unchipped on the tables and shelves. I walked through the entire house. My jewelry and makeup still lay on my dressing table, along with a splash of spilled face powder. A giant cask of salted vegetables still stood in the pantry, its heavy wooden cover sealed with red paper. A few shirts hung from the line in the kitchen courtyard, grimy from dust and bleached pale and crumbly by the sun but otherwise entirely whole. The broken tele-graph lay in the courtyard where Li Shi's soldiers had left it. The box of gold bars was still buried in the cellar, the marks of my fingers, which had smoothed dirt over its hiding place, still visible. Nothing had happened to my house, other than that it needed dusting. Finally I sat down in a chair, my stomach aching with relief, which can be as painful as distress. I clung to Guai's hand. Locking my door had been a magical act, I thought. Those fragile brass locks had kept the world outside.

That night, I stood at my gate and looked around me. I will never see some of these families again, I thought. They have been wiped from the earth, dead or scattered. How can an entire household disappear like that? Children, servants, animals, pots and pans, books, even the great stone jars of rice wine and pickled eggs in the cellars. I had a vague memory of something my mother had told me, about a household that disappeared as if they had been swallowed up, with all its worldly goods dissipated and the people scattered out into the world. Then I remembered that she had been talking about us.

In the next year or two, new houses were built on the sites of the old. The builders scavenged the bricks and tiles from the corpses of the former houses to make up the walls and roofs and doorways of the new. When I stood in my window before going to bed, I could not tell in the moonlight the difference between the bomb-broken husks of the old houses and the half-built shells of the new ones. But perhaps the difference is merely philosophical.

I found Yong Li and her family at our farm. When I received word that they still lived there, I went out immediately. Li Shi's car took me into the middle of a field, where the paved road stopped, and a mule and cart took me the rest of the way. Yong Li saw me from the window, and ran down the dirt path and threw her arms around me. She looked exactly the same.

"Elder Sister, I am so glad you are safe!" she cried.

"Can you ever forgive me for leaving you behind?" I whimpered, shamed by this undeserved display of affection.

"You didn't leave me behind," Yong Li said indignantly. "What choice did you have?"

I sat on a rickety wooden stool in her kitchen, crouched close to the clay stove in the corner, for while the winter sun was warm enough outside, the thick walls and brick floors of the kitchen in midmorning chilled the interior. Yong Li cooked eggs for me and boiled a pot of tea. "It was very hard," she told me somberly as she stoked the stove. "Rats as big as dogs. Hardly any food to be found. The Japanese stripped the fields and burned everything. Several families"—she paused a moment to clear her throat—"several families sold everything they had for one last meal, and then committed suicide together, children, grandparents, everyone. People I knew."

We sat in silence a moment, and I thought about how thankful I was that nothing on earth would ever induce Yong Li to commit suicide. Someone else might kill her, but she would never defeat herself. Inflexibility was against her nature, and what was suicide, except a final, unanswerable refusal to grasp the possibilities of change? But perhaps, for some people, death wears a kinder face than change.

But now Yong Li was laughing and digging around in a cupboard. "See here"—she grinned—"my homemade whiskey." The whiskey in my tea made me cough and seared the inside of my mouth, but I drank it gratefully, feeling its warmth spread through my limbs.

"I hid an American here while you were gone," Yong Li said, tapping her foot on the trapdoor that led into the cellar, half hidden under straw.

"An American?"

"An airman. He escaped when the Japanese captured Hengyang airfield, and I found him in the stable with the ox. I hid him down here until the war was over. The American had stomach upsets from the food I had to give him, but he never complained. I never understood anything he said. When the Japanese surrendered, I took him in to our army. That's when I found out that he had hidden for almost a month in the countryside before he found his way to me."

"That was very brave of you. The Japanese would certainly have killed you and your whole family."

"I know. I was frightened of that. I thought maybe I was being selfish, and I should think of my family more. But I knew the Japanese would slaughter him like a beast, like they did the other airmen at the field. I couldn't let that happen, what with him being all alone, and a guest in our country."

I supposed she meant stranger rather than guest, but to Yong Li, apparently, strangers were either guests or Japanese.

"What I couldn't understand," she continued, tipping a little more whiskey into my cup, "was how he could have hidden so long in the countryside. Why, he was twice as tall as my old man, and he had hair like yellow gold. It was amazing no one saw him."

"People only see what they expect to see," I said with a shrug. "You see everything because you expect nothing."

"Humph," Yong Li said. "Now you are drunk."

I slept that night in the farmhouse. Yong Li turned her husband out to sleep with their twin boys so I could share the bed with her. Outside, I could hear the insects and the birds of the night. They sounded very close, but also very faint, as if they were shy and did not have the courage to raise their voices.

"I'm going to give you this farm," I said.

"What? You have lost your mind."

"No, I will. It's yours. I'll make out the deed tomorrow when I get home."

"Don't do such a thing, Elder Sister. It's too good a piece of property. It's good farmland. You are never supposed to sell it, let alone give it away. I won't take it."

"You have no choice. I'm doing it. As long as I can always visit you. Now go to sleep."

Yong Li slid down in the bed, and I could feel the warmth of her happiness. I could not see her face in the darkness, but I could tell she was smiling. She leaned over to pull the quilt over me more snugly.

"I'm all right," I said.

"I don't want you to die of a cold before you can make out the deed," she chuckled. I lay quietly for some time, savoring the contrast between the warm air under the quilt and the frigid air on my face. The birds and insects fell silent as it grew later, and finally there was no noise at all except the creaking of the elm tree outside the window. I felt my chest expand with peace and freedom.

The next day I told Guai what I had done. "Do you object?" I asked.

"Certainly not," he said with a frown. "I'm very happy that you thought to do it. But I am bewildered. It seems out of character for you." His frown remained in his eyebrows, but his eyes and mouth began to smile.

"Well, I suppose it is," I said, flopping into an armchair and stretching out my arms in satisfaction. "Don't you always say that possessions are a burden? I'm lightening our load. Although I am at a loss to explain why." Then I leaned forward and caught his hand. "Are you sad? We won't be able to retire there now."

Guai squeezed my hand, a little absently I thought, and started to turn away. "We probably wouldn't have anyway," he said, with an infinitesimal shrug.

In the middle of the winter, early in 1946, on a day when I was at home doing my accounts and warming my feet on the little brazier under my desk, I received a telephone call on the new telephone that Guai had installed in our house. The raucous shout of the machine still startled me and made the hairs on the back of my neck rise. This morning the ringing was so sudden and fell upon such quiet air that I felt my heart flip in my chest. When I picked up the receiver gingerly, I heard a woman weeping hysterically on the other end.

"Who is this?" I demanded.

"They've killed him, he's dead!" Zao Zao screamed into the telephone.

"Who have they killed?" I cried, half rising from my chair.

"Father! They've killed my father! Li Shi killed him!" Then a long, drawn-out wail and the sound of a struggle on the other end. Then Li Shi's voice came on.

"Jade Virtue, it's me. Come quickly. Old Sui was shot in Chongqing yesterday as a Japanese spy."

"What?"

"Just come now." Then that lonely click that tells you that someone has hung up.

I hailed a pedicab and went directly to the house Li Shi and Zao Zao lived in now. She had come back from Chongqing ahead of her father to decorate the new home for her husband and to try to get pregnant. Old Sui had stayed behind in order to try to win new government contracts, now that the war was over. There had been no sign of trouble with him until now.

The maid let me in the door and I hurried down the hall toward the study, where I heard Zao Zao's and Li Shi's voices raised. Her voice was hoarse with tears and wildly veering from high to low, loud to soft, as if it were a car she could not control. His voice was firm and insistent, murmuring in low tones. Then she burst out of the door and ran down the hall toward me, throwing herself into my arms and sobbing into my shoulder. Behind her came Li Shi, his face white, his short silvery hair standing straight up where he had run his fingers through it.

"I called the doctor," he said wearily. "He should be here soon."

I held on to Zao Zao, all of us standing there in the hall with the servants watching us fearfully from the doorways. None of us said anything. When the doctor arrived, he put Zao Zao to bed and injected her with a sedative while I held her foot. So different from my youth, I thought. Then you simply cried until you were empty and then fell asleep out of sheer exhaustion. When Zao Zao seemed unconscious, I left a maid to watch her and went down to Li Shi, who sat in his study.

"How could such a terrible thing happen?" I asked, shutting the door behind me.

"What do you mean, how?" my brother asked wearily.

"Surely Old Sui was not a Japanese spy?" I sat down in a chair next to him and looked at him closely.

"Well, he was, in a manner of speaking. Old Sui traded tin and tungsten to the Japanese, but got back cloth and rubber for us. Information went back and forth like that as well. Some of that information I was able to use."

"Old Sui was a double agent?" I asked.

"That sounds almost too glamorous, but it's reasonably accurate. I don't think he thought of himself as a double agent, I think he thought of himself as a shrewd businessman. Same thing, really. But that is what he was."

"Couldn't anyone tell the Generalissimo? Didn't anyone know?"

Li Shi leaned forward and lowered his voice. "You heard Dai Li died in a plane crash just recently."

I nodded. Dai Li had been the chief of the intelligence branch.

"He alone knew who the double agents were. When he died . . ." Li Shi shook his head.

"You mean they just killed them all? Even the ones who were really working for us?"

"Yes." He ran his fingers through his hair again. "This whole country is insufferable. There were thousands of Japanese soldiers left in China after the war, and we are using them to fight the Communists. No wonder the common people in the countryside hate us. The Japanese soldiers are like windup toys. Just point them in the right direction and they kill." He threw himself back in his chair. "Yesterday, some men stole parts out of my jeep. My driver caught them. They stole the parts because they are starving, but we can't get spare parts and I can't countenance stealing from the army, so I executed them. Summarily. I shot them myself, right there in the street, and the bitterest part of it all is that I will never, never be called to account for my actions."

We looked at each other in dismay. Then I asked, "Why does Zao Zao think you killed Old Sui?"

"I don't know. Probably because I didn't prevent it from happening."

"Why didn't you?" I watched the lines at the corners of his eyes.

"How could I? I didn't even know about it. All these spy matters are conducted in complete secrecy. I only found out because one of the officers on the general staff is my friend, and called me to arrange to take home the body."

But Li Shi did not look at me while he was talking, and I felt wildly uneasy. We sat in silence for a long time.

"I'll come back when she wakes up," I said finally, getting up.

"Believe me," Li Shi said, as if he were speaking to someone else, "Old Sui was no great loss."

43

Guai and Li Shi and Zhao left for Nanjing in the autumn of 1946 to meet with the general staff about the war against the Communists, since all attempts to negotiate had failed. While they were gone, Zao Zao came to live with me, because her grief over her father's death was so extreme that Li Shi was worried about leaving her alone. She arrived with a suitcase of clothes and several bottles of scotch whiskey.

"You know why he went to that big meeting, don't you?" Zao Zao said, sprawled in an armchair and dangling her shoe from her toe. She sipped from her drink. She didn't seem particularly grief-stricken anymore, but her whole being emanated anger.

"Why?" I asked, looking at her over the tops of my reading glasses, from where I sat writing at my desk.

"To avoid sleeping with me." She sipped again.

"That's nonsense. Li Shi lives to sleep with you."

"Then why don't I become pregnant? I've been married to him for twelve years and I don't have a baby. Have you ever heard about Li Shi having any illegitimate children?"

"No, I have not. Zao Zao, try to think outside yourself for a change. Li Shi has fought a terrible war. You've hardly been together, in the last years, and when you have been together it's been under strained circumstances. Li Shi feels badly about it too."

"He just wants to keep me homeless." She exhaled in a bitter, ragged way and poured herself more whiskey.

"What do you mean, homeless? You have a large and beautiful house that he bought you, in the most fashionable part of town. You filled it with all these mechanical gadgets you ordered from America."

She threw me a derisive look, which was so unlike the old Zao Zao that I blinked in surprise.

"Yes, yes, all that's true," she said dismissively, into her whiskey glass. "But with no baby, I'm not really a member of your family. And I am no longer a member of my own, not since I married Li Shi. Especially not with my father dead. I no longer have ancestors, and clearly I will have no descendants."

I got up from my desk and went over to where she was sitting, and took her hand in mine. "Zao Zao, we are your family. I am your sister, as much as—more than—I am Graceful Virtue's."

"Who hates me, by the way."

"She was always jealous of you," I said.

"Why are you so nice to me?" she muttered into her glass, but she did not withdraw her hand.

I sat down in the chair next to her. "I don't really know. I don't know why I'm so fond of you, because you have such a temper. But I am."

"I want a baby."

"I know."

"I want a baby that I'll name after my father."

I nodded, watching her growing fury with anxious eyes.

"So that Old Sui's name will be in Li Shi's lineage forever. So I will be in his lineage forever. So our spirits will be entwined with his in the afterlife, and he can never get rid of us, no matter what he does. So he will fail in his attempts to keep me out."

I didn't know what to say. I sat next to her for the rest of the evening, reading, while she drank whiskey after whiskey. But she seemed to want to stay at my side. Well, I thought, many women get pregnant to hold a man, and often it works, in its own limited way. An honorable man, faced with his child, will often be unable to walk his flesh and bones away, even if his mind and his heart are gone forever. What was this plan of Zao Zao's, except a strange, spirit-ridden variation on that eternal theme?

Except for the evenings, when Zao Zao got drunk, it was actually rather a pleasure to have her in the house. She liked to play music on the new phonograph, and took my three children, who were now all teenagers, to the new cinema in Changsha. Jueh and Zhen adored this pretty, amusing aunt who dressed them in her own fashionable tight skirts and high heels. She taught Wan Li to dance Western-style to swing music records she had ordered from Hong Kong, taking the man's part to show him the steps he had to follow and commanding him, "Lead, lead! The gentleman must lead!" Wan Li's inexpressive face softened into a boy's face when she paid attention to him. I must have her come to stay more often, I thought, watching her dance with my son, even when Li Shi is at home. Wan Li was always difficult and rebellious, but the touch of Zao Zao's hand seemed to soothe him.

I sat in my study one evening a few days later, the windows at my back open in the unseasonably warm autumn weather. The sun had set, but glowed hotly from below the horizon, casting a red glow into the darkening evening skies. A light breeze blew in, but that air was hot too, and it was not refreshing. As I wrote, I patted my lip with my cambric handkerchief. In the small courtyard behind me, I heard the splash of water and Zao Zao singing as she took her evening bath in the bathhouse. When she had first gone in, I had glanced behind me and seen her candle appear in the little window high up in the wall, the flame suddenly resolving itself clearly inside the glass as she set it on the sill. Her splashes sounded companionable and actually rather comical, and the noise, obscurely, made me happy.

The furious scream that broke the calm of the evening was so sudden and unexpected that my heart seemed to miss its beat, and I spun around to the window. A string of violent curses followed. I leaned out into the courtyard, holding my desk lamp in front of me, and saw that Zao Zao had run out of the bathhouse in her silk robe and now had Wan Li by the wrist and was striking him, howling curses the entire time. I didn't pause to say anything, but whirled and hurried out of the study and down the hall to the door that led to the yard.

"How dare you, you little pervert!" Zao Zao screamed. "My husband will kill you!" She rained more blows on him with her fist.

"Who cares who sees you!" Wan Li shouted back, fending off her blows with blows of his own. They were clinging to each other with one hand and striking at each other with the other hand. "You're barren, everyone says so, even Mother! There's nothing to see!"

I started to run toward them, but I wasn't quick enough. Zao Zao shouted, "You stupid boy! You aren't even your father and mother's son! They got you from an orphanage in Shanghai! You are a whore's son!"

I came up to them as Wan Li drew back, his face stunned, his mouth open and his eyes wide. But worse still, as I watched, his face shifted into blankness, in a motion that was like falling, as if his features had fallen into the hard shape they would now assume forever. He and Zao Zao let go of each other, and drew back. She was panting with exhaustion, and I remember thinking that the utter stoniness of his expression somehow reminded me of when I first met Teacher Yang's daughter, Kai Hui.

"Zao Zao, how could you?" I asked wearily, near tears.

"He was peering in at me while I was bathing," she said brokenly, gesturing toward the little wooden kitchen stool that Wan Li had used to stand on to look in the window and which now lay toppled on its side in the wastewater ditch. "He said I was barren." She began to cry properly now, pulling the sleeves of her robe over her hands and burying her face in them.

I moved toward Wan Li, but at my first step he moved away, with the tiniest gesture of his fingers warding me off.

"It's not true, Wan Li," Zao Zao sobbed, looking up from her sleeves. "I only said it because I was angry. It's not true. I said it to hurt your feelings."

Wan Li's gaze slid toward mine, very reluctantly, as if seeking my agreement, but as my eyes met his I knew that we had turned a corner of some kind, and could not go back. I wish I had told you the truth from the first, my son, I thought. These old lies always come back to cut you. Everything comes back that has not been laid to rest.

I tried to move toward him again, and this time he turned and ran. He ran through the courtyards swiftly, in his bare feet, and I ran after him, calling his name desperately, calling to him of our love for him, but he did not turn his head. When he dived inside the house and leaped up the stairs, I shouted to the servants to help me, and they came running. Wan Li ran to the third floor and threw open the trapdoor to the roof. Then I heard one of the undergardeners running up the stairs behind me, passing me, shouting, "Young Master, Young Master! Come back!"

"Catch him, quickly!" I cried, breathless with the effort of running up three flights of stairs. The undergardener's cloth-bound legs disappeared through the trapdoor to the roof.

When I put my head out through the opening, I saw Wan Li running along the roof tiles, silhouetted against the last faint rays of gray-pink sunlight. He paused a moment at the edge and looked back at me, and even in the twilight I could see his blank white face, with his two stricken eyes looking out over his hard cheekbones. Then he leaped into the air, off the roof. I screamed. The undergardener threw himself forward, facedown on the roof tiles, and grabbed Wan Li's leg, clutching his ankle with desperate strength. I watched as the undergardener slid sideways down the side of the roof, still hanging on to Wan Li, coming to a stop against a drainpipe. I clambered out after them.

"Madame, don't go!" shouted another manservant from behind me, as he climbed out onto the roof. "Let me go instead!" We both stumbled toward the edge, where the undergardener was shouting for help. In the corner of my eye, I caught a momentary glimpse of Zao Zao's bright silk robe, huddled by the bathhouse. From every window in the house, the heads of various servants and my daughters craned, all of them calling advice and shouting in anxiety and excitement.

The three of us pulled Wan Li partly back onto the roof, with him struggling wordlessly the entire time to avoid our grasp. The upper part of his body was still hanging off the edge when we all realized that Guai was entering the gate to the front courtyard, directly below us, apparently having just come home. He set down his leather suitcase in the pool of light cast by the garden lamp and stared up at us with astonishment, then outrage.

The gardener shouted, "Quick, Old Master! Say something to your son!"

"Wan Li!" shouted Guai, a dignified figure in his Western suit and horn-rim glasses, clutching his English umbrella. "How dare you act this way? You should be ashamed—haven't you made enough trouble? Get inside! Get inside right now!"

The boy stopped struggling and looked at Guai with a flash of horrible fierceness. He reared his head back like a cobra and spat, "What would you do if I disobey? I am not even your son." And the whole household, peering from its various windows, recoiled in unison and was suddenly silent, realizing for the first time what had been at stake in this wild chase.

"Who told you such a thing?" Guai asked. I could tell he was trying to keep his voice even.

Wan Li stopped struggling and lay as if exhausted, pressing his cheek against the unyielding tiles of the roof, his ankle still in the grasp of the gardener.

Guai rubbed his face with the back of his hand, as if he were wiping away perspiration. "You are not my trueborn son," he called out.

"Guai!" I cried, but he ignored me.

"But we have loved you like a son. We have given you everything. More than we have given the girls, because you are the son in this family.

So now you know that everything was a gift, freely given by willing hearts, instead of an obligation. Why does that make you so angry?"

The gardener, realizing Wan Li no longer struggled, pulled the boy slowly back onto the roof, pulling like a fisherman whose fish has exhausted its struggles with the line and the net, and allows itself to be taken up into the hostile air.

The outcome of all this was that everyone acted as if Guai and I had done something wrong. Zao Zao went home to Li Shi and refused to speak to us for a long time. We sent Wan Li to Yong Li on the farm to live for a while, realizing that at least for the time being, the mere sight of us stoked his anger.

Almost every week, Guai had to rush out in the middle of the night to stop the confiscation of some man's worldly goods by the Guomindang collection agencies. The agents themselves were men of the worst elements, the kind that rise to power in days of confusion because they are not hindered by shame or scruple. Once, when Guai had been slow in arriving, he found the accused man hanging from a tree.

"They told me that he committed suicide in front of their very eyes," Guai told me when he got home early that morning. "Let me repeat that. Before their very eyes. Then they said that he had been a Japanese collaborator anyway."

"Did you believe them?"

"Who knows."

I rubbed his slumped shoulders. He took off his eyeglasses and put his head back to look at me, leaning it against my stomach.

"What is it, Guai? You look very distracted." I moved around to sit next to him.

"You know I've been working on a particular case these last few weeks. About an informant named Meng."

"Yes, but you haven't told me anything beyond that."

"Meng is a tough, greasy man. I had heard rumors that Meng had eaten fat throughout the war because he was paid by the Japanese. But he's valuable, he hears everything. I hesitate to act in investigations just because of a paid informant's word, but his information is always very accurate."

"How did the case begin?"

"He came in the other day and demanded to see me personally, wouldn't be put off by any of the police officers. Meng told me someone had slit the throats of all his pigs in the sty, because someone had found out that he was an informant for the police. 'I am a friend of the state!' Meng shouted. 'I demand an investigation.' I sent a young deputy, who found no clues.

"The next day, Meng appeared again. Someone had climbed over his fence and slit the throats of all his dogs in the courtyard. I sent the deputy again, but still there was nothing.

"When I arrived at the office on the third day, Meng was waiting for me. His manner was still belligerent, but now his eyes were wide with fear. His servant girl had disappeared, and he thought she had been kidnapped, because all her things were still in the house. The girl had been a mute, by the way. Now I personally went to Meng's house, and I brought in a team of investigators to look for anything which might help solve the crime. They didn't really recover anything useful. I told Meng to take his old woman—she's not really his wife, but they've lived together for twenty years—and leave town for a while, but he refused my advice.

" 'I can't leave,' he told me. 'I can't let them scare me. I'll sit up all night with a sword, and strike down this murderer.' "

"That was very foolish," I said. I leaned forward in my chair, frowning. "Why on earth wouldn't he just leave town?"

"Well, that's the true question, isn't it? As afraid as he was, he wouldn't go. Did he have gold buried under his house that he didn't think he could get out secretly? Had he been warned to stay? Meng, whatever else he was, was always very practical about his own skin. Why needlessly endanger it for his old shack and empty pigsty?"

"What happened?"

"I sent some police officers to guard the house all night—five of them, standing on guard outside. Meng himself sat up in his living room all night, armed, and heard nothing. At dawn, he went wearily to his bedroom, where his old woman lay, with her throat cut. The window was open. There was an inside latch on it, and it seemed as if she opened it herself, for what reason no one knows. I questioned the police officers, but they unanimously claimed to have seen and heard nothing. So I made plans to spend the night myself in the shack with Meng."

"No, you can't!" I shouted, grabbing his arm. "Guai, don't do this, or I swear I will leave you forever!"

"I'm not going to now, because Meng has fled. No one knows where he is."

"I'm glad for it," I said, calming down a little.

"But I wonder about why a woman who knew she was in danger would open the latched window of her house. To whom? For what? And then she obediently lay down on her bed so her throat could be cut? And five policemen standing outside heard nothing?"

We sat for a moment.

"Minister Yu," I said.

"What?"

"Years ago, Li Shi told me about Minister Yu. Guarded by a thousand men whose own lives depended on keeping Minister Yu alive. And yet he was assassinated in his bed, and all one thousand guards were executed. Li Shi thought it was a suicide conspiracy of one thousand men."

Guai leaned back. "So I have a conspiracy of five policemen?"

I shrugged. "Five policemen and Meng. And maybe one mute serving girl."

Guai gave a great sigh. "Anything is possible. But it seems I cannot protect either good men or bad ones."

"Don't feel bad. It's not your fault. Come into the kitchen, and I'll cook you some noodles. I have pickled cabbage and turnip, and cucumber in chili sauce to stir into the soup. I'll make the noodles myself, just like I used to in the old days." I stood.

But Guai did not move.

"What is it?" I said.

"You know we will lose this war to the Communists."

I sat back down again. "Surely not," I pleaded.

"We will. In fact, we lost it ten or fifteen years ago, when we first allowed the Triads to help us. They brought a worm of destruction into our government that ate away at our insides, and the business of government went from being a heroic nationalistic enterprise to being the building of vast personal fortunes through corruption. You see it yourself."

I said nothing, but I knew he was right.

"We lost the war years ago," Guai sighed, "only none of us knew it then. The future is actually prepared long in advance—that is why the fortune-tellers can sometimes guess at it. It's an odd feeling, really. It's as if we had died years ago, but kept on walking around as if we were still alive."

"But our army has seized Yan'an. Everyone said it was a great victory."

"The Communists let us have it. They abandoned Yan'an to us, and we seized that empty rock and proclaimed ourselves the victors. Yan'an only had value when the other side wanted it too."

Like so many other things, I thought.

"I heard that there is a Yellow Wind in Beijing," he said.

I was surprised. "Sandstorms from the Mongolian plains? But that only happens in the autumn."

"It is happening now, in the middle of the winter, sand mixing with snow. No one can remember the last time such an occurrence took place. I don't hold with worthless old superstitions, but it makes me feel as if the hand of heaven is against us. The grass bends before the wind, the wells and rivers choke up with sand."

I put my hand on his shoulder, and he looked up at me. "I would wish to see peace in my lifetime." He took his eyeglasses off again and wiped them with his sleeve. He leaned back with a mirthless smile.

"But then," he murmured, almost to himself, "why should I be different from any other man?"

$\mathcal{M}$y mother was now very old, and she almost never left her bed. I myself was getting old as well, but her continuing survival made me feel sometimes as if I were still a child. She was sick with many different illnesses, until finally Li Shi's doctor diagnosed cancer in her stomach, and I knew she did not have much time left. In her last days, she was in great pain, but she said little about it. I rubbed her legs for hours every morning, for her bound feet were beginning to feel pain again.

"It's strange," she said. "When you get your feet bound as a girl, you always think that they will stop hurting some day, and they go on hurting for decades, unceasingly. Then one day they finally stop, and it feels as if old friends have died. Now, for some strange reason, my poor legs have come back to life."

At night, I slept on the floor by her bed, helping her to the chamber pot, feeding her, bathing her, and dressing her, as I had done for Wang Mang so many years ago. Some nights, a maid slept there instead so I could rest in my own bed, but being away worried me so much I couldn't sleep in any event, and I gave it up. My pallet was next to my mother's coffin, which she had me buy for her ahead of time, in the old style, and set next to her bed, that its presence might comfort her.

Every morning, I opened the window for my mother to look outside. Every morning, I looked at her face against the pillow in the new light of day, and each time it seemed as though a little more of her had slipped away during the night, in spite of all my watchfulness. Finally, she seemed like a ghost, so thin and worn and wrinkled and desiccated, that a person just entering the room would have assumed she was already a corpse. Yet she continued to live, her eyes still alert and steady. She was still critical in her opinions, which I took to be a good sign.

In early spring, her appetite grew less and less, until one morning she waved me away weakly when I approached her with a bowl of rice porridge.

"Please, Mother," I said, my voice shaking with panic. Had we come, then, to that turn in the road?

She shook her head slightly but decisively. "Get me my hand mirror," she said, in a surprisingly strong voice.

I picked up her hand mirror, which I had plucked from the still-warm ashes of her old house after it had burned in the fire. It was one of the few things that had survived the blaze. It was quite old, made out of bronze, with a reflecting surface not of glass but of polished metal. On the back was a passage of intricate graven calligraphy. "Five Sons Pass The Examinations," it said.

She traced the words with her shrunken forefinger. "I was born in feudal times," she sighed, "when the Son of Heaven sat on his throne. And I die in the middle of this century, in the year 4645. In the old days"—she stroked the mirror's reflecting surface—"we preferred jade to diamonds, because diamonds were too glittery. We thought shiny surfaces were untrustworthy. And so they are, but now the entire world is in love with shiny surfaces. I received this mirror as a wedding present from my grandmother. Did you read the good luck it wishes, about five sons passing the examinations?"

I nodded and sat down on the edge of the bed. I felt my mother was very near the end. I dreaded losing her, yet I wished the entire ordeal over with quickly.

"How lost we have become," she said, "since the time when such a wish might be made." Then she looked at me keenly.

"Why are there tears in your eyes?" she asked.

I shook my head, and tears fell on the silk coverlet and rolled away on the glossy surface.

"You know I am dying, even as we speak? Don't shake your head. You will be sixty years old in a few years, and still you cry like a child. You never learned to resign yourself."

"Resign myself to what? I don't believe in fate," I mumbled.

"Neither do I," she said, sounding surprised. I sniffed at this and wiped away the tears. I put on a brave face for her to see, that false identity known as a dragon mask.

"Don't be unhappy, I've lived a long time," she said. "Immortality is for the gods. Frankly, I don't know how they stand it. Listen, Jade Virtue. Your father's box of scrolls. The one that's under my bed. The one I wouldn't leave behind when my house burned. Remember? I made you get them and carry them."

"Yes, what about them?"

"I'm leaving them to you. After I am gone, read through them all carefully. It is the wisdom of the past. It has all the answers you seek." Then it seemed to me that her sunken dark eyes glinted a moment, with what emotion I could not tell, but it was very unlike her. "Promise me when I am gone that you will read them all." A small smile crept onto her face, unobtrusively, as if she had thought something amusing but was afraid of offending someone by laughing out loud.

"Of course I promise. Will I be able to understand such ancient works?"

"Interpretation is everything," she said, without further explanation. "You are crying again."

"I'm sorry, Mother. But I cannot bear to be left alone here, without you." I was starting to sob, and soon I was weeping openly. But my mother did not scold me this time. She simply stroked my hand until I became quieter.

"Everyone loses their mother and father," she finally said. "It is the order of things."

"I feel an entire world is slipping away with you," I sobbed, trying to wipe away my tears with the corner of the bedsheet.

"Arrive without confusion, and depart without hesitation," she murmured.

She was quiet then after that, holding the mirror against her chest. I sat down on top of the coffin and held her hand. Toward the middle of the day, as the sun was reaching its highest point in the heavens, my mother died. I took the mirror from her hands. The sun was shining in through the windows; I trapped the light on its reflecting surface and bounced it back out again. The little bead of light caught for a moment on the shady garden wall, then lifted free and disappeared into the large golden eye of the universe.

I gave her only a modest funeral, as she had requested. I buried her with her mirror, which seemed right. For some weeks, I did not touch the box of scrolls beneath her bed. But I thought of them all the time. I was anxious to know the answers my mother had promised me, but I was afraid too, afraid that the answers would somehow be too erudite or hard to understand. But one hot day when I was alone in the house, I went to her room, which I had left very much as it had been before her death, apart from washing the bedding. I pulled the box out into the middle of the floor. It was long, rectangular, and made of polished wood. The brass lock still secured it—I had forgotten about losing the key during the fire. I plucked at the lock a few times, wondering what to do. I found other keys in the house, but none of them would open this particular lock, which was old and of primitive design. Finally, I went into the courtyard and found the small ax that Cook used, to break up kindling or to hack the limbs off poultry, and took that upstairs and chopped the lock off the wood.

There were perhaps a dozen tightly rolled scrolls in the box. I took them out one by one, unrolling them first between my hands, and then laying them out in full length, spreading them out on the floor, throwing them over the bed so that they lay like long paper banners, until the box was empty. I examined each scroll closely. Then I sat down on the carpet and gazed about me. I sat there until darkness fell, wondering, wondering, wondering, asking myself new questions about my mother that I had never considered or suspected before, for all the scrolls were blank.

45

*I*n 1948, my daughters Jueh and Zhen left home to go to college in Canton. Jueh was two years older, but I kept her at home so that both girls could go away together, for I did not want to send one alone. Jueh was our favorite, for she was pretty, charming, and eloquent, although her skill with words did not disguise her fundamental naïveté. Zhen was giddy and lighthearted and rather irritatingly silly. I had to scold her frequently, although I admit there were times when I wondered if I underestimated her. If they went together, I thought, they could at least look after each other. I had originally wanted to send them to Zao Zao's college in Nanjing, in the north, but Guai shook his head.

"The north is uncertain. Too close to our enemies. Better to go south. The Communists will have to go through us to get to them."

The only child of mine left at home then was my son Wan Li. He could not attend university, for he would not study. Always raucous and imperious in his ways, he became more and more troubled in the months that followed his sisters' departure for school. I had sent him for a while to live with Yong Li on the farm, and told her to treat him as freely as if she were his own mother. But she was too busy to watch him all the time, and he had begun to drink and whore and gamble with peasant boys older than he. He roamed the countryside with them, tormenting passers-by and getting into fights. His knuckles were always split and bruised, from hitting other boys, from pounding his fists into walls. Worried that some harm would befall him while he lived with her, she sent him back again to me. She brought him home herself, and stood in the hallway weeping for having failed me. I apologized for having put her to so much trouble, and begged her to eat dinner with us, but she had to return home to her family. After the door shut behind her, I looked at my son in dismay. He had always looked a little foreign to me, not quite Chinese. But now his face wore a prematurely dissipated expression, and I thought with a shiver that he looked like no one so much as Wang Mang.

"Come eat something," I said, touching his arm gently.

He made no response, but walked ahead of me into the dining room and sat down at the table. I signaled to Cook to get him some food and sat down across from him.

"I'm disappointed, Wan Li. You've given a lot of trouble to your aunt."

His eyes flashed at me. "Why do you call her my aunt?" he asked indignantly.

"What do you mean?" I asked, bewildered.

"Do you say that maid is my aunt because you think I am so low class?"

"That maid, as you call her, is one of my oldest friends. That is why I say she is your aunt."

"Do you force the girls to call her Aunt?"

"The girls do call her Aunt. I don't have to force them. They respect her."

He turned his gaze away and raised his chin. "Don't pretend to me again that I am related to that maid," he said.

I got up and went around the table and grabbed his shoulders, shaking him.

"How dare you?" I spat. "You are not worthy to empty Yong Li's chamber pot! Not because you are a servant, but because you are something worse than a servant!"

He tried to get up, but my fury had made me strong. I thrust him back into his chair. "Stay there!" I roared. "If you act like a whore's son I will treat you as one!" But as I glared down at him, I saw tears emerge from his eyes, slowly and gently, as if from a cocoon, and slide down his cheekbones.

"My son," I groaned, "what is wrong with you? Why are you so filled with contempt for those you should love?"

He rubbed his eyes like a small child, shrugging my hand off angrily. "Those that I should love? Who among them will love me?" he wept. And for a moment I thought of an evening many, many years before, when Wang Mang had forbidden me to leave the house. Why should anyone want to leave me? Wang Mang had asked me then, mockingly, and for the first time in my marriage to him, I had felt pity. Somewhere inside, I knew Wan Li's question spoke to me of the same sort of brokenheartedness, and I regretted treating him roughly. I drew him toward me and stroked the back of his head as he continued to weep, silently and terribly, with his shoulders shaking violently.

When Guai came home, I told him what had happened. Guai called Wan Li into the study. The boy stood on the carpet in the middle of the room and would not look at us, but only over our heads.

"My son," Guai said. "I know that finding out your origins was a terrible shock to you. I blame myself and your mother, because perhaps we should have told you from the time you were very small. But we felt as if you were our true son, and we didn't wish to make you think differently."

I nodded in agreement, watching Wan Li anxiously.

"When you thought you were our birth son," Guai went on, "you were vain and arrogant to others, because you thought you were better than they were. When you found out that you were once an orphan, it did not make you humble. It made you more arrogant than ever before. I do not understand this behavior."

Wan Li did not answer, but only stared all the harder at some mysterious spot above us. That entire night, in spite of our entreaties, he refused to speak a single word to us. But the next night, he came into the study again and told us he wished to be married.

We looked at each other anxiously. At seventeen, he hardly seemed old enough. "Let your mother and me discuss it together," Guai said, sending him out of the room. Guai turned to me as the door shut.

"Marriage? Where did he get such an idea?"

"I don't know," I sighed. "Maybe because the boys in the countryside that he gambled with had wives."

"They did?"

"Yes, they were older than he was, and anyway, the country people marry young. Much younger than us in the city."

"I wouldn't like to see him married. The responsibilities that come with marriage will be too much for him. Then we'll never get him to study." Now Guai was striding up and down in his office, waving a brush pen he had forgotten he was holding. Tiny spots of ink splattered onto his already ink-stained gray robe.

"Don't do that," I said, taking the brush and setting it down on its little blue-and-white china stand. "He doesn't study now."

"But we want to encourage him to apply himself. He's a smart boy—he's just lazy and irresponsible."

"But do you think he ever will apply himself?" I asked, suddenly sad. You hope and hope, and everything is bearable as long as you hope. Then you come to the end of hoping, and it feels like a death.

Guai thought this over for a minute, and sighed. "Honestly, no. It's breaking my heart. I don't know what to do with him."

"Well, if he won't be a scholar, and he doesn't want to do anything except spend money and fool around, he may as well get married. At best it may settle him down a little bit. A good wife can be a good influence."

"Yes, yes, that's true," said Guai, looking more hopeful.

"At worst," I said resignedly, "if he does something wrong, it won't be all our fault." I felt a twinge of guilt saying such a thing, but my sadness made me bitter.

Guai looked at me reproachfully. "How can you say that? That's no reason to find him a wife."

"Heaven and earth," I exclaimed. "I'm only thinking of you. If it wasn't for your position, I wouldn't care what people thought of us. But how are they going to trust you as an official when you can't control your own son? He is constantly getting into fights. He has made so much trouble already."

Guai's face fell at my words.

"I'm sorry, husband," I said then. "I'm a bitter old woman tonight. Forget what I said."

"Listen," Guai said, seating himself behind his desk and picking his brush back up. "I leave choosing the girl in your hands. You know more of that kind of woman's thing than I do. But I don't want to hear any more about shifting shame onto someone else. I am an iron-faced official, and that should be enough for everyone." He shook his brush again in agitation, and the ink flew.

"Don't," I said, taking the brush away again. "Don't pick it up until you are ready to write. I'll pick the girl. I'll look for good character in the wife rather than beauty or wealth. We don't need a daughter-in-law with a big dowry or white skin. I'll bring you something to eat in a little while."

"I'm glad you are seeing to this," Guai exclaimed, "beacuse I actually have work to do. Our nation is falling apart, and there are all these problems in my own home to distract me!"

I left without saying anything else. Falling apart in more ways than you know, I thought furiously as I walked down the hall.

.   .   .

But the more I thought about it, the more I decided I did want Wan Li to marry. Life tears through the generations, using up each one in turn and moving on to the next. With my mother dead, I felt that I would soon be next, and I was anxious to see my children settled. I told Yong Li of my quest to find a wife, and she immediately told me of a girl she knew living on the remains of a neighboring estate. The girl was named Lark, and she came from a good but faded family.

"Her aunt told me that her great-uncle was a high mandarin in the Ministry of Rites," Yong Li said. "You can see from the house that they used to be rich, but now they have no money. Still, they have a good name, and it is an old one."

Both of Lark's parents were dead. She lived in one wing of the former great house with her girl cousin, who was several years younger; the cousin's mother and father lived in another wing of the same house. I sent Yong Li to speak to them. After some suitably oblique conversations between Yong Li and Lark's ecstatic aunt—"Good fortune has returned to our house, husband!" Yong Li heard the aunt say to the uncle through the open window as she left—I went with Yong Li to see the family. I thought we should try to maintain some decorum, so I hired a sedan chair to take us there.

The rambling country house had clearly come down in the world, and the whitewash was peeling, but it was clean and well-kept. The courtyard was tidy, and there was a large reflecting pool about three feet deep in the center, planted about at its base with flowers. A few water lilies nestled on the surface of the water. These people know how to take bad fortune gracefully, I thought with approval.

The family, obviously incredulous at their luck, came out to greet us with utmost politeness, bowing deeply and murmuring fair words of welcome. "We are so honored," the uncle and aunt and cousin kept repeating. "We are so honored." They addressed Yong Li as Madame Go-Between.

Inside the house, we were seated in what I guessed was the best room in the house. There was a complete absence of any decorations—no carved boxes or cloisonné bowls, no lacquer or porcelain jars. Just shelves that held various household goods, cheap tin bowls and the like. No books, either, I noticed, frowning inwardly. Well, my son certainly isn't going to bring them any.

But when the young cousin brought in tea for the guests, the tea was served in two beautiful green porcelain cups of excellent quality. The cousin went out again and came back with cheap cups for the family. I saw that while the surface of my tea was thick with tea leaves, the cups held by the family contained only hot water, which they tried to disguise by sipping surreptitiously from beneath the edges of the porcelain cup covers. I thought: That's why the girl made two trips. No point in wasting tea on the family members. And suddenly I felt very tender toward them.

"Such good tea," I smiled. They all bowed and smiled their appreciation. There was a moment of shy silence. "What lovely flowers you have outside," I said after that.

"Thank you," said Lark's aunt. "They are just poor country flowers. But I like to garden, and in the spring we put flowers in the house. I wish we could have roses, but they are so . . ." Her husband looked at her, and the woman became embarrassed. "I mean," she finished lamely, "good specimens are hard to get."

"Yes, indeed," I said smoothly. "I had a terrible time finding mine. Perhaps you will allow me to send you a few cuttings?"

"Oh no. That wouldn't be right. It's too much trouble."

"Please. I have to trim them anyway. I usually just throw the cuttings away. How much more sensible to let you take them. They would just go to waste otherwise. And they would look beautiful outside by that reflecting pool you have."

"Well, if you are just going to throw them away . . ."

"I'll have the boy bring them to you tomorrow."

"Thank you, thank you," the whole family said, bowing in their seats as if I had offered them gold.

We spoke a little more about flowers. I agreed with Lark's aunt; we liked roses best. The cousin liked gardenias. "All young girls do," I joked. "It's romantic."

Everyone laughed appreciatively. If they are always going to be so appreciative, I thought, I imagine I'll enjoy being related to them.

"I'd rather plant vegetables that are good to eat," said Lark's uncle, and everyone laughed again.

"I'd like my son to take an interest in gardening," I said, looking modestly into my cup. Everyone sat up a little straighter. "He has been living in the countryside with Auntie here, and I think daily fresh air is good for him." Yong Li smiled and nodded.

"Gardening is a good hobby for a gentleman," said the young cousin.

Well brought up, I thought. Manners like silk. What a pity she's too young.

"Well, he's an adult now," I continued aloud. "He does not plan to enter the government like his father. He's very interested in the natural sciences. I don't think he'll become a doctor, but maybe he will do research."

"Yes, yes, research," everyone said, nodding profoundly.

"Of course, I would like to see him settled down before he begins his life's work."

"Yes, yes, settled down, of course," everyone said, nodding again.

"It's very important that he find a good wife. I hope the gods give me a daughter-in-law of great wisdom and virtue and filial piety. Someone who will take care of her husband's parents when they are old, and who will fill the house with grandsons." Oh yes, I thought, someone just like me.

Yong Li said innocently, "I heard you had a young lady in your house—your niece perhaps? Since we were passing by, we thought we would come to visit her. Everyone says she is a very fine girl."

"Yes, I do have a niece," Lark's uncle said. "She is a very good girl, very obedient. My dead brother's daughter. She has lived with us for many years. Uh . . . perhaps you would like to meet her, madame?" He looked at me, his eyebrows rising, as if he were afraid I might refuse, even at this point.

"Why certainly, if it is not too much trouble. What a nice surprise. Does she happen to be in the house?"

"Go call your cousin," they told the girl, who promptly ran off. Lark entered soon after, in what was obviously her best dress. Yong Li and I looked at her carefully. Her skin was not very white, but it was clean and fresh. And I liked Lark's mouth, neither hard and mulish nor soft and baby-like—I dreaded girls with soft, babylike mouths. When Lark looked up, her eyes were steady and calm.

Lark greeted us graciously and offered to fetch more tea. The young cousin was sent instead. They all sat down.

"Lark is nineteen," her uncle volunteered. Good, I thought. A little older was better.

"Such pretty girls in your family," I told them. The uncle and aunt shook their heads, but smiling.

The afternoon passed serenely. Lark answered my polite questions with equal politeness, interested but not overly eager. Lark, though not stupid, did not read books. Well enough, I thought. What good will books do her married to Wan Li?

The negotiations for the marriage were held several days later and proved very simple. Lark's impoverished family, eager to marry her into a big house, consented readily to my proposals. We settled on two new suits for the bride and one suit of new clothes for everyone else. I cheered them, however, with the promise of a fine feast and eight men to carry the bride's sedan chair. Lark, for her part, seemed perfectly willing. Her young cousin reported that the older girl was very agreeable to the match and had spoken of the upcoming wedding with every sign of satisfaction. I told Wan Li that his future wife was gentle and pretty, and he smiled for the first time in a long while.

The engagement was agreed upon. When my daughters came home from Canton during a school holiday, I took them to buy gifts for the new bride. We went to the street of cloth sellers, a chaotic little avenue that lay along a portion of the ancient city walls, behind a row of two-story gray stone houses not far from the Alley of Left Turns. It was crowded with the stalls of cloth merchants, ringing with the loud voices of commerce and choking with customers and traffic. Buyers jostled in and out carrying bolts of silk brocade, cheap cotton, gold braid, paper packages of buttons, balancing all these purchases with their other market purchases, so in the alley one had to skip nimbly to avoid large baskets of vegetables, pails of milk, and steaming bundles of bread. The cloth merchants were always shouting at people not to drop or splash food onto the cloth displayed in the stalls, and there was usually at least one pushing match every hour or so, gathering a large and vocal audience of advisers.

I went directly to one stall that I frequented and ordered the girl to bring the best brocades—"good enough for a bride." My daughters were ill-tempered at this. "She never buys such good things for us," Zhen whispered to Jueh as they stood across the alley from the stall.

Jueh whispered back, "Whoever heard of five kinds of cloth for a single dress? We always have only three."

I could hear them whispering in this disaffected manner and glanced over my shoulder at them. "Why are you loitering there?" I shouted to them. "People will think you are Shanghai dance hostesses. Come over here." The girls reluctantly crossed the alley, Jueh hissing under her breath, "I wish I were a Shanghai dance hostess."

·　　·　　·

There was some argument over whether or not to call the local astrologer to pick an auspicious day. I made a halfhearted stand against it.

"That old fake?" I exclaimed. "I hate these ancient superstitions, which only upset everyone." But the alarmed pleadings of Lark's family, and of Yong Li as well, made me relent. I sent for the astrologer, gave him a little silk purse with a few coins, and asked for an auspicious wedding day. The astrologer consented and went away, promising to return when he had cast his horoscope.

Days went by, and no one heard anything from the old man. "I knew this was a mistake," I told Yong Li. I sent the young undergardener for him, instructing the lad to bring the old charlatan forcefully if need be. When the astrologer finally arrived, I met him in the hall.

"Well, sir? I gave you good gold for a wedding day. I hope you are not trying to cheat me."

Without a word, the astrologer took the little purse from his belt and placed it on the floor between us in utter silence.

"Here, now," I said, suddenly alarmed. "There's no need for that. I apologize if I spoke hastily. But we are anxious to proceed with the wedding, and we need to know a good day."

The astrologer replied, "There is no good day. The girl will never enter the gates of this house."

"What are you saying?

"Your son will not marry her."

"Why not?"

"Why do you ask me? It is not my destiny to know everything. Not yours either." With that the astrologer left me standing in the hall, staring at the little bag of coins in the middle of the floor.

What could I tell Lark's family? I wondered. Could I get another astrologer? Should I make up something to tell them? I went to bed that night very worried and could not fall asleep. Finally, so that my tossing and turning would not wake Guai, I got up and sat by the window, watching the giant harvest moon that glowed on the horizon. The night appeared peaceful and quiet, the air cooling now that autumn was coming. But something about the size and whiteness of the moon, which at first had appeared beautiful—so beautiful I had sighed to myself in appreciation—started gradually to look unnatural, as if it had been painted into the sky to trick the eye.

·   ·   ·

Lark's cousin, who shared a bed with her, woke up suddenly in the middle of the night. The younger girl felt cold, in spite of the quilts, and saw that her cousin was not in the bed. She sat up and looked around the room. Then she got up and called softly down the vast old hallway. The faint echo of her own voice frightened her.

She walked down the hall, glancing into the empty, musty-smelling rooms, looking for a light and trying to sense if there was a movement in the darkness. She called Lark's name softly. Her heart leaped when she tripped over a small object in the hall and she almost fell.

The girl picked up the object and held it up to the faint early light just beginning to enter through the cracks of the old boarded-up windows. It was Lark's shoe. A little further along the hall, she found the other shoe. Where would Lark go without her shoes? the girl asked herself. For some reason, this small fact struck her so strangely that it made her panicky. She looked around wildly, expecting Lark to emerge at any moment from the shadows of the hallway. The mottled light from the windows confused her eye, and tricked her into seeing movement. When a cool breeze brushed her cheek, and lifted the hem of her nightdress, she suddenly became frightened, and ran screaming to the next wing for her parents.

The family, with the one old woman who still lived with them, was roused from their sleep. They ran about the great empty halls of the mansion, searching for Lark, calling her name. The slow-witted man who lived in a shed on their property and in return kept their vegetable garden ran up to them, startled by the noise they made and the lights in the house, and was told to join the search. Slow-witted as he was, he was the one who found her.

The shallow reflecting pool in the courtyard, the one newly planted about with my rose cuttings, had a knot of black floating on the surface, marring the perfect giant white moon whose reflection took up almost the entire surface of the water. When the terrified household drew nearer, the inky cloud clarified itself in their vision, and they saw that it was Lark's hair, floating on the water, spread out on the surface like a fluid fan. Lark herself was kneeling on the bottom of the shallow pool, and her upright torso leaned into the water, floating face down, as though she were resting in a kind embrace. Her arms were spread out and bobbed lightly up and down, her knees brushing the tiles as her body shifted in the liquid. When they pulled her from the water, there were no marks of violence on her cold skin.

When I told Wan Li the news, very gently, he stared at me for a long while, his eyes wide with shock. Then he simply started to laugh. He laughed so hard that the entire household came to see what was wrong. I was almost in tears myself, but I looked around, and I could see that the servants were all afraid of him, afraid of this wild laughter. Guai sent him away to his brother's house in Yueyang, where he stayed for several weeks. In the meantime, I paid for Lark's funeral. Then I thought about what she had done. The Japanese make a sort of religion of honor out of suicide. Westerners think that suicides are disturbed or mentally ill. Chinese suicides, though, are for revenge, and because the ghost of a suicide remains vengeful throughout eternity, it is a way of holding on forever. When I considered this, I paid a large sum of gold to have prayers said for Lark's spirit—paying the Buddhists, the Taoists, and even the Christian mission for their prayers. A girl so strong-minded that she could deliberately kneel and drown herself in a shallow pool—keeping herself still for that long, until she had forced the life out of herself—was the kind of ghost who would hold on forever, if you let it.

46

My brother's soldiers found Jin Yu in the mountains in late 1948, in the winter. It had started to snow in the mountains a few weeks previously. Acting on a secret message from a merchant's wife who lived in a nearby village, soldiers had conducted a raid on a little country town that roosted on the crest of a hill overlooking the rice fields of the valley below. They rousted the people out into the pathways and threatened to burn the grain in the warehouse. They searched the village and found Jin Yu, dressed as an old peasant. The young captain, who had not yet been born when Jin Yu became a revolutionary, looked at her face closely and compared it to the drawing he had of her. He brought her into Changsha in irons, on foot and walking in the snow, wearing only cloth shoes.

In the fourteen years that had passed since I last saw her, I thought of her often. But my concerns were about Guai and our children and my property speculation and my household of servants, about feeding and clothing all these people, about surviving a war and hoarding money and replacing broken dishes. So many things occupied me that my thoughts of Jin Yu, while frequent, were only in passing, in a way that now felt disloyal.

I sat thinking all evening after the capture, stirring the charcoal brazier and watching red overtake black on each coal. In bed that night, I asked Guai to let me see her.

"There's nothing I can do, wife," he said bitterly. "The army has her and they will execute her. The civilian branch can do nothing." He put his arm around my shoulders in the darkness, and I leaned against him and wished he had more power.

The next morning, I went to Li Shi. When I arrived at his house, Li Shi was signing the papers to promote the young captain who had accomplished the capture of this famous rebel.

"Well, why are you here?" he asked, more abruptly than usual, as if he already knew that I would be asking for favors.

"You know why," I said wearily.

"Oh, yes, your old schoolfellow. The one who loves the poor. Well, I'm sorry to say, the poor don't love her. When we threatened the headman, they gave her up to us in an instant."

"Yes, well. How very ungrateful of them."

"Maybe they were tired of her. All that Marxism-Leninism can be very dull if it goes on too long."

"Stop it, Li Shi. I cannot bear this meanness from you today. You know I want to see her."

"Why? You haven't seen her in years. Well, maybe that's why. I doubt your friendship would have survived without such a separation."

He might have been right. Jin Yu was trying to destroy everything that I possessed and relied upon, and had we been always together we would have one day come to blows. But our long separations had arrested the time that passed in between, so that it felt as though I had left her in the mountains only a few days ago, and helped her escape Changsha in the boat, wounded as she was, a few days before that. Perhaps that was why my feelings toward her remained the same, in spite of the events that divided us. In my mind, we were girls together still, in the world of our youth, when no one would ever change or die.

"Help me," was all I said to Li Shi.

"I can't do it."

"In secret. I want to see her in secret."

"No." Li Shi shook his head so firmly that I immediately saw that I would be unable to convince him. But I asked more questions anyway.

"Why not? The condemned always have people visit them."

"Now is not the time," he said warningly.

"She isn't even very important anymore," I pleaded, feeling shocked at how traitorous my words sounded. "She was a threat long ago, not now."

"She's something of a legend," Li Shi replied, looking out the window. "She's evaded us for many years. It's a bad time."

"That's the second time you've said that. Why is now such a bad time? We've been having a bad time in China for centuries. Why is this moment so very different?"

"Shut the door," my brother said. Surprised, I turned in my chair and pushed the wooden door behind me. It shut with a dull bang.

"We sent a spy to the Communists a few months ago," he said in a low voice, looking at me very directly, almost mouthing the words to me rather than talking. "A week ago he was able to send us a message, identifying two Communist spies in our government. Zhao invited the two suspected Communists to dinner. He left the table for a moment immediately after eating, and while he was gone, some of our soldiers burst in and shot them. But then our own spy's head was sent back to us in a box just a few days ago. The central government is rabid over this event. It was a bad time for this particular middle-aged lady to be caught. Another year, another month, I might have been able to just throw her into prison forever. But now I must kill her. Do you understand my position?"

I nodded.

"Anyway, I doubt Jin Yu would want to die in prison. From what I remember of her."

I nodded again.

"So I can't let you see her. I'm sorry."

When I left my brother's office, I thought that the only man in the province that was above him was Zhao Han Ren, and to him I would go. I went straight to the governor's mansion, almost running, and arrived panting, my breath thick and sticky in the winter cold. Beads of perspiration stood out on my lip, and I wiped them away with my hand.

Zhao saw me immediately, standing up behind his lacquered desk and bowing slightly. He was thinner than ever, wasted-looking, and his face was gaunt and seamed with lines.

"You will catch a cold if you run about in this weather," he said simply, gesturing me to sit down.

"I have come to ask you for a favor," I said, neither sitting nor taking off my coat. "If you have ever been my friend, help me now."

He looked at me steadily, without surprise.

"I want to see Jin Yu before she dies."

"Has your brother told you about our present situation?" he asked.

"Yes. Please help me anyway. She is a part of my life, and I don't wish her to die without someone to say something comforting to her." I took a step forward. "Please, Han Ren. I've never asked you for anything before."

"The answer, of course, is yes. Now will you sit down?"

I dragged my coat off my shoulders and sank into the chair across from him.

"Are you surprised at my consent?" he asked.

"Yes, of course. I thought you would refuse me."

"What would you have done if I refused you?"

"Bribed the jailers."

Zhao started to laugh, a hoarse cracking sound. "Well, that is no less than what I would have expected. It is lucky for you that I am near the end of my career and have no place to go as an official. I don't care if I get into trouble, but nevertheless, we'll have to be secret about it. She is supposed to die tomorrow afternoon."

"So soon?" I cried.

"It's a bad time. We can't delay. If you go to the gate of the garrison prison one hour before dawn, a man will let you in. You will still have to bribe him, but he will be told to accept the bribe." I shivered a little at how skillfully Zhao had ensured that blame would fall on the jailer if I were discovered. Still an old fox, I thought. "But you must leave at daybreak, before anyone can see you. Do you understand? If you disobey my instructions, you must take the consequences of discovery."

By that I understood him to mean that he would not help me if I were caught, and would deny that he had arranged the meeting. "Yes," I said. "Yes."

"It's a bad time. You know I had to have two men shot at my dinner table? I sat through an entire supper with them, talking and drinking and smoking cigarettes. I left the table to get a shot of morphine, and the soldiers hidden in the kitchen came in and killed them both. Blood everywhere, all over the dishes and food, all over the floor." Zhao closed his eyes for a moment, and I had the odd thought that he was picturing the scene rather than trying to block it from his mind. He lit a cigarette. "You still don't smoke? Well, good. I certainly hope we were right about those two being spies."

"I hope so too. Is there any doubt?"

"No. Our spy was always most accurate. He knew them well, you see. He had been a Communist once himself, and had gone to Paris with them when they were all young."

"Paris?" I fussed with my coat as if I were cold, pulling it up to drape around my shoulders, keeping my eyes on the floor and rubbing my hands together to conceal their shaking.

Zhao looked up from his cigarette. "Tai Yang—that was the name he used, even I didn't know his real one—was a very good spy, and not likely to make himself known. He became more and more secretive the older he

got. Hardly anyone knew he existed. In the last few years, most people
thought he was dead, a story he put out so that he could work among the
rebels. Well, he's dead now. His head was sent to me in a box. I was frightened when I saw it. Tai Yang was always the man who could never be
caught. The Communists are very formidable indeed if they could catch
Tai Yang."

The sun slanted in through the bare branches of the great oak that
stood outside Zhao's window. I sank back into myself. I knew now that
there was something that neither Li Shi nor Zhao had told me, some piece
whose absence I had sensed all along but that I could not guess until now.
Why bother to execute Jin Yu, who had not been an important Communist for many years? Who had lost power in the revolution as the result of
an unwise love affair? Who had been abandoned in the hills by her comrades long ago and fought on in her lonely fashion until a few days ago?
Who was now, like me, an old woman? The answer to my question sprang
into my head just then, fully formed, and I knew I was right. The spy was
a man whom people barely knew existed, invisible, like all good spies. But
once, long ago, when he was young and fervent, he had gone to Paris.
Now, twenty-five years later, Jin Yu had recognized him and denounced
him, and he was killed as a result—as a result of Paris, for the future is prepared far in advance. Almost with her last breath, she had become powerful again. Powerful enough to sting her enemies into angry vengeance.
Powerful enough to be chased down and captured and killed. How grati-
fied she must be, I thought.

"That oak has been there a long time," I said to Zhao. He turned to
look out his window.

"Yes, but it's winter," he said softly. "And all the leaves are gone."

The garrison prison was a squat brick building with a flat roof of corrugated tin. Its construction ensured that the cells would burn with heat
during Hunan's blistering summers and would be as cold as possible during the winters. I went there in the darkness of the early morning hours
and stood outside waiting in the icy cold. Waiting there for the man who
would let me in, I thought about warmth, about summer, about sunshine
and brightness. I remembered when I was still a teacher, and Jin Yu had
come back from Paris, and she came to find me to go and eat pastries. I
was alone in my empty classroom, correcting papers at my desk, the sunlight gracefully infiltrating the slatted windows. Through the open win-

dow, I could see a young student—Fragrant Forest?—reading quietly on the carved wooden balcony overlooking the small central courtyard, in the variable light under the outspread branches of a weeping willow. There was a slow murmur of voices from the courtyard below. I had looked up when Jin Yu walked in, and we smiled at each other, but remained silent a minute, both of us unwilling to disturb the quiet strength of the scene, breathing in the sense of calm that emanated from the very buildings of the school, that balm compounded of the smell and the sound of leaves, leaves that were both on the trees and between the sewn cloth bindings of the books.

Money changed hands. Then the jailer admitted me through the door and led me down a narrow hallway lined with heavy metal doors and lit by a few bare bulbs, which only increased the greasy gloom. Each door had a barred aperture, and I tried to see inside each one as I passed, but it was too dark. The cells were tiny and irregularly shaped. Small barred windows were set high up in the walls, too high for the prisoners to have a view of the outside, but a cold wind blew through them into the cells. There were no beds, and the men in the cells merely huddled into the heaps of moldy old straw thrown onto the floors. The cell block stank with mold and urine.

I kept my face carefully expressionless as I shuffled down the narrow aisle, clutching a small bundle under my coat. One cell was unlocked, and I was waved inside. The door was locked again behind me. I stood quietly, waiting for my eyes to adjust.

The bedraggled creature on the floor lifted her face. She was smudged with dirt, her hair was a tangled mess, and her swollen nose had clearly been broken. But Jin Yu's eyes looked out at me, as if from among ruins, and they still wore that expression of royal disdain so familiar to me. I squatted beside her and stroked her knotted hair, realizing with a slight shock that under the dirt her hair was entirely white.

"You knew it would come to this." She smiled at me.

"I was afraid that it would."

I took out a clean kerchief and gently rubbed Jin Yu's face with it, careful to avoid the broken nose. The kerchief became black almost immediately, but Jin Yu's face appeared no cleaner. I began to cry silently at this. Jin Yu patted my hand.

"Don't cry. My death will galvanize the masses. It will be worth it, if it stirs the boiling pot of revolution."

"Why do you talk like this, Jin Yu? You sound as if you are reading a speech. We are both almost sixty years old, and I am your dearest friend. Why can't you talk to me in a normal way?"

Jin Yu looked confused, as if she had just awoken, and a little hurt.

"I'm so sorry," I said at once. "I didn't speak properly. You look so terrible."

"I know," Jin Yu said. "The one thing I really hate is going to the toilet."

"What toilet?" I looked around. Jin Yu gestured at a corner of the little cell, where some straw had been neatly piled up.

"The men watch me when I go."

"What men?"

Jin Yu shrugged. "The guards. Sometimes the sergeant comes in from the guardroom to watch me. It's very embarrassing."

"Do they beat you?"

"They did. But I don't mind that as much."

I eased myself down onto the icy stone floor, making sure my fur coat was underneath me.

"What happened, Jin Yu?"

"Don't ask what happened to me. It would take too long, and we have so little time. Some disapproving wife heard that I instigated a free-love scandal in my youth, and she reported me." Jin Yu sighed. "These wives."

I could not help a sputtering laugh at this glimmer of her old spirit. I took the bundle out from under my coat and unwrapped it. "Look, I have some rolls for you. They're good—I made them myself. Remember, I used to make these when you came to my mother's house to visit me. They have bean paste inside."

Jin Yu smiled a little. "They smell wonderful. But when you leave, the guards will steal them."

"Then you must eat them all while I am here. I won't leave until you finish." Jin Yu nodded and began to nibble at the edges of one of the buns. She nibbled all around and ate the bread from around the filling first, and then licked the filling from her dirty fingers.

"How long do you have with me?" Jin Yu asked timidly, looking at me over the bun she was eating.

"About an hour. I have to leave at daybreak so no one sees me. I'm sorry, I wish I had more time."

"It's enough to say good-bye." She ate more, and I watched her. "You know, when I was in Paris, I would dream about your bean-paste rolls."

"Really?"

"I worked in a lightbulb factory there in the day, and studied at night, and met with the comrades. I had to eat potatoes all the time because I had no money. I was arrested three different times by the French police for taking part in demonstrations outside the Chinese embassy. I had to go into hiding for a while to avoid deportation." Her eyes lit up as she spoke, and she looked out into the dimness of the cell as if she could discern in it the bridges and squares and lights of Paris. I put my hand on her arm and smiled tenderly at her. She looked at me.

"It's all been worth it, you know."

I nodded without speaking.

When she had eaten another bean-paste roll, I asked her. "You were the one who denounced the spy, weren't you?"

"Yes."

"You knew him from Paris."

"Yes. He was my lover before I married. He was so fiery and radical then. We heard he had become a spy for the Guomindang, but then he disappeared for a long time. I was the only one left here who recognized him. The only one left here who had gone to Paris."

I leaned against the wall, and she leaned against me, draping herself in an exhausted way against my shoulder, like a child. She was even thinner now, while I had grown stout, and because of that I looked as if I were older than she, except for the fact that my hair was still black. But nothing could ever make Jin Yu less than completely beautiful. Her hair glowed in the faint starlight that dropped on us from the window.

"I want to warn you before I forget. Does Guai have some kind of plan to build dikes on the river?"

"Why, yes," I said, very surprised. "Every year the river floods the farms along the side, especially up near Tung Ting Lake. He thinks dikes will regulate the water flow and prevent floods."

"The comrades speak with disapproval of this plan, Jade Virtue." She twisted around to look at me earnestly. "They say he is trying to steal the soil from the very river itself, just as he and the other officials have stolen it from the peasants." Not only was the future uncertain, I thought, the past evidently was as well, always subject to new interpretations that made it something very different from what it had been before.

Jin Yu's voice broke in. "Don't let Guai fall into their hands, whatever you do."

"Thank you for the warning. I know you never liked him."

Jin Yu shrugged and leaned back against me. "It didn't have anything to do with him."

The sky began to lighten. I dreaded the moment when I would have to leave.

"Do you know what someone told me when I was in Paris?" she said, in a different voice than I had ever heard from her before. Wondering, childlike, dreamy.

"What, dearest?" I asked.

"Someone in Paris told me that there is a star in the sky that sailors used to steer by a hundred years ago. Then the star could be seen with the naked eye. But many instruments were invented to steer the ships. The star was no longer used, and as a result, we can now no longer see the star with just our eyes, even though the star has not moved. We need a telescope now. Some old men can still see it without a telescope, and some faraway tribes in the Pacific who still steer their canoes by it can see it. But except for those few leftovers from an earlier age, a human being can no longer see the star with just his naked eye."

As she spoke, the stars outside the window faded gently into the growing light of day. Like a stone-struck spark, or a flash of lightning, a brilliant but temporary glow. I began to take off my coat, thinking to leave it for her in the freezing cell. Jin Yu stopped me, and in her gesture was the slightest echo of her old command.

"Don't. I will soon be dead. If you give it away, I would rather you gave it to some poor woman who must go all winter without a coat."

I swallowed to keep my feelings down. "How can you be so calm about your death?" I held her hand tightly.

"I am looking forward to it. I know great things will come from my death. My death will be better than my life. It is what I have always desired."

My heart overflowed then, and I could bear it no longer. "My sister," I cried, "when can death ever be better than life?"

Jin Yu gave me her half smile, familiar to me from a lifetime.

"Death is my lover," she said.

"Why are you out here in the snow?" Guai asked, coming out to me in the garden, his breath forming a cloud around his head. "Where is your coat?"

"I passed a beggar woman on the street and I gave it to her," I said.

"You did? Your new fur coat?"

I merely nodded, too tired to explain. But Guai seemed to understand, for he said no more about the coat, but simply sat next to me and took my hand.

"Where will I bury her, Guai?" I asked, my voice breaking.

"Put her in our tomb," he said, his own voice edged with fatigue. "I doubt . . . I doubt we will lie there ourselves." I squeezed his hand gratefully, clinging to him, unwilling to let go.

I put my head all the way back and looked up into the cold face of the gray sky. A faint wail like a Tartar lament rose from the distant hills, from the towers of the city walls. Above me I heard a single wild goose, who had inexplicably lingered behind the rest. As I watched, it sailed all alone into the void.

47

At this point in my time on earth, more people were leaving my life than entering it. After Zhao told us that he had been ordered to leave for Taiwan, in order to prepare for the possible evacuation of the government to that island, I discussed matters with Guai, and began selling my property, in bits and pieces, quickly and for cash—or more precisely, for gold. I used the ingots to buy gold jewelry, which was lighter and more compact and would be easier to carry. I had never had to worry before about money being easy to transport, the way a thief might worry. I had spent the latter half of my life building things up, rooting things, accruing and gathering and stockpiling. Now I was tearing things down and scattering them to the four directions, as if I were a person who was nothing, as if all I had worked for was nothing. And perhaps it was all nothing, I thought. Depart without hesitation, my mother had said as she lay dying. And suddenly I understood what she meant by the blank scrolls. There is no past that can be understood, and no future that can be seen clearly. There is only this moment, and the fate that you write for yourself.

In January 1949, the Communists captured Beijing. In April, they captured Nanjing and were inexorably moving south toward Shanghai and Wuhan, which they would take in May of that year. I made arrangements with one of Li Shi's fellow officers to have his wife and sons fetch my daughters in Canton and take them on the boat to Taiwan. I wrote the girls lovingly, ordering them to pack their things and go with the officer's family, and to stay with them in Taipei until I arrived to get them. They wrote back, their letter tearstained, with Jueh's writing on the top half of the paper and Zhen's writing on the lower half. Jueh wrote that she could not believe that she would never see her home in Hunan again. Zhen wrote that she had seen a great monastery in the city of Canton catch fire, and that all the rats had fled the flames, running along the sewers, while above them the monastery swallows swooped and dived, screaming for the young trapped in the nests beneath the eaves.

But Wan Li refused to go.

"I won't leave China."

"We are going to China," Guai said carefully. "When we get to Taiwan, then Taiwan will be the real China."

"I won't go. I want to be a Communist. In Beijing, the crowds greeted the liberation army with songs and banners. I would rather be like them than like you."

"Wan Li, please," I pleaded.

"I am a man now," he said, speaking in a reasonable tone, as if everything he said was self-evident. Guai and I begged him all night, until the dawn arrived, but he refused to change his mind. I wept and wept, but he simply did not look at me.

"What will happen to you, my son, with all of us gone? Your father is a Guomindang official. It would go badly for you."

"I cannot bear your tears, Mother," he said, turning away. He walked out of the room.

"I'll stay here with him, Guai," I said.

"You can't. You have to go to Taiwan for the girls, who are waiting for you."

"What about you? What will you do?"

"As soon as I take care of matters here, I will go to Taiwan as well."

"And leave our son behind? Guai, we can't do that."

"Listen, Jade Virtue," Guai said, very seriously, taking my elbow and drawing me closer to him. "Wan Li is a man now. And it is in the order of things for a man to find his own way in the world, away from his mother and father. It's our duty to go to Taiwan, and we can't force him to come with us. He would certainly run away, maybe to the Red Army, and then we would have no control over his future. As it is, we can try to see him settled before we leave."

"When will we see him again?"

"When the Guomindang takes China back from the Communists. It can't possibly be that long—the Americans will help us. But we have to make sure he stays here, in Hunan, so we can find him again in a few years."

.   .   .

"We can't think of what to do with Wan Li. Everyone we know is going to Taiwan." I was sitting in my kitchen courtyard, adding tea to my cup from the little clay pot on the ground between us.

"I'm not even sure where Taiwan is located. Is there no one who could offer him a position?" Yong Li asked me. She was sitting on a low stool, and she leaned forward with her elbows on her knees.

"There will be no positions in existence anymore. An entire culture is fleeing China; we're all going to be crowding ourselves onto a tiny island, and all our structures will collapse after we are gone." I sighed. "I wish you would come with us, Yong Li. I am worried about what will happen to you afterward."

She shook her head and poured more tea for both of us. "I can't. It's different for you, you were the rulers, and so you must flee. My old man and I, we are just plain people, and so we must stay. We have so many children. Our farm is here, his vegetable stand . . ."

"I don't even know if such concepts will apply in the future, Yong Li. Your children, your farm, your vegetable stand. Will people even have those things next year?"

"Elder Sister, that is crazy talk. Those things are eternal. Haven't people always farmed and had children and sold vegetables? How can that change? Why, what would replace it?" She picked up the little teapot.

I didn't argue with her, because I didn't really know what the future held. My mind was groping toward the shadowy outlines of some grotesquely different civilization, some new and terrifyingly strange way of organizing human beings that I was only just beginning to comprehend. But I could not quite grasp the terrible whole, and so I said nothing and drank the tea she poured for me.

After a moment of silence, Yong Li spoke in a very low voice. "Elder Sister, when I come to visit you, I always insist we sit in the kitchen courtyard. That's because I don't want the servants to think I am putting on airs if you receive me in the great rooms." She looked up at me. "I hope you won't think I am putting on airs now."

"Nothing you could ever do or say would make me think that," I said, surprised.

"I feel some responsibility for Wan Li, because he lived with me and I was unable to make him feel better. No, wait until I finish. I know your heart is sore now, at the thought of leaving him all alone without any family. So I suggest he marry my old man's eldest girl. She's twenty, a virgin, and a hard worker. You know yourself what she looks like—she's not pretty, but she has no pockmarks or bucked teeth. Then he'll be in my family, and I'll look after him. It won't matter that his father was a Guomindang official, because he'll just be the vegetable-seller's son-in-law. When emperors change, it is better to be one of us than one of you."

I put my cup down, hearing its bottom rim click on the earthen bricks of the courtyard. I got up from my stool and knelt down in front of Yong Li.

"Elder Sister, what are you doing?" she asked, a little alarmed, and taking my wrists in her warm, work-roughened hands.

"Yong Li, you have treated me better than anyone else has in my entire life," I said to her soberly. "What do you get in return?"

She shrugged, suddenly shy, and looked down at our hands. "Well, I have known you for so long," she murmured. "You are the only person I have known since childhood, everyone else has come or gone." Then she looked up with a smile. "Now we'll really be sisters, if our children will marry."

"Yong Li, I give you my family name freely. But it will not be an advantage to you. The Communists do not love the highborn. It is your family name that will help my son."

"I am content for that," she said.

"Why are you doing this?" I asked, gripping her fingers in mine.

Yong Li put her head to one side. Her eyes were clear but sad. "Because you are leaving the soil of your birth, Elder Sister. I want to help you one last time if I can. I may not have another opportunity until the next world."

Wan Li married Yong Li's stepdaughter the following month. I had been afraid he would refuse, but I think the gravity of what he had determined to do—to stay here without us, without any protection or money—had begun to truly frighten him and he realized that he could not survive alone in the coming new world. He was, after all, still a boy in many ways. I was ready to give the bride a grand wedding, if that was what she wanted, but Yong Li refused. "Best in these times to be simple," she said, and I saw immediately that she was right. But I made a handsome present of gold and pearl earrings to the bride, and begged her to hide them away, in case one day she needed to sell them. Afterward, Yong Li took her new son-in-law home to live on the farm with her and her old man, and Guai and I waved forlornly from the gate of our house. Yong Li looked back to wave, and her old man looked back, and the new bride looked back, but my son did not look back.

In August 1949, Zhao left for Taiwan, without telling me. I found Li Shi in Zhao's office, clearing out documents to be sent to Taiwan or to be burned.

"Is it true?" I asked. "Is Zhao gone already?"

"Yes, he left yesterday." Li Shi did not bother to look up. He waved irritably to the aides who were carrying boxes of papers to the furnace outside.

"I see," I mumbled, frowning.

Li Shi glanced up. "Why, are your feelings hurt that he didn't say good-bye?"

"No. No, of course not. He's a very important man, and busy. I'm not surprised he didn't have time to speak to me." But still I frowned, and Li Shi laughed at me.

"You'll see him again in Taiwan," he said, smirking, and turned back to the documents.

"How close are the Communists?" I asked.

"They'll probably be in Changsha in a few weeks. What's left of my army is beginning to desert."

"To the Communists?"

"To them or just to the countryside, back to their own homes, where they can burn their uniforms and pretend to have been farmers all along."

"What about you?"

"I'll leave in good time."

"Where's Zao Zao?"

"I had Zhao take her with him."

"She didn't say good-bye to me either!" I cried, my feelings doubly hurt now.

"Now you know how I always feel. I thought it was best to get her out of the way sooner rather than later. She's pregnant, you know."

In spite of all my worries, I felt a spurt of joy at the news, mingled underneath with an uneasy sensation when I remembered why Zao Zao had wanted the baby. But I threw my arms around my brother and embraced him warmly.

"I'm so glad, Elder Brother," I said, burying my face in the warm, rough cloth of his uniform jacket. He stood still a moment, and then took my shoulders and put me back from him.

"What's wrong?" I asked. "What could be wrong?"

"I didn't think I would ever tell anyone this, Jade Virtue, but the meat is very close to the bone now, and I want you to know. A military doctor told me years ago, when I had been married a year, that I could never sire children."

"But what . . ."

"I never told Zao Zao either. She still doesn't know that I know."

"Doesn't know that you know what?" I cried, a horrible realization dawning on me.

"That the child she is carrying is another man's, which she will pass off as mine. Don't ever tell her that I know. It would destroy her, because she thinks she has beaten me at last. To deprive her of this victory"—Li Shi leaned against Zhao's desk and took a cigarette from Zhao's box—"would be too cruel."

"Why did you never say anything before?"

"It is not a thing a man brags about."

"And you don't care about the child not being yours?"

Li Shi put his head back and closed his eyes against the smoke of his cigarette.

"Does it really, really make a difference?" he asked. "In this world of ours, which is falling apart around our ears, does it really make a differ-ence?"

I leaned against Li Shi, the way I had seen swimmers in the Xiang River pull themselves onto rocks when they tired. I knew he always felt that he stood alone in the world, and was never surprised when people abandoned him, and indeed, did not waste much sentiment on it. But it hurt my heart to know that nothing ever relieved Li Shi's aloneness and that perhaps it was no longer even possible to relieve it, if it had ever been possible at all.

"Do you know what I think about, when I think about you?" I asked, looking him in the face.

His eyes crinkled into a smile. "What, then?"

"I think about when you were a boy. You studied so late at night that you would put your legs into empty wine jars to keep the mosquitoes from biting." I touched his face tenderly. "I remember seeing you as I went to bed, hunched over a book by the light of a candle, with your legs underneath the table, inside the wine jars."

Li Shi's face lit up in a way I had not seen in a long time. "Do you remember, Jade Virtue, how Mother got that old teacher to tutor me for the university entrance examinations? She hardly had any money to give him, and he kept refusing, so she bribed him with Father's old spectacles. His old, seamed visage smoothed out into pure happiness. 'It's as if I have regained my youth,' he exclaimed in awe. 'I see everything clearly, as I did when I was a young man.' He clapped his hands in glee, and wandered all over the room, looking at this thing and that thing, and marveling at the sharpness and clarity of all the ten thousand things that exist. He agreed to educate me, in exchange for the return of his youth."

When I left my brother in his offices, it was already nighttime. The fall of darkness had not cooled the summer heat, but seemed only to intensify it, so I felt as if I were walking through an immense oven, through waves of burning air unpunctuated by lights. In spite of the heat, in spite of my hair clinging damply to the back of my neck, my feet did not take me the direct way home, but all around the old part of the city. I passed near where my father's house had been, torn down decades ago to make room for government archives. I passed near the Pans' house, now owned by the former barber Cho. And I found myself outside the Pan family temple, a small stone structure down the street from the mansion. I had been inside only once, a year after I married Wang Mang, and they had opened the family temple to add my name to those carved on the stone tablets. But the family temple was opened only once every fifty years, I remembered, in order to revise the lineage, and so my name was still there, listed as Wang Mang's wife, and now there would never be anyone to change it. But the thought didn't make me uncomfortable or unhappy, as it might have once. I felt in my pockets. I had no fake paper spirit money to burn for the spirits in this place, such as was burned at funerals and ancestor ceremonies. I had only real government-issued paper money, which at this point was just as worthless, so I pulled out a few notes and burned them on the threshold of the temple. I had thought there was no breeze on this still hot night, but the blackened flakes of paper lifted into the air nevertheless, and floated there, dancing lightly up and down above my head, like dark butterflies, lit only by the fire that consumed them.

48

A few days later, late at night, there was a gentle knocking on the garden gate. Guai tried to get me to stay behind, but I refused and followed him out to the gate.

"Old Master, Old Master," a voice hissed over the wall. We opened the gate a crack, and saw outside in the dim night a man whom we recognized to be Yong Li's neighbor, a small farmer who held a tiny plot of land up the road from her.

"No, I can't come in," the farmer whispered. "But I came to warn you that they are very close. The first ones are outside the city outskirts now. What's left of the army is deserting in droves."

"I thought we would have more time," I gasped. "Li Shi thought another few weeks before they were in Changsha."

"They had a big breakthrough south of Wuhan," the old man muttered. "Never mind that now. You" he said, turning to Guai, "are an official. They will put you on a stage and accuse you of your crimes and beat you. They may execute you."

"I've done nothing wrong," Guai said. "I'll explain to them . . ."

But the old farmer, to my relief, shook his head firmly.

"There aren't any explanations. That time is long gone. You've heard what they are doing to the other landowners."

We nodded in silence.

"Old Master, you and the mistress must leave the city. There is no time to spare. Yong Li sent me to fetch you. I will take you to the countryside to her and her old man. My brother is a boatman—a member of the Triad, you know, like all the boatmen—and he will help you leave. Get a few things now, and I'll take you in my cart right away."

"What about Li Shi?" I whispered hoarsely. "How can we leave without him?"

The old farmer's crooked teeth suddenly gleamed whitely in the darkness. "The general is not a man to worry about," he chuckled. "He always leaps in time." True enough, I thought. I hope it stays true, unlike everything else.

Guai turned to me. "But everything in the house, all my books and papers?" he said.

"Never mind," I said. "Leave it all." And as the words left my lips, I felt a wave of weary relief.

The farmer grabbed Guai's arm. "You are endangering my life by talking. The time for words is over. Now there is only the sword and the strong arm. And"—he gestured behind him—"there is my bullock cart."

While the farmer waited just inside the gate, Guai and I picked out a single small leather suitcase, into which I carefully packed all the gold jewelry I had assembled over the last several months. I wrapped it all in the old clothes we would take. I left behind me on my dressing table a box of jade jewelry, which I had no room to take with me. I threw one last glance around my bedroom, at my fine European clothes, my bed and chairs, the laquered boxes of perfume reflected in the mirror on my dressing table. I noticed, just in passing, that the mirror had started to tarnish in one corner, and that the dim film had started to creep along one entire side. I must have that seen to one day, I thought, idly.

I found Guai downstairs, looking at his books, ranged neatly around the walls of the study. "Surely I can take just one?" he asked aloud. But he could not decide which one to take, and finally we left all his volumes there, alone on their shelves like lost children. All the windows were open because of the heat, and I left them that way. I left my house keys on the table in the hall, left the front door standing open behind me as I walked away, without a shiver or a backward glance.

We crouched in the back of the bullock cart, and the farmer threw a piece of old sacking over us. I pressed my cheek against the rough wood of the cart bed and smelled the earth and manure from the fields. The air grew slightly cooler, and I clung to Guai's hand. Then the cart pulled over to a side street in a poor section of town.

"We wait here for an hour or so," the farmer whispered, coming to sit in the back of the cart with us. "There is still nighttime traffic. In a little while, all will be still."

"Tell me," Guai whispered from underneath his corner of the sackcloth. "Tell me what's been happening in the countryside."

The farmer slid down further and lay next to us. I shifted to make room, and pulled some of the sacking over him.

"Many deaths, Old Master. They roused entire villages to go to the mass meetings, to kill the rich and give away their property to everyone. We took Old Cho out of his country house and put him up on a platform with a sign around his neck—I can't read—and he was faced with a hundred accusations, including old women who had never said a word outside their own four walls. Even Li Mao's wife, who doesn't dare look at anyone, shook her fist at him and said, 'He cursed me and drove me away when I went to glean grain in his field. My children and my husband's old parents were starving, what choice did I have? Why did you curse me and beat me when you had no use for the gleanings?' "

"Old Cho who used to be a barber?" I asked, as if it didn't matter.

"Yes, that's the one. That evening all the people went to Cho's courtyard. They heated an iron bar in the fire to torture him, but then he confessed and told us where his money was buried, and we dug it all up. We ate all the food he had stored in his cellars for holidays—he had crocks of wine, and preserved shrimps. Some of us had never seen this kind of food before. We lit bonfires, and set his roofs on fire. The flames shot up to the stars. It was very beautiful."

The farmer sighed happily and gazed at the night sky.

"And Old Cho?" Guai asked.

"Hmm? Oh, him. Cho's dead."

Later, the farmer started his cart again. We left the city by the little-used western gate, and crossed the Xiang River toward Yong Li's farm. We plodded along very slowly, to avoid rousing suspicion, and we arrived there only in the early hours of the morning.

Guai shook the farmer's hand warmly. "Thank you. Thank you. We owe you our lives."

The farmer shrugged. "You know, I am one of them. I believe in their promises. The empire of the laborer has come."

We stood in embarrassed silence for a moment.

"Then why have you helped us?" Guai asked.

The farmer's old eyes looked wet in the dim light of the stars.

"Old Master, you are a good man. I could not see you come to such an evil destiny."

Guai shook the old man's hand again. "I hope all their promises come true for you, my dear friend," he said. The farmer left us then. We stood by the side of the country road, listening to the rumble of cartwheels slowly fade in the direction of the town. Then we carried our suitcase through the trees of the orchard to Yong Li's house.

"I have to go to Yueyang," Guai said quietly. He took his spectacles off and polished them. "You know that. My elder brother is crippled with arthritis. If I don't go get him, he will never escape China. I'll join you in Taiwan."

"Please don't, Guai," I begged. "I'm your wife. If you ever loved me, then come with me. Yueyang is to the north—you are heading into the teeth of the Communists. Your brother is an old reprobate, I knew he would get you into trouble one day."

Guai shook his head in a way that told me there was no further point in arguing with him. My husband was a man who put all others before himself, and sometimes I hated him for it.

Yong Li's old man strung several dozen brightly colored enamel cups on a cord and gave them to Guai to sling over his back. He gave him a wooden rack to carry on his shoulder, with all the items of a brassware seller—cat's bells, knives, toothpicks, and earpicks, all dangling from the short pole.

"If anyone asks, you are a vendor of odds and ends," he instructed Guai. "These things are your stock you sell on the road. These cups are two coppers a piece. Remember that. Two coppers. If you don't have the right price, no one will believe you."

Guai and I left very early on the same morning. It was still dark when we rose and prepared to leave, but the heat was unrelenting. I wrapped all the gold jewelry around my waist with linen bands, under my clothes.

"You really won't go with me?" I whispered to Wan Li. He shook his head firmly, once, and went outside to wait until I left. Things that are not meant to be never get better.

The farmer who had brought us out of Changsha would take me in his cart to his brother the boatman, who would smuggle me in his boat downriver as far south as he could, to a spot near a branch railroad station in the next province. I would have to walk with my suitcase of old clothes a mile to the railroad station itself, and take the first train I could for Canton. I was wearing cheap summer trousers and a tunic, and my hand already hurt from the suitcase.

Guai would walk north, headed for Yueyang, dressed only in some old clothes of Yong Li's husband, and some cloth slippers that Yong Li had made him the night before. Only his spectacles looked odd, and he told me he would take them off whenever he saw someone suspicious. Seeing him dressed so poorly, pretending to be a small merchant with his spectacles still on his face, and carrying the rack of brassware to sell, I started to cry.

"Don't, Jade Virtue," he said softly, drawing me to one side, away from Wan Li and Yong Li and the rest of the family. "If you begin to cry now, you will weaken me, and I need all my strength to get to Yueyang and fetch my brother."

I nodded and wiped my eyes on my sleeve. "Be careful," was all I could say, because my heart was overflowing. "You are everything to me."

"The sooner we part, the easier it will be," Guai said. "The longer we linger here, the more unbearable it becomes."

He picked up his things and set off down the road that headed toward Tung Ting Lake.

"Wait!" I called out in the darkness.

Guai stopped and turned. I ran up to him.

"Will we ever see each other again?" I whispered, willing myself not to weep.

My old man smiled, and took one hand off his brassware rack, and caught hold of my fingers. I clung to him. "I will see you again, my love," he said. "In this incarnation, or in some other." And then he was gone, swallowed up into the unlit landscape.

I sat on my suitcase in the muddy courtyard and stared up the road, with Yong Li kneeling next to me and rocking me gently in her arms. Then the farmer came with his cart, and Yong Li's husband swung my suitcase up into the back.

"The faster you go, the better, Elder Sister," Yong Li said reassuringly, her arm around me as we walked toward the cart. Depart without hesitation, I thought. I sat on the back of the cart and watched as they receded into the distance, my son and his wife, my dearest friend left on earth and her husband and their children, all standing at the entrance to the court-yard. They all waved to me, even Wan Li. Although there were rays of light just below the horizon, the sun had not yet risen, and all my people faded back into the uncertain light. Watching them wave to me out of the engulfing dimness was like watching people drown.

The boatman took me through the southern gorges of the river. I sat in the prow with a needle and thread, repairing some of his trousers in a good imitation of a boatman's wife. My suitcase lay beside a heap of small fish. The riverbanks were bleeding red clay. The water was green as jade, and I thought about a line from a poem, something about pears as green as jade, and plums and apricots slowly turning yellow. There was no sound on the river. No temple chimes echoed in the canyons, no woodcutter's song sounded in the hills. For the better part of a day and a night, I was alone in the world with my boatman.

I carried my suitcase on my back from the boat to the tiny railroad station and bought a ticket to Canton. No one paid any attention to me, I was only one aging woman, among thousands of refugees. Everyone on the way to Canton was so panic-stricken that they left their belongings by the side of the road, and gave away their children to perfect strangers. I watched as they slaughtered their livestock by the railroad tracks and hacked off as much still-bleeding meat as they could carry, leaving the rest to rot. In the fields beyond, I saw only anthills and long grasses. The cries of angry and fearful men came to me over the wind, and the howling of distant packs of dogs. There is no limit to the amount of fear men and women can hold in their fragile bodies, and seeing all these things, sights I would not wish on the most evil of men, I thought that it was as if some dreadful mistake had been made.

At Canton, the entire city was convulsed by a bank run, with thousands squeezed into lines outside the various banks, trying desperately to get some money, any money, before they would have to leave forever. Guomindang officers sat on the docks with their baggage, waiting their turn on the boats. I saw one older officer in spectacles, spats, and leather gloves with his uniform, even in the heat. I found a young army major at the docks who knew Li Shi and Zhao, and although he had no news of either of them, he did get me a ticket on one of the boats leaving the next day. I spent the night in a doorway, hugging my suitcase, thinking of how I would use the gold next to my skin to buy a fine house for Guai and the girls in Taiwan, and how one day we would welcome Wan Li there, and Yong Li, and Li Shi, and Graceful Virtue and Mo Chi and Lily and everyone else.

I arrived at the boat early, and thanks to the officer, I got on without any trouble, crowding on board with hundreds of others. He escorted me on board himself, pushing aside the other refugees and shouldering my suitcase up onto the deck. Then he bowed to me, slightly.

"Please send my regards to General Liang," he murmured. "He is a great hero."

"Thank you for everything you've done," I said. "When you get to Taiwan, come find me, and I will do everything I can for you."

"I hope I will get there," he said, his poor young face somber, and then he left me alone on board, standing by the railing.

There was a scuffle at the gangplank as the crew attempted to pull it up. Some people who apparently had no travel papers had tried to board at the last minute, hoping to get past in the last-minute rush and confusion. They were shoved back roughly by soldiers on the dock, who held them back with the stocks of their rifles. But they were desperate and fought back, tearing at the soldiers' uniforms and trying to overwhelm them by sheer weight. The ship began slowly to pull away.

Then there was a cry from on board the ship. One man had in some way managed to climb on board by one of the ropes dangling over the side; he clutched the edge of the ship's railing and was trying to struggle over it. For a moment, it seemed almost as if he might succeed. But my own young officer broke free from the knot of soldiers and ran to the dock's edge and shouted, "Stop that man! Stop him, or I will order the boat back and make you all get off!" And a passenger—a woman who had come on board with several small children—stepped forward, picked up a length of wood from a stack on the deck, and brought it down with a crash on the man's fingers. He let go without a cry and plunged off the side of the ship onto the dock with a thud, where he lay with one leg dangling over the side. I gripped the rusty metal side of the ship and gazed at him lying there. His eyes were open and unseeing, and he did not move; from the way he lay, I guessed his back was broken. I strained my eyes to see him better, and I saw that his eyes glittered strangely. Then I saw that they were filled with tears, which still stood, even though the fearful spirit who had shed them was gone.

The ship continued to shift about slowly in its space, backing to and fro to get free of the dock. I went inside the cabin that I would share with several other official-looking wives, who sat on their bunks making up their faces. They threw me surprised glances, clearly amazed that someone as dirty as I would be sitting with them.

"Are you in the right cabin?" one asked me, trying to keep her voice polite.

"I certainly am," I said, as haughtily as I could. "Are you? Are any of you the wives of deputy governors?" There was silence. "I thought not. Now please make room for me on one of the bunks. I'm quite tired, and I wish to lie down."

They shifted sulkily to one bunk, leaving me the other. I lay down on the little bed, my head pillowed on my suitcase. The cabin was hot, and the woman across from me smelled like garlic. With my eyes shut, I could feel the salt in the air forming on my lashes and skin, and imagined it spreading all over my body, forming a crust, like the jade burial suit of an ancient princess. I fell asleep.

I dreamed I was at the house on White Crane Street. It was broad daylight, yet the halls and rooms were dim. There was no furniture in the rooms. In the dining room, there were many dishes and cups, laid as if for a family feast, but the plates sat on the floor, for the table was gone. In Guai's study, paper and pens and books lay scattered about the floor, with one pen still in the inkpot, but there was no desk and no chair. Upstairs in the bedrooms, the pillows lay on the floor where the bed had been, and the clothes were piled in the corners because the wardrobe was gone.

I wandered all over, but could see no people. The lamps had all just been lit, the wicks barely singed. An embroidery hoop lay on the floor, centered precisely on the spot where my mother had had her favorite chair. Pots and pans were stacked in the hall outside the door to the kitchen. I pushed open the back door into the vegetable garden. Where there had once been orderly rows of greens, there were now only furrows of earth, scattered with black lumps like giant seeds. I picked one up, and saw that it was a lump of coal. I rubbed the coal in my hand, and its blackness came off on my fingers. I hurled it away from me and wiped my hands on my skirt, streaking it with dark handprints.

When I turned around, the house had disappeared. In its place was only an empty field, with a cool damp mist beginning to roll in over the land. But in the distance, I thought I could see the front gate of Yong Li's farm, looming in the thickening fog like a prehistoric ruin, like a dragon, like a phoenix. I ran to the gate and then right through it, under the big wooden arch, and as I did so, the gate itself disappeared. But I kept on running down the dirt road, my eyes fixed on the distant glint of water that lay before me. I was rushing, rushing, rushing, like a river that finally nears the sea.

49

Changsha is very far away now, as far away as the days of my youth. My house, Patience wrote me, in her uneven straggling hand, has become a police station. No one tends the graves of my dead. I am free again, as free as the day my feet were unbound, as free as the day I left the mansion of the Pans for the House of Silk Fans. I think sometimes of what Teacher Yang told me, about my mind being a fortress. I know now that it is also an airplane, an unlimited wilderness, a heaven filled with stars. My house is the world, and the sky my roof. Any other resting place would only be a delusion.

Author's Historical Note

Some of the incidents involving historical figures in *Dream of the Walled City* are fictional. Xiang Jin Yu, for one, has a longer life in fiction than she did in history. However, the historical events that occur in the novel are facts.